HOUSE

8
OF

ORCHIDS

HOUSE

8

OF

ORCHIDS

JAMES THAYER

THOMAS & MERCER

Text copyright © 2016 James Thayer

Published by Thomas & Mercer, Seattle

www.apub.com

Amazon, the Amazon logo, and Thomas & Mercer are trademarks of Amazon.com, Inc., or its affiliates.

ISBN-13: 9781503948266
ISBN-10: 1503948269

Cover design by David Drummond

Printed in the United States of America

To my beloved wife
Patti
and our daughters
Alexandra and Annemarie

PROLOGUE

My brother and I were kidnapped off a street in Chungking, China, when I was five years old. Our amah, Mi Ling, was shoved into shelves at an open-air stall called the Prosperity Medicine Shop. Blue and white jars filled with herbs clattered to the cobblestones. A rough hand seized my neck. I was carried away, down an alley toward the Yangtze. Two-year-old William was under the kidnapper's other arm.

It was 1912. Our father was the American consul. My earliest memory is of playing in the consulate's elevator, the only one in Chungking. We never saw our father or mother again.

William and I were taken to the House of Eight Orchids, and from there we never entirely escaped.

1

The eunuch watched from the steps, half-hidden behind a stand that sold mustard tubers and oranges. He held a four-foot bamboo pipe between his teeth and was wearing a yellow silk jacket with mother-of-pearl buttons. In the Manchu fashion, his queue hung to his waist, and his temples were shaved. I could feel the weight of his stare. He had been watching me for twenty-five years.

The Wang Lung Men steps, green with slime, rose from the river to the Dragon Gate. Coolies carried water up the 360 steps, each coolie balancing two wood buckets on a pole over a shoulder, an endless procession of coolies wearing cotton shorts and brown shirts made from woven tree bark. At the bottom of the steps, a hundred bang-bang boys waited for the ferry from the south shore, ready to carry luggage. Chungking's ancient walls—a hundred feet high and whitewashed—lined some of the city near the river's edge.

A tie pinched my neck. The eunuch's Englishman had knotted it for me, put the cufflinks onto my shirtsleeves, and tied my shoelaces; I was wearing a pair of the Englishman's heavy leather brogans that were so tight I could scarcely walk without limping.

I held a black lacquered box that was inlaid with a teak dragon on the lid. The box was four hundred years old, dating from the Ming dynasty, and the ancient lacquer gleamed vermillion and black in the sun. In my other hand was a pole holding an American flag. That morning I had counted the stars—forty-eight of them—but I didn't know what they meant. I looked enough like an American, with green eyes and hair the color of straw, and I was taller than almost everyone else in Chungking.

Two steps above me, One Eye Gao Bai held a Japanese flag and a Kuomintang flag on bamboo sticks. On one of the eunuch's errands two years ago, Gao Bai had lost an eye, and his right eyelid was now stitched tightly to his cheekbone.

My brother William wasn't with us. This wasn't his kind of work.

At the bottom of the steps a steamer pulled in, and the deckhands threw lines to workers on the pier. Swift currents pulled at the boat, and black smoke drifted from the stack. The boat was about sixty feet long, with a raised pilothouse forward, and heavy machine guns mounted on the deck fore and aft. Fixed to the mast, a large white flag—the Imperial Japanese Navy's ensign, a red sun with sixteen rays—flew at the stern.

"I don't see him." Gao always spoke with his mouth pulled to one side, almost under his ear, as if everything he said were a secret.

A ferry steamed from the south side of the river, the bow pointed into the current so it wouldn't be swept away. A junk drifted down-river, its hull made of oiled yellow wood. The sail had been stowed, and twenty rowers were at their stations, their oars flashing in the sunlight. At the stern, a drummer beat a tattoo. Carrying furs or wood oil or silk, a dozen sampans moved downstream toward Ichang.

The line of coolies passed within five feet of me, chanting together in a low singsong and moving their feet in locksteps ever upward. On the other side of the steps, coolies with empty buckets returned to the river.

"There's the general," I said in Szechwanese, Chungking's Mandarin dialect. "His sword is almost as tall as he is."

As the steamer's lines were secured, the general stood on the deck as still as a statue, his chin lifted up and his mouth turned down. Leather belts crossed the general's khaki tunic, and his trousers were tucked into brown knee-length boots. His name was Fukudo, but he wasn't the reason we were standing on the Wang Lung Men steps.

Four men carried a red lacquer-coated sedan chair that appeared at the top of the stairs. After the chair was lowered, Chungking's mayor stepped out, with his Western suit jacket hanging crookedly on him, and his black hair parted precisely in the middle. Protocol demanded the mayor descend the steps to meet the general halfway, but he stayed at the top of the stairs, his hands behind his back, his gaze fixed on the distance. The mayor did not deign even a glance at the Japanese general. Four weeks ago, December 13, 1937, Nanking had fallen to the Japanese, and Chiang Kai-shek had moved the Nationalist capital to Chungking, where, because of the barrier of the Yangtze Gorges, he thought he was safely upstream. Three hundred years ago, Chungking was the last capital of the Mings. It was Chiang Kai-shek's third capital.

General Fukudo was here to try to negotiate the surrender of Chungking. There was more chance of it raining poultry than of Chiang Kai-shek giving up the city to the Japanese, and everyone in Chungking knew it.

One Eye Gao Bai rose on his toes, as if that would give him a better view of the Dragon Gate at the top of the steps. "Chiang isn't here."

I said, "He would never honor a Japanese general with his presence."

Chiang Kai-shek was probably in his compound in Huang Shang, a secluded neighborhood in Chungking. Below us, the Japanese general placed a hand on the sword's pommel, then stepped across the gangway.

Gao asked, "Are you ready with the box?"

Inside the lacquered box was a *senninbari*, a belt of a thousand red stitches, an amulet for a Japanese soldier going off to war, a gift. Usually the soldier's mother and other family members stitched the belt, but this senninbari was a gift from strangers, and the officer would be pleased.

"The colonel is the second officer," I said. "The one wearing spectacles."

I looked up to the tuber stand, but the eunuch was gone. He would be watching from somewhere else. White and tan stucco buildings lined the broad steps. Cured tobacco hung from the roofline of one shed, and shanks of horseflesh from another. Chungking smelled of hemp, charcoal, and garbage.

Colonel Tanaka Akiyo trailed General Fukudo up the stairs. Tanaka's uniform and helmet were almost identical to the general's. The colonel's Adam's apple bobbed with each step, and his spectacles flashed in the daylight. As if he were thinking about each step, he climbed with a slight hitch in his right leg, maybe hiding a limp. He, too, had a hand on a sword's handle.

The sailors had remained with their boat. The bronze latch on my lacquer box was unhooked. I saw the eunuch again, now standing behind a beggar who had no legs and whose arms were covered in green sores. The eunuch placed a coin in the beggar's wood bowl.

The general raked the sole of his shoe on a step edge, ridding the shoe of slime, which the Chinese would view as insulting. And only he and Colonel Tanaka came up the stairs, a meager delegation and another insult. Climbing and climbing, the general passed Gao and me, his gaze never leaving the steps in front of him. He wouldn't flatter this rotted melon of a country with even a sideways glance. Tucked under his sword arm was a tan envelope, perhaps Tokyo's surrender terms. A white-collared magpie—a good omen—shrieked from a tin roof above a cigarette shop along the steps.

As Colonel Tanaka Akiyo stepped up to my level, his mouth was open and he was breathing heavily.

I moved forward, through a line of moving coolies. "Colonel Tanaka. Welcome to Chungking from the American Iron and Steel Company," I said in flawless Japanese.

Tanaka looked directly into my eyes. Thousands of Anglos were in Chungking—businessmen and diplomats and their families, following Chiang Kai-shek, who had fled upriver with his army to Chungking. I was fluent in Japanese, and in Szechwan Mandarin and English. I bowed low, as did Gao; then I held out the lacquered box and opened it. Tanaka glanced up the steps, perhaps wondering how far behind the general he should allow himself to become.

"A gift from the American Iron and Steel Company, based in Pittsburgh, Pennsylvania, United States of America." I opened the box. "It is for your continued good luck. We understand you are the Imperial Army's railroad buyer."

He bent forward fractionally, peering into the box at the red stitches aligned in perfect rows on the silk belt. This senninbari was a masterful piece of art, the finest grade of Yunnan silk, and it glittered in the light.

I added, "And I hope that should the Imperial Japanese Army ever need iron and steel supplies, that it will give the American Iron and Steel Company due consideration."

I was making no sense, of course. An Anglo and a Chinese, making a gift of a senninbari to a lowly Japanese colonel in the middle of the Wang Lung Men steps? But all we wanted were a few seconds of hesitation.

Gao was on my right on the stairs, two steps higher. I gave the box to him, and he held it out as I lifted the silk belt.

"From the American Iron and Steel Company," I said as I placed the silk around his neck.

Then he must have understood. His eyes widened and he half-stepped backwards and brought a hand up to the silk, but it was too late.

Gao had already dropped the box and grabbed one end of the belt, and I the other. We yanked ferociously, and the silk cut into the colonel's neck so far that it almost disappeared into the flesh.

I said, "Your death has been paid for by the parents of Chen Bo-lin, who you beat to death three years ago at the Three Gate Prison in Harbin, Manchukuo." Manchukuo was the Japanese puppet state in Manchuria, which the Imperial Army had invaded in 1932. Colonel Tanaka had nothing to do with railroads but was with the Kempei Tai, the Japanese secret service.

The eunuch had doubled the price—to ten thousand Nationalist silver dollars—when the parents had insisted the colonel be strangled, instead of a death issued from a distance. Strangling was a shameful way to die, a woman's death. And *baochou*, or revenge, had to be extracted here on earth because none of China's religions offered a hell for those who deserved it.

The colonel's tongue protruded between his teeth, and both his hands were around the belt. His cork helmet slipped from his head and rolled down the steps. Gao and I leaped backward, dragging the colonel off his feet. We backpedaled toward the narrow alley between two mat-sheds, Tanaka skidding after us. Only ten seconds had passed since I had first spoken to Tanaka. Not one coolie had broken step.

The Japanese general was still climbing toward the Dragon Gate and the mayor. We hurried into the alley, dragging the colonel, whose arms were limp at his side and whose head was twisted at an angle. Alley filth covered his uniform. We turned a corner, then another, into a dark warren of alleys, the sky a gray stripe overhead. The click, click, click of a mahjong game came from somewhere, and I smelled the stench of sewage flowing down an open ditch.

The eunuch was waiting for us in front of a butcher shop, a meat axe in his hand. Six pig heads hung from the shop's ceiling still dripping blood. The parents would get the colonel's head in a woven basket in exchange for the last half of the payment.

"John, that was clumsy," the eunuch said in his high, warbly voice. His name was Chang Tao, and he was a short Manchu with a square head and deeply set black eyes, a narrow slip of a nose, and a knobby chin. We had celebrated his sixtieth birthday last autumn, but his face was still unlined. "You moved like a circus bear," he said. "Have I taught you nothing?"

Gao gripped the dead colonel's head to stretch the neck, the eunuch raised the axe, and I turned away.

2

The eunuch's penis and testicles were in a sealed jar in the compound's training room. His privates—called *pao*, which means "precious"—were always stored on a high shelf, symbolizing his desire to rise in wealth and position. I never let my gaze linger on the jar too long.

"The knife is too high." I stood in front of the shelves. "Put it down low, against your belly."

The boy held an eight-inch knife above his head. The edges and point had been dulled with a file.

He said, "When I do that, I can't swing it."

His name was Sun Bo, but was called Sixth Brother, and he was eight years old. Two months ago the eunuch had found him leaning against the compound's front gate, shaking with fever and his eyes leaking and red from trachoma. His mother had left him in the street because she couldn't feed him. Now his eyes were clear and he was eating as much as any of us. His head was shaved in the fashion of most Chungking boys, his feet were bare, and he wore a blue cotton shirt and loose black trousers. I was dressed the same way.

The eunuch watched from behind a bamboo partition.

"Then try it your way," the eunuch said.

The boy glanced at the eunuch. "With the knife? At Yellow Hair?"

"The foreign devil isn't as slow as he appears."

Four Caucasians lived in the compound, and we were each called *gweilo*, or "foreign devil." The Chinese always seemed to know which foreign devil was being referred to without clarification. My name is John, but I was called Yellow Hair by everyone but the eunuch and the Englishman. My brother William's hair was as brown as a dead leaf, but in sunlight it had a red cast, so he was called Red Hair. *Compound* was my word for this place, and no equivalent word exists in Mandarin. The eunuch called it the House of Eight Orchids and considered it his home.

My hands hung at my side, five feet in front of the boy, and my feet were squared beneath my shoulders.

Sixth Brother looked at the eunuch. "I like this foreign devil. I don't want to hurt him with a knife."

"Rush forward, and bring the knife down at him," the eunuch said.

"What if I cut him?" Sixth Brother asked.

"The question is not whether you cut John," the eunuch said. "The question is whether you obey me."

We stood on a woven reed mat alongside windows that were glass rather than paper, a mark of the eunuch's wealth along with his extensive weaponry. He kept a locked cherrywood armoire for pistols and rifles. Along the wall was a rack of lances, while two dozen daggers and short swords were stored in a sailor's trunk below a window. It was said that the eunuch had a blade for every day of the year, but that might've been only a story. Rumors swept through the compound like fires. Near the corner, a cherrywood armoire—its doors secured with a brass lock— housed the pistols and rifles.

Eunuch Chang said, "Let me show you what happens to disobedient boys."

A green phoenix was embroidered over the heart on the eunuch's red silk robe, and a sinuous green dragon circled the robe above the hem. The eunuch pulled the loops over ivory buttons, then removed his red robe. He wore yellow cotton trousers and green silk shoes. Because he was as thin as a whipping post, his ribs stuck out.

Eunuch Chang turned his back to the boy and reached over his shoulder to pull aside his queue. "I served in the Summer Palace, guarding the Morning Door, the eastern entrance to the empress dowager's chamber. The chief eunuch found me asleep there one night, sitting on a porcelain chair instead of standing at the door. He ordered a punishment called *raising the scabs*."

So many scars covered Eunuch Chang's back that it resembled a tray of noodles.

"I was striped one hundred times with a bamboo rod. A doctor then tended to the wounds with alcohol and salve. Three days later, another hundred blows were administered to my back. Raising the scabs is what happens when a boy is disobedient or fails in his duty." The eunuch slipped the robe around himself.

"Come on," I said to Sixth Brother.

The boy breathed deeply, then charged forward, the knife over his head, and he stabbed down with it. I half-stepped to the side, flicked his arm, and put my leg in front of his ankle. As his momentum carried him forward, I grabbed his collar and yanked him down to the mat, a maneuver I had practiced ten thousand times.

I put my hand lightly at his throat. "A knife coming down from overhead is lucky to find a target, and is easily pushed aside, just like now. Your knife held at your belly will find your enemy's vital organs." I released his neck.

The boy jumped up to his feet, the knife still in a hand. "I don't have any enemies."

"My enemies are now your enemies," Eunuch Chang said. "And I have many."

The eunuch's home was west of Chungking's old town. A thousand years ago, a Tang-dynasty poet had written that a sixth of a property should be for the home, a third for bamboo groves, and half for ponds.

Eunuch Chang had followed these directions to the square inch. The buildings were at right angles to each other, but the compound was at an oblique angle to the Yangtze, far down a cliff below, just as the geomancer had instructed. The Hua-ying Mountains rose beyond the river, forbidding granite peaks that seemed to fall straight to the shore. Chungking is built on a hill where the Jialing River meets the Yangtze. The city is too steep for automobiles and bicycles, and many Chungking streets end at precipices, the river far below.

The eunuch—and every other Chinaman I ever met—believed in the importance of walls and their proper placement, and the compound was surrounded by ten-feet-high plaster and wood walls with glass shards protruding from the top. Gate gods were painted on the front gate, and imperial regulations had forbidden a gate wider than one span—about three yards—so the gate was narrow. The last Chinese dynasty had been overthrown in 1911, but Eunuch Chang still followed its mandates. Just inside the portal, a spirit wall blocked the view from the outside and prevented entry by evil spirits, who cannot turn corners. When walking to and from the gate, we always went around the east end of the portal because the west end was booby-trapped, which the eunuch said provided a 50 percent chance of catching someone trying to sneak in the front gate.

The House of Eight Orchids had been placed in Chungking by a geomancer so that its courtyards and parks and buildings could not be seen from any nearby high point. The eunuch didn't want anyone spying on him. The only promontory visible from inside the compound was Xi Shan, a granite knob a mile west of town.

The eunuch dismissed Sixth Brother—who handed me the knife and hurried through a door to the kitchen—and stepped toward the west wall, where my brother William was at work.

"I don't see any progress," the eunuch said.

A white smock flecked with orange and brown paint covered William's shirt and trousers. William gestured with his palette. "Three more rebels today, on the riverbank. The paint is still wet on the one nearest the pier."

William's six-by-eight-foot canvas had been brought up the river from Shanghai and had been stretched over a frame. The painting was two-thirds completed, and depicted the 1864 battle for Nanking by Qing imperial forces, one of the rebels' last stands. I knew nothing about art, but even so, the force and beauty of the painting was clear to me: the canvas filled with fire, blades, muskets, charging soldiers, and the rippling water of the Yangtze red with blood. William's flare for art had been revealed early, and the eunuch had brought teachers to the compound, including Wang Zhen, a leader of a style known as the Shanghai school, who had lived at the House of Eight Orchids for two years while he instructed William and who once told me the eunuch was paying him vastly more than he could earn selling his own paintings. Three of William's paintings hung in the room. Often the eunuch would stand near my brother for an hour, watching him apply paint or ink to canvas or wood or paper, nodding.

William's gray-green eyes were canted, so he always appeared amused. His hair was curly, and on the streets Chinese would stop to stare at it. William's face was refined, with a narrow nose, ears tight against his head, and he had all his teeth. His face was a stark contrast to mine; my nose had been broken three times during my training, and so features a lump in the middle. My jaw is more square than William's, and some folks have mistaken it for a target. While my brother and I were the same height, I carried thirty more pounds than he does in my chest and arms. His pale skin flamed red at the least provocation. He was bantam thin, and I could circle his upper arms with my fingers, but I don't suppose it takes muscle to lift a paintbrush. His hair was walnut colored, but both his and my eyes were green and have the same angled cast. We looked like what we were: brothers. William was the only person in all of China who I knew—with utter certainty—loved me.

The eunuch had offered to build William an art studio in the compound, but William had said that he was alone enough in the forger's shop, and he enjoyed the activity in the training room. He stored a few of his brushes and oils and inks, tripods, and a canvas stretcher in a pearwood cabinet in a corner of our training room, but most of his art supplies were in his forger's shop.

William leaned forward, and when he lightly applied the tip of the brush to the canvas, a rearing horse magically appeared, and then he dabbed the brush on the palette, bent forward again, and the darker hooves and mane seemed to leap onto the canvas from his brush. He grinned at me. I was envious of his talent, and he knew it.

Eunuch Chang grunted approval, and William turned back to his painting. I followed the eunuch out the south door along a pebble path. A pond was on our left, some of the surface covered with water lilies. Orange fish called *long-lives* moved slowly under the surface. Fish are lucky because the word for "fish"—*yu*—sounds like the word for "plenty." Bulrushes lined some of the shore, and three black storks waded in the water. We crossed a wood bridge—I always walked several paces behind Eunuch Chang—then passed between camellia trees that had leaves so glossy they always looked wet. The sky was gauze white. For much of the winter a mist hung over Chungking, brought there by the two rivers, and the sun could disappear for weeks. Dogs even barked in fear and confusion when the sun breaks through. We passed a grove of pine, plum, and bamboo, planted together and called the Three Friends of Winter because they all bloomed in winter.

The compound had four courtyards, where men lived in the outer buildings, and the few women lived in interior rooms near the springs. The roofs were cedar with upturned edges and were decorated with glazed green and yellow tiles and small terra-cotta phoenixes along the ridges. When I was a child, I had counted forty-six carved stone dragon heads that served as waterspouts. I'd been told the women's bathhouse contained a Mosely folding bathtub the eunuch had ordered from an American Montgomery Ward catalogue. The tub had been shipped across the Pacific and up the river from Shanghai. The easterly courtyard is where the Rough Boys trained. I didn't go there much.

The eunuch entered the great hall, and I was close behind. We walked across shiny black tiles, passing four wall scrolls aligned perfectly, each with paintings of pink cherry blossoms so realistic that the scrolls might have been mistaken for windows. He sat on a blackwood chair, and I waited until he gestured that I should join him, and then lowered myself into a chair on his right. Between us was a wood table with green marble inlays on which was a silver bell. Displayed on both sides of the door to the kitchen were long scrolls showing Ming-dynasty empresses walking between purple-blooming azaleas.

"Will you eat first rice with me?" Eunuch Chang asked, inviting me to join him for the midday meal.

I bowed slightly. When he gestured at a chair, I sat next to him.

"When I was working the salt," he said, "a wise man whose memory I treasure told me that every man will have a year of three peaches," a phrase that means *bountiful along the Yangtze*.

The eunuch ran his hands along his lap, adjusting a crease in his robe. "But only one such year in an entire lifetime," he said, "and I believe this is my year." He brought out a yellow envelope from his sleeve. "This spring we have three projects that will bring the House of Eight Orchids prosperity."

I was always alert when speaking with Eunuch Chang, but I tilted my head toward him, the better to pick up his meaning. I knew of two projects—the disposal of Japanese colonel Tanaka and the planned robbery of an American gold shipment intended for Chiang Kai-shek's Nationalist government—and I had worked closely with Eunuch Chang on both of them. I was unaware of a third venture.

"A young woman will arrive here in a few minutes, and she is astonishingly valuable," he said.

I tried to hide my surprise and hurt that this was the first I had heard of this. "Perhaps I could have helped bring her here, Eunuch Chang."

"Snatching her was an easy task, and I didn't invest twenty-five years training you to send you on simple errands. Hiding her fate, however, will be more difficult, and it involves a graveyard. I despise graveyards, so you will indeed be called on, you and One Eye Gao."

"Perhaps I could have—"

He silenced me by raising a finger. "My loathing of graveyards is exceeded only by that of lawyers, but I tolerated one long enough yesterday to have my will drafted." He held up the envelope. "My bones have begun to ache on cold mornings, and clouds have begun to cover my vision."

I had never before heard him speak like this. Eunuch Chang was an immutable and eternal presence, and that he might be changing in any way was startling.

"After this year of three peaches, I will be less involved in guiding the House of Eight Orchids," he said. "I have no natural sons and so no natural heirs. Beginning this year, you will more and more be acting in my place, and when I visit a loathsome graveyard for good, my home here in Chungking will be yours. This document will see to that."

My eyebrows rose, and I stared at his black eyes. He had taught me to suppress emotions, calling them a weakness.

"You seem surprised," he said. "How could you be?" He offered his version of a smile, a slight movement of his lips. "Enough talk of my demise, and let's hope it is well into the future. Before first rice, let's meet our new student, the one worth her weight in gold."

When he rang the silver bell, the hall doors swung open to reveal a sedan chair carried by four coolies. The coolies lowered the sedan chair and stood with heads bowed, looking only at the floor, as was proper.

The eunuch stepped through the hall's door and pulled open the chair. A set of feet—tied together with rope and wearing five-inch Western high heels—kicked out at him, at his head. The eunuch dodged to one side, then grabbed the rope and dragged the prisoner out by the feet.

She landed on her back, and she stabbed at Eunuch Chang with her heels. Her hands were tied in front of her, and a strip of cloth bound her mouth shut.

A shiny onyx pin fell from her hair as the eunuch pulled her into the hall by her collar, sliding her on the tiles. Her white silk dress shimmered and was slit to the thighs, revealing glimpses of her long legs, a shocking thing. When Eunuch Chang released her, she kicked savagely, but he stepped adroitly out of range.

When he grabbed her hair and pulled her to her feet, she tottered unsteadily, but her gaze cut into him. The eunuch stepped behind her to untie the gag.

Her head whipped to him. "You will pay for this." Her words sounded like steam escaping. "I have friends who will come for you."

The eunuch shook his head, sort of sadly. "You no longer have friends."

"My family will—"

"Or family, except us." He spread his arms expansively. "We are your new family."

"You have no idea—"

The eunuch held up his hand. "Outside of my home, you have ceased to exist. You must reconcile yourself to this."

She yelled something incomprehensible and lunged at him, perhaps thinking she could seize his nose with her teeth, but she was still tied up. The eunuch stepped back, and she fell heavily to the floor, hitting her head sharply on the tile. She breathed raggedly. Again he lifted her by her hair, and he held her upright until she found her balance.

Since the Ming dynasty, the standard of Chinese beauty had been the melon-seed face—rounded and full—with faint new-moon eyebrows, a snubbed, almost invisible nose, and a mouth as rounded as a coin. This girl was certainly Han Chinese, but her face had a touch of foreign devil in it: prominent, angled cheekbones, slender nose, and wide mouth with a full lower lip. She lifted her chin and glared at him.

Eunuch Chang's voice was sweet and lilting, like a bird's song. "I will have nothing to do with you, and you are not to speak to me. You will now meet your teacher."

He returned to the blackwood seat and again rang the bell. At the east end of the hall were four two-hundred-year-old Qing-dynasty porcelain vases, cream colored with blue and iron-red patterns. Even in homes of great wealth, vases were brought out only for important events. A curtain near the vases was pushed aside, and Tuan Ning hobbled into the hall, her arms flung over the shoulders of two maids. Like all women born to noble houses, Tuan's feet had been bound when she was a girl. They were small and pointed, always hidden in satin slippers, and she could not walk on them.

"This is the girl, Eunuch Chang?" Tuan rasped. "She seems too frail for the work."

"It was a specific request," the eunuch said. "Not any girl. This one in particular. You will have to do the best you can with her, Madam Tuan."

"Who is this witch?" the girl said. "When I want to see a witch, I go to the cinema."

Eunuch Chang tried to hide a smile behind his hand. The maids helped Tuan toward the girl and set her up to her full height. Tuan Ning was known as Madam Tuan, never anything else. "Your name is Wu Luli. Is that correct?"

"I don't speak with witches." The girl haughtily turned her head away.

"But your name is not Wu Luli here. From now on your name is Fifth Sister. You will respond to Fifth Sister and nothing else."

Madam Tuan had been a great beauty in her youth, Eunuch Chang had once told me, but that had been decades ago, and now she was wearing a wig that sat low on her head. Underneath, wet starched cotton strips had been applied to her forehead, tightening her face as they dried. Her mouth looked like a gash with its violent red lipstick, and the dark purplish blush on her cheeks resembling bruises. Embroidered yellow chrysanthemums decorated her floor-length blue gown. On two of her fingers on her left hand were six-inch porcelain protectors, worn over her two long fingernails. They resembled dragon claws. It was said that her clothing filled three hundred camphor chests and that on her bedroom wall was a nine-hundred-year-old silk painting by Emperor Hui Zong called *The Five-Colored Parakeet Perched on an Apricot Branch*, a gift from the eunuch.

"Where have you brought me, witch?" the girl asked. "Take me home. I have plans for the afternoon."

Madam Tuan untied the girl's arms. I stared at the girl, at the newly named Fifth Sister, at her eyes and mouth, and her willowy grace, evident even though her ankles were tied together.

The girl said, "My uncle is the deputy police commissioner here in Chungking, and—"

With one swift motion, Madam Tuan dragged her nail protectors along the girl's right forearm. Embedded on the underside of the protectors were knife blades that Madam Tuan sharpened each morning. Two incisions instantly opened on Fifth Sister's right arm, from elbow to wrist, pink surgically straight wounds that abruptly filled with blood.

For two seconds the girl stared at her sliced arm, her eyes white all around; then she shrieked. Blood dripped to the black tiles.

Madam Tuan slammed her hand over the girl's mouth. "Our first lesson is to respect your betters."

Still smiling, Eunuch Chang rang the bell again for tea. I sat transfixed. Not at the blood, of which I had seen plenty over the years, but at the girl's face. Fifth Sister's face had opened a memory. I knew this girl, but I couldn't remember from where.

3

One Eye Gao Bai and I pulled the coffin, bumping in the cart behind us, along a road paved with granite. Many stones were missing, and the holes were filled with filthy water. We watched the roadway, trying to keep our feet from the holes. In Gao's jacket pocket, a cricket in a tiny woven cage made metallic clicking noises that accompanied our walk.

The Chinese do not bury the dead in towns, so that portion of Chungking that wasn't contained by the Yangtze and Jialing Rivers was ringed with graveyards. We were both wearing blue cotton pants and blue jackets, and oiled shoes, which is what leather shoes were called. They were a rarity in Chungking, even in winter. I was a head taller than Gao, but his neck was as thick as a stump, and his arms were hawsers. Also on the cart were a pot of wood glue and two brushes.

The bells of a rickshaw came from behind an outcropping. The puller was bent forward on the poles while a Nationalist Army officer rode in the seat. Gao and I pulled the cart close to the granite cliff face, right up against the green lichen that covered the rock. The rickshaw hurried past us, followed by a column of soldiers, twenty of them, walking swiftly. To a man, they were gaunt, and they wore blue quilted uniforms with cotton bandoliers for ammunition hung from their shoulders and bolt-action rifles across their chests. Army patrols were like locusts, stripping the land of anything that could be eaten or worn, and press-ganging anyone who could carry the loot, but they passed us without a glance.

Gao and I began again along the road when Gao asked me, "How long have you been at the House of Eight Orchids?"

"Since I was five, I think," I said. "Nobody has a calendar there."

"Twenty-five years for you, and fifteen years for me."

I looked at him.

"Have you ever disobeyed Eunuch Chang?" He was whispering, even though no one else was near.

"Do you remember what you looked like when you arrived at the House of Eight Orchids?" I asked him, an edge to my voice.

Gao pulled harder on his pole.

I had to increase my pace. "Most of your skin was open and leaking, and pus was crusted on your legs and arms. Your eyes were swollen shut, and your scalp was covered with lice. You couldn't close your mouth because of a tooth abscess. And you were naked except for a piece of dirty cloth around your waist. Do you remember?"

We guided the cart around a boulder that had fallen onto the road from the cliff above. Two Gold Tooth monks walked our way. All Gold Tooth monks had one gold tooth and wore gold-colored silk robes. They always traveled in groups of four, the eunuch had told me: the two who could be seen and the two who couldn't. I averted my eyes because they were too dangerous to even look at. The monks silently passed us, heading into Chungking.

I went on, "Eunuch Chang took you in, and he gave you medicines and food. At the House of Eight Orchids, you have been taught to read and to figure. You have your own bed." To yell would be to lose face, but my words were clipped with anger. "I have never disobeyed him, and I never will. And neither should you."

"Are you going to spend your entire life at the House of Eight Orchids?" he asked.

I spoke slowly, so each word would register on him. "We are his sons."

"And aren't some of the things Eunuch Chang has us do . . . Aren't they wrong?"

I turned away, scowling. Our missions for the eunuch often involved violence. Others were swindles, extortion, or thievery. Eunuch Chang never used these words, and preferred euphemisms. For example, stealing a wealthy woman's diamond jewelry was called *lightening her burden*. For twenty-five years I had done what Eunuch Chang has told me to do, in whatever language he used to describe it, and hadn't thought much about it.

"Does he trust us, big brother?" he asked, turning the spokes by hand because the grass was high and the ground soft.

"Why does that matter?" I leaned forward on the poles.

"Most of the time he doesn't tell us why we do things. He just sends us out."

Five coffins were aboveground in the cemetery, each resting on stools or a stack of mud bricks. Today was the fourteenth day of the month, and even though it was a calculation made on a Western calendar, fourteen was the unluckiest number, and nobody wanted to put a dead family member in the ground on such a day. Tomorrow, the grieving families would appear to dig the holes for the coffins, the precise position of the holes revealed by geomancers.

Gray haze hid everything beyond three hundred yards, even the Yangtze far below us. As the cricket trilled in his pocket, Gao Bai grunted against the poles, and the cart moved forward in fits and starts over the rough ground. Three burners were in the cemetery, seven feet tall and made of brick, used for burning clothing and facsimile money to send to the spirit world with the deceased. White mortar had leaked down the bricks.

"Here it is," I said.

We had come to a plain wood coffin sitting atop stools at the edge of the graveyard, against the line of trees. The coffin had been nailed shut. Eunuch Chang had told us that inside the coffin was the body of a twenty-five-year-old woman who had drowned when she slipped into the Jialing River while washing clothes. Eunuch Chang hadn't told us her name and probably didn't know it. Yellow and white holy papers had been pasted onto the coffin to ward off evil spirits. I lifted the glue pot from the cart and set it on the ground, and then Gao and I pulled off the strips of paper from the woman's coffin, brushed new glue onto them, and pressed the strips onto the coffin on our cart, which contained three gunnysacks of sand.

We lifted the woman's coffin from the stools and put our coffin in its place. Tomorrow the woman's family would return to the cemetery to dig the hole and light a white candle and burn joss sticks, and lower the sand-filled coffin into the ground.

Gao and I pulled the cart away, the woman's coffin behind us. A green and gold bee-eater landed on a stone grave marker, flicked its long tail feathers, then took off again. We reached the road and turned back toward town.

He said, pulling on one pole, "We don't have any idea why we do most of the things he sends us out to do. Eunuch Chang points, and we go."

"Why do we need to know the reason for anything?" I asked, pulling the other pole. "The eunuch wants us to do this, and that's enough reason."

"Don't you think Eunuch Chang owes us—"

I cut him off. "You are forgetful of yourself, little brother. Pull this cart, and be silent until you are thinking properly."

捌

Eunuch Chang never spoke to me much about his life before he arrived in Chungking—just a sentence here and there, usually as a caution against something I was doing—but the Englishman, when he was feeling talkative, and Madam Tuan, after she had had her fill of Four Rice Wine, ended up telling me stories about the eunuch's past.

He either had been banished from the Summer Palace in Peking, which Madam Tuan believed, or had escaped just before his planned beheading, which the Englishman had told me. That Eunuch Chang traveled west into the wilderness rather than to Peking—where he would surely have been found—meant he was running for his life. He moved at night, reaching Datong in Shan-hsi Province—150 miles west of the Summer Palace—in two weeks, and climbed over the Great Wall four days later. He stole handfuls of millet and barley from storage sheds but never had enough to eat. His plan, the Englishman had said, was to find the Yellow River and follow it south. The imperial court was Manchu, and even though Eunuch Chang was Manchu he would hide among the Han in south China where the empress dowager's spies were fewer and loyalty to the imperial court was weak.

Bandits have always roamed the wasteland between China and Mongolia, the steppes at the end of civilization. Peng Pao-chia led three hundred deserters from China's army there during the war with Japan in 1894 and 1895. Peng fashioned himself a warlord, but he was an outlaw who led outlaws who knew they would hang together or they would hang separately. Peng and his bandits discovered Eunuch Chang hiding in a goat shed. They tied the eunuch to a donkey's tail, and three of the bandits took him west—traveling five days—to Otog Qi, where Eunuch Chang was sold to a salt man.

The eunuch worked at the salt well for eight years, from 1896 to 1904, I estimated. The well was a foot-wide hole in the ground. Four men on a wheel drew up the salt brine from the ground, which was collected in a pond. Using hoes, the men spread the brine onto a bed of stones, where it dried in the sun. After the water had evaporated, salt was scraped up and packed into bags, which were draped over asses or camels for delivery east to barges on the Yellow River.

Arigh—he used only one name, as do most Mongols—owned the salt spring, and he owned Eunuch Chang. Because it was cheaper for Arigh to buy a new slave than to maintain one, the slaves were worked until they could work no longer, and then they were thrown into a ravine where wolves howled at night. The eunuch outlived a dozen other slaves during those eleven years.

One fellow was as resilient as the eunuch. His name was Fu Yong, a monk from Luoyang, on China's central plain. The monk often joined Eunuch Chang on the wheel, and a friendship grew between them. Fu had lived for twenty years at the Batua Monastery and had left the monastery as penance for something he never told the eunuch about. The monk had walked northwest toward the desert, seeking further punishment. Bandits found him, and he was sold to Arigh. The monk claimed he was happy working the salt because he deserved it. Fu Yong was sturdy and hard and took it upon himself to teach the eunuch those things that couldn't have been learned at the Summer Palace.

Meditation, singleness of purpose, and patience—topics one would expect from a monk, the Englishman told me. But there was one other course of instruction. For much of its six-hundred-year history, thieves had tried to prey on the Batua Monastery, and the temple and other buildings had been destroyed many times by the authorities. Over the centuries the monks had developed a form of defense that came to be called Two Arts. One art was the fist and the other the knife.

Eunuch Chang enjoyed remembering a particular conversation with the monk, Madam Tuan had told me. The eunuch and Fu Yong were leading two loaded camels toward the salt-gabelle station, where the salt would be weighed and taxed, when Fu told him that all Batua monks carried knives.

Chang had laughed. "Except for you, a slave working the salt."

"Even me." Fu had smiled. "Even now."

And so Fu instructed the eunuch in the use of the knife: where to hide it, when to use it, and how to use it. Fu's knife was a double-edged dagger with a blade precisely as long as the monk's hand. "A knife blade is most useful when it is the length of the hand that it grasping it," he told the eunuch.

The monk died in the summer of 1904. His body was tossed into the ravine, and that same day, Eunuch Chang used Fu's knife to disembowel Mongol Arigh, jammed the body into the salt well—tamping it again and again with his foot until Arigh's head served as a stopper in the brine hole—and then walked toward the Yellow River.

He followed the river south, and when it turned east for its great run to the sea Eunuch Chang continued south, crossing the Qinling Mountains to the Yangtze. Then he walked upriver to Chungking, barefoot much of the way. His worldly possessions consisted of one tattered shirt, a set of trousers ragged at the cuffs, his privates, which he carried in a pouch tied around his waist, and the monk's dagger. The journey took two years.

The same day he arrived he read in the *Chungking Morning Flower* of the brutal murder of a seventeen-year-old boy, the son of the owner of the Yangtze ferry. The murderer had not been found. The eunuch attended the funeral, drawing scowls because of his peasant clothes.

He pulled aside the father, who tried to brush him off, so Eunuch Chang came to the point quickly: "I will find the murderer of your son, and deliver him to you."

The father said, "I would only want to see him in a box."

"Then tell me the size of the box."

"I should have said two boxes." The father stared at Eunuch Chang, perhaps noticing something feral in the eunuch's midnight-black eyes. "Two wicker boxes. Each the size of a pig's head."

The eunuch delivered the boxes to the father two weeks later, both dripping blood. The Englishman didn't know how Eunuch Chang had found the murderer, how much the eunuch was paid, or which parts of the murderer were in which box.

The eunuch had found his calling.

捌

The Englishman's hands began to shake every day at five in the afternoon. Years before, the eunuch had been given a Danish Bornholm longcase clock as payment for some service, and he placed it against a wall in the library. Every day at five o'clock, the first gong would sound and the Englishman's fingers would begin to twitch slightly, and by the time the last of the five notes had been struck, his hands would be shaking violently.

As the last knell faded, the Englishman moved his left hand under his tattered corduroy vest, trying to hide the shaking. It was now evening of the day of my visit to the cemetery with Gao. We had left the stolen body in the compound's icehouse, near the cistern. The completion of our mission would wait until midnight.

The Englishman's name was Robert Smyth. Not only did his hands shake when the clock struck five, but also his mind wandered. "But, you see, John . . . the Anglo-Frisian that is the nucleus of English . . . was altered in the year 1066, when a great shift occurred because—"

"You've already taught me this, *laoshi*." I smiled at him. The word means "professor," and is a mark of esteem. He had never learned Mandarin, and viewed his ignorance of the language as a point of honor, and so we always spoke English.

"Then I may be entirely out of things to teach you." He tapped his head with a trembling finger. He was shaking so badly that the wattles under his chin wiggled. "The tank is empty. I knew it would happen someday." He had been saying this for years. Our daily meetings were no longer lessons, but he always began them with some arcane piece of history, claiming I had forgotten it.

William, who had been sitting next to the clock, put the heavy novel he had been reading aside and came over to us. "Can I help you, Robert?"

Smyth gestured shakily towards his room. He was in his sixties, but his hair was still as dark and thick as a badger's, and was swept back in waves kept in place by Two Bridges pomade. His face was as white as a skull and marred by deep creases. He wore round tortoiseshell spectacles, and I washed the lenses for him once a week. At no more than 110 pounds, he was a skeleton draped with flesh. Even though Chungking was so hot in the summer that it was called one of China's three furnaces, Smyth wore a wool jacket and trousers year-round, and always seemed lost within his heavy clothes.

A library, such as the one we studied in with Robert Smyth, was rare in Chungking. I had never seen another, though I have a memory of being in a room with a wall of books at the American consulate when I was a child. Eunuch Chang's shelves contained about two hundred books and a thousand scrolls, some five hundred years old, kept in rolls with black string. The twelve-foot-long Pearl Sutra—yellow paper that had been stamped with wood blocks, made in 882 and found at Dunhuang on the Silk Road a hundred years ago—was his rarest scroll. William's painting of the Kangxi Emperor—a Manchu who ruled for sixty-one years, portrayed in yellow-and-blue court robes and sitting on his throne—was near the black Remington typewriter proudly displayed on a stand that no one dared touch. Cedarwood smoke rose from a copper tortoise-shaped incense burner.

Among all of the eunuch's possessions, one was missing. I had noticed its absence years ago. The knife he had carried on his long journey from the saltworks wasn't at the House of Eight Orchids. When I had asked him about it, he had replied, "Don't concern yourself with it," in a tone indicating the subject was closed forever.

A kitchen girl brought a bowl of rice topped with pork slices and green beans. A blue scarf covered her hair. She tried to give the bowl to the Englishman, but he waved it away. She glanced at William's curly hair, as she always did.

"You've got to eat." William took the bowl from the girl and pushed it at him.

His hands shook too much to use chopsticks, so a large wood spoon was in the bowl.

I said, "Eunuch Chang won't let you go to your room unless you eat. Otherwise you'll starve yourself to death."

The Englishman sighed heavily, then lifted rice with the spoon. He studied it with apparent distaste before eating it.

"Have you ever seen the back of Eunuch Chang's neck?" I asked.

"The big scar, almost hidden by the queue?" he said around a mouthful of rice. "Back in 1911, when the Manchus were overthrown, the revolutionaries filled the country with cries of 'Off with the queue.' Two fellows with knives ambushed Eunuch Chang and tried to cut off his ponytail, and that's how he got the scar."

"What happened to the two revolutionaries?"

"I suspect their bodies were found at the bottom of a well, discovered only when the well water began to putrefy. That's what Eunuch Chang usually does with bodies."

Smyth had attended King Edward's School in Birmingham and Exeter College, Oxford, and had taught literature at the University of Leeds. Looking for something to do for half a year, he had come to China just to come, he had told me. This was thirty years ago. He had found a reason to stay in China—opium—and had never gone home.

From our first day in the compound—when I was five years old and William was two—Robert Smyth had spent several hours a day with William and me, usually in this library. During those early years, Smyth mostly made sure William and I didn't forget English. Then he had instructed me in literature and history, though he often said that the history he taught on Tuesday he had learned on Monday. And when William got older, Smyth taught him, too. He also taught us how to use a knife and fork and napkin at the dinner table, and how to shake hands, and how to walk like a Westerner. Teaching me not to spit on the street only took him one month.

The Englishman wasn't my only teacher. A Chan Buddhist monk from the Shaolin Temple had taught me to fight. More precisely: he had taught me to make fights one-sided and short. His hands moved so quickly I rarely saw them, only felt them when I failed to block his strikes. I still studied with him each day.

William was only three or four when it became clear that he would walk a different path. He didn't take to fighting—refused to learn it—and, later, would chide me for my devotion to the skill. William's talent became clear one day—I recall him being about eight—when, using several pencils and bottles of watercolors, he precisely duplicated a one-*kuan* Ming-dynasty banknote, dating from the 1640s, that the eunuch had framed and hung on the library wall. My brother had done it for fun, but the eunuch saw profit. That day, the eunuch began assembling the compound's forger's shop, where William spent most of his time.

My instructor, the Shaolin Temple monk, knew hands and fists but not knives. Eunuch Chang taught me how to use a dagger, and how to drink tea. He also made me learn mathematics, and he drilled me on the Mandarin language. I memorized Sun Tzu and Clausewitz. I had studied the eunuch's knife technique perhaps more closely than he knew. He preferred his number-two knife, a double-sided blade with an ebony handle. Whenever he was about to draw it, his right eye twitched—the slightest of movements, of which I think he was unaware. So, I made sure I didn't telegraph my movements. He showed me how to swing the blades and how to throw them.

Tarir Vishut was a Bombay fakir who taught me to set snares for wild pigs and hares, and to identify which wilderness plants could be eaten. When Vishut was forty years old, he heard a voice in his head ordering him to witness the sun rise over the Eastern Ocean, the Pacific. He had been walking fifteen years when he reached Chungking. Tarir Vishut had convinced the eunuch of the utility of snares, and so we have four traps in the compound, including the irresistible snare—as the eunuch termed it—near the whipping post.

Another one of my teachers, Ito Yoshimasa, had jumped ship at Chungking in 1915. When I was growing up, Ito had spoken Japanese with me an hour each day. But five years ago, Ito's forehead had begun to grow bumps. He had contracted leprosy. Eunuch Chang burned the compound to the ground, all the buildings and all their contents, even the ancient scrolls and the Danish clock. The eunuch's face had been grim as he watched the plum trees being felled and burned. The philosopher Lao Tze had been born beneath a plum tree 2,600 years ago, and plum trees were revered. He had the walls around the compound torn down and the rubble carted away. The ponds were drained, and a statue of Buddha was carried away. The grounds were covered with lime, half an inch deep everywhere. The only thing saved was the Eunuch's pao, his privates in the jar. Then he rebuilt a perfect replica of the entire compound. A new clock came from Denmark, the ancient scrolls were replaced at a huge cost, and he stocked the place with statuary, pots, books, and knives. The compound now looked as it always had. Ito Yoshimasa vanished, and the Englishman said he was probably at the bottom of a well.

William and I weren't the only children who had been brought to Eunuch Chang's compound. There were always four or five of us. Most were Han, but also some Manchu. There was a Russian boy who had wandered off at a train station on the Trans-Siberian Railroad and a French youngster who had been stolen from his family off a Chungking street, just like me. An Uyghur from the Altai Mountains had come to the compound when he was eight, and had lived with us for twelve years. He went off on an assignment eleven months beore and hadn't returned.

Under Madam Tuan's supervision, several girls usually lived in the compound. One had hair the color of fire and was sixteen years old when she arrived. I was smitten with her, but Madam Tuan was vigilant, and I was only able to speak to her a dozen times during the three years she was in the compound. One day she disappeared, and not even the Englishman knew where she had gone. I have had almost nothing to do with girls since. The eunuch saw to that.

Eunuch Chang rented out his students, and sometimes he sold them. We were trained to perform specific tasks. The instruction often took years, and the fees the eunuch charged for our services were exorbitant.

The main reason I was valuable to the eunuch was that I was a foreign devil and could go places and do things no Chinaman could. Just three weeks before, I walked into the Long River Shipyard in Jafong, downriver five miles from Chungking, with an English passport and a letter from the maritime insurance club West of England, and I asked if I could inspect the premises for a survey the club was doing of Yangtze shipyards. Both documents were William's forgeries, and an hour later I walked out of the shipyard office carrying forty vessel blueprints. Eunuch Chang didn't tell me who the client was.

Last winter, dressed in brogans and a striped tie and using a plum-stone accent the Englishman had coached me in, I addressed a Limey on a Chungking street with, "Edward? Eddie? It's me, Joseph Bartlett. Remember? Christ's College, three years behind you." He was walking with a woman who had curly blond hair and lips the color of a pomegranate. Smiling widely, I had stuck out my hand, and when he tentatively reached to shake it I savagely shoved back his index and ring fingers, loudly breaking them. He screamed, and I said, "Keep it in your pants, Eddie." I nodded at the blond woman and walked away. Eunuch Chang usually didn't tell me anything about my errands, but this time he mentioned, with a smile as narrow as a knife blade, that Eddie's wife—a woman with brown hair—had been the client. My brother had shaken his head in disgust.

"I'm done with this slop." The Englishman cut into my reverie about the instructors at the House of Eight Orchids. I placed the bowl on the table. He had eaten three spoonfuls of rice.

William asked, "Do you know who the young lady is? The one who was brought to the compound this morning kicking and fighting?"

"She is tall and haughty. And now that Madam Tuan has laid open her arm, she's still tall but less haughty, I would imagine."

"Where did she come from?" my brother asked.

"Somewhere she'll never see again, if history is a judge."

William said, "I know her from somewhere."

"Half my life here, and I still can't tell one Chinese woman from another." The Englishman drew a leg under himself. "Help me to my room."

William put a hand on his arm. "Can't you wait awhile, Robert? I'll beat you at chess again out here in the library."

Smyth shrugged off William's hand. I pulled the Englishman to his feet and placed an arm across his back to steady him. I helped him out of the room and along a path.

William followed us. His voice was taut. "Why won't you help him, John? He needs help. With his problem."

The gravel sounded under our feet as we passed William's forging shop and the tailor's shop, which had a Singer treadle sewing machine. Once a week, Eunuch Chang played a game with the tailor, Xiong, giving the tailor a magazine photograph of a uniform or a suit or a dress or a jacket, then returning in two hours, expecting that article of clothing on a mannequin, down to the buttons and lace and insignia. And he always found it there.

We walked around the glass and iron greenhouse that had been brought from England. Inside were eight white orchids in eight Ming-dynasty porcelain pots, and nothing else. Eight was the luckiest number, but I didn't know why the eunuch favored orchids. The greenhouse contained only those eight orchids, and if one faded or died it was immediately replaced with another. Nobody but the eunuch was allowed to enter the greenhouse, and he spent many evenings here, often just staring at the orchids, smoking his long pipe.

The Englishman's room was near the whipping post and the irresistible snare, loaded with a double-bladed axe as bait. The eunuch believed that anyone coming into the compound for nefarious purposes would find the axe impossible to resist, and would suffer for the impulse when he tried to lift the axe, which leaned against a pear-tree trunk next to the room's outside wall, as if forgotten. The snare's propulsion was a two-hundred-pound boulder balanced atop the compound's wall behind our room. We all stayed away from the noose, buried under half an inch of loose gravel under the axe.

I pushed open the Englishman's door and guided him inside. Usually William left us at this point, but he came into the room, too. Tar paper had been nailed over the windows, and the gloomy room stank—a thick chemical odor that always caught in my throat. A silver tea service, a gift from the eunuch, was on a dresser. He never used it, but dusted it every day. A Union Jack covered the wall behind his bed. Huiqing—the same girl who had brought him his dinner—followed us into the room. She moved to a brazier where coal pellets were glowing.

"I'd invite you in for tea," the Englishman said, "but next time it might be me hanging on the whipping post."

I helped him down to his bed. A chest of drawers and a three-legged stool were the only other furniture in the room. When I was fifteen years old, the Englishman had offered me his opium pipe. I had inhaled hugely three times. When I woke up, Eunuch Chang and Madam Tuan were there, and after I had gathered my senses I told them that I had demanded the opium pipe from the Englishman and had threatened to smack Smyth if he didn't share it. I was then chained naked to the whipping post behind the men's privy, my arms over my head. The eunuch then nodded at Madam Chang, who ran her fingernail guards down my back four times, the blades leaving bloody trenches. I hung from the post for two days, and then I was taken to my room. Fever and infection brought me close to death, and only after two weeks could I return to my education. The Englishman told me he owed me his life. Just like the eunuch, I carry scars on my back.

Once Smyth was lying in bed, he looked up at me. "I've got a brother in Gloucester."

"On the River Severn, the longest river in Great Britain, which rises in the Cambrian Mountains in Wales." I smiled. "You've taught me more English geography than King George knows."

"I don't have long, and—"

"You've told me about the photos and your last will and testament."

He slid out from under the bed his Russian cigar box, which weighed two pounds and was made of solid silver. *Regalia Elegante* was inscribed on the front of the box. He opened it to reveal his will. Also inside the box were his passport and the three photographs of his family. A British passport was called Old Blue.

"You are killing him, helping with his pipes," William said.

"I will make sure your brother in Gloucester receives your will and the photos should anything happen to you," I said. "You have told me fifty times."

"You benefit from repetition." He pushed the cigar box back under the bed.

My brother crossed the room and said, "Listen to me." He knelt by the Englishman's bed. "Pay attention a minute."

I looked at William. "We've tried this dozens of times."

The girl cut a pea-sized piece of opium tar from a black stick and pushed it into a pipe bowl, glancing at me. Using tongs, she placed a charcoal ember next to the opium, then blew on the bowl until the charcoal glowed.

William whispered, "Robert, we can get you out of here."

She handed him the pipe and left the room, silently closing the door. He propped himself up on an elbow. The mattress was made of straw covered in coarse cotton.

William gripped his arm, as thin as a broom handle. "You can get away from here."

He smiled, revealing remarkably yellow teeth. "Where would I go?"

"We can find a place. Somewhere safe, away from the eunuch."

I said, "He's heard all this many times, William. From you and me. It's too late."

"A place safe from the eunuch?" The Englishman laughed, more a gurgle. "And why would I go?" He drew in opium smoke and held it in his lungs.

"Look at yourself," William said. "You are dying, but it's not too late."

"I'll go nowhere." He closed his eyes. "Life is perfect right here."

William snatched the pipe from the Englishman's mouth. His voice was reedy. "Why won't you listen to me, Robert?"

"We've tried everything, little brother. It's no use. Give him some peace." I gently pulled the pipe from William's hand and inserted it between the Englishman's teeth.

William's anger had turned his face red in blotches. He rose to his feet and fled the room. I stared at Smyth, then patted his arm. The sweet smoke followed me out the door.

4

One Eye Gao Bai called from the darkness behind me, "Where should we put it?"

We were carrying the coffin stolen from the cemetery. The wood was still cold from the icehouse, where it had been stored that evening. Gao and I had turned to this task soon after the Englishman had fallen asleep, and it was nearing midnight.

We were in a saloon that looked as if it would fit in more in California than Chungking. The bar was twenty feet long, with a brass foot rail near the floor and a shiny spittoon at the corner. Behind the bar, shelves held dozens of whiskey bottles. A bartender had draped his white rag over a hook below the moose head above the bar.

Wood captains' chairs surrounded a faro table where a deck of cards was fanned out on the green felt with chips stacked in front of the dealer's chair. Five sets of spurs—some with discs and some with rollers—hung on the wall behind the table.

I crossed the floor—painted to resemble planks—to run a hand along the feathers and beads of an Indian war bonnet on the wall near the spurs. I'd never seen such a thing before.

Stepping over electric cables, I passed a Bell and Howell camera on a tripod, and ducked under a sound boom. An overhead gantry supported spotlights, and two tripods held more lights around the stage. Yet the set was dimly lit by a single bulb hanging on a wire. I returned to the hallway. Gao and I lifted the coffin, and I walked backward into the studio, the coffin between us. The pry bar hanging from Gao's cloth belt banged against the coffin, and Gao grunted under the load as we carried the coffin across the set and lowered it to the floor. He lifted a cotton rag from a pocket and held it to his nose. With his other hand, he jammed the pry bar under the coffin's lid. The nails ground loudly.

I left him there, returning through the hall and passing another stage, where a mock-up of a Japanese G3M bomber was mounted on tall sawhorses. A government agency called the China Film Company had hired this studio—Two Rivers Film Production Company—to make propaganda films. Most of the time, though, Two Rivers' stages had sets of the Summer Palace, as the studio specialized in melodramas about the empress dowager—usually portrayed as a merciless and cunning villain— and the intrigues and romances of the imperial household in the last days of the Qing dynasty, just before the revolution threw them out in 1911. The studio also churned out detective movies—often set in Shanghai—and westerns, where both cowboys and Indians were played by Chinese actors.

I came to the studio's side door, which I had kicked in a few moments earlier, and lifted a five-gallon wood keg that had *Harbin Brewery* stenciled on its side. Near the door was a poster of Zheng Zhengqiu standing in front of a cart and mule, from the movie *Romance of a Fruit Peddler*. I placed the keg over my shoulder and walked back to the western set.

Gao was bent over, his hands on his knees, and his mouth opening and closing like a fish. He wiped his face with his sleeve. "I can't get near it again."

I approached the stinking lump. Her family had probably gone deeply into debt to buy the white silk for her burial robe. Eunuch Chang had ordered me to find a female corpse, and Madam Tuan had said the easiest way would be to find a young refugee and use a knife to turn her into a corpse. Chungking was filled with tens of thousands of people who had fled inland when the Japanese had taken Nanking. No record existed of them anywhere. They lived on the streets, and when it rained they got wet. I had preferred robbing a grave, even though it meant convincing Gao Bai.

He said again, "Eunuch Chang never tells us why we are sent on these missions. Doesn't that bother you?"

"Why do we need to know anything?" The odor of rot caught in my throat. The beer keg contained gasoline, and I poured some over the body, then onto the bar, the faro table, and the floor. "You know the way out?" I tossed the keg onto the floor. "I don't want you to have to stop and think about the route to the door."

I pulled out a set of brass knuckles from a pocket and threw it onto the floor. The Blue Rooster, one of Chungking's gangster organizations, used brass knuckles as their signature. Eunuch Chang detested gangster societies, saying the members were inept and boorish thugs. Once every five years or so, one of the gangs would try to take over the eunuch's business, and six or eight gangsters would be dealt horrible deaths, and the gang's survivors would beg for mercy and pay a huge indemnity.

Gao lifted a length of twine from his pocket. At least, I first thought it was twine. He held it up. Even in the low light, it glittered.

"A necklace?" I asked. "Where'd you get it?"

The chain was made of thick gold links, and a sizable jewel hung from it, maybe a diamond.

"I took it from the new girl, the one whose arm Madam Tuan sliced open. Eunuch Chang told me to leave it at the body tonight." But he didn't let go of the necklace.

I asked, "When was the last time you were handed an empty rice bowl, One Eye?"

He hissed through his teeth, then tossed the necklace onto the corpse. "You are right, big brother. I don't need to know these things."

I brought out a sulfur match and scraped it with my thumbnail. It flared into life. "Let's go."

I dropped the match onto the corpse. Fire erupted high, crackling and hissing, and brilliantly lighting the stage. Flames raced across the floor toward the saloon's bar and the piano.

I followed Gao down the hall, past the Japanese airplane, the roar of the fire following us. We pushed through the door and ran out onto Heping Road.

捌

The next day I was walking toward the dining hall when a child's crying came from the other side of the wall.

"Hear him?" William asked. "That's probably the boy. I saw Ham Fist bring him into the compound yesterday."

A few minutes before, William had come to my room and had asked me to follow him. When we walked along the kitchen building toward the sound, the scent of grilled duck skin followed us.

I asked, "How else will the House of Eight Orchids find recruits?"

William grabbed my arm to stop me. "The boy was taken off the street, just like we were."

I shrugged. "That's how things are done around here. Thousands of orphans are in Chungking's streets. He'll have a better life here in the compound than outside."

"Yesterday he was crying for his mother, and he is still crying for her. He may not be an orphan, and maybe his parents live nearby. I want to help him."

Harsh words came from the other side of the wall, which halted the crying.

I was wearing cloth shoes and could feel the gravel under my feet. I smiled. "What are you going to do?"

He winced. I—with my muscles and knives and training—had insulted him. The words had escaped me before I could stop them.

His words were clipped. "You know as well as I do that I'm powerless against Ham Fist and the Rough Boys. I'm an artist—pushing paint around on a piece of cloth—but you . . . you are . . . whatever the eunuch has made you. Please get that boy out of the Rough Boys' Yard and take him home."

I pulled at my chin. "Ham Fist won't like it. And neither will the eunuch."

"You need to do the right thing."

"I always do the right thing."

He said, "I'm talking about something else entirely."

I looked at my brother, standing there in Chungking trousers, his eyebrows up and his mouth partway open, ready to argue more. Much as I held fast in my allegiance to Eunuch Chang, I still could never get rid of the idea that I might've been responsible for William and me never seeing our parents again, those years ago. I was only five when the eunuch took us, but I was the oldest, and he was my charge. I loved him like no one else on earth.

I said, "You wait here."

He smiled broadly, and I left him there. On the door to the Rough Boys' Yard was a red-and-blue painting of General Guan Yu, with his curved sword and square mustache, from the time of the Three Kingdoms. The gates were always open, but the Rough Boys seldom came into the main compound. I walked into their courtyard, looking for the child. Unlike the rest of the eunuch's grounds—where you couldn't walk in a straight line due to all the ponds, hillocks, trees, hedges, and statues—the Rough Boys' courtyard was a gravel plane. Three wood striking posts—each six feet tall—were planted in the ground near the dormitory door. A young man named Always Hungry was smashing his fist into a post. All the Rough Boys had to strike a post five hundred times each day with a fist or foot, but if Ham Fist, the yardmaster, couldn't hear a strike—if it weren't loud enough—he cuffed the boy to the ground, and the boy would start his five hundred again. The Rough Boys had half-inch calluses on their knuckles. A young man named Always Hungry was smashing his fist into the board.

The child was sitting on the gravel next to the privy tender's hut. He kept his eyes on the ground as I approached. His hair had been cut off, and his scalp was still red from the lye wash meant to kill lice. His cheeks were remarkably round, as if he were hiding oranges, and they were wet. He was maybe five years old.

I knelt next to him. "Did you come here today?"

He kept his eyes on the ground. "Yesterday."

"Are you getting enough to eat?"

"I want to go home."

At the other end of the yard, two boys—about twelve years old—carried a thirty-pound stone back and forth in a relay. With his back to me and his hand in the air with three fingers up, Ham Fist counted the times the stone was carried across the yard. He might've been the largest man in China, a head taller than me and half again as heavy. From my distance, Ham Fist didn't appear to have a neck, and his head was a stump on top of his sloping shoulders. His hair was black and bristly, cut almost to the skin. When he yelled at the boy carrying the stone, the boy lifted the stone over his head four times before passing it to the other boy.

Ham Fist's lieutenant, a Mongol who always wore a Royal Navy cutlass in a scabbard he had found somewhere, was overseeing three boys at the striking posts. His name was Munokio, which means "ferocious dog" in the Mongol language. He was a wiry fellow who only smiled when he was about to slap one of the Rough Boys.

I asked the boy, "What's your name?"

"Yang Hai. I want to go home."

"Do you know where you live?"

I kept my eyes on Ham Fist, who was still running the drill, where the boy staggered under the stone. When it slipped to the ground, Ham

Fist kicked the boy, then scooped up the stone to toss it to the other boy, who almost fell to his knees under the weight.

"I live on Brown Dog Street."

"Where on Brown Dog Street?"

"I don't know." The boy pushed the back of his hand against his mouth. He wasn't going to weep in front of me.

"What does your father do?"

"He's dead."

"Your mother?"

He brought up his gaze. "Momma sells canaries."

"Does she have a shop?"

"A canary shop." His small voice was almost lost in the yard. "Momma and I live behind the canaries."

"At the back of the shop?"

He nodded.

"Do you have brothers or sisters?"

"Just canaries."

I pointed at Ham Fist. "Did he find you?"

"I was chasing a chicken, and that man grabbed me."

The House of Eight Orchids was in fact two houses, the front—where the eunuch and I and fifteen or sixteen others lived—and the Rough Boys' compound in back. Eunuch Chang liked to believe that his business was founded on intellectualism. His genius was the reason for his success. Students recruited for the front—One Eye Gao Bai, Sun Bo, a dozen others, and me—were taught to read and write because the eunuch had concluded we were bright. We learned languages and comportment, and if we showed interest in a subject, the eunuch arranged for tutors. When he had seen me staring at maps in his library, he had the Englishman teach me geography. The eunuch prided himself on outsmarting his rivals and victims.

But there was another aspect to the House of Eight Orchids: the Rough Boys. Every year Ham Fist plucked several orphans from the

Chungking streets, and most became intensely grateful for the food and shelter. They were taught violence and obedience and became ferocious fighters. The eunuch believed teaching the Rough Boys to read or write was a waste.

So when Eunuch Chang's plotting and cunning weren't enough, the Rough Boys were used to give a shopkeeper a black eye or start a seemingly spontaneous riot that destroyed a block of buildings owned by a wealthy trader. I suspect Eunuch Chang was embarrassed by his need for the boys, as he almost never mentioned them.

Ham Fist wasn't cautious in his recruiting. Most of his captures were orphans—Chungking had thousands of them living on the streets—but some weren't, and the eunuch might not have cared too much either way.

I said, "I'll take you home."

"That man said I can't go home." He pointed at Ham Fist. "He said this is my home now."

From a shed near the striking posts, Ham Fist brought out two sledgehammers. Each of the Rough Boys swung a sledgehammer half an hour a day, striking the ground again and again. Ham Fist still hadn't looked in my direction once.

"Come with me." I pulled the boy to his feet and hurried him along behind the privy tender's hut toward the gate. I was going to return this boy to his home, and it wouldn't be the first time I had taken a boy back.

I pushed him along for a few steps, and he must have realized the stakes because he sprinted out ahead of me, his short legs churning. We ran through the General Yu Gate, and I led him over the pond on the White Swan Bridge, past the Great Hall and a stone statue of Kuan Yin, the goddess of compassion, where William was waiting. He only smiled as the boy and I ran out the main gate, rushing by the gate gods.

Near the compound's wall just outside the gate, Madam Tuan was shopping at Red Face Zixin's cosmetics wagon. Her maids—who had carried her out here—waited nearby. Red Face visited once a week, precisely at this time. Madam Tuan's makeup held her face together, and without it I suspect the skin of her face would shatter like a broken window. She never missed the appointment, even when she had dysentery and was carried to the cosmetics wagon on a cart. Madam Tuan usually spent five silver Mexes during a visit. Red Face's vest had pockets for dozens of samples, and he wore a black cap and black vest over a skivvy shirt. The vest had a dozen pockets for samples. He pulled stoppers from bottles to allow Madam Tuan to sniff the perfumes.

The cart displayed brushes, little appliances used to press eyelashes into shape, manicure scissors, rouges, lip colors, and a hundred perfumes, the bottles always clinking together when the cart moved. Madam Tuan was known to spend two hours making her selections. Three years ago, Madam Tuan had suspected Red Face Zixin of diluting her new bottle of lilac water and had Ham Fist bring him to the compound, where she had lopped off one of his big toes with a bolt cutter. Limping and bowing, Red Face had appeared at the gate at the appointed time the following week.

Madam Tuan didn't look up. Gesturing widely, two scholars—who always wore gray robes slit up the sides and black skullcaps topped with a black button—leaned toward each other as they walked. The boy ran between them, and then so did I. We turned onto Woodblock Lane, a narrow dirt road with sewage running down the middle in a gutter. The lane was squeezed between straw-and-mud huts. A sedan chair's lead bearer called out a signal, "There is a cloud in the sky," and the rear bearer answered with, "Someone's on the earth nearby," and both men stepped to the side of the road, out of our way. The boy was too winded to go farther, and he knelt with his hands on his knees. I scooped him up.

At the corner I hurried south, and ran past a butcher's stall where ham hocks hung from a pole. The street ended at a cliff down to the river. Across the Yangtze, the gunboat USS *Ingram* was moored at the Lung Men Hao Lagoon near the American navy club, with a coal barge alongside. At the Big Power Bath House I turned west, passing three children playing *bao* with a rubber ball. The boy bounced along in my arm.

"Yang Hai, there's your corner," I said, breathing heavily.

He grinned and pointed at a blue *Victory in Resistance* banner hanging from a telegraph pole. A traveling salesman—wearing bells sewn to his trousers to attract business—carried a ten-foot bamboo pole from which hung bowls and dishes. We passed an old woman bent under a load of sunflower stems. A man in filthy rags lay in the street, his hand at his throat, in the last throes of cholera. He was ignored by passersby because by custom the last person to touch him before he died would have to pay for his funeral.

At a temple for the Dragon King, who rules the weather, we turned onto Brown Dog Street. The chattering of canaries carried down the street, and the boy pushed himself out of my arm, ran along the cobblestones, and dashed into the canary shop. A dozen cages of red and yellow birds hung from a wood crossbeam near the shop's door. Across the street, a man in a tattered black jacket fried onions over a charcoal brazier in front of a fortune-teller's stall. Smoke drifted from the brazier.

I stopped to gather my breath. A joyful whoop came from the shop, then Yang Hai's laughter. His mother emerged between the canary cages, Yang Hai in her arms, pressed tightly against her blue apron, which was speckled with bird guano. A strawberry birthmark was on her cheek. She stared at me, a foreign devil, then hesitantly stepped my way.

The boy yelled a warning, too late. A giant hand grabbed the nape of my neck and spun me around. Ham Fist bunched my shirt and almost lifted me off the ground. His black eyes were sunk deeply into his skull, and his nose was flat. His lips flapped as he breathed. His hair was black and bristly, cut almost to the skin. He smelled of cooked cabbage.

He raised his massive fist to my nose and said, "Don't ever come into the Rough Boys' Yard again." He cocked his fist, about to smash my face.

I have carried three knives since my second day at the House of Eight Orchids. One time Eunuch Chang found me with only one knife, and I went without food for a day. All of them are sharp enough to cut a maple leaf in half edgewise. I had trained with knives for thirty minutes a day for a quarter of a century. The eunuch insisted I also always carry thirty hundred-yuan notes for emergencies, rolled tightly together and placed under my belt. Same with One Eye Gao, my brother, and everyone else who might journey from the compound.

A knife had already dropped into my hand, and I thrust it forward into Ham Fist's raised wrist; then I shifted on my feet to press the knife deeper, pinning his wrist to a pole next to a canary cage. Blood squirted down the blade. He tried to bring up his other hand, but I hit him in the solar plexus, and he groaned and would have fallen to the cobblestones were it not for his pinned wrist.

I grabbed both his ears and brought up his head so he had to look at me. Blood ran down his sleeve.

I said in a low voice, "If you ever visit Brown Dog Street again or have anything to do with that boy, I'll peel the skin off your back and fry it over that brazier."

I yanked my knife from the pole. He collapsed to the stones, groaning like a wounded water buffalo. I wiped the knife on his jacket, and it disappeared up my sleeve.

Still in his mom's arms, Yang Hai wore a wide grin. His mother's eyes were wide. I waved at them and turned back to the House of Eight Orchids, anticipating the pleasure of recounting this rescue to William.

捌

"Your father will never let you go." The soldier tapped the handle of his *liuye dao*, a Ming-dynasty willow-leaf saber. Seashells decorated his leather breastplate along the shoulders.

"I am coming with you." The young lady was wearing a phoenix-tail skirt made of satin strips of different colors—or at least, I thought they were different colors, as the film was in black and white—and embroidered with flowers and birds. She lowered her gaze, then caught her lower lip in her teeth, the fetching mannerism that had made her famous throughout China. She reached for his hand. "And I am not going to tell my father."

The audience gasped. Loyalty, not love, was the basis of relationships in China, and for the girl to fail to ask her father for permission for anything—much less running away with a soldier—was outrageous. We were in the Great Wall Theater on Prolong Life Road, two hundred yards from the Wang Lung Men steps, three hours after my run-in with Ham Fist. The projector clicked at the back of the theater. Someone near me smelled of fish.

Sitting in the third row, we stared up at her colossal image. Her hair was pinned up with jewel-encrusted combs, and her fingernails were dark and an inch long.

William leaned my way and whispered, "Watch what she does with her eyelashes. She doesn't blink but instead slowly lowers them and then brings them up."

I scratched my nose. If I had worn a wristwatch, I would've checked it.

"She is luminous," my brother whispered. "I'd like to paint her."

Once in a while the eunuch allowed William to paint what he wanted, but much of my brother's time was spent forging old Chinese art, which the eunuch sold through complicit brokers in Hong Kong and Shanghai. William's record price was 450 British pounds, obtained from one Earl Pomeroy of Gloucester, who was visiting Hong Kong to add to the collection that his father had begun decades before. The earl purchased *Along the River During the Qingming Festival*, painted by the Song-dynasty artist Zhang Shengwen eight hundred years ago. At least, that's what Earl Pomeroy believed. About once a month the eunuch's brokers would find a wealthy buyer for another of William's forgeries. My brother provided steady revenue for the House of Eight Orchids. Not as much as me, but steady nevertheless.

One Eye Gao Bai snored softly in the seat next to mine. He had left his cricket in his room. William and I seldom left the compound alone. The eunuch said we were accompanied for our protection, but over the years I had come to believe he was afraid to lose his investments: William and me. The eunuch could never entirely trust a foreign devil, even ones he treated as sons. William went to a movie every week, and I usually came along to keep him out of trouble, I liked to tell him, though he never got into trouble. Gao Bai always came with us and always slept through the movies. He was the best man with his fists at the House of Eight Orchids.

I had seen the young lady up on the screen in a dozen films. Her name was Wu Luli, or Tsingtao Lily, because she was born in that port city on the Yellow Sea across from Korea. In the first decade of the century, Wu Luli's father had become wealthy distributing Tsingtao beer, brewed by German settlers. At fifteen, Wu Luli was cast in her first film, and then she went to Hong Kong, where a dozen studios were located, though now she also made movies in Chungking and Canton as well. Her daily affairs were reported in the newspapers. She rode horses at the Shatin course near Hong Kong and owned a Packard Deluxe Eight. She had been seen at the Peninsula Hotel restaurant in Hong Kong with Clark Gable and at the Raffles Hotel's Long Bar in Singapore with Somerset Maugham. The *Chungking Daily Press* had breathlessly reported that Tsingtao Lily had worn a bias-cut gown designed by Madeleine Vionnet to the China Relief Ball at the Renmin Hotel. A month ago she was spotted on General Chiang Kai-shek's motor yacht, speaking with his wife, Mei-ling.

On the screen, the soldier mounted a horse, then held his hand down to her. She looked up at him with those eyes and gripped his hand. He pulled her up, and she sat sidesaddle in front of him. He put his arm around her and kicked the horse's flanks. After a glance back at her home, she turned toward the west and her future. She and the soldier rode toward the mountains. The music swelled, and the credits began to roll.

When I elbowed One Eye Gao Bai, he jerked awake. The three of us rose from our seats, and Gao pulled on his black wool cap. We followed the crowd up the aisle toward the lobby, then out onto the street.

I narrowed my eyes against the sun. The movie had been a matinee—
Eunuch Chang didn't want us out at night unless on business—and it was
the middle of the afternoon. William brought a handkerchief to his nose
against the smell of sewage rising from an open ditch at the side of the road
where Mengyao Xu, known lately as Four Finger Xu, stood in front of a
dough stick pot. Four Finger Xu was the red pole, or enforcer, for the gang
Two River 14K, which specialized in bringing country girls to Chungking
to sell to whorehouses. He wore a black felt bowler and a red vest.

William said, "Don't start anything, One Eye."

One Eye—the person who had lopped off Xu's finger two years
ago—menacingly stepped toward Four Finger, who fled between two
mat-sheds. One Eye laughed and nudged me. He deserved some favor-
able sign, and so I smiled at him. We walked up Red Bayberry Street
toward the compound.

"John, do you remember when you were sixteen years old, and on
the eunuch's orders you approached a Western businessman on Hoolan
Street? You yanked his briefcase from his hand and ran away through
the crowd. I watched from on top of a tobacco shed."

My brother was recalling a day that was painful and humiliating
for me.

I asked, "What of it?"

"And later that afternoon when you asked the eunuch why he had
wanted that briefcase, he boxed your ear."

My head had rung for two days, and I couldn't look at Eunuch
Chang in the eyes for a month.

"You swore then you'd never again ask about Eunuch Chang's business," William said. "Maybe we'd better make an exception today."

"Not a chance."

"That girl Eunuch Chang kidnapped. I thought I'd recognized her
earlier today in the compound. Now I'm sure of it." He put his hand
on my arm, stopping me. "She is the actress Tsingtao Lily."

5

"*National Herald*, mister?" Even speaking just three English words, Sun Bo's accent was thick. "Only two weeks old." His shaved head reflected the electric bulb overhead.

William waved a hand. "Leave me alone, you unwashed street urchin." He was following the script.

He and I had just returned from the theater, and were in time for Sun Bo's lesson.

"Fresh newspaper. Only two weeks old, mister." Sun Bo moved toward William, holding a stack of newspapers in front of him. The boy's trousers and shirt were made of blue cotton, and his sandals were woven straw. "Newspaper, mister?"

William was wearing some of the Englishman's old clothes, including a worsted three-piece suit with a watch hanging from a fob. The Englishman was the usual pickpocket victim during practice, but Smyth was indisposed, undoubtedly due to too large of a pipe last night. William stepped along with a walking stick that had an ivory boar's-head handle, also on loan from the Englishman.

William wasn't supposed to laugh, but he did, and he said in English, "Be gone, you slit-eyed heathen."

As William raised the stick threateningly, the boy tripped over his own feet and tumbled into him, the newspapers and cane flying. William tumbled backwards, Sun Bo falling with him and crying out in alarm.

William grunted as he landed heavily on his rump.

"Sorry, mister. Sorry." Sun Bo scrambled to his feet and rushed away, leaving his scattered newspapers.

Eunuch Chang held up his hand and asked in Mandarin, "Did you get it, Sixth Brother?"

Sun Bo smiled widely as he held up a leather wallet.

The eunuch lightly cuffed Sun Bo's head. "I have no interest in his wallet. What could be in a wallet? Five yuan and a photo of some gweilo's ugly wife. Where is his passport?"

"My fingers only found the wallet, Eunuch Chang."

William pushed himself to his feet and made a production of dusting off his sleeves. He had told me he always enjoyed playing the pickpocket victim. Between William and the Englishman, they had had their pockets picked five thousand times at the House of Eight Orchids.

"We are only going to have one chance to get the real passport, Sixth Brother," the eunuch said. "The man will be at the train station only a few minutes. You cannot fail."

William picked up the walking stick and planted it firmly on the floor. "I didn't feel your hand, Sixth Brother, so you are getting better." He pulled the passport from his jacket pocket and held it up. It was Robert Smyth's passport, also on loan. "You'll snare it next time, Sixth." William was wearing an ascot, something he had seen in a Fred Astaire movie. It was vivid scarlet, and it made his suit look even more shabby.

Sixth Brother asked, "Why doesn't Yellow Hair lift the passport? I've seen him steal a watch off a man's wrist. He can take anything off anybody."

Eunuch Chang again cuffed the boy's head, more a pat. "You ask too many questions. But you are getting older, so I will tell you this time. You will take the passport from an American, and then John will be visiting the American after we take the passport. The American can't have seen John at the train station."

Two thousand Americans were now in Chungking: diplomats, factory representatives, reporters, engineers, contractors, and military personnel—so many Americans that Chinese restaurants on the south side of the Yangtze near the foreign consulates were serving ham and eggs for breakfast.

Almost as soon as Chang dismissed the boy, a girl entered the hall carrying a tray. Her head was down, and she crossed the hall to us, taking the deferential short steps. She gave Eunuch Chang a glass from the tray, then one to William, and I don't think she meant for me to see this, but her fingers pressed into William's hand as he took the glass, an outrageous breach of servants' decorum. She brought her head up to stare into William's eyes.

The actress's hair was pulled up with tortoiseshell pins in the fashion that girls adopted at nineteen to indicate they were ready for courtship. She wore a servant's white blouse and knee-length black skirt. Bandages were still around her arm where Madam Tuan had sliced her open. William was as still as a tree stump.

"Madam Tuan's lessons in deportment have succeeded." Eunuch Change lifted a palm toward Tsingtao Lily and spoke as if she weren't in the room. "When this so-called actress came to our home, she was haughty, disrespectful, and filled with corrupt Western notions.

"Here she is now, doing her duty obediently."

Tsingtao Lily crossed the room and handed a glass to me. She smelled of jasmine. As she passed me the glass, she pressed my fingers, too—more a caress—and lifted her gaze. Her eyes were unlike anyone else's in the compound; they were straight and untamed, and burned into me. Then she dropped her eyes again to the floor.

The eunuch said, "Madam Tuan has done a masterful transformation."

The actress moved toward the door. William's gaze followed her.

"We now have a proper young woman," Eunuch Chang said.

I wasn't so sure.

捌

The eunuch's robe was decorated with the Eight Immortals crossing the sea on their way to the Conference of the Magical Peach, a design popular in the Qing-dynasty court two hundred years ago. The House of Eight Orchids' tailor had worked on the robe ten months, and had presented it to the eunuch a week ago. The robe would be fobbed off to a wealthy collector in the American city of San Francisco once the eunuch had worn it enough to lessen the sheen.

Eunuch Chang said, "William, your brother and I have business to attend to. Do you have work in your shop? Perhaps on those US military procurement orders?" The eunuch raised his palms toward William to take the sting from the dismissal.

It didn't work this time. William brought himself up and squared his shoulders, as if trying to make himself look larger. Now that he was no longer playing the pickpocket victim, William switched to Szechwanese. "You don't need to dismiss me, do you, Eunuch Chang?"

The eunuch slid his hands down his silk robe, his display of vast patience. He said in his silvery voice, "Your brother has his specialty, and you have yours, William. You are included in everything that befits your skills."

"I paint and draw things." He wore a look of ill usage. "So I fiddle with horsehair brushes and paint pots all day. I could do more."

The eunuch's eye twitched, and I involuntarily took a step away from him.

He asked, "What do you have in mind?"

William worked his mouth without a sound.

"What else can you do for the House of Eight Orchids? Tell me what you can do for me, and I'll let you do it."

I said, "William, let's you and I talk about this later." I feared for him. This was a wild breach of accepted behavior. He was questioning Eunuch Chang. Tsingtao Lily's scent—lilac—was still in the room. I stared at my brother.

William stepped forward. "I don't like being sent away all the time."

The eunuch's face was a mask of innocence. I'd seen it before, this utterly blank expression with the corners of his mouth lifted slightly. It never boded well for whomever his gaze was upon.

My brother said, "When you and John and One Eye talk about the House of Eight Orchids—its plans and its future—I'm always sent out of the room."

"Perhaps you are right. You may stay today."

William and I followed the eunuch to the six-panel black lacquer screen that divided the room. Instead of the usual scenes from the imperial dynasties, this screen was painted with Kuomintang soldiers holding their rifles and banners high. The eunuch liked to laugh at this clumsy propaganda. He often repeated the ancient maxim "The mountains are high, and the emperor is far away." He didn't care who ruled China. His queue swung behind him as he walked. Then he folded the screen to one side, revealing the back of the room.

A Japanese pilot was lying on a table, his arms and legs strapped down with rawhide cord. He wasn't wearing clothing, but his abdomen and legs were wrapped in white bandages. Madam Tuan sat next to him on a high stool, a long black dress hiding her bound feet. She bowed to the eunuch but didn't give William or me a glance. William stopped as if he'd run into a wall.

The eunuch gestured toward the pilot. "His airplane's engine failed, and he landed the plane in a field on the road to Chengtu. I bought him from the farmers who captured him for two thousand yuan."

Madam Tuan said, "He has been given the bowl of tea, though I had to hold his nose and drop it down his throat, as he wouldn't drink it without my help."

The eunuch nodded. "The herbal tea deadens the nerves, though not as much as I had hoped when I drank it those many years ago."

She said, "I've also washed his privates with pepper water."

"What are you doing?" William whispered, barely audible.

The eunuch stepped to the foot of the table and stood over the prisoner, whose mouth was opening and closing but who didn't make a sound.

The eunuch said to us, "I met Madam Tuan when she was a girl. She and her father lived in the Imperial City just outside Forbidden City gates."

Eunuch Chang seldom told me anything. Most of my information about him came from the Englishman, who liked to stretch tales, so I never knew whether I was hearing the truth.

Madam Tuan smiled at Eunuch Chang. "I remember my first sight of you. You were so afraid your brother had to pull you into the room. But you were determined to improve yourself so you could serve the empress dowager."

A tea table was next to her, on which were a stack of bandages and a metal plug, which was round and shiny, nothing I'd ever seen before.

The eunuch said, "Madam Tuan's father was a knifer, one of five men licensed by the imperial court."

"As was my father's father, and his father," Madam Tuan said. She waved her long nail protectors, emphasizing her words. "For each operation, my father received six taels. It was a good living."

"What operation?" William asked.

"The one that allowed me to serve in the imperial palace," Eunuch Chang said. "We will need your help, William. After the procedure, the pilot will need to walk for two hours. He will want to lie down, but you can't let him."

"Eunuch Chang," William said, "forgive me, but I don't know what you are talking about."

Madam Tuan always looked at William and me as if we were prey. From a fold in her dress, she brought out a curved knife that had an ivory handle.

"Madam Tuan was taught the procedure by her father," the eunuch said. "She will slice off the pilot's privates as close to the body as possible, then insert the metal plug into the urethra, and cover the wound with wet paper and then bandages. The plug will keep the passage from closing so he will be able to pass water."

I held up my hand, but William brushed it aside.

He stepped forward. "Eunuch Chang, why are you doing this?"

His mouth was pressed into a thin line, and he looked at William closely, as if taking an inventory. "You asked not to be sent away, and you weren't. But I don't owe you or your brother or anyone explanations."

"John told me you paid two thousand yuan for this prisoner," William said. "And now you are going to mutilate him?"

The eunuch's chin came up. "Where I come from, it is not a mutilation. It is an elevation."

I said out of the side of my mouth, "Why don't you and I go outside, William. We don't need to be here."

My brother said, "He is a prisoner of war, Eunuch Chang. He doesn't deserve this."

"He is not a prisoner of war," he said. "He is a prisoner of Eunuch Chang, which is to say, me."

Madam Tuan laughed.

"Have you heard nothing of what is happening in Nanking?" the eunuch asked. "I am going to take his privates and then set him free. It is a better fate than the Japanese are offering anyone in Nanking."

The eunuch had showed me a photograph taken several weeks ago in Nanking, of a Japanese soldier carrying a sword, standing in front of forty severed Chinese heads displayed in rows on the ground. More news of atrocities there arrived in Chungking each day.

William turned to me and yelled, "Don't you see how wrong this is? Do something."

I brought up my hands in what I hoped was a gesture of reason. "He's a Jap, and he was on his way in his plane to kill as many people in Chungking as he could."

"This is barbaric." William's face was red and bunched. "Don't you know that, John? And, Eunuch Chang, it is beneath you."

"My privates are in a jar on a shelf. So I am simply the result of barbarism, a monstrous aberration? Is that what you mean?"

William inhaled loudly, then bowed to him. "Eunuch Chang, please don't twist my words. This is a mutilation, and it is deeply wrong."

Madam Tuan said, "Listen to your foreign devil waver and quail, Eunuch Chang. You should have drowned him and his ignorant brother years ago, just as I suggested back then. You, gweilo"—she jabbed the knife in William's direction—"close your big stupid round eyes if you don't have the nerve for this."

The Japanese pilot moaned. His arms were shaking so violently that his knuckles were rapping the table.

The eunuch stared at William. "Four years ago—near Yellow Tooth Teng's home—your brother deliberately jumped in front of me, receiving a bullet that had been intended for my head. The bullet went entirely through his shoulder. The pistol had been so close that the muzzle blast also set his shirt on fire."

"I remember all too well, sir." William nodded in my direction.

"John spent one month in a hospital, and then three more months went by before he regained his full strength."

William waited.

"And, I seldom discuss money in my home, but I want you to know that since the New Year, I have sold your art for the equivalent of two thousand silver Mexes. So I am aware of my obligation to you and your brother. It is a debt of gratitude, a large debt."

I had never before heard him say anything like this.

"What is this I am hearing?" Madam Tuan said. "A debt of grati-tude? These foreign devils are servants, and they are due nothing. Eunuch Chang, let me do the procedure before the pepper bath wears off."

The eunuch held up his hand to silence her, then said to William, "You can unburden me of that debt right now and save this Japanese pilot from the procedure. His privates will stay attached to him, and I will then owe you nothing."

The pilot opened his eyes and pulled his mouth back in a rictus. He must have been brave. He wouldn't let himself cry out. Bushido is the way of the Japanese warrior.

"You can stop this procedure, William," the eunuch said. "Accept my offer, and I will then owe you nothing."

"I don't know what . . ."

"But someday you may wish I were still in your debt."

"I can't let this mutilation happen." He inhaled deeply. "I'll settle the debt. Don't do it. If you ever owed me anything, you no longer do if you stop this procedure, Eunuch Chang."

"I wish things were that simple." The eunuch rearranged his lips into what might've been a smile. "But they seldom are."

Madam Tuan laughed lightly. She tapped her nail protectors on the table next to the Japanese pilot's ear. The pilot flinched.

"Or you can have the girl," the eunuch said.

William stepped back as if punched in the chest. "Pardon me, sir?"

"You heard me quite clearly, I suspect."

"Which girl, Eunuch Chang?"

"Do you think that along with my testicles, I lost my eyes? The girl who stares at you every chance she gets, hoping you'll stare back. The girl who touches you whenever she thinks no one is looking. The girl who whispers to you when you pass her on the walkways. The girl who smiles at you whenever she gets the chance."

"Eunuch Chang, I'm sure that . . ." William glanced at me.

"Tsingtao Lily, the actress in the film you saw at the Great Wall Theater. The girl who scandalizes all of Hong Kong by appearing at Western nightclubs on the arms of French and British diplomats. The girl who the *Straits Times* said broke the heart of every Singapore man who saw her in *The Malay Pirate*. The girl who the newspapers say owns one thousand pairs of earrings. She is trying to encourage you. She thinks you will rescue her. Soon she will proposition you.

"I brought her to the compound because a Shanghai businessman—the founder of Three Blossoms Steel Company—wants her," Eunuch Chang said. "He has seen all her films and reads everything he can about her. He wants her for himself, just as an art collector might want a painting for his home, where only he can look at it. The world thinks Tsingtao Lily died in a fire. This businessman will pay me, and I will deliver her to him."

"I hope she is ready," Madam said. "She still has much to learn about humility and duty."

"But I will give her to you now," the eunuch said. "Tsingtao Lily can be yours, and my debt to you and your brother will be extinguished. I will refund the businessman's payment, and he will simply have to understand."

William stammered, "I c-can't—"

I said, "Eunuch Chang, perhaps there's another way, and—"

Such was his power over me that he cut me off with a glance. Then he said, "Or you can save the Japanese pilot's privates."

William looked again at the pilot. Madam Tuan was holding up the curved knife, and the pilot's eyes were on it. He was shaking, forehead to feet. The rawhide straps were sunk into the flesh of his arms and legs.

"One or the other, William. Make your choice."

"I can't let you castrate the pilot." His voice was as tight as a wire. "It's not right, Eunuch Chang. He is China's enemy, but it's still not right."

"Is that your choice?"

He asked, "Is there any way—"

"Life is filled with difficult choices. Make yours now."

He chewed on nothing. "I can't let you do this . . . this surgery."

"That's your decision? Tsingtao Lily still goes to Shanghai with the businessman?"

He nodded, the slightest of movements.

The eunuch laughed in a small way. "You've been twenty-five years with me, William, and I still find you inscrutable." He gestured toward Madam Chang. "There is to be no new member of the society of castrati today, Madam Tuan. The pilot keeps his privates."

William stepped back and hunched his shoulders, seeming to shrink.

"So please take care of him," the eunuch said to the old woman.

Her arm a blur, Madam Tuan brought the knife across the pilot's neck, instantly opening a gaping wound from side to side. The pilot jerked against the restraints. Blood rushed out of his neck and spilled onto the table. The sound was of bubbles and gasping and drowning. Madam Chang shifted so blood wouldn't get on her skirt as it fell to the floor and splattered on the tile. The pilot jerked once more, then was still.

I was rooted to the floor.

The eunuch opened and closed his hands, as if testing the air. "I feel lighter, no longer being obligated to you and your brother."

"Eunuch Chang, you said the pilot . . ." William's words tumbled out. "You said that if I—"

"I said the pilot would keep his privates." He started for the door. "And he still has them."

捌

My room at the House of Eight Orchids was in a tiny building—more a shed—and contained only my quarters. It was separated from the wall across from the axe snare by twenty feet of loose sand. An intruder who managed to climb over the wall in sufficiently healthy shape to continue—an unlikely prospect—would leave his trail in the sand, alerting us to his route. The room contained my cot and a French chest of drawers that the eunuch had presented to me with a flourish, saying the chest dated from the time of Louis XIV, and it indeed might have because William could forge a lot of things, but he couldn't forge furniture. The room didn't have a chair, because either I was lying down in my room or I wasn't there.

It was after midnight, and I was having trouble sleeping, wondering about my brother. He had seemed giddy in his shop, showing off the documents. William had the brains in the family—I say by way of understatement—and learned anything from a book twice as quickly as I could. But he was often melancholy, sometimes sitting in his shop for a day, his mouth turned down and doing nothing, and I couldn't coax him from the room. And sometimes I would catch him staring off at the clouds, as if he wished he could be released from the ground and float up toward the sun. The Englishman said my brother was a dreamer. William might be happy once in a while, but he was never giddy. I was my brother's self-appointed guardian—he would despise me mentioning anything like that to him—and I worried about him, as I was lying there twirling my number-one knife.

Last year at the Great Wall Theater, William and I—with One Eye asleep next to us—had seen an American short film about Benny Goodman. His drummer twirled his sticks in his fingers when not pounding the drums. I had taught myself to twirl my number-one knife, not without cutting my right index finger to the bone three times, but I could spin it so quickly that it was scarcely visible. The knife whirled in my hand, around and around.

Someone pushed open the door. My knife flipped to ready. Her scent came in before she did. Tsingtao Lily squeezed into the room and closed the door behind her as if she owned the place. She didn't appear to walk, but rather drifted to my cot and stood above me. Even in my darkened room, her clothing seemed bright.

I tucked away my knife and sat up. "What are you doing here?"

She held out her arms and spoke in English. "The man who is buying me will like this, don't you think?" The line was from *The Tea Schooner Girl*, Tsingtao Lily's first movie, which had played in Chungking for six weeks.

"Where did you get the *guju*?"

The robe was made of crimson silk, with loose sleeves. The lapel was trimmed in black. Below the *guju*'s black hem were red velvet slippers of a style indicating they were brought from Kashmir on the Silk Road more than a hundred years ago. Pins inlaid with mother-of-pearl held her hair high on her head.

She turned a slow circle. "I stole the robe and slippers from Madam Tuan's room." She held up her wrist. "Same with the hairpins and the jade bracelet. Does the robe look better on me than on that old hag?"

"Madam Tuan is going to badly hurt you."

"She's already sliced open my arm. What more can she do?"

"You have no idea," I said.

Lily smiled. "She'll never know. I'll put everything back just as I found them." She swayed her arms. "I just wanted to show you this *guju*. It fits as if it were made for me, don't you think?"

She, the cot, her scent, and I filled the room.

"Have you seen *Follow the Fleet*?" she asked. "With Fred Astaire and Ginger Rogers? Irving Berlin wrote the music."

Her hand was at her hair, toying with an ivory pin that held her hair up. Her face—with her almond eyes and finely planed cheekbones—was as close as it had appeared in her films up on the screen.

"Ginger tap-dances to the song 'Let Yourself Go,'" she said. "I can't dance, but I could learn in a week or two. Someday maybe you can see me dance."

She half-stepped closer along the cot. "May I sit down?" She lowered herself to the cot and pushed her hip against mine. "Someday I want to go to the Golden Mountain and make American movies. They are seen around the world. All the world knows who Joan Crawford is."

I squeezed back against the wall.

She said, "I met Myrna Loy once, did I tell you? She was in *The Thin Man*, a fabulous role. She suggested I come to America. I already know how to eat with a fork." She put her hand on my elbow. "Did you see *Women in Arms*? The director was George Swift. When he was in Singapore I spent three days with him at the Raffles Hotel. He promised he would give me the lead role in his next Dracula film."

Her clothing was so bright I had to squint. "You will gain nothing in my room. Go back to the women's quarters."

She moved her hand up and down my arm.

"Mr. Swift said he was sure he could get Clark Gable to play Count Dracula," she said, "and Clark and I would receive the same billing. Maybe someday I'll go to America."

Her fingers moved, and she pulled the pin from her hair, which fell to her shoulders. Then she released the sash around her waist.

"My pony could be shipped to Los Angeles," she said. "My maid and cook would come with me, and I'll buy a new car when I get there. I'm thinking of the new Cord 812 sedan."

I lifted myself by my elbows. My face was inches from hers. "You won't get help here. Go back to your room."

"Have you heard of the Sunset Boulevard House of the Manicure in Los Angeles?" she chattered on. "I read about it in the Chinese-language *Screen Stars* magazine. There are twenty seats for manicures and ten for having toenails done. Can you imagine? And Antoinette's on Wilshire Boulevard sells gowns directly from Paris."

In *The Manchurian Bride*, Lily had played a heartbroken runaway who saves herself with charm and intelligence. In *The Dowager's Handmaiden*, Lily's character escaped servitude using the force of her intellect. In *The Jap's Puzzles*, an evil Japanese slave lord offered Lily freedom if she could solve three deadly puzzles. I had watched the movies at the Two Lucky Dragons Theater and the Great Wall Theater in

Chungking. In each of these films Lily had used her powerful mind to prevail, with William and I and One Eye sitting in the tenth row.

And here was the real Lily marveling at the number of chairs at a manicure shop. She tried to knead my chest, but I caught her hand.

"You'll help me get out of here, won't you?" she asked. "You and I could be very happy tonight."

"You've come to the wrong room, I'm afraid."

She pouted with her exquisite lower lip out. She leaned forward, her hand on the back of my neck, pulling me toward her. "I can make you help me."

Her skin seemed to be glowing, and she languorously lowered and raised her eyelids. Her lips were an inch from mine. Her perfume—jasmine—wrapped around me.

But I'd had enough. "Eunuch Chang once ordered me to steal an envelope of money from a Catholic nun. The money was the Chungking mission's funding for a year. If I can take money from a charity, how is it that I could betray the eunuch by helping you escape?"

I lifted her off the cot. She gasped, her eyes wide. She had been turned away, maybe for the first time in her life.

I opened the door and pushed her through, but a fearsome thought hit me, so I gripped her arm. My voice was low. "Stay away from my brother."

"You're a thug." Her face flamed red. "Take your hand off me."

I tightened my grip, and I know how to do it so it hurts, and she yelped and tried to twist away. I fairly lifted her from the gravel and dragged her along the walkway, her feet skittering on the pebbles.

Her voice was iron. "Are you threatening me, you thug? What will you do, break my nose with your fist? Or maybe you'll use one of your knives the kitchen girls told me about. They say you carry fifteen of them."

"I never make threats, but I do give advice. Stay away from William. He won't help you, either."

"Or what'll you do?" She sliced me up with her eyes. "You can't hurt me. I'm too valuable to your master."

I fiercely shoved her away, and she scrambled to stay on her feet.

"Thug. Ignorant peasant." She pointed a long finger at me. "No, you're worse than a peasant: you're a eunuch's slave."

I bit down, my jaw muscles so tight my chin rose. The blood beat in my temples. Trying to calm myself, I flexed my fingers and inhaled hugely. I managed to say, "You heard me. Leave William alone."

She narrowed her eyes and bared her teeth, the same look—her trademark—that had conquered the pirate captain in *The Golden Bounty.* The pirate had gathered her in his arms, pleading for forgiveness.

I stepped back inside and closed the door.

Though I had hidden it from her, I was unaccountably worked up, embarrassment and need working on me in equal measure. I gripped the door handle. A moment ago the Manchurian bride had been in front of me, inches away and there for the taking. It had been close, her lips almost on mine and her scent enveloping me. She had come within a breath of breaking me. Then, confronted with my own weakness, my anger had flashed, and I had gripped her arm so that she had cried out. Eunuch Chang taught that anger was dangerous and unprofessional.

I returned to my cot and pulled the thin blanket over me. The eunuch had been trying to rid me of these red flares of anger for a quarter of a century, but he obviously had not succeeded. I stared at the ceiling, and it was a long while before I slept.

6

"Does it look real?" the eunuch asked. "I don't read the language."

The document, which was in English, was titled *United States Department of State, Office of Procurement, Distribution Order*, and it was dated ten days from now. Several lines of text were printed, and signatures were in ink. An embossed blue seal on the bottom was of a steam locomotive in a circle of stars.

"But of course it looks real." The eunuch answered his own question, tilting his head toward William. "The master forger created it." Prominent cheekbones and low brows protected the eunuch's dark eyes. He was wearing his topaz-blue robe, made in Soochow, the southern town known for embroidery. A mulberry tree in green and gold thread adorned the robe front.

William's shop shared quarters with the sickroom, on the other side of a wall. A clamshell jobbing press—with a big iron wheel—stood against a wall near an open cabinet containing stacks of paper in dozens of grades and colors. The shop was filled with the tools of his trade: from an apothecary cupboard containing two hundred bottles of ink and dyes, and jars holding brushes made with horse, rabbit, and deer hair, to drawers of knives and razors and rulers, and, mounted in a wood frame above William's drafting table, a Leica Schraubgewinde camera.

I lifted the forged order and held it to the light. William laughed lightly. His spirits had returned. I didn't have the knowledge to tell an authentic US State Department order from a fraud, and he knew it.

"What about this one?" The eunuch placed another document on the table.

Department of the Army Payroll Headquarters was printed in green, as was the line for the signature. The rest of the document had been typed.

I pointed. "The typewriter has a faulty *M*. All the *M*s in each sentence are a little crooked."

"The typewriter in the army payroll office has a faulty key." My brother's voice was jubilant, a tone I seldom heard from him. He was smiling and rocking on the balls of his feet, switching his gaze between Eunuch Chang and me, as if savoring the knowledge of a great secret. I had expected him to be withdrawn and sullen after his humiliating attempt to save the Japanese pilot the day before. But as he displayed the forged documents, he grinned and laughed, beaming. Something had changed in him, something I didn't know about.

The eunuch slid a document on the table closer to me. "And this document cost me one thousand United States dollars."

I lifted it. A photograph of me had been attached to the document, and green squiggly lines covered the lower photo and the paper on which it was mounted so that the photo could not be removed and replaced with the same squiggly alignment. The photograph was of my head and shoulders. I was wearing a United States Army major's uniform. The document was titled *United States Army—United States Consulate Transfer Identification*. Printed under the photo was Ronald Case, Major, Quartermaster's Office, 2nd Infantry Division, United States Army.

"United States Army officers do not carry identification containing their photographs," William said. "But when this much money is involved, this document is issued, identifying the army officer who will take custody of the gold when it is removed from the ship."

William had taken the photograph last week with his Leica. I held the document up to the light. I looked like an American army officer.

The eunuch smoothed an eyebrow with a finger. "William says these documents are indistinguishable from the real ones." He turned to me. "My question to you is: Are you indistinguishable from a real American?"

I returned the document to the table.

"The Englishman says that sometimes you act more Chinese than American," he said. "And you often act more English than American. He says there are profound differences."

I said, "He has told me I should laugh louder."

"He also says you drop your eyes too quickly when you approach strangers," Eunuch Chang said. "And you stand too close to people when speaking with them. And your breath smells like ginger instead of something called Ipana."

"I'll be American enough, sir, and—"

He gestured, inviting my silence. "The tailor tells me your uniform will be identical to a real one. At great expense I have purchased an American-army–issue Colt .45 and a holster American officers wear. Should the ship's guards detect the slightest amount of Chinese in your mannerisms—or English or Japanese or any of your other tutors' nationalities—you will fail. You must be an authentic American army major."

I stood straighter. The Englishman had told me American army officers act as if they had bamboo poles down their spines.

The eunuch folded his hands together. "I now have a friend employed at the San Yun telegraph relay station, and another is working as a translator for the British-American Joint Military Advisory Office. It is a rare combination."

"We've rehearsed everything," I said. "I know the words I will speak. I know the documents and how to present them to the American guards."

"One hundred thousand United States dollars are on that steamship. It will be my largest prize ever."

I said, "I thought the actress was going to be your largest prize ever."

"Let's meet this peddler from Shanghai."

He held up a hand toward William, indicating he was to remain in the forger's shop. I thought he might puff up like a rooster and protest at being excluded, but, still smiling mysteriously, he brought out a sheet of tan paper and bent over the table, beginning a new project.

I followed the eunuch from William's shop along a walkway. The kitchen was near, and the wind carried the scent of ripe skin eggs, which are duck or chicken eggs coated with lime and flower and left to ripen for eight weeks, which turns the yolks black.

We entered the great hall. The owner of the steel plant was sitting on a blackwood chair next to the marble-inlaid table.

Between his blunt fingers was a factory-made cigarette, and he tapped it so the ashes fell onto the black tile. His Western double-breasted herringbone suit with broad lapels and square padded shoulders made him look top-heavy. The knot in his red silk tie was the size of a fist. Pomade kept his slicked-back hair in place. His nose was flat, and his lips were moist above his small and unstable chin. On the table was a suitcase.

He pushed himself up from the char. "The legendary Eunuch Chang." His bow was a small movement. "I had hoped you weren't merely a fable—the product of a hundred stories—and here you are."

"Shih Heng. I am honored to meet the founder of the Three Blossoms Steel Company."

"But not sufficiently honored to serve tea." Shih Heng's voice was silky.

"An unforgivable oversight," the eunuch said. "My staff will be punished."

Shih jabbed his cigarette my direction. "Who is the foreigner?"

"My bodyguard."

"The great Eunuch Chang needs a bodyguard?"

"I learned many years ago never to be alone with gold bullion," Eunuch Chang said. "Strange things can happen, few of them good."

"But a round-eyed, white-haired foreigner?"

The eunuch flicked his thumb in my direction. "This gweilo body-guard will do until a better one comes along."

The businessman stroked his tie. "I have heard stories about you, Eunuch Chang, about when the buttons were torn from your cap at the Summer Palace." Shih laughed and turned a palm up, an invitation to the eunuch to tell tales.

Buttons on a palace eunuch's cap signified rank. To have them torn off was a disgrace. The eunuch's mouth was pressed into a white line.

"Is that true?" Shih waved his cigarette. "I would like a story to tell my wife and children about the legendary Eunuch Chang."

"It was many years ago," the eunuch said.

"You were caught five *li* from the palace, leading a Mongolian pony carrying a cousin of the empress dowager. You and she were traveling west, away from the palace. Is that true?"

The eunuch stared at Shih.

"Running away with a girl?" Shih said. "And you, a eunuch? What would be the point?"

"Is the gold in the suitcase?" the eunuch asked.

"And so you were brought back in chains before the empress dowager, and she expelled you from the Summer Palace. The story is that your queue was cut off and that you were carried out through the palace's livestock gate and thrown into a pigsty."

"Open the suitcase. Let's see your payment."

"Your queue has grown back," Shih said. "How about your privates?"

I flicked my wrist, and the knife in my sleeve dropped into my hand. The eunuch held up his hand in front of me. "This is a business transaction, John."

"But, Eunuch Chang," I said. "This vulgar and surly—"

"I'll have no wind or waves," the eunuch said.

The knife was back up my sleeve, and the cigarette was in Shih's mouth, the smoking tip bouncing as he spoke. "I left my guards at your gate. I am insulted you believe you need a bodyguard." He untied the case's straps and pulled open the lid. "Here is your payment. Let's make the exchange and be done with it."

Twelve gold bars were in the case, each stamped with an imperial dragon, meaning they had been cast at the Peking mint sometime before 1911. He removed them from the case two at a time and let them fall heavily onto the table.

He tossed the cigarette butt onto the floor. "My boat leaves shortly, Eunuch Chang. I am in a hurry."

The eunuch glanced at the door that was between the Ming scrolls. "Bring in Fifth Sister."

"I have prints of all her films," Shih Heng said. "I had to buy them for outrageous amounts from film distributors. I have seen *The Maiden in Moonlight* thirty-two times."

The young woman came into the room, her head down and her hands clasped in front of her as a servant would.

Motionless, he spoke as if she weren't there. "I bought her costume from the last scene in *The Banishment of Jia*. She is going to put it on for me."

Her peasant's blue cotton skirt and white blouse were a stark contrast to the portrait Shih drew of the actress in glamorous costume. Tsingtao Lily lifted her chin. Shih hissed, a long rattling inhale between his teeth. Her skin glowed in the light. Her mouth was relaxed, and perhaps a small smile was on her lips. Even in the coarse and bulky clothing, her form was willowy. She didn't cast a fraction of a glance at Shih Heng or the eunuch. Her eyes locked on to me.

I looked away, at a scroll on the wall, then the black-tiled floor, then at a lacquer cabinet, then back to her. She was still staring at me. Eunuch Chang made a small sound, maybe a laugh.

Shih crossed the hall, approaching her slowly, ducking his head and squeezing his hands together, scuttling closer, a grin frozen on his face. He touched her arm tentatively.

The eunuch said, "I will have her delivered to your boat later today."

"I'll take her now," Shih said.

"I won't have you leaving my home with this woman in tow and parading her through Chungking. She will be hidden under a brace of bamboo poles on a goat cart and delivered to the Yangtze dock."

Perhaps Shih wondered whether he should trust Eunuch Chang to deliver his purchase to his boat. He glanced at me, then said, "Good." He looked at Tsingtao Lily again, then left the room, heading back toward the gate.

The eunuch dismissed the girl with a wave of his hand and said, "Carry the gold bars to my room, John."

She cast her eyes at me before passing through the back door. I lifted the gold bars. I thought I would never see Tsingtao Lily again, but I was wrong about that.

捌

Later that day we rang the consulate's bell. The butler opened the door, bowed, and invited One Eye Gao Bai and me to step from the porch into the hallway while he hurried away to alert the consul. I remembered this hallway, with the olive-green tiles, the French side table, and the crystal lamps on the wall. The last time I had ever seen my mother, she had been standing in this hall, wearing a blue dress and white pearls, tucking in my shirt, and laughing at something my amah, Mi Ling, had said. I hadn't been in the building since then, twenty-five years ago.

Gao and I were at the United States consulate on the south side of river on consulate row, across from the Wang Lung Men steps. Enormous flags covered the consulates' roofs like protective tarps. The United States and Great Britain and France weren't at war with Japan, and the consuls didn't want their buildings destroyed if the Japanese targeted Chungking.

"You look frightening in that uniform," Gao whispered.

My United States Army uniform was perfect, down to the thread count on the jacket. I made sure that my backbone was as rigid as a lancer's pike. My cap was under my arm, and my shoes reflected lamplight.

The butler reappeared at the end of the hallway and invited us to follow him. I led the way, the eunuch having told me that an American army officer would always step forward first, and a Chinese officer would follow, irrespective of rank. My heels clicked on the tile. Gao Bai followed. He was wearing a Nationalist Army uniform, a Sam Browne belt over a tan tunic, and knee-high boots. Collar tabs of three gold triangles on a red patch identified him as a colonel. Gao was young for a colonel, but young Chinese officers were being promoted as quickly as the older officers were being killed by the Japanese.

As we walked by the elevator, I pressed the "Up" button out of habit, as I had done a hundred times as a child.

The butler signaled that we should enter the office. The American consul, Rupert Burkland, rose from his desk. I introduced myself as Ronald Case, making sure to shake his hand firmly—a peculiarly American trait, the Englishman had said. Then I introduced Gao as Colonel Pan Bingweng of the Nationalist Army Distribution Office, and said the colonel did not speak English. The scents of tobacco and leather were the same as the last time I had been here, and memories of my childhood rushed back. I inhaled sharply and tried to focus. The consul stared at Gao's eye flap only a few seconds.

Burkland said, "When this gold reaches Chungking and is given to General Chiang, I'll no longer have to think about it, and that'll be cause for celebration." I handed him my meticulously forged documents, and he studied them carefully. The office, too, brought back fully formed memories of the dark-red oak desk, the pleated leather chair, and the green banker's lamp. Burkland's skin was almost burgundy. His eyes were flinty, and I suspect they didn't miss much. Next he accepted Gao's documents.

On the wall behind the chair were a framed photograph of President Roosevelt and five other photographs, all of men in business suits.

"May I look at your photo of the president?" I asked. "It's different from the one at the base."

The consul nodded.

I stepped to the wall. "Who are the men in these other photos?"

"The consuls who preceded me," Burkland said. "If you serve here at least three years, you get your photograph put up on the wall. It's supposed to compensate for the lousy pay."

The man in the photograph in the middle was William's and my father. I had no memory of his face, only of his vests and a silver belt buckle. The photographs weren't labeled with the consuls' names, but I felt I was staring into a mirror. Same nose as me—at least before mine had been broken three times. Same square jaw, same mouth and canted eyes, in black and white on the wall. Maybe William looked more like our mother. I couldn't ask the consul my father's name because the eunuch had insisted I say as little as possible to avoid traces of the English accent I'd adopted from Smyth. I moved away from the photos, but my eyes remained on my father.

The consul placed all the documents on his desk and gestured toward the door. "So you both will be at the dock when the gold arrives? And the army will provide an armed escort and a truck or cart?"

Gao glanced at me.

I finally pulled my gaze away from my father's photo. "Of course, sir."

"I'll be at the dock, too," Consul Burkland said. "I've never seen a hundred thousand dollars in gold before."

He bid us good-bye, and the butler showed us the door.

As we walked between privet hedges toward the street, Gao said in Mandarin, "You needed to study a photograph of President Roosevelt? What happened back there?"

"Nothing." I pushed open the iron gate and turned down the street. "Nothing at all."

捌

Etched with two lobsters, the brass lock was called a carpenter's lock because of its toolbox shape. I'd been taught how to pick vastly more complicated locks, and this half-century-old carpenter's lock was mostly for decoration, a bright flash of brass on the cherrywood armoire doors. I pushed the key into the lock, and when springs released the bolt I slid the lock off the doors. The rack of lances hung on the wall near the armoire. The eunuch's private parts were in the jar on a shelf, and as always I kept my gaze away from them.

I opened the doors. Stored on the armoire's racks and shelves were two rifles with scopes, a German submachine gun, and a dozen pistols. Boxes of shells covered the bottom shelf. I lifted out a Luger Parabellum, manufactured during the Great War. I moved to a table, then pulled off the pistol's magazine and disassembled the Luger in five seconds. Then I reassembled it in six seconds. The eunuch held firearms in contempt, admitting they were useful on occasion but saying they were inelegant.

William relaxed by reading books. I relaxed by doing this, rapidly taking apart and putting together the eunuch's firearms, the parts clicking together soothingly, and I could think about other things while doing so. I had lately taken to the notion of approaching Eunuch Chang about sending William to the École des Beaux-Arts in Paris, which has trained many great European artists, the Englishman had told me. William had a gift, remarkably perceptive vision, and adroit hands. Maybe he could go beyond forging passports and producing fake art for gullible collectors. As I took apart and reassembled the Luger, I was coming up with a plan to approach the eunuch about William's future.

The door was pushed open, and the Englishman hobbled in, planting his cane on the floor, a hand on the boar's head of the handle. He was breathing quickly, and his face was redder than usual.

I smiled at him. "You are probably here to instruct me on the shift from Middle English to Chancery Standard English in the late 1400s." I liked to make him laugh.

"John," he said, more a gasp. His hands trembled. It was too early in the day for his hands to shake. He blinked hard, as if trying to marshal his thoughts. "It's William." His voice crackled like electric sparks. "The eunuch's got him." He bent over his cane, trying to catch his breath. "Ham Fist and a couple of the Rough Boys caught William outside the compound, and he was with the actress Tsingtao Lily. Ham Fist brought them back here."

I dropped the Luger. "Where's William now?"

He pushed his spectacles back up his nose. "Eunuch Chang has him, down near the lily pond. You'd better—"

I was already out the door, sprinting past the kitchen, where two cooks leaned out the door to look down the path. I turned the corner and passed the irresistible axe and the whipping post. As I approached the White Swan Bridge, a fearful cry came from the south, my brother's voice. I moved through the Three Friends of Winter toward a blue flash visible through the leaves. When I came to a clearing near the pond, I stopped, breathless.

William was on his hands and knees, his head down, touching the gravel. When he tried to rise, the eunuch lashed his back with a bamboo rod. William collapsed.

The eunuch was standing over him. His lips were pressed so tightly together his mouth had disappeared. He brought up his head. "Your brother has betrayed me." His voice was as high as a whistle. "He is a traitor to the House of Eight Orchids."

William brought up his head, and his eyes fluttered. He opened his mouth but made no sound. A stripe of blood appeared on his back.

I cautiously moved toward the eunuch, and I bowed. "Eunuch Chang, what happened?"

"The Rough Boys spotted your brother and the harlot actress running down Horsehide Street toward the ferry. William had steamboat tickets with him. They were fleeing downriver to Shanghai."

Drops of blood fell from the rod.

"The Rough Boys brought William back to me, and then One Eye delivered the whore actress to Shih Heng's junk," he said. "Now I'm teaching

William a lesson about loyalty, and I'm not going to stop until his backbone is exposed to the air." He gestured with the bamboo. "Look at him. I've only caned him three times, and he's ready to faint."

"William has done many things for the House of Eight Orchids," I said. "He's created much wealth for you."

William tried to rise, but the eunuch sent the rod onto his back again, and my brother again dropped to the ground, his arms and legs splayed out.

The eunuch's face was a grim mask. "I have been betrayed twice before in my life: once when a good friend reported to the Summer Palace captain that I had fallen asleep at the dowager's west door, and then by that Bombay fakir. And your brother is the third time. It will be the last time."

I said, "There's been a mistake, Eunuch Chang. William would never—"

"Running away with a movie whore." His words were so choppy they sounded like bamboo trunks clicking together in a wind.

William groaned.

"He is a traitor to me, and to you. I take you and your brother in, and I make you both prosperous." The eunuch kicked William onto his side with his foot, and he looked at me. "You are loyal to me, are you not?"

"You should not have to ask, after all my years here, Eunuch Chang." I dipped my head again.

"Then you finish this." He handed me the bamboo rod. "Lay his backbone open to the air."

I struggled for words. "Eunuch Chang, he's my brother."

"And you would never betray me." He stepped aside.

I waited for more from him, but he was silent.

I said, "No, I never will." I moved toward my brother, the bamboo rod in my hand.

A bunting called from the Three Friends of Winter. I had lived thirty years by then, and in all those years I had never struggled with myself as I did then. Standing between my brother and the eunuch, I was overtaken with doubt. The House of Eight Orchids—my brother's and my home for twenty-five years—was cemented together by duty and loyalty. The place was less a compound filled with buildings and gardens than it was a testament to those canons. Eunuch Chang had instilled them in us from our first day in the compound back when we were children, and he had drilled us in them year after year. And now China was crumbling, with the Nationalists, the Communists, and the Japanese warring against each other, and with the Americans and British and Germans protecting their interests along the Yangtze with gunboats and soldiers, and with heavily armed bandit and deserter gangs roaming the countryside. But Eunuch Chang was serene, as he always was, because duty and loyalty would carry the House of Eight Orchids through the turmoil. If waves of anarchy and war were to wash over Chungking, we would be safe here in our home. He would see to that. Duty and loyalty—to Eunuch Chang and the House of Eight Orchids—were the sun rising and the moon setting: unquestioned and eternal.

But my life had begun before the House of Eight Orchids. That life in the American consulate was mostly blurred by time, but my brother William was in my every splinter of memory from back then. He was my one connection to my parents, to my history before the compound. He was the one person whose feelings toward me, and mine toward him, were not based on the eunuch's conception of duty and loyalty but from something far deeper—a blood bond. My vision blurred, and I had to shift a foot to catch myself.

But I braced myself to my duty. I inhaled hugely, and said, "Sorry, William."

When I raised the bamboo, the eunuch nodded.

My elbow hit the eunuch's nose so sharply the snapping of the cartilage might've been heard down at the river. He pitched backward, fell against a pine trunk, his silk robe up to his knees, revealing his trousers.

I lifted William by his arm. "Get going."

He found his feet and tried to reach around to the wounds on his back. I caught his hand, then shoved him along. "We don't have time for you to check yourself."

"John, what—"

"Move. Run." I tossed aside the rod. "We don't have long."

I glanced over my shoulder. The eunuch had already risen to his knees. His hand was at his nose, and blood poured down his sleeve. William wasn't running fast enough, so I prodded him along. We rounded the west end of the pond, heading for the Tang gods at the gate.

William stopped so abruptly I almost ran into him. He turned to me. "Tsingtao Lily was taken to the steel fellow's junk a few minutes ago, after the Rough Boys caught her and me. Shih Heng's junk. He's going to take her upriver. I'll never see her again."

I stared at him.

William said, "Promise me you'll help me get Lily away from him."

"What do you mean?" I struggled with the idea.

"We love each other." He pushed out his chest. "I'm not leaving the House of Eight Orchids unless you promise to help her. And to help me."

I looked again back at the clearing. Trees hid the eunuch.

"William, she's using you." I tried to push him toward the gate. "Can't you see that?"

He shook off my hand. "I'm not leaving Lily in the hands of that depraved Shih Heng." Drops of his blood fell to the ground from his shirttail.

"She's duping you." My voice rose. "She would tell you anything to get you to help her."

A bell rang, piercing and insistent. I had heard it only once before, when the compound was immediately evacuated because of the leprosy fright. I knew what it meant: the eunuch, Gao Bai, and the Rough Boys would be after us in a moment.

William said, "Help me get Lily. Please."

I grabbed his arm and yanked him along. "You're a fool."

He tried to resist, but his feet slid along the gravel, and he swatted my arm, to no effect. The bell rang and rang.

"I've got a fool for a brother." I pulled him along, my hand around his wrist. I looked across the pond. One Eye Gao Bai was running toward the bell, and Ham Fist was coming through the Rough Boys' gate. His hand still at his nose, the eunuch ran across the White Swan Bridge toward them.

William tried to stop, but I kept tugging him forward.

"A fool," I said between deep breaths, "and I never knew it until now."

捌

When Chiang Kai-shek and the Nationalists—the Kuomintang—arrived in Chungking, they renamed the streets. Our route was along Patriotic Strength Boulevard, formerly Glazed Tile Factory Street. We turned south toward the river on Death to Imperial Japan Road, which had been Whisk Broom Street. The air smelled of tripe stew.

Three pigeons flew overhead, the bamboo whistles attached to their pinion feathers piping eerily. This was the Heavenly Berry market. William and I pushed past a roasted duck vendor and stepped around a man selling dental bridges on a blanket. A mynah bird in a cage hanging from an eave called out an oath as we hurried past. My brother was running a few feet behind me. We passed the whitewashed mud wall of a restaurant now used as a missing-persons bulletin board. With luck we could get lost pushing through the hundreds of relatives who stood near the wall, most dressed in rags. William bent over to catch his breath, his hands on his knees, but I grabbed his arm and pulled him along.

We reached the Fan To steps and descended past a line of coolies carrying sacks from a junk. These steps were narrower than the Wang Lung Men, and they were steep, and they twisted and turned, carved out of the granite cliff. The Morning Star Bathhouse—a cave fitted out with tubs and iron pots of water hanging over fire pits—was halfway down the steps at a landing. This was a clear day with no haze, a rarity in Chungking. The sky was pale blue above clear yellow. The Hua-ying Mountains across the river were close.

I glanced behind me, up the steps, fearing the eunuch was already chasing us. Ficus trees clung to the cliff, some of the boughs hanging over the steps. Below was the Yangtze. A sandbar in the middle of the current was a landing strip during low water. A Junkers Iron Annie was on the sandbar, and coolies were removing its cargo of machine parts to transfer to a sampan. Houses on stilts lined the shore. Tethered to a fisherman on the shore, a cormorant bobbed on the surface of the river, then disappeared below it. Depth markings had been carved out of the granite and were painted white, one on top of the other, rising eighty feet up the cliff.

Two junks were moored to a dock at the bottom of the steps. The one upriver belonged to Eunuch Chang. It was the smaller of the two, and it was made of eight—no more or less—species of hardwoods brought from India. The deck rail was inlaid with silver dragons. Silver is called *the obstinate metal* and is rare in China. On the mast a red phoenix pennant flapped in the wind. Sometimes Eunuch Chang would take his junk out into the middle of the Yangtze and just sit there, trackers keeping the vessel in one spot. I didn't know why.

The second junk was larger, about forty feet long. The boat had two masts, a square stern, and a raised poop. Unlike most junks on the Yangtze, this vessel was bright with paint. The deck was crimson, and the rails were yellow. A red phoenix with outstretched wings perched on a boulder was painted on the stern. Sailors believed the phoenix represented speed, and the boulder safety.

William and I descended the last steps to the dock, where a dockhand in a black jacket waited for orders. I held a sack in one hand. The river gorge funneled cold wind from the west, and waves washed over the lower boulders. Jagged rocks broke the surface, water foaming around them. The Yangtze was white with swift currents. A man in a wide straw hat was at the junk's rudderpost, and a drummer was on the deck. Two half-mile-long plaited bamboo hawsers were attached to the junk's prow. Upstream, on a narrow towpath on the old-town side of the river, fifty trackers gripped the line, waiting for the drumbeat. On a sandbar near the other shore another fifty trackers were arrayed along a second hauling line.

Wearing a cotton cap and a bulky blue coat padded with straw, the drummer lifted the sticks high over his head, then beat the drumhead five times, then five times again. The sound echoed between hills. The drumhead was probably made of ox hide, which was stretched over a wood barrel. Hawsers were lifted to shoulders, and the trackers turned to face up the river.

Two sampans swept by, oarsmen keeping them off the rocks. The ferry was on the other side of the river, and its doleful whistle sounded and sent steam shooting into the air. A flock of Siberian cranes lifted off the far shore.

The drummer beat the hide three times, the signal for the port trackers to pull the junk away from the dock. I ran along the dock with the cliff and the city above me. A dockhand unwound a line from a bollard and cast it onto the junk's deck. The junk slipped away from the dock. The river rushed against the boulders along the shore and the dock's pylons.

I held up a hand to William. "Wait here."

I leaped over water and landed on the deck, the sack bouncing against me. The junk drifted away from the dock. The hatch into the poop was closed, and the sails were on the deck, folded back and forth at the battens. I stepped around a coiled line and a wood deck hatch. A cage of pigeons—used to send messages to the home port—was secured to a mast. The drummer was facing forward and didn't see me coming.

I said right into his ear, "Do you know of the eunuch Chang?"

He started, holding his sticks motionless in midair.

"I am from the eunuch Chang," I said. "He wants this junk returned to the dock. He will consider it a great service if you do so."

"Eunuch Chang?" He stared at my green eyes. This might have been as close to a foreign devil as he had ever been. "I do not know if I believe you."

A knife dropped into my hand, my number-one knife. "Make up your mind if you believe me. Do it quickly."

He glanced down at the knife. He brought the sticks down and beat the tattoo for reversing course, six beats, a pause, then two more. The trackers along both sides of the river straightened in unison, shifted their grips on the hawsers, then began giving way, easing the junk back toward the dock.

I removed ten one-hundred-yuan notes from my currency role, probably a half year's wages for him. I pushed the bills between the button loops into his coat. "I dislike bringing out a knife. Eunuch Chang says weapons are a display of weakness." I slipped the knife back up my sleeve.

The drummer grinned thinly. As the Yangtze's current pushed the junk back toward the dock, I moved aft to the superstructure. Heng Shih opened the hatch and rushed out, rage on his face, aiming himself toward the drummer. He was still wearing his business suit, though the brogans had been replaced with red cloth slippers, and he was carrying an oddly shaped drinking glass, the kind the Englishman had once told me was used for gin.

He never saw me. My fist crashed into his temple, and he fell to the deck like a pole-axed steer.

I walked through the hatch into the salon. Lit by kerosene lamps, it resembled a seraglio, with orange and red silk cushions and purple draperies, and a bead curtain covering the hatch to an adjacent compartment. A red brocaded chair with legs made of elephant tusks stood in a corner, and a large brass plate hung from a wall, with the design of a rooster hammered into it.

Tsingtao Lily was sitting on a cushion. Her mouth opened, and she placed a hand over her heart. She was still wearing a peasant's blouse and skirt. She smelled of jasmine. I grabbed her arm and dragged her out onto the deck, then to the rail.

The junk's hull timbers creaked as the boat bumped the dock. The drummer raised a stick in our direction and smiled again. We stepped over the rail and jumped onto the dock. William embraced her, and she laughed with joy. The Fan To stairs rose to Fetching the Lantern Lane. I started up the steps, and my brother and the actress followed.

When she laughed again, I turned to look at her.

Her eyes seemed to be lit from within. "I knew your brother would make you help me." She laughed again, without covering her mouth with her hand, a shocking thing.

The Japanese bombed Chungking for the first time that day. I never heard a siren or saw a warning lantern. As I stood there, staring at Tsingtao Lily on the steps as she smiled at me in her knowing way, a plane with an orange disk on the fuselage became a blur in the corner of my vision. Then a blast blacked me out and catapulted me into the Yangtze River.

7

The Chinese love rocks. Every granite precipice, every jagged outcropping, every boulder along the Yangtze had been named before the era of recorded history, and carries the name to this day.

The bomb's concussion sent me sailing at a cliff wall called the Emperor's Hand, next to the steps, and I slid down to a boulder called Widow's Tear Drop Number Three, and then rolled into the current. When I regained my senses—the bitterly cold current swirling all around—I was being swept downstream a few feet from shore. Blood marked my path down the stones, and the bubbling current at my shoulders was pink. I gasped for breath, then sank below the surface. I had never learned to swim. Nobody in Chungking could swim. The suffocating water pulled me down, and I scraped against a boulder. I broke the surface again amid foaming white water, and I banged against a granite ledge on the shore. The current pulled me away from land. I tried to breathe, but my mouth filled with water and I sank into the river.

I was yanked to the surface by my hair, my face and head burning with pain. Water fell from my eyes. Tsingtao Lily had anchored herself to the shore by gripping a banyan branch, waded up to her knees in the water, and pulled me toward land. I stumbled up the loose stones below the surface. She grabbed my shirt and tried to push me onto a boulder. Something blocked my right eye. I collapsed to the stone, my feet still in the river. Blood poured from my head onto the rock and mixed with river water before being swept away. William had already climbed from the current onto the rocks. He leaned against a boulder. His clothes were sodden, and his hand was gripping his face, as if he were disoriented.

"You're badly hurt," Tsingtao Lily said over the din of the rushing river. She gripped my arm to steady me.

She squinted against the sight of me. "I can see your skull. You are bleeding all over." She tried to lift me off the boulder. "We've got to find a doctor." She tugged me upward. "William, can you follow us?"

William stumbled, but caught himself and began to follow us. His face was blank.

The ground seemed to lurch and spin. Blood dribbled down the granite steps, where bodies lay everywhere, mostly dead coolies—some still twitching, some missing arms and legs. A woman held her head in her hands, moaning, next to the body of a fellow whose intestines hung out. By gingerly feeling my head, I discovered that a piece of shrapnel had ripped open my forehead—a flap of skin was hanging over my eye—and another had torn my scalp above the temple. The shrapnel had rattled my brain, and I blacked out for some of the climb while the other two had to wait for me.

A teahouse named the Pavilion of Harmonious Virtues was on fire, the beams cracking and falling. Bodies lay about, some with ghastly wounds, others with not even their hats and caps misplaced.

I stopped walking—the city spinning around and around—and leaned against a shop wall, unable to go farther. Blood ran down my cheek and spilled off my chin onto my shirt.

William steadied himself with a hand against the wall, but he was apparently gathering his wits. "John, you need help."

"Come on." Tsingtao Lily pulled my sleeve. "Do you know this street? Where is a doctor?"

I couldn't move my legs, and nausea seized me. I leaned over, gripping the wall trying to stay on my feet. My forehead pumped pain into me.

"You must walk," she said. "Your brother and I will lead you."

She put her arm around my waist and struggled forward. We stepped over a crimson plank that had been part of a shop floor. The flap of skin slapped my cheek.

"Concentrate, Yellow Hair," she said.

William was on the other side of me, leaning against me to keep me upright. "Lift your feet, John. Keep moving." He slurred his words, and he seemed a few seconds behind everything. The bomb blast had addled him. Maybe his head had hit the same boulder mine did.

Thousands of blue roofing tiles littered the street. A vegetable cart had spilled cabbages. A fifty-foot wall of flame was one street west, on Old Clothing Lane. Smoke columns rose in all directions, merging in a growing black cloud. Air-raid sirens blared.

Tsingtao Lily pulled again at my arm, but I toppled to the cobblestones, landing on my side. The flap of my forehead hung in my eye. I groaned, and my insides felt as if they had been stirred with a stick. She and William tried to lift me, her wet skirt against my back. Blood fell to the stone beneath my head, and I gasped with pain.

She knelt beside me. "You are going to bleed to death if we don't get help."

My voice was ragged. "Eunuch Chang will be looking for us. Go. Run."

She shook her head.

"We'll find you a doctor first," William said.

I worked to get out the words. "His vengeance will be terrible. I can handle myself. Get going."

Tsingtao Lily reached for the skin hanging above my eye and gently held it up to the exposed bone, as if the flap might stick. It fell away, back across my vision. My brother was blinking steadily, as if trying to clear his mind.

"He will be looking downriver," I said. "So go west into the country."

"Not until you are sewn up," she said. "Not until I know you will not die. You saved me, and now I'll save you."

She never had the chance. A bowler hat appeared above her on the steps. It sat atop a gangster's head. He cackled, a sound that merged with the hiss and pop of nearby fires. He grabbed her by the hair and brought a finger down her cheek, tracing the curve of her cheekbone. He grinned, probably recognizing her.

When she pushed away his hand, he struck her face with his fist. It was Four Finger Xu, the red pole. His organization, Two River 14K, was always looking for women.

William lurched toward Four Finger, but the gangster savagely pushed him backwards, and William tripped over a beam on the sidewalk.

Four Finger Xu pulled Tsingtao Lily upright. She tried to strike him, but he slapped her so hard she staggered. He prodded William to his feet, then pushed him and Tsingtao Lily down the street, but then he glanced back. He laughed again and stepped back to kick me in the head. I blacked out for the second time in fifteen minutes.

捌

Chungking residents had hoped the mountains surrounding the town and the mist that covered the city most days would protect them from Japanese bombers. That day—the first Japanese attack on the city—the air-raid sirens had begun wailing only after the attack had begun, too late for many.

Two minutes before, I had been lying on the road trying to gain my wits, unable to bring my mind to bear on anything other than the pain in my head—the skin of my forehead still hanging across my eye. The blast that had thrown me into the river had scrambled my brain, or maybe it had been Four Finger Xu's boot to my face, or some combination. Then, prone on the cobblestones, my mind still in a fog, I could swear I saw Eunuch Chang hurrying down the street, his Manchu blue robe standing out like a beacon among the fires and rubble. One Eye Gao Bai—a dagger in his hand—was close behind him.

The eunuch sidestepped a pig that had been killed in a blast, and stepped over a dead postman in his green uniform. Eunuch Chang pointed at a man sitting on a step who was holding his head in his hands. A pool of blood was at his feet. Gao Bai lifted the wounded man by his throat and held him up to the eunuch. They were too far away for me to hear, but I knew what Eunuch Chang was asking him. The eunuch was already searching for William and me.

Dizzy and lurching, I went through the first door I saw, Tailor Meng's shop, and I pulled out my roll of yuan notes. Tailor Meng had been killed by a bomb blast, his right leg torn off at the pelvis, and his right arm at the elbow. His body—still warm—was on top of the tailor's rag pile. The all-clear whistles sounded. Smoke poured down the street outside the tailor's shop, and across the street the Cloud Gate Restaurant was hidden behind orange and purple flames. I could just make out Tailor Meng's wife picking up spools from the floor. She righted a woven-bamboo mannequin. She held a white rag to her hip as she worked. The window facing the street had blown inward, and glass shards had punctured her hip and leg. Her pants were damp with blood. She was steadily cleaning the shop, ignoring her injuries and not glancing at her dead husband. He had called himself Tailor Meng, but his wife Peizhi had done most of the sewing. Bolts of cotton leaned against a wall, and a dark-green bolt had fallen onto the floor. She looked up when I stumbled in.

I shoved five hundred-yuan bills at her. "A man is coming to kill me. Hide me." She said, "I do not trust this money, with the Japanese coming." But still she tucked the bills into her blouse, then shoved me down into the pile of rags where her dead, dismembered husband lay, and sprinkled pieces of cloth over me. Then she dragged her husband's body out onto the rags on top of me. His body lay there, visible to anybody who entered the shop. I was right under him, somewhat hidden. She placed her husband's leg across his body, at a right angle to him, and positioned his arm on rags above my eye, severed tendons touching my face. A visitor might see the horror of the mangled body lying on a pile of rags and turn away. After she had arranged the rags, she returned to her broom.

Eunuch Chang swept into the shop. In his tenor voice he said, "I am looking for a yellow-haired gweilo who I believe is injured. Bamboo Merchant Wailin said he was standing in front of your shop. Where is he?"

Her voice was steady. "I have been a widow fifteen minutes, and you dare speak to me that way?"

Gao Bai came into the shop, and he circled it, opening a thread cupboard with the point of the dagger. Then he moved toward a stack of boxes against a wall, and I lost sight of him. Tailor Meng's body pressed down on me. The arm leaked onto my face.

The eunuch's hands were up his sleeves in the Manchu fashion. "If you have seen him, and you do not tell me now, we will come back. It will be bad for you."

"Get out of my shop," Peizhi said. "Leave me to my grief."

Gao Bai crossed the floor into my patch of vision, and he turned for a last look at the room. He stared at Tailor Meng's ruined body, and then his one good eye shifted slightly, from Meng's slack face to something an inch or two nearby, to bits of cloth on the rag pile. He snorted and shook his head.

Then he tucked the dagger into his pants and followed the eunuch from the shop. Gao had often called me his brother. He may not have seen me buried below the body in the rags. Or he may have.

8

The monkey gripped the mule's mane, right in front of me. The monkey's fur was yellow, and so were his teeth, which he had bared at me every two minutes all day. Whenever I had lost consciousness and had leaned forward over the pommel, he had hissed, and I had jerked upright in the saddle. The monkey weighed forty pounds and wore a red cotton jacket with a yellow fringe, and every ten minutes he peed down the side of the mule. I would've swatted him off the mule, but then the caravan boss would have shot me out of the saddle and not given me another thought. Sixty horses and mules were in the freight-hauling caravan, which in China is called a *horse gang*, and I was on the lead mule along with the hissing, peeing monkey. The mule had six brass bells hanging from the saddle, and two dozen round mirrors, all designed to frighten away spirits.

Fifteen drovers kept the horses and mules moving, walking alongside and tapping the animals' flanks with willow switches. The last pack animal in line was a donkey, a horse-gang tradition, as its braying frightened away beasts and spirits. Over a hundred different items were loaded on the horses and mules in cotton sacks and woven bamboo boxes: cured tobacco, soy sauce, chili oil, dried fish, knives and spoons and pots and scissors, bottles of medicines, boxes of sewing needles, a dozen wire-framed eyeglasses, an artificial leg, and a box of the new Zippo lighters. I was the only passenger, and I had paid a hundred yuan for the privilege of sharing a mule with a monkey.

A gweilo traveling upriver was news along the Yangtze. Farmers and fishermen had told me William and another man—Four Finger Xu— and a woman were a day or two ahead of me.

The caravan was approaching Red Cloud Ferry, a village on the Yangtze—no more than a hundred mud-and-thatch huts, a few shops, and an inn. A dock jutted out into the river where the ferry landed. We rode on the trackers' trail near the river and passed the rapids just downriver from the village. Granite boulders protruded from the river surface, and white coursed between the rocks and sent mist into the air. The rapids were called White Horse Rocks because the water was churned to white and because one of the boulders resembled a horse's head.

A team of trackers was pulling a salt junk through the rapids. We passed them, keeping just inland of them. Polemen kept the junk off the rocks as it was hauled upriver through the treacherous river course. The trackers were chanting as they stepped and pulled, stepped and pulled. A trackers' path here was only on one side of the river because some of the opposite shore was lined with cliffs too high for the trackers. The White Horse Rocks took up half the river's width. The other half was deep and swift. Only motor vessels could make it upriver past Red Cloud Ferry without trackers.

The caravan's gang boss fired his rifle into the air, and three other drovers also shot off rounds, a warning to any lurking bandits that the caravan was armed. The animals' hooves raised dust, which the wind blew back at us, and we moved in a yellow cloud so thick I couldn't see the river just fifty yards west. Up ahead, a warning bell rang. The villagers would hide until they knew it was a trading caravan and not soldiers or bandits.

The road was deeply rutted. A dead dog lay against the trunk of a camphor tree, its eyes eaten out. Bamboo trees lined the road on the inland side. Farther east were terraced fields of sugarcane rising up to Eagle Talon Mountain, with a peak of three granite columns. I knew the mountain was there, but I couldn't see it through the dust. My mule pushed through a herd of white goats.

The gang boss, Yee Pengfei, cupped his hands around his mouth and called out his own name. He never put his Lee-Enfield rifle across his back or in a scabbard, but always held it in his hand. He wore a leather vest over a cotton shirt, and his breeches were tucked into leather boots. A cartridge belt hung around his neck like a scarf. His eyebrows grew together over his nose, and his four front teeth were missing. He walked toward a hut, where a pale face could be seen behind a partly open door. Words were exchanged, but I couldn't hear them. Yee Pengfei's caravan traveled through Red Cloud Ferry four times a year.

Someone shouted an all clear. The villagers emerged from the bamboo grove and from behind boulders on the riverbank. Yee Pengfei waved the horse gang toward an inn, the village's only two-story building, and the only one made of wood. The innkeeper emerged from a door and smiled at Yee, a hand already extended for payment. He wore a filthy white apron, and he was missing the end of his nose, so he had one hole instead of two nostrils.

My forehead was leaking blood, and dust was caked over the wound. Yellow dust covered my blue shirt and the monkey's red vest. My mule moved toward the inn's stable, which was nothing but a lean-to and a hayrick where water buckets hung from hitching posts. Yee pulled a leather purse from under his shirt.

The monkey slid down the mule's neck and hurried across the ground to the stable. He ran along a pile of loose hay, then to the manure pile. He shrieked and whooped and jumped up and down, then ran back to Yee Penfei, who angrily jammed his own coins back into his purse, shouted something at the innkeeper, and grabbed his horse's reins. The monkey had just warned Yee that sick horses had been quartered at the stable. Foal pneumonia or moon blindness or horse bots—the monkey could sense them all. Yee tossed the monkey back onto my mule's neck, then mounted his horse, leaving the innkeeper scowling. Sixty animals behind me, the donkey brayed and snorted, perhaps sensing he had farther to travel this evening.

Loud voices came from up the road, near a scrub oak. A wicker cage was suspended from a pole that was held up by two bearers. A woman was gesturing widely and arguing with the lead bearer. I thought maybe the dust was coloring my vision, as the woman had red hair with gold streaks in it. She was taller than any woman I'd seen in China, too, and her fingers were too long. She had one of her fingers right in the bearer's face, and she was moving them angrily.

Yee dug his heels into his horse's flanks and caught up with me. "That's the crazy doctor. She's an ocean ghost, like you." He laughed, revealing most of his tongue because he had no front teeth. "She's so skinny, everyone calls her the bamboo doctor." Yee was from His-An, up north, where Anglos were called *ocean ghosts*.

The mule's bells chimed when I brought up the reins and slid to the ground. My head jolted with pain. The monkey instantly placed himself on the saddle. I was wobbly, but I made it over to the doctor.

She was speaking in bad Mandarin. "You must let me look at her."

The pole bearer said, "There is no help for her. The stuff is all over her." An orange-sized goiter on his neck tilted his head so that his right ear almost touched his shoulder.

"Put that child down," the lady said. Her lips were narrow and her chin large, or maybe I just wasn't accustomed to Anglo chins—rugged promontories compared to Chinese women's. Her eyes were gray or green, I couldn't tell. She wore a skirt down to her ankles and a man's black jacket. She stood in front of the bearer, blocking his way.

"She is my daughter," the bearer was telling her. "She will go where I tell her to go."

At the edge of the village, fifty yards away, two people emerged on a path that led into the forest. They did not come closer, but waited near a silver eucalyptus tree. I couldn't make them out clearly, but one was leaning on a crutch, and the other wore a blue bandana over his face, and only his eyes and forehead were visible, and even at this distance I could see the forehead was deeply cracked. They were dressed in rags that hung off them, some ends trailing in the dirt. A woman at that end of the village yelled, then threw a stone that bounced off a tree trunk near them.

The woman doctor pointed at the bearer, her fingernail half an inch from his nose. "Put down the cage."

He chewed on his cheek, then slipped the poles off his shoulders. The cage was lowered to the ground. A girl was in the cage, her fingers around the bamboo. She peeked out.

I lurched forward on weak legs, my forehead on fire and my thinking fuzzy.

"Doctor? I need help."

She raised a hand in my direction. "I'll be with you in a minute." Mud had caked the hem of her long black skirt. She said to the bearer, "Don't get in my way."

She tugged apart the knot on the hatch and reached into the cage to pull out the girl, who was about fifteen years old and who hid her face behind her hands. She wore only a peanut sack, with holes for her head and arms. The lady doctor stood the girl upright and gripped her thin wrists to pull her hands down.

"What's your name?" the doctor asked.

"Sing," the girl whispered—a name that means *starlight*—shifting her feet, embarrassed.

"Be still." The doctor lifted her chin with a hand. "Let me look at you."

I could no longer stand. I sank to the ground and had to use an arm to keep from falling face forward into the dust.

"She has leprosy," the bearer said. He stood well away from the doctor and his daughter. "It's all over her face and neck." He pointed to two people wearing rags hovering near the eucalyptus tree. "They will take her away. They will feed her. There's a place where they all live, one li up the road toward the mountains."

The doctor ran her thumb along the girl's cheek. The girl tried to bring her hands up again to hide her face, but the doctor pushed them away.

The bearer said, "If my wife has caught it, I'll send her to the leper colony, too,"

With her fingernail, the doctor scraped the girl's cheek once, then again. "How long have your cheeks been this red and brown?"

The girl stared at the ground.

The bearer said, "Ten days."

The doctor leaned even closer to the girl, then kissed the girl's red cheek, a firm kiss, accompanied by a loud smack, lest anybody miss it. The girl's father—his face open—stepped back.

"She has tinea." The doctor patted the girl's shoulder. "It is a reddening and roughening of the skin, a minor rash, caused by a common fungus. I'll treat her skin with sulfur, and she can return to your home in seven days, completely cured, her skin as lovely as a rose petal. I'm not going to let you banish her to the leper colony."

Scowling, the girl's father lifted his poles, as did the other bearer. They hurried away, disappearing around the corner of a mud hut, scattering chickens.

From my spot on the ground, I managed to say, "You just caused him to lose face. He's now your enemy."

She looked down at me. "Who are you?"

I spoke in Mandarin. "The girl will be beaten when she returns home." The ground was spinning. I could feel the fever in me, coursing up and down. I was about to pass out again.

"What should I have done? Let the lepers take her?" She knelt next to me and pressed my forehead with her finger.

I yelped with pain.

"This is badly infected." She rubbed the skin below my hairline, none too gently. "Who sewed you up?"

I inhaled slowly, trying to focus on her words. "A tailor's wife."

"What's this dirt on the wound?"

"Earthworm dirt."

Still on one knee next to me, she pulled out a piece of cloth from her sleeve and pressed it onto the wound. She brought down the cloth so I could see it. It was soaked with yellow pus.

My voice seemed far away. "The dirt thrown up by earthworms was made into a plaster, which was pressed onto the wound with a piece of burning wood."

"Did the tailor's wife do this, too?"

"I paid a country doctor for the earthworm plaster yesterday." I leaned sideways, but she caught me. "Isn't it healing the gash?"

The horse-gang boss, Yee Pengfei, walked up to me, his horse behind him. "We are going on another hour, to Face of the Cliff. There's usually a clean stable there. Are you coming with us?

She switched to English. "Are you English or an American? A Canadian?"

I replied in English. "I'm Chinese. My home is in Chungking."

"You're as Chinese as I am, and I'm from Idaho."

She pulled me upright—lifting me right up from the ground—and arranged my arm over her shoulders. "The hospital is just up the road, not a hundred yards. I'll look after your forehead when we get there."

Yee turned back to the caravan. He laughed and called over his shoulder, "The monkey will miss you, Yellow Hair."

I tottered, but she gripped me tightly.

"Help me get back on the mule." I didn't have the strength to lift my head, and was speaking to the ground. "My brother is lost upriver. I'm looking for him, and I can't stay here. He might be only a day ahead of me. I need to go."

The doctor gripped my chin as if I were a child. She stared at my forehead. "Unless you come with me, you won't last a day."

捌

"What is that?" I asked.

"A syringe." She held it up. "Haven't you ever seen one before?"

"What does it do?"

"It contains a nerve block called procaine. I'm going to inject it into your forehead using this needle."

She wore a white apron over a white cotton blouse and a round mirror attached to her head with a band. I was perched on a stool and had to concentrate on staying upright.

We were in a hospital examining room, a phrase I learned later. Books were displayed in a glass-fronted case. Storage cabinets lined the wall. A white sheet covered an examining table that had metal stirrups sticking out, near a blood-pressure unit on a wall. A white metal cabinet held bottles and tubes. A human skeleton—pieced together with wire—hung from a wood frame near the window, its left hand gripping a fly whisk. I lifted my nose and sniffed. The room was the first place I had ever been that didn't have an odor.

"I don't want that big needle stuck into my head."

She said, "Your wound must be opened and cleaned, and it'll be far too painful without the anesthetic."

Sing, the girl who the doctor had saved from the leper colony earlier that day, dusted a steel autoclave. To keep warm, she carried a fire basket made of woven bamboo in which was a saucer of burning coals. She opened the glass case and adjusted the books and medical journals, aligning them perfectly. She was humming as she worked, and glanced at the doctor—adoration in her eyes—every few seconds. The doctor had already bathed the girl and had given her a white skirt and a blue blouse. Sulfur had been applied to her cheeks, but the marks on her face—the tinea—were still red swirls and criss-crosses.

"Then I'll clean it without the anesthetic," the bamboo doctor said. "Can you handle it?"

She was a large-boned woman, with wrists as thick as mine, and she was almost as tall as me. Her face was peculiarly angular, with stony cheekbones and drawn cheeks. Her eyes were green with gold flecks in them, matching the gold streaks that lightened her red hair. She was attractive in a foreign-devil way.

"I just spent three days on a mule with a monkey," I said. "So I can handle anything."

"Handle anything?" She smiled crookedly. She pinched a fold of my forehead and yanked the flap of skin away from my skull, ripping out the seamstress's stitches.

Pain slashed through me, and I yelped, jerked back on the stool, and fell onto my back, toppling the stool and clutching at my head. I rolled onto my side and groaned.

"You handled that well," the bamboo doctor said. "Now to the painful part, cleaning it out."

Gasping from pain, I crawled off the floor and back onto the stool. My forehead felt as if a rat were eating it. I struggled to remain upright, and whispered, "Maybe I'll try the needle."

She pointed. "You dropped your knife."

I slowly bent to retrieve it, the blood rushing to my head, pumping in more pain.

"And your other knife," she said. "How many knives does one person need, I wonder?"

I picked up the second blade, too, and returned to the stool. She inserted the needle several places into my forehead, pressing on the plunger. If the needle caused any pain, it was lost in the cosmos of suffering in my head. The flap hung over my eye.

She poured clear fluid from a bottle onto a cotton ball. "How's your head now?"

I could unclench my fists. The pain was lessening.

She touched the wound with the swab. "Does that hurt?"

"I can't feel anything."

She rubbed the cotton across my forehead.

"Does the anesthetic do anything to the brain?" I asked. "It's not going to make me more stupid, is it?"

"How would that be possible?" She tossed the bloody swab into a bin and prepared another.

The agony above my eyebrows—my constant companion for the past three days—had vanished. I could move my head without a jolt of misery. I could blink without pain. I asked, "Why is a foreign-devil doctor in the middle of China?"

"The money for this hospital comes from a group of Idaho and Montana churches. I've been here five years."

"Did you go to school to become a doctor?"

"Tufts Medical School." She scraped my forehead with the cotton. "I've never seen so much pus from one head." She used tweezers. "Or gravel." She held up a bit of stone, then dropped it into a metal bowl on a tray.

I indicated an overhead light. "You have electricity here. First I've ever seen outside Chungking."

"We have a Delco generator donated by the churches."

A nurse in a starched cap helped a young man into the room. The man was as slender as a crane, but his belly was bloated, pushing out his blue shirt. His wrists were wrapped in filthy rags. His face was knotted. The nurse helped the man onto the examining table.

The doctor glanced at the new patient and said in Mandarin, "Hsui, take off the bandages. I'll be there in a moment."

"What's wrong with him?" I asked.

"He has roundworms, giving him a distended stomach." She lifted a threaded needle from a tray. "The village healer slashed his wrists to let out the worms."

"How else are they going to get out?" I asked. We were speaking English.

"So now he has roundworms and slashed wrists." She pushed the needle through the skin of my forehead. "I'll give him santonin over several days, then purge him with calomel."

I was giddy from the lack of pain. "I can't feel anything above my nose."

She tugged at the thread.

"I'm looking for a man who is missing a finger," I said. "His name is Mengyao Xu, but he goes by Four Finger Xu. He's traveling with two other gangsters from the Two River 14K, up the Yangzte on this side."

Making noises that sounded like tsk-tsk, she dabbed my forehead with cotton again.

"They have kidnapped an actress and my brother and are going to sell them," I said. "Maybe to a Japanese battalion, which would have a place called a 'comfort house' for the officers. Or maybe to a slaver working the river. The actress would bring a high price. I don't know about my brother. I need to find him." I was chatting on and on, which would've earned a narrowed glance from the eunuch—one of his maxims was "Reveal nothing"—but the absence of pain had loosened my tongue.

"This morning I treated a fellow who had only four fingers," the doctor said, peering closely at my forehead.

"Was he wearing a round black hat, a bowler?"

She laughed. "It looked like a skin egg on top of his head."

"I hope whatever you treated him for turns out to be fatal," I said.

"Not a chance. A broken bone in his foot." She worked away on my forehead. "After the bombing in Chungking, a wall fell on him, crushing his foot. He'll be fine."

"Was he with a young lady?"

"I saw a lady on a horse over by the toolshed. I didn't get a good look at her, didn't give her much thought. There were some other people nearby, three or four of them, but I didn't pay them any attention. I can't say if an Anglo was among them." The doctor pulled the thread, making my head bob. "When you find this Four Finger fellow, are you going to use those knives on him?"

"Only if he gives me the opportunity."

She tied off the last suture. "I can find a bed for you in the main ward. In three or four days, your fever will disappear."

"I'm leaving this afternoon," I said.

"Heading upriver?" she asked. "Follow me."

She led me past the roundworm patient and through a door into a strange garden. With my head numb, I could walk readily. The garden was without flowing water, scholars' rocks, chimes, a statue, or a wall around it—all requirements for any garden I'd ever been in, including the eunuch's. And there was no bamboo. A boy about fifteen years old was on his knees, pulling weeds, his rear end toward us.

The doctor said, "This is my bit of home, an American garden, a replica of my father's garden." She indicated a row of plants. "Roses and violets and gardenias. They'll bloom later in the year." She walked into the garden and nodded toward hundreds of short blue and yellow flowers so thick they hid the dirt below them. "Those are crocuses, the first flowers every year."

When I hesitated at the edge of the gravel, she said, "The grass is meant to be walked on."

I stepped after her, between rows of bare rose stems.

"I've added a few things my dad doesn't have in his garden," she said. "That banana tree, and that guava tree by the generator shed, and the wisteria that grows over the door to the examining room. It's too cold in Boise for wisteria. In the fall, this garden is filled with dahlias. And sometimes I can get a *lan-hua* to grow, the orchid with the strong scent."

The hospital was a one-story yellow brick structure with a blue tile roof and a chimney, rare in China. The doctor pointed to a second building, on the other side of the garden. It, too, was made of brick, but walls had been painted red. Mosquito netting, not glass, was over the windows. Ragged coughing came from within.

She said, "That's the contagious-disease ward. It has two rooms, one for malaria and the other for whatever disease is in town. This week it's breakbone fever." She looked at me. "What's your name?"

"John."

She smiled. "Do you have a last name?"

"Not that I remember. Sometimes I'm called Yellow Hair and sometimes Third Brother. Depends on who is talking. And I know an Englishman who calls me Yank, though I don't know what that means. I hope nothing bad."

"How can you not remember your last name?" she asked as she plucked a weed from the edge of the path.

"I haven't heard it in twenty-five years." I touched my temple and couldn't feel a thing.

We neared the young man who was weeding. Whenever he pulled a weed, he carefully smoothed the dirt with his fingers.

She switched to Mandarin. "Feng, stand up, will you, please?"

He only half-turned toward us, and kept the right side of his face hidden. The doctor pivoted him by his shoulders so that I could see his face. Bandages covered his right cheek from his chin to his hairline. He did not bring up his eyes. He was wearing a black jacket, and his hands were covered with garden dirt.

"Bandits came to his town—called Deer Horn—six miles up the river," she said in English. "When the town couldn't pay the bandits' so-called tax, one of them cut open Feng's face. Three long slashes, cut through to his tongue. His cheek looked like fish gills." She patted the boy's shoulder, and he returned to his weeding. "That's what waits for you upriver."

"I'm more competent than my forehead would suggest," I said.

"Up the Yangtze are hundreds of square miles that the Nationalists can't control, and the Communists haven't dared to invade. Only the bandits and warlords hold sway."

I leaned over to pick a weed from the grass, enjoying the new freedom from the agony in my head.

"They're deserters from the Nationalist Army, most of them," she said. "If they leave their outlaw packs, they'll be caught and hung. So they roam the countryside in bands, burning and killing."

"Where can I buy a horse?"

"Who is the actress this Four Finger Xu has kidnapped?"

"Her name is Wu Luli. She is known as Tsingtao Lily. She's been in dozens of films. Maybe you've heard of her."

"The nearest movie theater is in Chungking. I never have time to go there."

The doctor looked directly at my eyes when she spoke. I wasn't used to it, not from a woman.

I said, "Tsingtao Lily saved my life, pulling me from the river. I was too close to drowning to be surprised at the time, but I look back now, and I am surprised. Maybe my brother saw things in her that I hadn't." On and on I chatted. This foreign-devil doctor had heard more words from me in the past five minutes than the eunuch heard in a month.

We neared the end of the garden. A line of people waited to enter the hospital. Women carried babies on their backs. One man carried a woman on his back. Several men were on crutches. An old woman sat in a wheelbarrow. Several lay on the ground.

"Are those folks more patients for the hospital?" I asked.

"Sometimes only six or eight people are waiting at the door. Sometimes fifty. People at the front of the line have camped there overnight. We serve them tea and rice. We don't have enough beds, and I'm the only doctor here. Almost every day someone dies in that line."

I could feel the new stitches with my finger, but my forehead was still numb.

"They come here with malaria, dysentery, tuberculosis, typhoid, and trachoma. And scabies, broken bones, intestinal parasites, bad teeth, and malaria. I've contracted malaria myself."

"Are you ill now?" I asked.

"It comes and goes. I'm fine now."

The low growl of a motor came from a hut at the far side of the garden. Black smoke rose from a stack atop the building, and west of the hut was a shed on posts, with a roof but no walls. A mound of coal was under the roof. Five men near the hut rose from stools as we approached them. One jabbed a shovel into the coal, and another withdrew a rag from a pocket.

"That's the generator shed," the bamboo doctor said. "So we have electric light. I have to send to Hong Kong to get replacement bulbs. Those men keep the generator running."

"It takes five people to maintain a generator?" I asked.

"I employ fifty-three people for the generator. Three shifts of foremen, mechanics, oilers, wipers, coal shovelers, and wheelbarrow men. And another twelve on the *wupan* that brings the coal to Red Cloud Ferry."

We turned back to the hospital, walking along a row of azaleas not yet in bloom.

"This hospital is the only employer within a day's walk. So fifty-three people are making something of a living. The Idaho and Montana churches don't mind."

I asked, "Do you have a name, other than Bamboo Doctor?"

"Elizabeth Hanley." She pushed back a lock of hair. "Nobody calls me Betty or Betsy or Liz. Not even my father. Only Elizabeth. Maybe I'm too starchy. And why are you staring at me?"

"I've never spoken with a foreign-devil woman before. Not more than a word or two."

"Never?"

"The eunuch wouldn't let me. And the bound-foot cripple, Madam Tuan, said they were all ladies of the night, anyway."

She crossed her arms. "I'm having trouble following you."

The door from the examining room opened. Ham Fist filled the door frame. One of his gigantic hands was around Sing's neck, and she gasped for breath. She hung above the floor, suspended by her neck. Ham Fist's other hand held a revolver, and it was pointed at me.

"The eunuch wants you back," he said. "Put your knives on the ground."

Ham Fist was wearing a black jacket lined at the neck with a rabbit fur. Bandages were around one wrist. His head was massive, but his ears were too small, the size of coat buttons. His nose was shapeless, and his eyes were deeply sunken. I dropped two knives onto the grass.

"All of them," he said.

A third knife fell from my clothing.

"You are soft, gweilo, and you care about things you shouldn't care about. The eunuch has never been able to rid you of that silliness." Ham Fist waved the pistol at me, maybe afraid I hadn't seen it.

Sing struggled for breath, wheezing and gasping. She clutched Ham Fist's arm, to no effect. Her legs swung wildly.

He said, "Come with me now, or I'm going to pop off this child's head, right in front of you and this foreign-devil woman."

The bamboo doctor said in Mandarin, "Look at the girl's face. Look closely." Her voice, soft and lilting when we strolled in the garden, was sharp.

Ham Fist stared at Dr. Hanley, then looked at Sing. A tuck of suspicion formed on his brow. He looked at the doctor, then again to the girl, squinting.

"She has leprosy," the doctor said. "Now you do, too, probably."

Ham Fist caught his breath.

"The disease has left her face and crawled up your arm," the doctor said. "Your face will be red and rippled in a day or two, just like hers. Then your nose will rot off, and then your ears will turn black and drop off."

Ham Fist's mouth fished open. He jerked his hand away from Sing's neck, and she dropped to the ground.

The doctor said, "The leper colony is one li inland. It's called Precious Peace Colony. Thirty lepers in various stages of disintegration live there. You will be number thirty-one."

The pistol was lowered, apparently forgotten. Ham Fist stepped back.

"I'll walk you there, if you would like," the doctor said. "You'll be able to make it to the colony before the disease strikes."

Ham Fist disappeared into the examining room. I could hear him trip over something that clattered to the floor, maybe the stool. A far door slammed.

The doctor hurried over to Sing to help the girl to her feet. "You know I was lying to him, don't you, Sing? About you having leprosy." She pressed her cheek against Sing's red cheek, hugging her. "We won't see that fellow again."

Sing returned the hug. My knives were already back in their places.

Still embracing the girl, the bamboo doctor said over her shoulder, "A donation box is at the front door. Most of my patients can't pay, but perhaps you can."

I stepped toward the door.

She said, "I hope you find your brother and the actress before the bandits find you."

9

The bandits didn't find me, but the army did. A platoon of Chiang Kai-shek's Nationalist Army was arriving—an officer on horseback leading the way—just as I stepped from the hospital. The officer pointed a quirt, and two soldiers ran from behind his horse, their rifles aimed at me. It was too late to duck back into the hospital.

The soldiers—in ragged greatcoats and olive caps, and carrying stick grenades tied to cloth bandoliers—circled behind me and used their gun muzzles to push me toward the officer.

"Oiled shoes." The officer, a lieutenant, indicated my feet with his quirt. He spoke without removing a bamboo pipe from his mouth. "So you should be good walking." When the lieutenant signaled again, the soldiers prodded me toward the column of Nationalist troops coming up the path from the river.

They were a frayed lot. Some wore dirty puttees and others wore trousers. A few were barefoot. Some carried bolt-action Chiang Kai-shek rifles, and several had no weapons. One soldier wore a washbasin as a helmet, and another had a black bowler. Rice straw was visible at the sleeves and necks of many uniforms, where the soldiers had padded their uniforms against the cold. This was a foraging party.

Into the clearing came a line of porters, about twenty men tied together by a rope at their necks. The first porters were carrying wicker baskets, but the remaining men were empty-handed. They wore filthy cotton clothing, and most were barefoot. Four Finger Xu was last in line, and a rope trailed after him. His head was bare, the soldiers having had appropriated his bowler. Behind Four Finger was a soldier with a bayonet fixed to his rifle. If Four Finger recognized me, he didn't let on.

Three days had passed since the bomb blast that opened up my forehead, which still issued pain into the rest of me with every step I took.

I said to the lieutenant, "I am an emissary from Eunuch Chang of Chungking. Perhaps you have heard of him." I looked for some sign of recognition from the officer, but there was none. "He will be grateful if I am given free passage. He is known to reward favors generously."

The lieutenant laughed, and a soldier behind me swung the stock of his rifle into the back of my head. I fell to all fours, my mind blank. When the soldier kicked me in the stomach, I collapsed to my side.

Two soldiers slung their rifles, then lifted me by my arms and dragged me to the end of the porters' line, the tops of my feet dragging on the ground. They stood me upright, and when I tottered, a soldier slapped my ear so hard it rung. I'd been selected, I supposed, because I was larger than anyone else at the hospital and so could carry more weight. I was pushed into line behind Four Finger Xu. The tail end of the rope was cinched tightly around my neck. In front of me, Four Finger Xu was standing on one foot.

"Where's my brother?" The rope made my words raspy. "What'd you do with him?"

He didn't look at me. The rope around his neck had sunk into his skin. He held his foot off the ground. The soldiers spread out, some entering the hospital, others heading for the outbuildings and the barn. The generator workers ran into a bamboo glade. The soldiers threw a nurse through the hospital door. She managed to get back on her feet, brushed her apron and righted her cap, and then hurried into a stand of tallow trees. Feng—the boy with the bandaged cheek—was marched from the garden to the line of porters. Another rope was produced, and he was tied to the line behind me. The lieutenant called orders, pointing at the buildings.

The soldiers returned with plunder. One carried four live chickens, upside down, the wings flapping. Another came back with a gunnysack of rice. The ox lumbered toward us, a soldier flicking a bamboo cane at its flanks. Quarters of a butchered hog that had been hanging outside the kitchen were brought in a wheelbarrow. Four bags of wheat were found, then another four. A basket of cabbages and another of peanuts were brought from behind the hospital, then a box of Swatow mandarins. Starvation was the main killer of Chinese troops, far more deadly than the Japanese.

The soldier in the bowler lifted a box of medicine bottles under one arm and the old surgical set, from the examining room, under another. The doctor's Statue of Liberty wall clock came next, then small bags of spices in a wood box. The lieutenant directed his men with his quirt, and loot was handed over to the porters. I had to balance a fifty-pound bag of flour on my shoulders. A soldier handed Feng the wall clock, then laughed and slapped Feng's bandage. The boy gasped with pain but didn't drop the clock. I looked along the line of porters for Ham Fist, but he must have disappeared before the foragers arrived.

A shriek came from the hospital. A soldier pulled Dr. Hanley from the building by her flaming red hair. She swatted ineffectually at his hand as the soldier dragged her toward the lieutenant. When the soldier released her, she struck his face so hard with her fist that he fell to the ground. The lieutenant laughed. The soldier rose unsteadily and scurried away, likely ashamed.

The bamboo doctor pointed up at the lieutenant. "I have permission in writing from Madam Chiang Kai-shek to operate this hospital. How dare you strip all our food and supplies."

Still holding the pipe between his teeth, the lieutenant said, "Madam

Chiang—may she live a thousand years—is five days' march away. My colonel is one day's march. I fear my colonel more than Madam Chiang."

"I have patients I must attend to," she said, folding her arms across her chest. "Let me return to my work."

"You will return to your work, but for us," the lieutenant said. "Our battalion doctor was killed in a Japanese strafing run. Our unit has many sick and injured soldiers. Welcome to the National Revolutionary Army."

She shook her head. "You can't make me go."

He leaned low in the saddle. "Doctor, you can walk behind my horse, or I will tie you to his tail and you will be dragged behind my horse. Which will it be?"

She lowered her gaze, hugging herself more tightly.

The lieutenant smiled. "Then we are agreed."

Rain began to fall, and large drops hit the dry ground, throwing up puffs of dust. The wind picked up, and bamboo trunks clicked together.

Carrying a cotton bag of rice, a soldier approached Four Finger Xu. The bag was tossed at Four Finger, who cried out and fell to the ground. The bag landed next to him. Favoring his broken foot, he managed to stand again, huffing with pain.

The lieutenant rode his horse along the line of porters, and when he reached Four Finger, he asked, "Can't you carry the bag?"

"My foot is broken," Four Finger said, lifting it off the ground, as if the officer might see the fractured bone under the skin.

The lieutenant pulled out his pistol, aimed it at Four Finger's nose, and pulled the trigger. The sound of the gunshot fled quickly. Four Finger collapsed, bone shards and brain matter already on the dirt. A hole had replaced his nose.

The lieutenant's arm swung toward me, and the pistol barrel was pointed at my left eye. "That looks like a bad wound on your forehead. Do you think you can keep up with us?"

I was feverish and weak, but I said, "I'm sure of it."

The lieutenant blew the whistle and turned his horse. Dr. Hanley followed the officer, her hair already glistening from the rain. The foraging party formed up, their rifles over their shoulders. Tied to one another, we porters started forward, the slack rope between each of us lifting off the ground.

I shifted the bag of flour on my shoulders and moved with the line, and I had to step over Four Finger's body to do so.

捌

I pulled off my right shoe, trying not to draw away skin. When I held it upside down, blood dripped out. My sock was sodden and in tatters, and I peeled it off to reveal blisters. I removed my other shoe, and that foot was fine. Feng was already curled up and asleep on my right. Both our necks revealed collars of open sores from the rope's chafing.

I was sitting on the shingle, leaning back against a boulder, a few yards from the river. The other porters had also collapsed on the beach. Most of them stared vacantly out at the river. Carrying a tin pot, a soldier walked toward us, with wood bowls in a fishnet bag slung across his back. He gave me a bowl and used a ladle to drop rice and two bits of stringy meat into the bowl. The soldier kicked Feng's legs to wake him, then handed him a bowl. When Feng asked for chopsticks, he was kicked again. I fed myself with my fingers.

The Yangtze was a li wide here, a third of a mile. Weeping cypresses were along the riverbank, the wind pushing the branches out over the water. Wild peppers and bulrushes also grew along the shore. A bloated water-buffalo carcass floated by, bumping into boulders, then drifting on. In the middle of the river was a *tow-shu*, a tea boat, about fifty feet long, with a sharp prow and stern to negotiate rapids, a poleman at the stern. A patchwork of rice paddies and cane fields was on the far side of the river, and higher up the slope were green fields of winter rye, rising to the stark purple mountains.

I tossed the empty bowl onto the pebbles. Feng finished his meal and instantly fell asleep, his back against me. We had walked for nine hours. Two of the porters had fallen on the road and were unable to rise, and had been shot, their loads given to soldiers.

Just as my head sunk to my chest, I heard, "I have some tincture of iodine. Let me look at you." A bag of medical supplies hung from her shoulder.

Dr. Hanley lowered herself to my side. Behind her a soldier carried a bayonet on a rifle. Her hands were covered with dried blood, and gore dappled her sleeves and apron. Her gray-green eyes seemed faded.

"Raise your chin."

I struggled to lift my head. She applied the iodine to the rope burns, and it stung. Then she dabbed iodine on my forehead and feet. She pulled a bandage roll from the bag, ripped off a length, and tied it around my foot. I gritted my teeth against the pain.

"Why does only one of your feet have blisters?" she asked.

"You're the doctor."

She said, "I treated the lieutenant for an abscessed molar, pulling the tooth, and I heard him say the foraging party is going to go out again tomorrow, to a town called Mountain Peace. A rice warehouse is there."

Feng was still asleep. I nodded in his direction. "He won't survive a second day."

"How about you?" she asked. "Can you survive another day?"

I shrugged, not sure of the answer. The sun was low over the mountains in the west. Arrayed along the river's shoreline were four tents, all of them white with large red crosses on the tops. Wounded Nationalist soldiers lay on the ground near the tents. Orderlies moved among the wounded, dispensing water and changing dressings. The army's flag—a white sun on a purple rectangle on a larger red rectangle—flew from a pole. Moans and cries carried in the wind.

"Are you all right?" I asked.

"I walked all day, though I didn't have to carry anything." She put the cap back onto the iodine bottle. "Since we arrived here I've amputated a gangrenous leg, set a fractured wrist, cleaned out three wounds, and wired up a shattered jaw."

"Battle wounds? I didn't think the Imperial Army was that close."

"Yesterday Japanese planes strafed a regiment downriver near Red Cloud Ferry. This is a hospital company. And I just treated the regiment's colonel for trench foot." She smiled. "He was chatty, and I asked him about your actress, this Tsingtao Lily."

"She's not my actress."

The doctor laughed, a tired sound. "Your brother's actress, then." She was wearing something around her neck. I later learned it was called a *stethoscope*. "I told the colonel that Tsingtao Lily might be in the area, and asked if he had seen her."

I touched my neck, which was stinging.

"The colonel beamed at her name, and he went on and on about her while I worked on his foot," she said. "He called her a beautiful river pearl and China's devoted maiden. He is smitten, just like your brother. But he hadn't seen her, and he didn't think any of his men had, either, as he would've heard about it. And he hadn't seen an Anglo, your brother. I don't speak Mandarin as well as you do, but I think he was telling me the truth."

"Tsingtao Lily knows how to act in front of a movie camera, and she knew how to act in front of William. He was the minnow at the sandpiper's legs, as we Chinese say. She inveigled and promised and beguiled him."

The doctor said, "Do you realize you've made fists with your hands, and your voice has hardened. Are you angry at the actress?"

"My brother never had a chance."

"How do you know she inveigled him?"

From experience. Tsingtao Lily had appeared in my room, her wiles on display, and that's how I knew what she was capable of. It was too tawdry to talk about. I said, "William doesn't know how some things in life work, including worldly women." I rubbed my calves. They were sore. Everything was sore. "Do you have brothers and sisters?"

"Two brothers back in Idaho. I'm the oldest."

"And parents?"

"Sure." She dug around in her bag.

The guard followed us back and forth as we spoke, interspersed with glances at the mess tent.

"William is the only person at the House of Eight Orchids who ever laughed. He laughed loud and often. Laughter weakened character, Eunuch Chang believed." I rubbed my jaw. I looked at her. I was perilously close to confiding personal matters, behavior which at the House of Eight Orchids was as foreign as skipping rope. Unburdening yourself burdens someone else, the eunuch liked to say. "I need to sleep." I looked up at the guard and said in Mandarin, "The doctor is ready to go."

The guard—a corporal wearing a quilted blue winter uniform—said in Mandarin, "Lady, I have to bring you back right away."

The guard's head was covered by a wool cap with earflaps. She simply smiled at him. He fidgeted but apparently didn't know how to move her along.

A quartermaster's wagon—with wood-spoke wheels and oxen in the traces—was being unloaded near a tent. A Ford truck with sweeping fenders and a red cross painted on the side was parked near the wagon.

"Are you ever going back to the Beautiful Country?" I asked her, using the Chinese term for the United States.

"Every other year I visit Idaho for three months." She put the ends of the stethoscope into her ears and, without a word of explanation, pushed aside my jacket and shirt and placed the other end on my chest.

"What are you doing?" I asked.

"Haven't you ever had a physical examination? I'm listening to your heart, and lungs and gastrointestinal system."

"I'd rather you not." Had she no modesty?

She pressed the thing onto my chest. "Take a deep breath."

I did as she ordered. She moved the stethoscope and asked me to inhale again, and I did. A pheasant clattered from high grass inland a few yards.

"You carried that bag all day." She pulled the stethoscope from her ears. "I need to check you for hernias. Stand up and lower your pants."

Maybe Madam Tuan was correct: the foreign devils were lunatics. I vigorously shook my head.

"Later, then." She brushed back hair from her face, and I couldn't help staring at the freckles along her long nose.

"Are you going to stay here forever?" I asked.

"China is wearing me down." She rubbed her neck. "I don't laugh much anymore, and I don't sleep much, and my malaria comes and goes. I'll go back to Idaho for good, sooner than I'd planned."

"This army hospital unit isn't going to let you go," I said. "They're going to work you to death."

"When I was treating his feet, the colonel said I could go back to the hospital in a couple of days. He said it, and I made him promise."

"You might be traded between regiments, but the Nationalist Army isn't going to let you go, not a doctor. Not ever."

"But my patients are back at the hospital." She leaned closer to me. "The colonel promised—"

"He is lying to you."

They came out of the west, five or six of them. There was no sound, not at first, and they were almost invisible, lost in the brilliance of the setting sun. The huge red crosses on the Chinese tents made no difference. Yellow tracers streaked in from over the river. The ground erupted all around, spigots of sand and pebbles. Bullets ripped into tents and soldiers, plowed the ground, and ricocheted off the boulders.

I grabbed the doctor and shoved her down, my arm across her shoulders. A hole the size of a dinner bowl was punched through her guard's chest, and he fell to the shingle.

I yelled, "Feng, get behind a boulder."

It was too late. A tracer ricochet had found his head, and the phosphorous burned furiously inside the half of his skull that remained. Only then did the sound of the Nakajima fighters reach us, first the stutter of the machine guns, then the whine of their engines that dropped to a low growl as they flew over and sped inland. The planes rose and banked, readying for another strafing run. Dr. Hanley tried to crawl toward Feng.

"You can't help him." I levered myself off the ground. "Get up. Let's go."

"I need to—"

I hooked my hand under her arm and dragged her across the beach, weaving through boulders, then climbing an earthen bank. The Japanese planes were turning sharply, about to fall from the sky again. I pulled her along, her long skirt trailing behind her.

The tents had been ripped apart. Chinese soldiers that had been lying on the riverbank wounded were now lying there dead. Only splinters remained of the surgical table. Four horses lay on the ground—one still kicking—and a fifth horse was unscathed, snorting and dancing against its hobbles. Cook pots and bandages, rifles and blankets were strewn about. The hospital's only vehicle, a Ford, had sunk to its axles and was on fire. The Japanese planes had somehow missed the supply wagon and the oxen.

We crossed the driftwood on the high-water line, then ran through yellow saw grass. The bag of medical supplies bounced against the doctor as we moved along. I led her into a bamboo thicket, pushing aside the trunks to get deeper into the glade. The planes roared in again, their guns pounding.

I had to lean against a trunk to gather my breath.

She gulped air and pointed at the ground. "You forgot your shoes."

10

As night closed in we walked through cotton and wheat fields and along dikes, keeping away from the dirt road at river's edge to avoid army patrols. It was too cold to stop. I stumbled along in an exhausted daze, but the doctor didn't seem weary. We had traded a farmer a pair of long scissors from the doctor's bag for cloth shoes, which kept my foot from shredding further.

As the moon rose above the eastern hills, lights came into view a hundred yards inland from the river. It was a hamlet: a dozen mud-and-straw huts and one larger building. We passed a slaughter pen, stepping around a heap of offal as we neared the homes. A stream ran down from the mountain, and a forty-foot-high waterwheel turned slowly, creaking and splashing. A rotating log at its hub ended in a mud-brick mill house, where sugarcane was crushed into syrup. The wheel was still turning, the paddles rising and falling. Water dripping from the turning wheel looked yellow in the moonlight.

The doctor put her hand on my arm and whispered, "I don't hear any dogs."

She gestured toward a hut that had no light visible through its paper window. I couldn't make out anything.

"I've been to a dozen villages, treating people," she said. "Dogs always howl and bark and come out to investigate. Where are they?"

I moved toward a hut. Out of the darkness a head protruded, a human head, with no body beneath. The eyes were open and dead. The mouth was pulled back in a grotesque smile. Strips of skin hung from under the jaw. The head was stuck on a pitchfork.

"There're more," the doctor said.

We moved along a row of heads, six of them, all men, and all mounted on pitchforks and shovels. A moan came from a doorway. A woman was sitting on the threshold, holding her head in her hands. At the end of her building a dozen dead dogs, each ridden with bullet holes, were stacked like wheat sheaves. As the moon rose, its light cast the hamlet in dull silver.

The doctor and I stepped along a hardpan walkway, passing mud-brick huts with palm-frond roofs.

"Who did this?" the doctor whispered.

We rounded a hut's corner to find red embers and smoke where a building had been. Fishing nets had been thrown onto the fire, and curled bits of net popped and hissed, sending sparks into the night sky.

A voice came from the door of the next hut. "The inn has been burned down, if that's what you are looking for." An elderly woman came into the red light of the dying fire. "It wasn't an inn anyway. Just a room that belonged to the ferryman. But he's dead." She spoke Mandarin with a strong up-country accent. She looked like a pile of sticks, weighing eighty pounds at the most.

"Who did this, elder sister?" I asked. "Who killed all the men in your village?"

"Bandits." She was missing two front teeth. "At first they only wanted money, but then they found the vats of fermented sugarcane juice, and they all got drunk and started shooting us. They shot some of their own, too." She pointed at her mouth. "I had a gold tooth. They knocked that out, and the one next to it, too, with a rock." Her upper lip was swollen and red. An old burn scar along her neck was purple. Her face was deeply lined. She dipped her chin with every word.

"May I look at you, ma'am?" the doctor said. "I'm the doctor from Red Cloud Ferry."

The old woman leaned closer to the doctor, eyeing her up and down. "You're a foreign devil." That apparently settled the question.

A nightjar flew overhead, and the waterwheel rumbled. The wind coursed along the Yangtze canyon, moving the tree branches overhead and carrying the odor of molasses, the scent of a sugarcane village. The river valley was narrow here, and we were on the only path up the river.

I addressed the woman again. "Elder sister, I'm looking for my brother. He is thinner than me, and his hair is darker, though not as dark as yours. He may be traveling with a woman, and they may have passed through here today. The woman is tall, with a long nose."

"And no calluses on her hands? Never worked a day in her life?"

"That'd be her."

"The bandits put her up on the toolshed roof and made her dance for them. They banged their bottles of cane liquor with sticks, and that was their music. They yelled at her and laughed, and some of the bandits danced on the ground below her. More staggering than dancing."

"What happened to her?"

"The bandit captain dragged her down from the roof and took her away on his horse. I didn't see a foreign devil."

"Do you know where the woman and the bandit went?"

"Are you going after her?" The old woman stared at me, moving her gaze up and down, as she might a hog haunch at a market. "Do all foreign devils look like you?"

I said, "Most are better looking."

The old woman said, "You look like a hard man, someone not to be fooled with."

"Sometimes," I said.

"Come with me."

She walked along the stream toward the waterwheel, proving she was stronger, less rickety than I had guessed. A man's body was partly submerged in the creek, facedown, the water streaming over his head and shoulders. A third of his skull was missing, probably shot off. We walked alongside azaleas and gentians, the waterwheel looming over us. The water passed under the paddles, pushing the wheel.

Frogs sounded from the stream.

Ivy grew up the mill's brick walls. Next to the mill were ricks piled with cut sugarcane. The axle entered the mill through a circular hole in the wall. It turned slowly, given torque by the water. The old lady pulled open the mill door. Dr. Hanley and I followed her into the mill. The lady lifted a sulfur match from a box on the wall and lit an oil lamp. She adjusted the wick, and the flickering light revealed the mill machinery.

Wood-spoke gears were above a gray-green stone wheel that rolled around and around on a granite bed. The wheel must have weighed as much as ten mules and was as tall as I was. It moved slowly, with majestic force, and its rumble filled the room. The stone bed was lined with wood to prevent juice from spilling, and a gutter was along the bed's west end, where juice flowed into barrels.

I didn't see the body until the old lady moved across the wood floor to the wheel and pointed at the granite bed. The doctor covered her mouth with a hand.

"I had plucked a chicken for dinner," the old lady said. "The bandit chief tried to take the chicken, and my husband hit him in the face. And so the bandits brought my husband and me to the mill and fed my husband feet first to the millstone. They made me watch."

The body was as flat as a leaf. The skull was reduced to powder, and blood had drained off the bed into the gutter. The massive wheel completed another circuit, and rolled over the body once again.

"I don't know how to stop the wheel," the old lady said. "Everybody who knew is dead."

I looked toward the ceiling, at wood cogs lacing together. Maybe I could figure it out. The wheel trundled around again, a massive presence in the room.

The woman's face was pinched with anger. "My husband's name was Tao Wuzhou. We were married thirty-two years and had five children together."

"I'm sorry, ma'am," I said.

"The bandit chief goes by the name Wood Leg."

I had read about him in Chungking newspapers. He had been a sergeant in the Nationalist Army, and had lost a leg in a training accident, and so had been dismissed from service.

"I know where Wood Leg's camp is," she said. "That's probably where he has taken the girl you are looking for."

Maybe my brother was still with her. "You'll tell me where the camp is?"

"Only if you swear to bring Wood Leg back here to me." Her voice crackled like fire. "Alive."

捌

Trailing a spray of silver sparks, the rocket raced across the river, shot upward, and exploded, a chrysanthemum of green sparks that dazzled, then flickered and faded. Laughter came from up the river, and drunken hooting and hollering. A splash was followed by more laughter, then rifle shots. Three rockets soared into the black sky—two red and a blue—and they wove together, in and out, spewing sparks, then raced higher and burst apart, filling the sky with shimmering light.

I moved along the shoreline, pushing against the current in water up to my knees. The bandits were once soldiers, and perhaps they had placed sentries on the road and maybe the pier, but I didn't think they would guard the crease where the river met the land. Boulders the size of oxen were along the shore, and I walked between them, in and out of the water, keeping boulders between the bandits and myself, but steadily moving closer. Sharp stones were beneath my feet, and I caught myself from slipping on river weed beneath the surface.

Another rocket bomb ignited over the river, setting the sky alight for an instant. Then the darkness covered me again, and I pushed upriver. Three men were on the pier, one of them holding a bottle, visible for only an instant as another rocket erupted overhead. I waded up the shore and ducked behind a beached sampan. Along the shore, a bandit sat astride one of the wooden barrels lining a brick building. He had a bottle between his knees and a rifle across his lap.

I left the water and climbed up a stony bank, moving between dove trees. When another flash lit up the area, accompanied by cackling and laughter, I could see the rooster painted on one of the four buildings in the complex, the symbol of the Happy Rooster Fireworks Company. The slow wind carried the scent of black powder.

A building was burning—maybe the manager's office—casting a nimbus of flickering yellow light. Two men stood near the fire, warming themselves. I walked behind another shed, staying out of the firelight. Crouching, I moved along a stack of empty wood boxes behind another shed. Shivering, my jacket and pants wet and sticking to my skin, I moved into a grove of pine trees at the edge of the fireworks plant, traveling upriver along the beach. My three knives were in place.

I found the man with the wood leg on a sandbar fifty yards from the plant. He was pouring black powder onto the beach, onto a mound there. He laughed and walked backwards, pouring the powder, leaving a trail of it, wood leg sinking into the sand with each step.

A teacher at the House of Eight Orchids, Ito Yoshimasa, had taught me to walk silently: rolling my feet, bent at the knees, placing one foot right in front of the other. I emerged from the trees, jumped from the bank onto the sandbar, and walked toward the bandit captain, making no more sound than a rabbit. Another rocket burst overhead, but the bandit captain held a glowing punk in one hand as he watched the black powder draining from the bag.

I got within three feet of his back. "Where is the Anglo?"

He started, then spun on the axis of his peg leg.

"The Anglo, and the woman who you forced to dance at the mill town. Where are they?"

His nose was so crooked that it looked as if it had been broken and badly set, and his head was shaved to the skin, probably against lice. His eyes alert with malice, he pulled back his coat and reached for a pistol tucked behind the rope that held up his drooping trousers.

I can move a knife quickly, from nowhere to business, then back to nowhere before the eye can register it. Before the bandit could touch the pistol grip, his right ear was falling toward the sand, sliced from the side of his head.

I stepped closer. "Bring that pistol out, and it'll be your intestines on the sand next. Where's the Anglo and the girl?"

His hand found the hole where his ear had been. Blood came away on his fingers. His voice was strained by pain. "I sold them."

"Who did you sell them to?"

"A KMT captain on a junk, the boat who patrols the river between here and Green Grove Crossing." KMT were the Kuomintang—the Nationalists, Chiang Kai-shek's outfit.

"When?"

"Yesterday," he replied.

"What's the KMT captain's name?"

"We call him Purple Scar because there's a dark scar all along his face."

"Was the wine part of the deal?"

"We took it off a trader's barge, not from the KMT captain."

I lifted the pistol from him and put it in my waistband, then pushed him forward, along his trail of gunpowder, toward whatever he had planned to detonate, a lump on the sand. The gunpowder trail led to a dog, one almost as large as a donkey, the biggest I'd ever seen, though with only half a tail. Its feet were bound together by a leather cord, and he was covered in the black powder. It snarled at me with fangs as long as my index finger and stared with eyes that glowed like burning coals. A bullet hole in the giant animal's shoulder leaked blood onto the sand.

The bandit inhaled deeply, as if ready to shout a warning, but my blade was at his throat.

"Not a sound," I said.

Pistol shots came from behind the plant, followed by inebriated cackling.

"You were going to burn up this dog with gunpowder?" I asked.

He shrugged. "He growled at me so I shot him."

I shoved the bandit captain toward a bank of fir trees on the shore. Then I kicked his wooden leg out from under him, shoved him to the ground, and said, "Wait here. You make a sound, I'll use your own pistol on you."

I returned to the dog. I don't like dogs, especially mammoth creatures like this one. In the sputtering red light, the dog looked as if it had risen from a crack in the earth, a hell dog. With a knife I cut the cord around his legs. The dog scrambled to his feet, still staring at me, then shook himself mightily, casting black powder from its fur. He didn't seem to notice the bullet hole in his shoulder.

I crossed the sand to the bandit, lifted him by the arm, and pushed him toward the darkness of the fir glade. Rifle shots came from the fireworks plant, and more laughter. I looked over my shoulder again.

The giant dog was following me.

捌

"Have you ever looked into a mirror?" Dr. Hanley lifted an almond with her chopsticks. "And asked yourself who you are?"

"The House of Eight Orchids doesn't have mirrors. Evil spirits might emerge from them."

"I'm not being literal, and you know it."

"You are about to give me a lecture." I smiled. "I don't need a lecture from an ocean ghost."

We were in Xingjian's hut. She and other women in the village had cleaned our clothes, and Xingjian had served us chicken and rice. It was the hamlet's last chicken. The bandits had killed her husband by feeding him into the sugarcane press, and had taken away everything they could carry, but this chicken had somehow escaped the bandits, so it was our dinner, served with almonds and leeks, as we were honored guests. The old woman came and went, always hovering, making sure our bowls were never empty. A tallow candle on the table threw a meager light. The floor was hard-packed dirt. Five or six children took turns peeking through the door. Smiling and nodding, Xingjian brought in a bowl of sliced pineapple and placed it on the table. She bowed once, bowed again, and backed out of the hut.

"Have you ever been to church?" the doctor asked.

"Like the Presbyterian church where the Americans go on Sunday? Not likely."

"You've never attended a church service?"

"The eunuch doesn't favor churches or temples. Or shrines, though he has several at his home because the cooks and gardeners insist on them."

She chewed a bit of chicken and seemed lost in thought. I passed the bowl of pineapple to a child at the door. He whooped and disappeared with the bowl, the other children chasing after him.

"How about school?" the doctor asked.

"The House of Eight Orchids is a school."

When she laughed, her angular features softened. Her hair was auburn in the candlelight. "A school for what? Picking pockets?"

"I can recite from memory more than three hundred lines of *Hamlet*." I sounded like a braggart even to my own ears, but I couldn't stop. "I can read the poetry of Matsuo Bashō in Japanese. I'm familiar with calculus and can chart the motion of the stars. Eunuch Chang saw to it that I was educated. Same with my brother, William."

Xingjian came into the hut. She was wearing a blue apron and brought in a bowl of roasted peppers. She asked, "Is that your dog outside, beloved brother?"

"He's not my dog, that's for sure," I said.

"He won't go away." She placed the bowl on the table. "He's too big and ugly for this town."

"He followed me here from the bandit camp, running along the bank as my boat drifted downstream," I said. "But that doesn't mean he's my dog."

Xingjian left the hut, and I could hear her trying to shoo away the dog. The huge animal growled, and the old woman cursed it, then padded away.

"You honestly don't see it," the doctor said.

"I have no idea what you are talking about, and not for the first time."

She held her palms up, as if inviting understanding. "Eunuch Chang is a gangster."

I stared at her.

She said, "His gloss of sophistication doesn't hide that fact. You've told me about his ancient scrolls and his artwork and his lovely gardens, but those things don't disguise who he is."

I felt as if she had grabbed my throat. "I don't need to hear your judgments about the man who—"

"For God's sake, John, he stole you from your parents." She reached for my hand. "Isn't that proof he's a gangster? And he raised you from a boy, and he was kind to you, and he taught you things, so you've forgiven him the awful and essential fact of your existence."

"You don't know about—"

"And he never gave you a moral compass," she said. "He never taught you life's most important lesson: right from wrong."

"I'll take you downriver back to your hospital in the morning." I rose stiffly from the bench.

She said, "Your Shakespeare and your calculus don't change anything."

I stepped to the door. "Two River 14K is a gang. And so is Blue Rooster. The House of Eight Orchids is nothing like them."

"And I'm telling you, only a veneer of refinement is the difference between the House of Eight Orchids and those other gangs. He taught you to be a gangster, and that's what you are."

I stepped around the table and headed for the door, my jaw clamped so tightly my face ached.

She said, "You need to get right with God and the world, John."

"Is there any wonder we Chinese hate missionaries?" My voice rose. "Nosey, sanctimonious, and tiresome, all of them. Even you doctor-missionaries. Go back to lancing boils and leave me alone." Could I have sounded more childish?

I left the hut, pushing through the group of children, who stared at my round eyes and my hair. Their bowl of pineapple was empty. Sitting to one side under a banyan tree, the dog—its half tail as thick as my arm, and its head as large as a hog's—looked at me, too. I crossed the ground toward the cane press, propelled by anger and moving quickly. I caught up with Xingjian at the door to the mill building.

She was smiling. "It's my turn again."

Five other village women waited at the cane-press door. They wore scarves and blue skirts. One of the women handed Xingjian a shoe awl. It had a round wood handle and a two-inch blade. They all nodded and smiled, and one of the women opened the door for Xingjian. I looked over the heads of the ladies into the mill room.

The bandit Wood Leg was in a chair near the enormous millstone. His hands were tied behind his back, and his good leg was bound to the chair legs. His wood leg was on the floor in a corner. His head was bent forward, and his body was twitching. His eyes were open. Blood stained his shirt and his pants. Some of the blood was dried and flaky; some was wet. Bloodstains colored the floor under the chair. A hole had been punched into Wood Leg's right cheek, and blood had dried along his jaw. He moaned. When Xingjian approached him, he brought up his head. His lips parted. The mill worker's body—Xingjian's husband—had been scraped off the stone.

She stood over him. "This is for my husband, Tao Wuzhou, again. You and your men killed him, remember?"

She raised the shoe awl over her head, allowed Wood Leg's eyes time to find it, then slashed down with it, sinking the short blade into his right biceps. She twisted the awl and yanked it out. The bandit groaned, and his head sank to his chest.

"I'll be back tomorrow morning, and I'll remind you about my dead husband again," Xingjian said. "Have a good night." She left the building and passed the shoe awl to a woman whose hand was held out.

This was the death by shoe awl, a common punishment along the Yangtze. Every hour on the hour, night and day, a widow stabbed the bandit captain once with the awl. The women took turns. The condemned might last three days. Most of Wood Leg's suffering was still ahead of him, and he surely knew it. Then his body would be tossed into the river.

I turned away from the mill house and said "Get out of my way" to the dog, who had followed me there. I was headed to the stables, intending to cover myself with rice straw and fall asleep.

The bamboo doctor was wrong. I indeed knew the difference between right and wrong. Death by shoe awl for the bandit who had emptied this village of husbands and fathers was right.

11

"Have you ever been with a woman?" Elizabeth asked.

I looked at her. "I'm with a woman now, aren't I?"

"Don't be thick." She smiled. Wind lifted strands of her hair. "You know what I mean."

We were side by side on the *wupan*'s thwart seat. The boat was square at both ends. Behind us, the boat's owner was standing on the deck made of plaited bamboo mat, a twenty-foot pole under his arm. The pole trailed behind us in the water. We were floating with the current, and he only used the pole to keep us away from the shore. I carefully studied the shoreline.

"Are you going to answer my question?" the doctor asked.

"Don't they have manners in America? How can you ask that?"

"I'm a doctor. It's a clinical question asked in the interests of science."

"That huge dog has been following us." I pointed at a stand of dwarf pines on the shore. "He stares at our boat, then moves along the shore. I don't much like dogs. How about you?"

She laughed. Water washed against the *wupan*'s hull. The poleman hopped on one leg and pushed the pole against a granite boulder above the river's surface. The boat slid away from the rock. His left foot was the color of bark, shriveled and leaking. It had been crushed between a barge and a pier. When he had learned one of his passengers was a doctor, he had offered to take us to Red Cloud Ferry if she would amputate his foot when we arrived. He grinned crazily each time I looked at him, perhaps at the prospect of survival. I was escorting Elizabeth back to her hospital—it was too dangerous for a woman to walk alone along the Yangtze between villages—and then I would continue upriver to Green Grove Crossing. I calculated that I would only lose several hours in the search for William.

Elizabeth said, "You know so much about some things and utterly nothing about other things."

"Ask me something about geometry. The Pythagorean theorem. Go ahead."

"This imbalance in your brain is startling."

The *wupan* drifted toward the hamlet's pier, which was made of logs lashed together. When the poleman pushed against the riverbed, the boat's stern swung toward the shore, and the boat sidled up to the log. We left the boat and walked along the log pier, then onto the beach. In water up to his knees, a fisherman hauled in a net hand overhand.

"Do you want to eat dinner with me?" I asked.

She smiled. "What are you having?"

"A fellow from Bombay taught me to catch food. Let me check."

Elizabeth followed me as I walked around the stone shrine where I had set a snare. I ducked under a pine bough and brushed aside undergrowth, looking at the pine needles and leaves that had hidden the twine loop. They had been disturbed, and the bit of carrot used as bait was off to one side. A sapling that I had bent almost double had acted as the spring. A wharf rat—twelve inches long, not counting the tail—hung from the sapling by the twine. It was dead.

"I was hoping for a cape hare," I said, "but it looks like we are having wharf rat. They're not bad, with ginger sauce and mushrooms."

She said, "I'm busy tonight, it turns out."

I tossed the rat aside, and we walked back through the trees toward the road.

The doctor stopped at a palm tree. "I'm going to visit some patients here in the village before I go back to the hospital." She extended her hand, her green eyes shining mischievously. "If you get wounded within a day's walk of my hospital here—and I don't doubt you will—I'll probably see you again."

She gripped my hand. "I hope you find your brother."

"The answer to your question is no," I said, shifting on my feet.

"I've asked you dozens of questions." She raised an eyebrow. "Which one are you answering?"

"The eunuch said women were a distraction," I said. "And that if living without women was good enough for him, it was good enough for me."

She ran her fingers through her hair, so red and yellow it seemed on fire.

"He's never let me have anything to do with women," I said. "And I mention this only because you are a doctor."

A bullet smacked the palm trunk. An instant later the sound reached me.

I lunged at her, roughly shoving her toward a banyan tree, her legs scrambling to keep herself upright as I pushed her. I pinned her against the trunk. Her eyes were wide, and her mouth opened, maybe to protest my rough handling of her. I leaned out from behind the tree to look in the direction of the shot.

Fifty yards away, half-concealed behind a hut wall, the Rough Boys' yardmaster, Ham Fist, was staring at me along the barrel of a pistol. He fired again. The bullet creased the air near my ear.

"He's here for me, not you," I said to the doctor. "Stay here until he's gone."

I lit out of there, sprinting around a fish-drying shed, then ran across nets spread to dry, then through a stand of dogwood trees, my legs pumping. I glanced over my shoulder. Ham Fist was running after me, pumping his arms up and down, with a revolver in one hand.

I ran through knee-high grass and past a bamboo-sided shack, leaped over the handles of a plow, then sprinted through a copse of pine, my arms in front of my face to ward off the boughs. I dodged around a tree of heaven, then pushed myself through brushwood. The sound of another pistol shot came from behind me. I was breathing hard. I could hear Ham Fist plunging through the brush behind me.

I ducked under dove-tree branches. Some animal in the underbrush skittered out of my way. Roots and vines tugged at my feet. I plunged deeper into the forest. Ham Fist yelled something, but I couldn't make it out through the ragged sound of my breathing. I jumped over a creek, sinking into mud on the far side, then pushed myself through a thick stand of trees, the forest getting darker as it closed in on me. My lungs felt as if they were collapsing.

I came to a clearing. Several dilapidated huts were in the distance, and a lean-to made of branches was near a pink pig that was rooting the ground with its nose. Standing in front of me was a man without a face. I had come to the leper colony. I may have yelled in fear; I don't remember. I turned on my heels, aiming north to parallel the river, desperate to flee Lian-jao, the evil spirit that spreads leprosy. I only took five steps before Ham Fist—stepping from between two camellia trunks—brought the butt of his pistol down across my head. I collapsed to the dirt.

He lashed my face with the pistol barrel, then grabbed my shirt and yanked me upright so that we were nose to nose. I was dizzy and couldn't gather my feet under me. He slammed my temple with the pistol.

"Eunuch Chang wanted me to bring you back alive," Ham Fist said, "but I just don't think I can manage it."

I tried to drop a knife into my hand, but I couldn't gather my wits to grasp it. It fell between my fingers to the ground. He poked the pistol's muzzle into my cheek and began to tighten his finger around the trigger.

"Good-bye, round-eyed foreign devil."

I never heard a thing. One instant Ham Fist was standing there, his pistol pressing into my head, about to scatter my brains all over the leper colony, and the next instant the air was filled with fur and fangs. Snarling—then Ham Fist's scream—filled the forest. The monster twisted and snapped and rolled, and Ham Fist was under it, shrieking in pain and fear.

It was that monstrous dog. Its ears were black, and its dewlaps were flying, flinging saliva. Its fangs must have been three inches long, and they sank into Ham Fist's arm, then his shoulder, then the back of his neck. The pistol had disappeared in the brush.

The monster dog backpedaled. Ham Fist screamed and kicked. The dog shook him so hard I could hear Ham Fist's molars snap together. The animal spun, lifting Ham Fist from the ground, then slamming him back down.

I ran back into the forest—more staggering than running—my legs wobbly and my vision still blurred, leaving Ham Fist to his fate, and hoping it was horrible. And while I don't much favor dogs, that one had risen in my estimation.

捌

The whore boat docked at the town, but I didn't see it right away because I had built a bonfire, starting it with rice straw, then using as many green boughs as would burn. Acrid black smoke rose from the fire. Standing in the smoke was the only way to blind the leper spirit Lian-jao so it would wander away and thus not attach itself to me. My eyes were burning, and tears poured down my face. My lungs were filled with smoke, and I stood there as long as I could before leaping out of the smoke and inhaling the cool air. I wiped my smarting eyes and blinked several times until I could see again.

The boat was a paddle-wheel steamer, about eighty feet long with a shallow draft. Vines were wrapped around the smokestack, but only as a symbolic attempt at camouflage, because Japanese planes never targeted whore boats; Japanese officers would be all too willing to patronize them if they conquered China. Smoke rose from the foreward deck, where joss sticks stuck in sand buckets burned for good luck. On a whore boat, a hundred were burned whenever the ship was moving down the Yangtze, the perfumed smoke drifting with the wind, advertising the boat's imminent arrival.

Two young women were on the deck below the pilothouse, both wearing crimson robes that fluttered in the breeze. Their lips were red, and their hair fell in oiled ringlets down their backs, a style worn only by prostitutes. They were smiling and chatting and taking in the air.

I kicked sand onto the bonfire. Smoke still drifted off my clothing. That a whore boat would pull into Red Cloud Ferry was odd. No one here had money for such entertainment, and this wasn't a coaling port. A deckhand slid out a gangplank after the boat was secured to the pier. Two fellows emerged from an amidships hatch and stepped onto the pier, one from this century and one from the last. The modern man was tall, wearing a Western business suit, a blue tie, and leather shoes. The second fellow was as squat as a toad. He wore a loose cotton jacket the color of eucalyptus leaves with matching gray-green trousers. He was barefoot and his head was shaved, and he walked behind the modern man with his head low, seemingly in utter deference to this man and the world in general. But he didn't fool me.

The man in the suit carried a stack of posters, and he held one up to a nearby farmer. I couldn't clearly see it, but the poster appeared to have a photograph of a face on it. The farmer waved a hand, indicating *no*, but the fellow shoved the poster into the farmer's hand anyway. Then the man, always followed by his deferent companion, approached an elderly man who was bent under a sheaf of cured tobacco leaves. Again he held the poster up and pressed it upon the tobacco hauler.

When the man in the leather shoes drew nearer, I could make out a photograph of Tsingtao Lily on the poster. I stepped from behind the tree and crossed the sand toward him. The river soughed by. He was showing the poster to the ferryman, who was standing beside his beached sampan. I stepped around boulders and an uprooted tree trunk.

As I neared them, the man in the eucalyptus shirt half-stepped forward, his right hand as rigidly straight as a knife blade. He looked at me.

I said in Mandarin, "Last I heard, Tsingtao Lily was traveling with my brother."

The man in Western dress turned to me. "Her name is Wu Luli. I despise the name Tsingtao Lily. You will refer to her as Miss Wu."

I said, "You would be her father, I take it."

"I deal with round-eyed brewers in Tsingtao every day, and I tire of it."

He may have been unaccustomed to anyone holding his gaze, but I stared straight at his eyes, at the small uncharitable mouth, all set within a face so long and compressed it was as if his ears were squeezing his cheekbones together.

"What do you want?" he demanded. "Get to the point."

I didn't understand his Tsingtao dialect well, but I wasn't going to lose face by admitting it, so I just continued in Chungking Mandarin. "Do you always travel with a Gwo Dai monk, Mr. Wu?"

The monk in the eucalyptus-colored jacket smiled slightly. To an untrained eye, the monk might have appeared relaxed, standing there on the sand, a half smile on his face, but he was as coiled as a spring.

"When I visit a piss hole such as this town," Wu said in Mandarin, "I don't come alone."

"And on a whore boat?" I asked. "I'm surprised."

The monk said, "You have a knife in your sleeve. I can tell from the way you hold your hands."

The monk's voice, as pleasant as a bamboo flute, didn't fool me, either. He was tiny, not five feet one, and the giveaway: his hands were covered in scars and calluses.

Wu said, "I hired a Junkers to fly me to White Pleasant Rock, the nearest airstrip. So then I paid for passage on the next vessel headed downriver, which was the whore boat. But I don't suppose I need to explain myself to you."

I said, "Maybe Tsingtao Lily . . . Miss Wu . . . and my brother, William, are still together. I'm looking for him. "

"You can't even find the right continent," Wu said. "How will you—a foreign devil—possibly find my daughter? You don't know enough about China and the Chinese."

"I know much about China," I said.

He appraised me, his gaze stopping at the gash on my forehead, then my shoulders, and hands and legs, something he must've learned from the German brewers in Tsingtao, as a Chinaman would never be so rude.

He said, "Come with me," and he led me toward the whore boat, folding up the poster and putting it into a jacket pocket. The monk followed me, too closely.

"Don't step on my shadow, monk," I said over my shoulder. "It's bad luck, and I'll take offense."

He let the distance widen between us, but only a little. The Gwo Dai Temple on the Yangtze River near Tongli had been used as a hiding place four centuries ago by Prince Li-yu, who believed his father, the emperor, and his brothers were conspiring to kill him. The prince ordered the monks to defend him. He lived at the temple forty-two years before he passed away. During that time the monks became formidable fighters, and after the prince's death the temple was sustained by hiring out the monks as bodyguards. Standing near a bald fellow wearing a eucalyptus jacket was usually sufficient protection for anyone.

I crossed the gangplank onto the boat's deck, following Wu. One of the young ladies on the deck lifted aside her blouse to expose a breast, and raised an eyebrow at me. I smiled and wagged a finger. I once met a prostitute at the Three Leaf Teahouse in Chungking. She waited for me to make an offer, and I waited for her to say something interesting. After one minute I left the teahouse, and I haven't had anything to do with whores since.

Mr. Wu walked to the boat's aft rail and beckoned me to follow. "Spies are everywhere, even in this filthy town. We can talk here."

The monk again placed himself between Wu and me, a little to the side, against the rail. "Who are you?" Wu asked.

"I'm a friend of the eunuch Chang Tao."

The monk's eyes left my hands for my eyes. "The eunuch's gweilo apprentice? You are he?"

"Do you know if my daughter is alive?" Wu asked. "I heard a report she was seen in Red Cloud Ferry, and that's why I came here, but rumors are more common than flies along the river."

"She did not die in the cinema theater fire."

"You know that?"

I held a hand to the sky. "On Buddha's blessed memory, I swear to you that I saw her alive six days ago."

Wu ran a finger along his upper lip. "Why are my daughter and your brother traveling together?"

"Because William is immature, a naïf, and she used her beauty to entrance him, and she—a woman who is as famous in China as Sun Yat-sen, a woman who Errol Flynn took to dinner when he was in Shanghai, and who the *Shanghai Film Talk* called the most beautiful woman in China—manipulated him and took advantage of him, and made him do a dangerous and silly thing. He didn't stand a chance, with her targeting him."

"Yes, that sounds like my daughter."

I didn't mention my own predicament: I should have known—I did know, and had pushed the terrifying thought aside—that Eunuch Chang would come after me, and that nothing I ever could do would redeem myself in the eunuch's estimation, and nothing I could do would ever save me from his vengeance.

He said, "I want you to find her."

"I'm only looking for my brother."

"They are likely still together," he said. "Finding one won't be any more difficult than finding them both."

"I'm not interested."

He said, "If you will find her, and return her to me, I will pay one fortieth of a *shi* in gold. And you will have a powerful new friend." He curled his index finger at himself.

A shi was 132 pounds. No one knew who would be controlling China in a few months—Chiang Kai-shek, Mao Tse-tung, or Emperor Hirohito—and whoever it was would declare the other's money to be worthless.

"Make it a twentieth of a shi," I said.

He inhaled slowly.

I smiled at him. "You said I didn't know much about China, but I know as much as anyone."

A Gwo Dai monk would be fast, of course, but I was faster. My fist hit the monk square on his forehead, a massive blow that sounded like a gunshot. The monk pitched backward against the rail, and I shoved him over it. He cartwheeled into the river.

"For example," I said, "I know that no monk in China knows how to swim."

Wu leaned over the rail. The monk surfaced, slapping the water and sputtering, then sinking again. The current moved him alongside the whore boat's hull. He came to the surface again, water falling from his face, his eyes rolling skyward. Down he went again.

"A twentieth of a shi in gold on Luli's return to me alive," Wu said. "We have a deal."

I hurried along the deck, and just before meeting the gangplank I reached into the water and pulled the monk to the surface, then hauled him up to the deck. His eucalyptus jacket had turned dark green with the water. I rolled him away from the edge. He coughed and gasped, and wiped water from his face. He caught my eyes, then looked away.

As I walked across the gangplank back to the pier, I said over my shoulder to the actress's father, "Not having the gold ready when I bring her to you would be a mistake."

"That is clear," he said.

12

I hurried through the hospital ward and pushed open the door to the surgery. The doctor had hired a sampan to bring her back to the village. She was bent over a patient, instruments in her hands, a white mask on her face, and her abundant hair under a cap. A nurse sat near the patient's head, monitoring gauges. The patient was draped in a white sheet, except his thigh, which the doctor sponged. After she dropped the sponge into a bucket, she lifted a needle that had thread hanging from it.

She looked up. "Put on a mask."

"I need a rifle," I said. I had the pistol, but it might not be enough. "And ammunition."

She stuck the needle into a flap of the patient's skin. "You came to a hospital to find a rifle? What sense does that make?"

"China is flooded with weapons. Somebody in Red Cloud Ferry must have firearms. Do you know who?"

"I have just put"—she switched from English to Mandarin, asked a question of the nurse, and continued in English—"a hundred and twenty-seven stitches into this patient."

I stepped closer. A cone was over the patient's nose and mouth. The nurse used an eyedropper to add fluid to a cotton ball at the tip of the cone. It must've been making the patient sleep.

Elizabeth looked up. "He was horribly mauled. I've never seen anything like it. We don't have bears in this part of China, and no tigers around here. I can't imagine—"

I swatted away the cone. Ham Fist was on the table. Fresh surgical stitches were keeping his face together. They ran from his temple to his jaw, from his jaw to his ear, from his ear down his neck. Other stitches were on his shoulder, disappearing under the cloth that covered him.

"What are you doing?" Elizabeth asked. "He showed up here two hours ago, crawling out of the pine grove behind the hospital. I'm almost done. He'll survive."

My knife dropped into my hand. I put it at Ham Fist's neck. "I'm going to save you some trouble."

The doctor's hands stilled. "Put that knife away, John."

"This fellow is named Ham Fist. You were there: earlier today he was one second away from blowing my brains all over the forest floor, and he'll start hunting me again the minute he leaves your hospital."

"This is a hospital. We save lives here, not take them. Put the knife away."

I stared down at the Rough Boys' yardmaster, at the big stupid wad of a head. Then I pricked Ham Fist's neck below his Adam's apple, just a drop of blood. The knife went back up my sleeve. "If he ever catches me, my blood will be on your hands."

She glanced at my wounded forehead. "I've already had your blood on my hands. What's a little more?"

Her eyes smiled above the mask. She worked the needle—pushing and tugging—and said, "I'm done. I've sewn up everything that can be sewed."

She gave instructions to the nurse, then pulled off her gloves and mask as she left the surgery, and dropped them and her blood-smeared apron into a woven grass hamper. "I need to get away from this place."

We walked into her garden, past the generator shed and all its attendants and toward the river. She was wearing a blue-and-black plaid skirt and a white blouse buttoned to the neck. She pulled a tortoiseshell clip from her hair, which fell to her shoulders.

She asked, "You weren't really going to kill my patient, were you?"

"Of course not." Eunuch Chang had also taught the art of a judicious lie.

"There's your dog again." She pointed toward the bamboo glade that bordered the hospital property.

The giant dog was sitting between two bamboo trunks, staring at me. I said, "That's not my dog."

"He's following you around like he is."

"Mosquitoes follow me around, too, but that doesn't mean they're mine."

The Yangtze was in the distance, sparkling silver in the light. Mist spurted from the White Horse Rocks below town.

"Are you going to give him something to eat?"

"If that were my dog, I might. But that's not my dog."

"He's ugly enough to be your dog. That's my medical opinion on the issue."

The dog was fifty yards away. I've seen smaller horses. Most dogs in China—the dirt-brown garbage-pile mongrels—have pointed muzzles. This dog's muzzle was blunt, like a bear's.

"He's been injured." The doctor stepped toward the bamboo thicket. "There's blood on his shoulder. Old blood. It's caked and black."

"Shot by the bandit captain, I think."

"Maybe I can do something for him. I've pulled bullets out of people. Dogs can't be much different."

I grabbed her arm. "Don't go near that dog."

"He's probably in pain."

"He's vicious," I said. "Trust me, I know. I've never seen anything like it."

She looked at me. "The patient I just sewed up?"

"I would have tried to stop the dog, but I was laughing too hard."

"If there's a bullet still in that dog, I'm going to remove it. I want you to go over there and get him. Go on."

"It's more likely that I sprout wings and fly to the top of a tree."

"And then lead him to the hospital."

I stepped toward the dog, as tentatively as I've ever done anything, intensely aware of Elizabeth's eyes on me, of her standing there with her arms crossed. I was vastly relieved when the huge animal huffed mightily—dewlaps flapping, scattering a cloud of yellow bamboo leaves on the ground—and turned half a tail and disappeared into the bamboo.

I said, "With any luck, that's the last I'll see of that monster."

She shook her head for my benefit, then glanced at the line of patients near the hospital door—at least three dozen—but apparently decided she could spare a few more minutes. We walked along, passing the inn where a woman was selling yellow peppers and roasted sweet potatoes spread out on a red cloth, her back against the inn's wall. The innkeeper with the missing nose swept dirt out through the door with a straw broom.

As we made our way toward the river, I told Elizabeth about my deal with the actress's father. I said that once I found William and Tsingtao Lily, I could use the gold her father would pay me to escape China and start a new life somewhere. I had no idea where that might be, but nowhere in China would be safe from the eunuch's revenge.

"What are you looking at?" Elizabeth asked.

I forced myself to look away. Once again, I had found myself staring at her oversized face with the merry gold-green eyes, strong cheekbones, and wide mouth, so different from the Chinese women's faces, with their triangular chins and rosebud lips.

"Is there an army outpost nearby?"

"I'm not going to help you find weapons, John. That's not why I was sent to China."

The river spread out before us—the cropland, foothills, and peaks on the other side. A team of trackers was coming up the river, pulling a boat through the White Horse Rocks. They stepped and heaved to their chants. They wore slings around their waists, attached to a line connected to the boat's bow. The boat—a small junk—was just coming into view, pitching and yawing in the rapids, water slapping against its hull.

The chanting grew louder as the trackers approached along the path at the river's edge. I was about to lecture Elizabeth on the necessity of being armed in these difficult times when the junk came fully into view, pulled upriver by the trackers. A red phoenix flag was on the mast, whipping in the wind. It was Eunuch Chang's boat. White water rushed against its bow, and it rolled and righted as it was brought through a chute of water. The eunuch had come for me.

My largest knife dropped into my hand, but I knew it wouldn't be enough, so I tucked it back up. I left Elizabeth, sprinting toward the butcher's shop. I ran between two mothers carrying their babies in slings on their backs, and around a water buffalo whose owner had pushed him to the side of the path so the trackers could pass.

I leaped over a hog-carcass stretcher and ran into the shop. I grabbed the largest blade I saw, an axe with a heavy steel blade, which had been leaning against a wall. The oak handle was shiny from use. Before the butcher had time to protest, I ran from the shop and sprinted along the path, the river on my right and mud huts on the left. The trackers stepped and heaved, singing over and over a Szechwan Mandarin rhyme: "I pull the line. The river will take me."

Naked except for black cotton trousers, the last tracker in line—the nearest to the eunuch's junk—was usually the strongest, and was called the *wheelman*. He anchored a single-file line of fifty other trackers arrayed along the river's bank, all attached to the line with slings and leaning into their work, pulling the junk upriver. The wheelman looked up from the path. At the sight of my axe, he yelled a warning, slipped out of his sling, and jumped away from the plaited line. The other trackers looked back, and some took off their slings and left the line, and others stood at their posts. The hawser slackened, sinking to the path. Out in the rapids, the junk's two polemen turned in my direction.

I wound up and sank the axe into the hawser. Strands popped apart. A man in a teal-green robe emerged from the junk's hatch and walked forward to the prow. It was Eunuch Chang. River spray doused him, and the junk dipped and rolled as if trying to buck him off. His gaze found me.

I swung again and again, slicing through more of the plaited bamboo strands. The current began pushing the vessel downstream. The line lifted off the ground, but I brought the axe down again, cleaving the hawser's last strands. The length of hawser still connected to the boat snaked off the path and into the river.

Freed of the trackers, the junk swept back into a boulder, then spun sideways into the boulder that had given the rapids its name—White Horse. The deck rail ripped away, the junk tilted, and the starboard gangway dipped under the foaming water. The polemen let their shafts slip away, and they seized the aft rail. Eunuch Chang gripped the mast with both hands. Water rushed along the deck, sweeping the eunuch's feet out from under him. Another blast of river water slapped him against the deck, but he still held fast to the mast.

The junk was hidden by a water spume; then the vessel rose against a boulder, its prow pointed at the sun and a third of its aft under the foaming water. The hull grated against the stone, a shriek and groan sounding above the rushing river. Slipping sideways off the boulder, the junk spun in a whirlpool. The polemen hung on. The prow came around again, facing upstream.

Then the current rolled the junk and pushed it against another boulder, snapping the mast and crushing part of the superstructure, and the junk almost foundered. But it caught a merciful current, and the boat righted. The vessel slipped over a stone ledge and into a raging trough and disappeared behind a wall of water. The junk was gone, and so was the eunuch.

捌

Elizabeth led the trackers to her hospital, treated one of them for tapeworms, set a broken thumb on another, and paid their wages for the days of tracking since they had left Chungking, using hospital funds, and I suppose she did so because I had cut the trackers' line. She made me write an IOU to the hospital for the money, a term and concept I'd never heard of before. Eunuch Chang often loaned money—enormous sums—and nobody ever signed anything. If payment were overdue, One Eye Gao Bai and I visited the borrower, and we never had any trouble to speak of.

Then Elizabeth and I ate first rice at Red Cloud Ferry's inn. The dining room contained three tables, chairs, and a mud stove. Once a month the doctor treated the innkeeper's piles, and so he served us plates heaping with food and would accept no money from her for the meals. As we ate, I tried to make the doctor laugh, telling her about the time I cut my cheek with a pick learning to open a door lock, but she stared at me as if I were five-legged goat.

A boat's prow appeared across the river, then its two stacks, which poured out black smoke as the boat struggled against the current. White water broke on the vessel's prow. Only powerboats could negotiate the west side of the river. An American flag flew from the stern. It was the USS *Ingram*, a gunboat based in Chungking, which chased after bandits and warlords who threatened United States vessels. The US Navy called it the Yangtze Patrol. Eunuch Chang had warned me to stay away from its gweilo sailors in Chungking.

I was desperate to get upriver after William. Elizabeth had said that the *Ingram* would call at Red Cloud Ferry in a few hours. No one in China traveled on the country's primitive and dangerous roads if a water route were available. The bandit had sold Tsingtao Lily to a KMT junk captain. I couldn't think of a way to negotiate with the junk master without a gunboat's help, so I waited for the American vessel to dock.

When I asked why the United States Navy would possibly have any interest in Red Cloud Ferry, Elizabeth said that the skipper was a friend of hers, and he liked to visit, and she sometimes treated the sailors for their maladies. British and German boats also docked in town, she had said. Medical doctors weren't on board.

She rose from the table and smiled her thanks to the innkeeper. The *Ingram* crossed the river above the rapids and neared Red Cloud Ferry. I followed the doctor out to the pier. The people of Red Cloud Ferry emerged from their huts and walked from their fields, headed to the pier, carrying chickens and baskets of corn, beans, rice, and squash. A young man opened the sty next to his home and poked a brown pig with a bamboo stick until the pig started for the pier.

When the *Ingram* was still two hundred yards from shore, an officer on the forecastle put a megaphone to his mouth. "Is Dr. Hanley in the village?"

She was often away from her hospital in Red Cloud Ferry, on her route that served five other villages. She waved her hand widely, and the officer returned the wave.

The captain stepped from the pilothouse onto the deck next to the Chinese pilot who had steered the *Ingram* into port. He wore a blue jacket and a peaked cap, and he waved at the doctor. The steam engines' thrumming carried across the water.

The gunboat was about 160 feet long, with a twenty-seven-foot beam. Her draft was only five feet, allowing her to negotiate the treacherous river. The gray steel hull at the prow was fifteen feet high, but the hull was stepped so that the aft two-thirds of the main deck were only four or five feet above the waterline. Three-inch guns were mounted fore and aft.

The captain said into the megaphone, "Our wiper has fractured his left leg. It looks bad."

Elizabeth cupped her hands to her mouth. "Can you move him to the hospital?"

"The bones are sticking out of the skin. Will you look at him first and decide if he can be moved?"

The pilot wiggled his finger, and the steam engines lessened their rumble. The gunboat drifted against the dock, and sailors jumped off the ship to secure mooring lines. A sailor tossed a coin onto the beach amid a crowd of young men holding chickens upside down, the chicken's legs tied together with braided straw. A wrestling match followed, and then one fellow held up the coin and yelled out in triumph. He threw his chicken to the sailors. Another coin was tossed at the vendors, and another scramble ensued.

Deckhands set a gangplank into place, and the gunboat's captain stepped across to greet the doctor. They shook hands and smiled at each other. He guided her onto the gangplank. The bluejackets on deck removed their caps. She saluted the quarterdeck in the proper military manner, which brought huge smiles from the sailors, some of whom she had likely treated in the past.

Then she signaled me to follow her. I was halfway across the gangplank when the gunboat's skipper held up his hand.

"The Japanese have taken Hankow lower on the river," he said, "and I've been ordered to only allow American citizens on board the *Ingram*."

"John is an American," the doctor said. "I don't know his last name, and neither does he." She introduced the skipper as Frederick Beals.

He asked me, "Do you have a passport?"

"Four or five of them that I've used in the past. Three of them are American."

The skipper was a lieutenant commander with bushy eyebrows, a jaunty look with one of those American square jaws that made me want to poke him. He had tucked his blue shirt into work dungarees.

"Then you'll need to stay shoreside." He gripped the doctor's elbow, guiding her toward the deck.

I said, "But I can prove I'm an American."

He looked back at me, his hand still on the doctor's elbow. He smiled—revealing big, square, white teeth—and glanced sideways at the doctor, perhaps soliciting a grin. "You can prove it?"

"You use the ship's safe as a bedside table in your quarters on board the *Ingram*. On top of the safe is a framed photograph of your wife and two children. A General Electric portable record player is on top of your trunk."

The commander's smile fell away.

"Inside the safe is the one-time pad used for the *Ingram*'s radio transmissions."

His voice low, he said, "How can you possibly know that?"

"The one-time pad is made of blue tissue paper. You keep it in the safe next to a gold pocket watch inscribed on the back, *To FB from his father*, and there's a date I don't remember."

"I will have you arrested," the commander fairly sputtered.

"My employer in Chungking was hired to take the one-time pad from the *Ingram*. He assigned me the job."

"You will be put in chains," the commander said. "You will be tried before a YangPat military tribunal and then hung."

"Getting on board the *Ingram* and into your quarters was easy," I said. "Then I sprung the safe door. Took me fifteen minutes. I didn't need to hurry because you were at the reception for the Belgian console at the navy club. Probably a nice affair, with crystal goblets and everything.

"But I stood there in your cabin, your safe door open and the pad in my hand, and I figured that I was too much of an American to take a US Navy codebook from a US Navy gunboat, thereby ruining a US Navy officer's career. So I put it back and closed the door. I even left your pocket watch, which was against my better instincts."

The commander's neck had turned a gratifying purple.

"So that makes me enough of an American to board your boat, I figure."

The commander inhaled hugely, staring at me until a grin slipped onto his face. "Welcome aboard the USS *Ingram*." He shook my hand. "Perhaps you would like a tour."

"Let me look at the wiper's leg," Elizabeth said.

"He's on a cot in the wardroom." Commander Beals walked aft along the deck. "He's been given morphine, and a lot of it." He turned to me. "Please don't talk about the *Ingram* or anything you see on board once you leave the boat."

"I wouldn't think of it," I said.

"The Office of Naval Intelligence believes someone in Red Cloud Ferry is being paid by the Japanese. So make no mentions of the ship or our cargo to anyone."

"A gunboat has cargo?"

The commander moved ahead. I followed him and the doctor along the deck. Two coolies swabbed the deck with yarn mops, and another coolie polished the brightwork on the starboard side, a soap pot in one hand and a rag in the other. The *Ingram* had a complement of fifty sailors. Fifteen or twenty coolies also lived aboard, hired to cook and clean. The Yangtze Patrol was one of the few places in the US Navy where a gunner's mate had a butler. The coolies bunked in the forward hull.

The steam engines made the deck hum beneath my feet. We passed the fire hose and stepped through a hatch into the wardroom where the injured sailor lay naked except for white skivvies, below a world map on the wall.

"This is Bosun's Mate Miller, one of the ship's best hands," the skipper told Elizabeth and me. "I can't do without him."

The doctor stared down at the fractured leg, the exposed bones reflecting light from the overhead bulb. She checked the pulse in his wrist. "I'm Dr. Hanley. I'm going to set your leg. You can't be moved, so I'm going to do it here."

A sailor who'd been wiping Miller's pale face with a washcloth said, "He ain't said anything in an hour."

The doctor placed her hand on Miller's sweaty forehead. "I'll return to my hospital to gather equipment. You'll need a couple months to recover, but you'll be good as new." She patted the sailor's arm and said to the others, "You keep him as comfortable as you can."

She said to Commander Beals, "I'm going to the hospital, and I'll return with a nurse and a surgery kit. I'll be back on board in twenty minutes."

Beals stepped to the hatch and assigned two sailors to accompany the doctor to help with the lifting. He asked me, "Who was your employer, assigning you to steal a US Navy codebook, if I may ask?"

I didn't see any reason to hide the truth. "The eunuch Chang."

He stared at my face, then my hands, then my face again. "And you are his apprentice, the one some call Knife Ghost and some call Yellow Hair?"

"I prefer John, actually."

"Are you carrying knives right now?" he asked.

"Not so you'd notice."

Commander Beals pulled at his ear. "Four months ago the Office of Naval Intelligence asked about you."

"An American intelligence agency? What did they want?"

"I made some inquiries around Chungking, and I concluded you didn't exist."

"I'm often accused of this; sometimes I even believe it myself."

He stepped toward the wardroom's aft hatch. "I've been having trouble with the feed pumps. Two days ago I had to haul fire. Since you seem to be so all-knowing, do you know anything about steam engines?"

"I know how to steam rice. Would that help?"

I followed him forward through a hatch, ducking under electric light cages, then to a companionway and down a ladder. The odor of grease hung heavily in the air. A coolie carrying a canvas bag of laundry pressed against the bulkhead to get out of our way. The noise was of a thunderstorm, with deep echoing reverberations. I followed Beals into the engine room.

The steam engine was a monster of brass, glass, and steel. Commander Beals obviously loved this machine, beaming as he pointed out valves, pistons, and levers. The steam engine's roar seemed centered between my ears. This was a place of powerful joss. In the next compartment was the fire room, with the boilers and ash pits, and beyond them the coal bins.

The engineer sat at a workbench filling out a form. Wrenches and screwdrivers hung from the bulkhead above the bench. He wore greasy white trunks and leather boots. Sweat rolled down his breastbone.

He rose from the chair and touched a knuckle to his forehead. "I've jury-rigged the feed pump again, Skipper. We'll see how it goes."

Commander Beals gestured toward two coolies, one of whom was wiping a piston and the other tending a pump. "We added a couple of coolies an hour ago. We're training them to be wipers."

I looked at the coolie wiping the piston, his back to me.

"We fished them out of the river just below White Horse Rapids," Beals continued. "Their junk had foundered and—"

I understood, just not in time. Eunuch Chang spun away from the piston and hit me in my abdomen with his fist, a blow that would fell an ox. I bounced back against the workbench, and he chopped the side of his hand into my neck. Pain shot down my arms and legs, and they instantly quit working. I collapsed to the deck.

Beals hollered something, but the eunuch jabbed two fingers into Beals's breastbone, and the commander folded like a jackknife.

Eunuch Chang seized my shirt collar and lifted me toward the engine. He flipped open the blowdown cock. Steam roared from the engine, a pencil-thin blast of water vapor hot enough to scald Satan, filling the engine room with a piping scream. Steam also blew out from under the grates. He jerked my head toward the steam jet.

"You betrayed me," the eunuch said in Mandarin. "You betrayed your father."

"The hell?" yelled the engineer. He yanked a red handle on a cord next to the workbench, and a klaxon sounded above the noise of the steam and the engines. A two-foot open-end wrench in his hand, he rushed the eunuch.

Chang's foot stabbed into the engineer's kneecap, and the shattering of bone sounded above the steam. The engineer's momentum carried him into Eunuch Chang and pushed one of the eunuch's feet sideways on the grate, lessening the eunuch's purchase. But he yanked my head toward the cock's steam. Sizzling bits of vapor landed on my cheeks and forehead. The steam jet was four inches from my eyes, then three inches. The eunuch grunted with the effort of moving me toward the steam. His blows had paralyzed me. Beals rolled over and struggled to all fours, his mouth hanging open. Billows of steam rose from the grates under him. He tried to lift a leg.

The engineer must've been a brawler in his younger days, and he still was. With his good leg, he kicked up, and his foot smacked into where any other man's privates would've been. Eunuch Chang ignored the blow, and he yanked my face nearer the shrieking steam jet. The skin on my forehead—an inch from the howling steam spout—began to parboil.

The engineer slashed the eunuch's leg with the wrench, then again; then he thrust up with the wrench, catching the eunuch under the rib cage. Eunuch Chang tottered back, and my head sank away from the blasting steam. A coolie tackled the eunuch from behind, gripping his legs. A sailor—the water tender from the fire room—rushed through the passageway, put his arm around the eunuch's neck, and fiercely yanked back, the sailor's curses lost in the hissing of the steam. Another engine-room sailor appeared. The eunuch crushed this man's nose, flattening it against his cheekbones with a pop, before the man could grab the eunuch's arms. Another sailor appeared and helped pin the eunuch's arms. Eunuch Chang disappeared under the pile of Americans.

Commander Beals used the edge of the workbench to right himself. He worked his jaw several times before he could say anything. "Take him topside. Tie his hands behind his back, and throw him overboard."

Eunuch Chang was hustled out of the engine room, surrounded by sailors and coolies. I lay on the deck grate, facedown.

When Beals closed the cock, the jet of steam disappeared. "Dr. Hanley will be here in a moment," he said to the engineer. "She'll fix you up. You won't even miss a watch down here." He helped the engineer sit upright.

I tried my arms again. They worked in a haphazard manor. The left side of my body was buzzing and out of my control. The eunuch had taught me how to do this—paralyze someone—but I never thought I'd be on the receiving end of it. My much-abused forehead felt as if the skin had been peeled away again. A sailor called down that the doctor had returned.

I coughed raggedly and said, "Tying his arms . . ."

Beals turned his head to me. "Say it again, over the engines."

"Tying his arms and tossing him into the river."

"Yeah?"

I said, "It won't be enough."

13

"Richards, you are on corpse patrol," ordered Commander Beals.

"Skipper, I'm a machinist's mate in the United States Navy. I didn't sign up for no corpse patrol," Richards said.

"If I want sniveling, I'll visit my father-in-law in Tacoma," Beals replied. "Grab the pole."

Richards lifted a pole off a rack next to the fire hose and walked forward on the starboard side, peering down into the water between the *Ingram*'s hull and Red Cloud Ferry's pier.

The skipper told me, "If we tie up any length of time, bodies foul the lines and get jammed against the hull. The river is cheaper than coffins."

Elizabeth and a nurse were in the wardroom setting the sailor's leg. The doctor had applied a salve to my burnt forehead, smiling as if she thought a steamed forehead was funny. Tattered clouds slipped by overhead, and the wind was picking up, pushing waves down the river. A white plover flew through the masts, then dipped toward the shore.

On the other side of the river, a village on a log raft moved downstream. Dozens of huts had been built on the raft, home to two or three hundred people. They were floating their lumber to a mill near Chungking. The raft would also be carrying barrels of molasses, baskets of rice and millet, piles of rabbit pelts, and anything the villagers could sell.

Smoke from their cooking fires drifted along with them, and they beat drums to warn vessels downstream, and the sound rolled across the river.

A sailor in *Ingram*'s pilothouse called down, "Skipper, a junk is off the port bow three hundred yards. It just turned our way."

The skipper called back, "Can you tell what it's carrying?"

"KMT, rail to rail."

"That's Purple Scar's boat." Beals rubbed his jaw. "The Yangtze River has an ironclad rule: just when you think things are going pretty well, a boatful of KMT shows up."

From the pilothouse came, "The junk has requested permission to pull alongside, Skipper."

"As always. Signal approval."

I asked, "What do they want?"

"Their squeeze. Only ten dollars, if we're lucky. That's how I knew we'd find your junk; Purple Scar finds us." Commander Beals had agreed to help me because assisting Americans along the Yangtze was the *Ingram*'s mission. He had added, "It's how I earn my pay, such as it is." Elizabeth had loaned me a physician's black bag and a stethoscope.

"Why do you pay it?"

"It's just easier to pay than to object. The other YangPat gunboat does the same thing, and so do the Limeys. I carry cash for the purpose. It's like a toll to use their river. This one's the only KMT junk between here and Green Grove Crossing. So you really think your brother is on board?"

"I don't have any better information."

The junk slid into view. Its freeboard was higher than the *Ingram*'s. A rudderman was on the junk's elevated aft deck. Only one sail was raised for steerage. River weeds had attached to the hull at the waterline and streamed along with the vessel. Deckhands dropped an anchor aft, and the chain played out loudly from the locker. Battens clacked together as the sail was lowered. American sailors lowered truck-tire bumpers over the *Ingram*'s rail.

Soldiers jammed together on the junk's decks. Some wore straw conical hats, some wore brown cloth caps, and some wore the M35 German helmet with steel flaps over the ears. Germany had helped build the Chinese army in the early 1920s. Many carried Mauser bolt-action rifles, but some only had pitchforks and axes. Their captain was at the rail amidships, a pistol on his hip, his chest puffed out with importance.

Commander Beals called to the KMT captain, "Me habbee no ching ching."

And then he whispered, "Don't tell him we are looking for your brother until the junk is secured alongside." He turned back to the KMT captain and held up two fingers. "Two Goldie mon-mon ching ching, all habbee, no more."

"I speak fluent Mandarin," I told Beals. "Let me do my business before you start talking in pidgin about ching ching."

"All right, but take it easy. These KMT louts are unpredictable and dangerous."

As the junk drifted closer, I switched to Mandarin and said in a voice that the KMT captain—but not many of his men—would hear, "I'm looking for my brother. A bandit at the Happy Rooster Fireworks plant said he sold him and a woman to you."

When the boats were abreast, the KMT captain peered down at the skipper, then at me. A deep purple scar ran from his hairline down past his ear to his jawbone. He was bandy-legged, as if he'd been in the cavalry. His service cap was tilted jauntily to one side. "They were my guests for less than a day." He smiled with the benevolence of superior knowledge. "But they are no longer on board."

"Where are they?"

"I traded them away. I made a tidy profit, too, because the woman is exceptionally fine."

And because the farther up the Yangtze River she was, the more she would be worth.

"Who did you trade them to?"

"That would be my businesses, wouldn't it?" The captain pushed out his chest even farther.

I signaled to a chief gunner's mate named Red Leery, who then moved to the forward three-inch gun, and in theatrically large motions wiped down the traversing gear. Purple Scar's eyes flicked to Leery.

"My friend—the redheaded gweilo at the gun—has offered to blow your junk out of the water, should you fail to cooperate. All I need to do is signal him, and he will lay the gun right at your prow." I looked at Beals and switched to English. "Isn't that right, Commander?"

Even though he couldn't have understood my Mandarin, Beals offered a firm lieutenant-commander nod. American sailors were lining the deck rail to watch the negotiations.

The KMT captain narrowed his eyes. He looked at my yellow hair. He asked, "How is it you speak the language of heaven, foreign devil?"

"Answer my question," I said in Mandarin. "Your life depends on it. Who has my brother and the woman?"

The KMT captain's face turned moon white. He glanced at the *Ingram*'s three-inch gun on the forward deck. His hand twitched toward his pistol but stopped before it touched the grip. He lowered his voice so that I had to lean out over the gap between the vessels to hear him.

"The papermaker at Green Grove Crossing. He wanted her, and I threw in the Anglo as a bonus. He wasn't worth much."

My number-one knife dropped into my hand. The KMT captain's throat was fifteen feet away, an easy target. I would not let such comments about my brother pass.

Commander Beals had apparently noticed the flick of my wrist. He said, "Put it back, John. Don't let this fellow rile you into a rage."

I'd heard the same words from the eunuch on several occasions. I asked Purple Scar, "How can a papermaker afford the woman?"

His narrow smile returned. "He paid in dark tar."

Opium. The KMT captain would probably sell it in Chungking. Or—and this was just as likely—the captain was lying, and Tstingtao Lily and William were still on board the junk.

I said, "I'm going to search your vessel for my brother and the woman he is traveling with." I lowered my voice so he wouldn't lose face in front of his men. "Tell your men that I am an American doctor." I held up Elizabeth's leather bag, pulling out the stethoscope. The KMT soldiers may never have seen such an instrument before, but it looked official and important. "And tell them that I have been ordered by the Golden Mountain navy and by the KMT Department of the Navy to search for a man who is spreading typhoid fever up and down the river."

The KMT captain's face paled again, making his scar appear even more livid. He glanced at the *Ingram's* forward three-inch gun, Red Leery polishing the barrel with a rag and grinning evilly at the junk captain.

He said, "A United States gunboat would never fire on a Kuomintang vessel. You are making an empty threat." His voice, too, was low, meant for me and not his troops.

"If you try to sail away without allowing me to search your vessel for my brother, you'll find out how empty the threat is." I looked at him the way Eunuch Chang stared at the doomed.

His jaw was clamped so tightly the vein on his neck stood out. He inhaled loudly, then yelled at his soldiers, "These bowl-eyed dogs are searching for a typhoid carrier, and this Western doctor is going to search our ship. General Chiang has personally ordered that all KMT vessels oblige him." He pointed at one of the sailors. "Put a gangplank in place."

I didn't wait for the gangplank, but instead lifted a leg over *Ingram's* rail and leaped up toward the junk's deck, using its bulwark to lever myself onto the deck. The black bag was under my arm. Purple Scar grinned and gestured me farther onto the deck, as if my search for typhoid victims were his idea, another attempt at retaining face in front of his men. He troops shifted about, staying out of my way. I stepped over a coiled line and bent to enter the hatch to the aft cabin.

A ladder led me to the junk's lowest deck. Cotton sacks of rice were stacked against the wall, as were six-inch shells. Bending under beams, I moved forward, passing the galley. I lifted away a cloth curtain to reveal the forward compartment and a chain locker that smelled of linseed oil. Other than the chain and bags of eggplants, it was empty.

"You, there." The KMT captain had come below deck. His voice was loud, as he was broadcasting to his troops on the main deck. "You've had enough time. There's no typhoid on this boat. Get off."

A black drawing was on the wood of the hull, a foot above the bilge water line. It was a drawing in charcoal—with wide black lines—of a dragon boat, and it looked like the same boat that was in the *Southern Inspection Tour* that was mounted on the wall of the House of Eight Orchids' training room. I rose to my feet as the KMT captain approached.

"Your time is up," he said. "Leave my boat."

"Was my brother kept in the bilge when he was on your junk?"

Purple Scar spread his hands. "Where else could I keep him and the woman? This boat carries eighty soldiers, all with young men's needs and desires." His expression was one of stupid determination. "I had to keep the Anglo and the woman away from my men. Where else on board could I do that?"

I slowly drew in a breath.

"It was for their own safety. Even a foreign devil such as yourself must understand that."

"Yes, of course." I smiled at him. "I appreciate your concern for their well-being. What else could you have done, after all?"

My fist hit him square in the stomach. His cap flew from his head as he doubled over, but before he could collapse to the deck, I grabbed his head and pushed him down through the hatch into the bilge well, stuffing him down as if loading laundry into a bag. He splashed into the foul water. I tossed his cap after him, then closed the hatch. I grabbed three bags of rice and put them on the hatch.

I returned aft toward the ladder, passing the galley. The cook was still peeling vegetables.

I said to him, "Let your captain soak awhile."

Purple Scar wouldn't have appreciated the cook's smile.

捌

American sailors are a companionable lot. Always willing to share their opinions, always ready to boast about their hometowns, always offering a quid, particularly after they learned I didn't chew tobacco. San Diego is bursting with beautiful women, and Norfolk boardinghouses have signs that say "No Dogs or Sailors." I learned a lot aboard the USS *Ingram*, things not even the Englishman knew.

Later that same day I had boarded the KMT junk, I was on the *Ingram's* fantail watching a sailor whittle a chain from a tree branch. Ten links had already been carved from the branch, each link the size of an O made with the finger and thumb. The links were interlocking just like a steel chain. The sailor had been working on it a week. Many of the Americans' duties aboard the *Ingram* were done by coolies. Carving the chain was Red Leery, whose white cap sat atop red hair, and whose forehead was peeling from the sun. The base of his nose was as wide as his mouth. Wood shavings covered his lap.

I said, "Carving would be easier if you sharpened your knife."

"This knife is sharp." Red Leery held up his knife, a steel blade with a walrus-tusk handle with a sailing schooner scrimshawed on it. "I grind the blade on a stone every week."

"Your coolie probably grinds the blade," I said.

I sharpened my knives twice each day even if I hadn't used them. We were passing Old Man's Beard, a stream of water that fell from the high cliff next to the Yangtze, the flow breaking up and turning white as it coursed down the stone face to splash on boulders at the river's edge. The Gold Tooth monks lived behind the waterfall, the eunuch had told me—though, looking at the waterfall, I didn't see how. Farther upriver, swallows flitted in and out of hundreds of holes in the cliff. A few stubby trees clung to the cliff side.

"I can only do two things well in this life, John." Leery dug the knife's point into the wood. "I can send a three-inch gun shell up a rat's ass at a thousand yards, and I can whittle chain links out of a branch. So I don't need no lessons on knives from anybody."

The aft three-inch gun was mounted on a turret, its barrel pointed at the sky, and the rest of it was a compilation of wheels and levers, all painted gray. From a pocket, Leery lifted a book of matches and a pack of Old Gold cigarettes. He ripped out a match from the book, scraped the match against the book, and when the match flared, lit the cigarette. I'd never seen a book of matches before, only stick matches.

Leery hugely inhaled the smoke. "I'll bet you never even carved a turkey with a knife, John."

I said, "A peach pit is sharper than your knife."

Leery smiled. "You can tell us sailors all about the heathen Chinee— you speaking their language chop-chop and all—but don't go telling us about using no knife."

Leery was sitting on a bench, leaning back against the bulkhead. Next to his head—suspended on the wall—was a life ring made of cork and covered in red canvas, with USS Ingram stenciled on it. A coolie who had been polishing the aft rail brought over a broom to whisk the bough parings from Leery's lap. He cleaned the shavings from under Leery's chair and swept them overboard through a scupper. He bowed and returned to polishing the rail.

"That's what I like about China," Leery said, drawing the knife along the inside of a link, cleaning out the last splinters. "Folks know how to bow. I can go a month without anyone bowing to me back in Omaha."

The Ingram was sailing upstream only fifty yards from a cliff. Bird guano streaked the granite, and a few dwarf pine trees grew from the cliff face. The gunboat was steaming twelve knots against the current but only four knots over the ground. Coal smoke and sparks whipped around the fantail.

Leery's voice was kindly. "You stick to your Chinee talkee, and I'll handle the knives. We don't want you to cut yourself or nothing." He ran his blade along a length of the bough, peeling bark.

The eunuch would have caned me for what I did next. Showing off was undignified and, worse, a tactical mistake. "Never reveal your strengths," he liked to say. But this US Navy bluejacket was easy to like, and I had an unaccountable urge to impress him.

I said, "Red, take a good look at the life ring hanging next to you."

Leery raised an eyebrow, but he pivoted on the bench to stare at the red life ring, the center links of his wood chain drooping almost to the deck as he turned.

Leery said, "It says 'USS *Ingram*,' the boat you happen to be standing on. What about it?"

I was eight feet from him. One instant the life ring was hanging there, Leery's eyeballs ten inches from it, and the next instant the life ring was hanging there with a knife buried to its hilt in the cork, accompanied by a sharp clap. The knife blade had split the letters *USS* from the word *Ingram*.

"Where'd that knife come from?" He touched my knife's stag-horn handle, perhaps making sure it was really there. Leery blinked, then twisted toward me. He looked at my hands, empty and hanging by my side. He pulled at his jaw and held out the wood chain. "You want to carve the rest of this wood chain? It'll go quicker, I'll bet."

I left him to his whittling and climbed the ladder to the pilothouse. A sailor was behind the wheel, gripping spokes with both hands. The Chinese wheelman was standing next to the brass binnacle. On a shelf next to the hatch was a wood box containing a Zeiss Asiola telescope and a folded wood tripod. Commander Beals was making entries in a log on a stand next to the engine-room telegraph. He was wearing a peaked cap and a blue jacket with the stripes and star of his rank on each sleeve.

He put down his pencil. "That walled town up ahead is Green Grove Crossing."

I peered through one of the pilothouse windows. On the western shore half a mile upstream was a yellow wall about twenty feet high.

"The town has no dock, so we will sparmoor," Beals said.

"Do you know where this opium merchant lives?" I asked.

"I've met him before." He smiled. "He's charming. You'll like him."

"Maybe so. But he won't like me."

捌

"Is that the papermaker?" I pointed at a man passing by who was wearing lantern pants, which had more cloth than straight pants, meaning the fellow might be prosperous.

Commander Beals shook his head. "Don't worry. I won't miss him. Hold the ruler next to the nose. It'll tell us the scale."

The wood ruler was precisely twelve inches long, and I positioned it next to the face of the life-sized gold Buddha.

Beals bent over the Leica, which was mounted on a tripod. "The light is low in here, so the shutter speed will be slow. Hold still."

The sitting Buddha's hands were pressed together. The statue was about my size, made of clay and painted gold. Next to the shrine's west wall was a red lacquered offering stand. A stone incense burner emitted a trail of smoke. Behind Beals, just outside the shrine's door, blue and red prayer flags hung from poles. The shrine was across the road from the papermaker's shop.

"Robert McDermott is a professor of antiquities at the University of California at Los Angeles. He and I are writing a book on Buddhist shrines. I do the research here, and he does it in the States. This is the sixty-third Yangtze River temple I've photographed."

"I hear a street kitchen approaching," I said. "Do you want a rice bowl?"

He fiddled with his camera and didn't reply, so I left the shrine, squinting against the sun's white light outside. The shrine was up against the town's river wall, near the main gate, and across from the paper-maker's shop. An old woman leaned back against the wall, a basket of pig bristles at her feet. A barefoot man with bells on his ankles carried a bamboo pole over his shoulder. A stove—the fire smoking underneath—a teapot, wood bowls, and a cloth bag of chopsticks hung from hooks on one end of the pole. Wicker bags of vegetables and pork cuts were suspended from the other end.

"Pork and rice, please," I said in his language.

He stared at my eyes. I'm used to it. The price was two yuan, and I didn't feel like haggling. While the vendor was stirring the rice with a wood spoon, a woman wearing a purple scarf over her head walk toward the town gate carrying a basket of leeks. Massive hinges—painted black and studded iron—held the gate doors in place. The wood slabs of the gate had been painted red at some point, but the decades had faded the door to dusty pink. A fishmonger squatted on the road near one of the gate hinges, his live fish swimming in oiled paper troughs on the cobblestones. The *Ingram* was moored a hundred yards out into the river in front of the gate. The motor tender was beached near a banyan tree, the line tied to an exposed root. The sailors hadn't been granted leave, Commander Beals saying Green Grove Crossing "holds only trouble for gobs."

Another fellow crossed the courtyard. He wore a silk jacket, the only one I'd seen in Green Grove Crossing. I glanced at Beals, still over at the shrine. He nodded. This was the papermaker.

I gave the bowl back to the vendor. An orange and black tiger was painted on the shop's front wall between two small windows covered with tar paper. Next to his shop was a fifteen-foot-high pigeon coop, with a hundred birds flapping and cooing and pecking, the owner standing in front, ready to wring the necks of as many pigeons as he could sell. I followed the papermaker into his shop. Green Grove Crossing had no electricity, and the dim room was lit by rapeseed oil lamps attached to the walls.

I said in Mandarin, "I have a business proposition for you, paper-maker."

His eyebrows rose at my use of his language. He looked at my eyes and hair. He wore spectacles—unusual for someone in an impoverished river town—and his thatch of shiny black hair was parted in the middle and swept to the sides, a Western look.

His hands clasped together, he bowed, slipping his arms into the sleeves of his yellow silk jacket. "I am a simple paper manufacturer. What business might a Westerner have with me?"

Drying sheets of bamboo and rice paper covered three of the shop's walls, and the shop smelled of something long dead, as did all paper shops. Wooden tubs filled the room where bamboo and tree leaves soaked.

Standing against a back wall near a rack of drying paper, half-hidden by the shop's gloom, was a young man with a pistol in his hand. He didn't take his gaze off me. His shirt and trousers were dark blue, and he wore straw sandals. The pistol was a big revolver, maybe a .44 or .45 caliber. The muzzle was pointed at the floor, but the hammer was back.

The papermaker bowed again. "Please do not mind him. I must take precautions. These are dangerous times."

I said, "A papermaker needs a bodyguard?"

"My name is Wu Ming," the papermaker said. "This is my shop."

Wu Ming was a common alias. The phrase sounds the same as the Mandarin word for *nameless*. My hand flashed, and my knife appeared stuck in the wall three inches from the bodyguard's eye.

I pointed at him. "If you raise that pistol, my next knife goes through your right eye and pins your skull to the wall."

The bodyguard didn't move, not one twitch. The revolver hung in his hand, aimed at the floor.

I crossed the shop. Wu Ming stepped back, but he wasn't fast enough. With both hands I grabbed his neck, jerked him toward a tub of soaking leaves. His feet skidded on the tile floor. I pushed his head down toward the oily red liquid.

"Where's my brother?" I said.

I plunged his head under the surface and held it there. Bubbles rose from his nose and mouth. I glanced at the bodyguard. His arms still hung loosely at his side. He shook his head and looked away.

I yanked the papermaker's head out of the fluid. "You bought him and a woman from the bandits. Where are they?"

He burbled and coughed and swatted weakly at my arm. Red oil flowed off his skull. I shoved his head back under the surface and held it there. More bubbles, but fewer.

I lifted his head out again. "Where's my brother?"

He gagged and spit and inhaled. I let him wipe his mouth.

"I sold—" He gasped for breath. "I sold the woman to Pole-head Song. She's an actress. He wanted her."

I brought him up to standing. Red oil flowed down his neck and into the yellow silk of his jacket. He wiped his eyes and nose and coughed again. He swayed, but I held him up.

I asked, "And the gweilo who was traveling with her? My brother?"

Trying to clear the oil from his eyes, he blinked and blinked; then he bent over to cough and spit. He said in a bubbly voice, "I sold him, too. To Pole-head Song. I didn't get much for him."

I shoved him away, stepped to the bodyguard to yank my knife from the wall, and started back toward the shop door. I wagged a finger at the bodyguard, another warning.

As I reached the door, Papermaker Wu Ming said, "A sailor earns less than a papermaker, I have heard. Perhaps we could assist each other." He tried to stand upright but had to shift a foot to catch himself. He drew a hand across his eyes again, bringing away oil.

"My boat leaves in twenty minutes. What do you want?"

"These days—with the turmoil in China—I must always go in the back door. I have a delivery to make to Chungking, and perhaps you would help." The papermaker brought up a cotton sack from under the table. He turned it upside down, and three stacks of American currency fell out, each tied together with a straw. "How many years does it take a sailor to earn three thousand dollars in American money?"

The currency—ten-dollar bills—was grubby. The money had passed through many hands. I had just roughed him up, humiliated him in front of his bodyguard, yet he still wanted to do business with me. Huge profits must've been involved.

"I will give you half this money right now. It is fifteen hundred dollars. It is yours."

"In exchange for what?"

This time Wu Ming brought out from under the table four cubes wrapped in oiled cotton. Each was the size of a building brick.

He said, "Take these to Chungking. Deliver them to a friend there, and he will give you another fifteen hundred dollars."

"Opium tar?" I asked.

"What does it matter? I am a poor papermaker trying to make a living for myself and my family." He coughed and spit again. Oil dripped from his hair onto his shoulders. He laid his hands flat on the table, ready to negotiate.

Eunuch Chang had spent twenty-five years warning me about my temper. A sudden rage could ruin a business transaction, and could be dangerous, and displayed weakness, and was not the Chinese way. Over the years I had made progress controlling the abrupt anger.

Most of the time. My friend, the Englishman Robert Smyth, was a slave to opium. Each lighted pipe leached him of life, and day by day he was closer to death. Weak and sick, his breath rattling in his throat, he was so thin his chambermaid could lift him. He journeyed toward his death willingly—happily—each night, lying there in his dark room, his vacant eyes on the far wall. I had tried and tried over the years to help him break his addiction, but there was no hope for him.

I said to the papermaker, my voice rising uncontrollably, which I hate, "Our deal is this: you lose."

When the papermaker opened his mouth to protest, the air blurred in front of him, and his lovely silk jacket was instantly cut open, three large slits, one each side and one just under his neck. The front of his jacket was now a loose flap that fluttered to the floor. My blade hadn't even nicked the skin of his chest. The papermaker looked down at the patch of yellow silk on the floor.

I scooped up the money and the opium bricks. The point of my second knife was a quarter inch from his eye. My voice was low. "Don't you move, either, or it'll be the death of you."

I hurried from the shop, carrying the money and the opium. I passed a goat cart filled with watermelons. I was so angry my jaw ached from being pressed together.

At the town gate I placed the three stacks of bills into the blind beggar's hand. The cook raised a pair of chopsticks at me and held up the rice and pork on a dried lotus leaf, but I ignored him.

I walked through the gate. Commander Beals was waiting at the motor tender near the banyan tree, the mooring line in his hand. The camera hung from on a strap around his neck. His tripod was already stowed. I walked to the water's edge and threw the bricks one by one far out into the river. They quickly sank.

"That's what I figured." Beals laughed. "And on my first visit to Green Grove Crossing two years ago, I tossed the papermaker's bricks into the river, too."

I helped him push the boat off the beach. The hull scraped on stones as he got into the tender.

"I'm down to two knives," I said. "I don't like it."

"We can find you another."

I waded out a few steps, pushing the boat in front of me. The *Ingram* was dead ahead, the boarding ladder hanging from hull amidships.

I climbed over the tender's transom and took a seat. "Commander, I need to ask another favor from you."

14

The warlord Song Mu was known as Pole-head Song. Carrying a fifty-pound gunnysack of baking soda over my shoulder, I approached his headquarters, walking inland from the river, stepping over driftwood the sun had bleached white. Commander Beals's pocket watch—the one I hadn't stolen from his cabin aboard the *Ingram*—was in my pocket. The *Ingram*'s cook had given me the baking soda.

At the edge of the shingle, three human heads were mounted on poles. They were blackened with flies and rot, and their mouths were pulled back, and their eye sockets churned with maggots. Two of the heads wore Japanese army field caps. The third head was above a sign tied to the pole that read, "Deserter."

The only brick building in sight housed Pole-head Song's headquarters, which Beals had said had been a Qing-dynasty armory. Iron bars covered the windows, and rifle crenels lined the roof. A gun slit had been cut in the iron door, which was partway open. I could see a Benz limousine parked alongside the armory as I walked by a dozen soldiers who squatted around a fire.

Behind me, the Yangtze was flat and yellow under the high sun. A stone outcropping called the Dowager's Nose hid the river to the north.

The ledge was empty except for a heron's nest, a stack of sticks almost as large as a gun carriage. The heron ran its beak down its feathers.

I carried the sack of baking soda up to the armory's door. "I'm here to speak with General Song. Let me see him."

Eunuch Chang knew that his countrymen would automatically obey an Anglo who spoke the language. A guard walked around me, apparently looking for firearms, then pushed the door farther open. With the bag over my shoulder, I entered the armory, and the guard followed.

A warlord was a man who ruled an area because he had an army that would fight for him. The warlord might be of the nobility or might be up from the ranks, but most had a magnetism that drew soldiers to them. They might rule a thousand square miles or ten square miles, and their territories were usually distant from the central government. They collected taxes, and they were absolute rulers of their land. In 1926 the Kuomintang and the Communists banded together to try to eliminate the warlords, invading many of the warlords' territories. Rather than fight, many warlord armies joined the KMT or the Communist armies until the KMT and Communists retreated to their strongholds, and then it was back to normal for the warlords.

Pole-head Song's army was called Song-chun, the army of Song. Commander Beals had told me Song commanded three thousand soldiers and owned two British Mark V tanks that had served in the Great War, and six water-cooled Browning machine guns. His headquarters were always decorated with at least one head on a pike because—it was said—his father had once told him he was so stupid he should have been born with two heads so he would have had at least one brain.

General Song was bent over a desk, a pencil in his hand. He didn't look up. His blue tunic was decorated with gaudy military decorations: a gold sunburst, a silver chrysanthemum, and a red-and-silver sash across his breast.

A chain bound the actress Tsingtao Lily to a chair. She was haggard, barefoot, and dressed in a soldier's blouse and pants. Her chin came up, and she grinned hugely at me, a smile of victory. A wood comb held up her hair, and somewhere she had found some red to apply to her lips.

"What do you want?" Song asked as he made notations on a document.

"I want to purchase Tsingtao Lily," I said. "And the Anglo who came with her."

He dropped his pencil and came around the desk to stare at me. "Round-eyed devils don't fare too well this far up the Yangtze."

The armory's rifle racks were empty, but an ancient howitzer on spoke wheels was in a corner next to a dusty stack of canisters. A banner on the wall read *Use all our bullets, then our bayonets, then our fists, then our teeth.* The double doors at the back were closed.

General Song said, "If that is food you are carrying, you have just donated it to my soldiers."

"Where's the Anglo? I want to purchase both of them."

I lifted the watch from my pocket. I had to stare at it. Despite his Bornholm longcase clock, Eunuch Chang was contemptuous of time-pieces, and I had never owned one. It was five minutes to one o'clock. I had five minutes.

"I'll trade your camp for the actress and the Anglo," I said.

This time his laugh did not sound genial but mean. "I have thousands of soldiers to feed. The actress will bring me enough money for a month's supplies. I have the sale arranged. She is a swan's feather brought from a thousand li away." The phrase was an ancient one, meaning *a lucky find.* "And unless you can explain your presence here, you will be put in chains."

I brought out the pocket watch again. Three minutes.

"Why don't you raise taxes on the peasants to feed your soldiers?" I asked. "You can let Tsingtao Lily go. You don't need her. The great General Song doesn't deal in hostages, does he?"

Of course he dealt in hostages. All warlords did.

He said, "We collect the pig-rearing tax, the pig-slaughter tax, the pig-inspection tax, the pig-sale tax, the pigsty tax, and four hundred and thirty other taxes. There is no more tax to be had." He directed his thumb toward Tsingtao Lily. "She is worth her weight in gold, and I intend to get it."

"And the Anglo?"

"He left last night."

"Where is he?"

"I gave him to my men last night. They told me he disappeared a few minutes later. They don't know what happened to him. But why am I explaining things to a dead ghost man?"

I looked at Tsingtao Lily. "Then I'll just take her. I'll trade your camp for her."

"You are speaking in riddles. Perhaps you should be thrown into the river."

"Will you do me the honor of accompanying me outside?" I asked.

His eyes narrowed. "I still have not determined why you have appeared at my camp."

"Listen carefully, General." I looked again at the watch. "Leave the armory right now, or die."

He stared at me, and the calculation was plain on his face. Something about my tone—combined with the bizarre nature of my visit: an Anglo in the middle of China carrying a big sack and looking at a pocket watch—must have abruptly registered on him as dangerous.

He yelled, "Bring the girl."

The guard unhooked the chain from the chair and lifted Tsingtao Lily to her feet. He pulled her along like a goat. The general rushed after them, and so did the guard who had escorted me into the armory. We stepped into the sunshine. Tsingtao Lily cursed her guard and kicked him in the shin. He grunted but kept his hand on her chain.

Again I brought up Commander Beals's watch. It was one o'clock, right on the mark. I looked across the beach toward the Yangtze. The *Ingram* was just drifting out from behind the Dowager's Nose. The gunboat was gray and menacing.

I smashed the gunnysack against the armory's wall. Baking soda burst out, dusting the wall in white. Marking it as a target.

I ran toward the campfire.

General Song backed away from the building. He ordered my guard, "If anything happens, shoot the gweilo. Then put his head next to those Japs' on the poles."

My guard was no more than fifteen years old, with a shaved head. Ringworm circles marred his scalp. He had an open, worried face.

I smiled at him. "Don't shoot me. I'm a nice fellow when you get to know me."

He whispered, "What if the general orders me to?"

"I've been shot a couple of times. Two years ago, a bullet went right through my thigh. Hurt a lot, I don't mind admitting. And another time, right through my shoulder."

"I've never fired a rifle, anyway," the young soldier said. "Not once. We don't have enough bullets to practice." He stared at his rifle's bolt. "If I have to shoot, maybe I'll miss you."

The *Ingram*'s forward gun blew gray smoke. Red Leery manned the gunsight. He would want to show his skill, and he did.

The shell must have entered a window, because the armory's front wall burst outward, the concussion knocking me back. Bricks filled the air and then scattered across the ground. My young guard had to pick himself up from the ground. Dust swirled over the front wall's wreckage. The heron lifted into the air, dove toward the water, and glided away just above the surface. Soldiers ran inland toward the barracks, abandoning the meat on the spits. General Song stared at the destruction.

The gunboat slid fully into view. Leery's gun again spouted smoke, and an instant later the armory's back wall blew apart.

I said, "Once again, General: your camp in exchange for the actress."

He looked at me, his mouth turned down. He swiveled his gaze toward the river.

"My friends on the gunboat are going to fire into your camp until I begin walking toward the river with Tsingtao Lily. If I don't walk with her, or if they see me fall, they will keep firing the *Ingram*'s guns."

Song's mouth was a narrow line, his lips pressed white. He dipped his head, and his chin ballooned like a frog's.

"My friend behind the forward gun could hit a butterfly out of the air," I said, "and he'll be happy to reduce your camp to cooking chips."

Another shell hit the armory, churning the debris and blowing up dust. The sound of the explosion rolled out across the camp. The soldiers who had been marching had disappeared into the tree grove beyond their drilling field. General Song's hands were bunched tightly.

The gunboat's next shot smacked into the Benz limousine parked against the armory. The car shot into the air, the front window erupted into glittering shards, and the iron plates rose skyward and spun around and around before landing heavily. The engine block cartwheeled twice and then came to rest thirty feet from the undercarriage. My ears rang when the fuel tank exploded.

"Your house up on that hill will be next," I said. "Then the barracks, the mess, and anything else the *Ingram*'s gunner can find. Your camp is going to resemble a plowed field."

He inhaled so fiercely the air rattled in his throat. He pointed at the river. "Go, and take the wicked actress with you."

I grabbed her chain, but she scowled at me, so I dropped it and took her arm.

"Run, before he changes his mind," I said. "Toward the ship."

We hurried away from the camp and onto the beach, dodging boulders and deadheads. I pulled her along through a patch of river weed. Gun smoke drifted downriver. *Ingram*'s tender started toward shore, two sailors manning it. At *Ingram*'s forward rail, Red Leery waved his cap at me, and I could see his smile even at this distance.

捌

A gong's deep rumble came from Red Cloud Ferry. The gong ringer was hidden from my view by the inn. Villagers emerged from their homes and shops to listen. He was too far away for me to hear his announcement.

Elizabeth and I leaned against a boulder on the Yangtze's bank. She was shivering from malaria and had told me that sitting in the sun would help rid her of the chills. I had bundled up dried river weed to use as cushions. We kept our shoes on to protect against sand fleas. *Ingram* was moored downriver to our left at the village's pier. A sailor wearing a tool belt climbed the mast, perhaps headed to a radio antenna.

The doctor spread out her arms and raised her chin to catch more sun. A turtle's head popped above the river surface. The turtle eyed the doctor, then slid back into the water, leaving only an expanding ripple. Sun-grayed wood drifted past in the current. Behind us, across the trackers' path, was a pigsty and a farmer's hut. The pigs squealed and snorted.

"Do you think about your kidnapping all the time?" the doctor asked. Her eyes were closed. The malaria had drained her color, and her face was wan, making her freckles more pronounced.

"Only when someone forces me to recall it by asking questions." I touched my forehead and received a touch of pain, not a jolt. The skin was healing. "Most people know better."

"Sometimes it helps to talk about things."

"The Englishman told me Americans were big talkers." I twisted a wrist, and my number-three knife slipped into my hand. "Talk, talk, talk, is what he said."

The blade was three inches long, and the butt at the end of its staghorn handle was half of a large pearl mounted on a cap. I twisted off the cap to reveal a tiny compartment in the handle. I dumped out the contents and held it up to Elizabeth.

She opened her eyes. "A button?"

"I don't remember why, but the day Eunuch Chang kidnapped me—back when I was five years old—I was holding two mother-of-pearl buttons. I gave one to my brother when he was five, when I thought he'd appreciate it. It's the only thing we have that belonged to our parents. William keeps his under his cot in his room at the compound, in a candy tin."

Elizabeth reached for the button, then stopped her arm.

"It's okay." I dropped the button into her hand.

She said, "We don't see mother-of-pearl this far up the river. I'll bet your mom brought it to Chungking from Hong Kong or San Francisco."

The button flashed iridescence. A yellow bittern waded downstream, its long legs looking rickety and its beak just above the water, ready to stab down. The gong sounded again.

"I don't remember my mother's clothes, but I've imagined she owned the buttons and that they were on her nicest dress. I've played out a lot of imaginary scenes about how I came to be holding the buttons that day." I smiled. "In some of them, I'm quite the hero, rescuing my mom from terrible villains."

"Eunuch Chang let you and William keep these remembrances of your early lives?" She passed me the button.

"We never told him about them." I looked at the button—probably for the ten thousandth time—and then dropped it back into the knife's handle and screwed on the cap.

She said, "A button isn't much to hold on to, is it, John?"

"Sometimes I wish there were more." I generated a grin. "But there's no point going over the past—I can't change it."

A wagon wheel's creaking came from downriver. I returned the knife to its place and rose from behind the boulder. Gong ringers wear red sashes across their chests, which end in red tassels. A donkey pulled the ringer's cart. Brass camel bells hung from the donkey's neck and chimed as he walked. Carrying a mallet in one hand and a bamboo switch in the other, the gong ringer walked alongside the cart.

"Hear the news," the ringer called. "Hear the news." He swung the mallet into the gong strapped onto a framework on the donkey's back, and its fluid note rolled out along the beach. "There are profits to be made and lessons to be learned. I bring profits and lessons." His chant was as old as the land and delivered with a monastic cadence.

The ringer continued in a singsong manner: "I speak of rewards and punishments. Hear me: rewards and punishments. The good eunuch Chang of Chungking sends his best wishes to the people of this village and offers a five-hundred-Mex reward for information about a foreign devil known as Yellow Hair."

I dipped behind the boulder. Elizabeth struggled to rise from the sand, using the boulder to pull herself up.

The gong ringer announced, "And to those who would be tempted to assist this foreign devil and to those who would even speak with him, the eunuch Chang invites you to see the fate of one who did." The gong ringer stepped aside, revealing the bed of his cart.

The woman with the cabbages winced and turned away. I sidled between two boulders for a closer look. A body was on the cart, under the gong. The torso was covered with a yellow silk jacket stained with blood. The head had been cut from the body and was nearer the donkey's tail. He had been recently killed, as his blood still dripped from the cart.

The gong ringer called in singsong tones, "Yes, come and see the fate of one who did."

The eyes were open, and flies rimmed the mouth. The hair was still perfectly in place, with a Western part down the middle. It was the fellow from Green Grove Crossing who had called himself Wu Ming, the papermaker who had asked me to smuggle opium.

15

"Here's your daughter," I said. "Where's the gold?"

Tsingtao Lily's father, Wu Longwei, was at a table at Red Cloud Ferry's inn. He said, "I have been thinking about our deal, and I have a problem with it."

I said, "Your only problem is if you don't have the six pounds of gold."

We were sitting at a table in front of plates of grilled lamb strips and gelatinous strings of shark's fin. We had only partly eaten, and the next course—wine-soaked dates and candied persimmons—was already on the table next to an abacus with ivory beads.

"When Luli was four years old, I was so poor that I could not raise her, so I betrothed her to the young son of a Tsingtao horse-trolley owner, and she moved to their home," her father said. "They would raise her, and I would be freed of the burden of feeding her." He was using Tsingtao Lily's given name. "But she fussed and carried on, and I had to take her back into my home."

He said, "When she ran away to become a so-called actress, I was humiliated. I could not walk in Tsingtao's streets for a year. My friends and even my brothers laughed at me. You can see, then, that Luli has already cost me a great deal."

"I may have to use the gold to buy my brother somewhere," I said. "I'm not leaving here without it."

Over on the bench, Tsingtao Lily wept into her hands, as she had done in *The Red Lantern*, where she played a palace girl with the rank of *kuei fe*, which means "honorable concubine." She peeked through her fingers at me.

"Your history with your daughter isn't my concern," I said. "Where is my twentieth of a shi of gold?"

"The best cooks in China come from Tian Liange"—he gestured at the food—"and as you can see, I have one in my employ. When I was poor I ate straw soup, and now I eat shark's fin, and this happy turn of events didn't come about by being careless with money."

I said, "Nothing would be more careless with money than not paying me."

"So, let me see." He reached for the abacus. "Every injury has a value. Luli's canceled betrothal." He flicked an ivory bead. "The years of her food and clothing." Another bead, which clicked against the first one. "The value of her room. My mortification when she left home. The years of embarrassment when her photos appeared in the newspapers, showing her hanging on to a liquor glass or to an actor or film director. The cost of coming here to find her to take her home."

He clicked a bead with each item; then he held up the abacus. "An extraordinary coincidence: Luli has cost me precisely a twentieth of a shi of gold."

He lowered the abacus and picked out a persimmon. "So, unable to obtain reimbursement from my daughter or anyone else, I must cancel our bargain."

His joke with the abacus had been elaborate, tabulating all his daughter had cost him in money and humiliation. He undoubtedly hoped to regale his Tsingtao friends with it for years.

Only then did I sense a man standing behind me. I glanced over my shoulder. He filled the inn's doorway. A machine pistol was in his hand, an old German Mauser with a wood stock and a stick magazine, common in the Nationalist Army.

"I have heard of your knives." Wu looked at the man in the doorway. "If the round-eyed devil raises a hand above his waist, kill him." He rose from the table. "You Westerners have corrupted Luli."

"I'm not a Westerner." I stood up. "I was raised in China and speak the language as well as you do."

He came around the table and pushed me toward the door. The man with the pistol stepped aside but didn't lower the weapon. He wore a gray coat to his knees and a blue bandana tied over his skull. His chin was the size of a fist, and his lips were so thin his mouth was a slit.

The two men escorted me outside and pushed me along the path at the river's edge. And why was I allowing them to push me along? The machine pistol had something to do with it, sure, but there was another reason. I was being cheated, and I was dumbfounded. Nobody ever cheated Eunuch Chang, because the consequences were terrible and certain. And so, acting for the eunuch, I had never been cheated, had never dealt with someone welshing on a deal, until now, being shoved along the Yangtze path with a Mauser machine pistol pointed at me, and this strange turn was taking me time to comprehend. It was as if Tsingtao Lily's father had switched to speaking Polish. I did understand one thing: without the fearsome Eunuch Chang behind me, I was just another fellow to cheat.

A rat boat—with a poleman at each end—floated by on the river. Gray haze hung low in the valley, hiding the mountains behind the Yangtze's far shore. We reached a tangle of uprooted trees on the shoreline. River weed hung from the trees' roots. The wind blew down the river valley, carrying the scent of tobacco from a drying shed upriver.

Wu hit me on the back of the head, not much of a blow, as he wasn't much of a fighter. He yelled, "You did this to Luli, you and the other foreign pig entrails."

He struck me again, a glancing blow that stung rather than staggered me. The smiling man with the machine pistol—the muzzle was still aimed at me—was four steps away.

Wu was spitting with anger. "You devils from across the ocean lured my daughter from Tsingtao, and my humiliation has been endless. It's the same thing you gweilos have been doing to China for a hundred years."

Here was another episode with which he would regale his Tsingtao friends: the gweilo's savage beating on the banks of the Yangtze. In his telling, his heroics would become another Boxer Rebellion against the Westerners. He drew his fist back for another shot at me. I was ready to begin teaching the two of them today's lesson. A knife dropped into my hand.

Wu didn't see it coming, and neither did I. The bounding and twisting giant dog flattened Wu, who shrieked surprise. The animal furiously snapped its jaws and snarled, and sounded like one of the electricity-generating dynamos in Chungking: low, mean, and all business. Wu cried out in pain.

As the guard tried to raise the machine pistol, I stuck a knife through his hand into the Mauser's wood stock. He opened his mouth to howl, but I slammed my fist into his forehead. He collapsed to the path as if he were boneless.

I sprinted back toward the inn. The dog's tearing and scuffling and Wu's shrieking was loud behind me. If Wu wasn't going to give me the gold, I wasn't going to give him his daughter. Maybe I'd give her to my brother when I found him.

捌

"Doctor?" I stepped into the hospital ward. "Elizabeth?"

Every bed was occupied and covered with mosquito netting. The room smelled of antiseptic. Two ceiling fans stirred the air. Sing, the girl who the doctor had saved from the leper colony, had lifted aside a net and was drawing a washcloth across a patient's forehead. She signaled to me.

I walked to the bed. It was Elizabeth under the net. She was shivering so violently that the bed frame was shaking. She licked her lips, and when her eyes found mine, she smiled in a small way. Sing tucked the net aside and brought a three-legged stool for me.

"What's wrong?" I asked. "You don't look good."

"I have malaria, as I told you." Her words were breathy. A brown blanket was over her. "It comes and goes."

"Are you taking medicines?"

"I've done what I can. My muscles ache, and sometimes I'm nauseated." When she stopped talking, her teeth clattered together. "Mostly it's the cold waves that go up and down that keep me in bed."

"Have you chased out the cold spirit?" I asked.

"I've taken quinine."

"That's all you've done? No wonder you are shivering." I scooted the stool closer to her bed. "You haven't rid yourself of the horned-frog spirit that brings malaria."

She was pale but her gray-green eyes were lively. "We don't allow folk medicine in the hospital. It usually does more harm than good."

"But I've seen this work." I reached for her arm. "We have to snap out the frog spirit."

"John, honestly, you can't believe—"

I pinched her arm, and lifted the skin, then let it snap back.

"John—"

I did it again, pulling up the skin higher. "When we get done with both arms, we'll do your neck. It only takes about an hour." I grabbed the skin of her biceps again, lifted and released.

"That hurts," she said. "Don't be foolish."

The patient in the next bed groaned and rolled onto her side. Her head was on a wood block. Other than for Westerners and whorehouses, pillows were unknown in China.

I said, "The frog spirit won't leave until your skin starts to turn purple."

"Who taught you this nonsense?"

"It's the bruising that convinces the frog malaria spirit that it must flee." I snapped her skin again.

"Ouch. Stop that." Her red hair was spread on the pillow. "You're a nut to believe this." She tucked her arm under the blanket.

I leaned back on the stool. "You don't want to get better? This cure is thousands of years old. It's been proven over the centuries."

"Bring over the wheelchair." She pushed herself up on her elbows. "Take me to the garden. I need sun."

Sing helped swing the doctor's legs off the bed, and we lifted her into the chair. The doctor was wearing a white cotton top and bottom that the Englishman called *pajamas*.

I shoved the chair between the beds to the door, then pushed her in the wicker wheelchair out into the garden. The generator crew rose and took off their caps. A breeze shifted the rose branches. A gardener was smoothing the path pebbles with a bamboo rake, and the wheelchair's wheels sank into the pebbles, forcing me to lean into the job to move the chair. A collared crow clacked in a pine tree behind the generator.

"I contacted an attorney in Boise, my father's lawyer," Elizabeth told me, "and he has purchased a small building for me in the town. My parents loaned me the money."

"Where's Boise?" I asked.

"In Idaho."

"Where's Idaho?"

She looked at me.

I said, "An Englishman taught me geography. I know where Nottingham and Salisbury are. Ask me about England."

"I can't stay in China much longer, not with this malaria. I'm going to open a clinic in Boise. It's hot there in the summer, and not so humid. I won't ever be rid of the disease, but the attacks won't be so frequent."

"Are you married?" I asked.

"I'm in the middle of China suffering from malaria and chatting with a moron." She grinned. "How would marriage fit into that?"

Across the garden, three birds rose in a rush from the bamboo glade and flew toward the river, squawking.

"But I was married once," she said.

"What happened?"

"His shirtsleeve caught in a wheat combine's thresher, the spinning blades in a drum that separate wheat from chaff. The blades yanked him in and ripped him up so badly that his coffin remained closed at the funeral. I couldn't even look at him one last time."

I pushed the chair off the path, then between two rows of roses, which weren't blooming yet. Blue crocuses lined the rose beds and cherry trees, and pink blossoms covered cherry trees near the shed. Sing followed us. The doctor looked better out in the sun. Her freckles glowed, and her cheeks and chin regained their ruddy hue. Her hair was a lively red. The sun didn't do anything to shorten her nose, though.

She was looking at the bamboo glen. "There's your dog."

I spun toward the bamboo, half-expecting to be tackled and torn apart. But the animal was motionless. The massive head was bracketed by bamboo trunks. The ears were black and tight against its skull. Steam came from its nostrils, or maybe not. He moved out from the trees and stood at the edge of the garden.

"He's as big as a horse," I said.

"He's staring at you."

When I took three steps sideways, the dog's head moved fractionally. He indeed had me locked in his gaze.

I said, "I wonder what he wants."

"Food, maybe." The doctor switched to her bad Mandarin. "Sing, bring a bowl of pork from the kitchen, will you?"

I said, "I wouldn't feed that dog were I you."

"He looks hungry."

"If you kick a dog, you'll never know where he is," I said. "But if you feed him, you'll always know where he is, and that's close by. I don't want that dog close by."

"He has rescued you twice," the doctor said. "He's earned a bowl of pork."

The brindled animal huffed and blew. Blood dripped from the fangs, but I'm pretty sure that was my imagination. The generator crew hurried away from him, disappearing around a corner of the hospital. The gardener dropped the rake and fled into the hospital ward.

"He scares the demon out of me," I said. "I mean, look at him."

Sing appeared with a wood bowl of pork strips. I couldn't pull my hands away fast enough, so I had to take the bowl when she passed it to me.

"What's wrong, Sing?" the doctor asked.

The girl's chin was on her chest, and her cheeks were deeply flushed. "That lady in the kitchen . . ."

Tsingtao Lily was eating pork and rice in the hospital's kitchen.

"What happened?" the doctor asked.

Sing whispered, "She told me I was pretty."

"And so have I." The doctor squeezed the girl's arm. "It's unanimous."

Sing's face was scarlet with pleasure.

Elizabeth shifted to English. "John, walk that pork over to the dog."

"If you think this is such a good idea, you can walk it over."

"I'm in a wheelchair."

"You can roll it over."

"Eunuch Chang's fearsome enforcer is afraid of a puppy?"

She was having a fine time at my expense, but the dog was still there and the pork bowl was still in my hands, and the pitiable truth is that I am susceptible to a goad. So I willed my legs to work and put one foot in front of the other, and crossed the garden, passing a peach tree.

The dog got bigger and uglier as I got nearer. He lowered his head and his half tail and blew up dirt with a snort, and then he loosed a searing snarl, a sound straight from hell that stopped me as if I'd been yanked by a rope. The dog's red eyes bored into me.

I could hardly hear my own voice. "I'm not taking one step closer to that animal, I guarantee you."

I set the pork bowl on the ground and back-stepped away, my palms toward the dog in a gesture of utter meekness. I dodged around the peach tree on my way back to the doctor.

She was still shivering, but she laughed. "In Idaho, it's called being a fraidy-cat."

I'd never before heard the term, but I knew it wasn't flattering. I pushed her chair onto the path toward the hospital. Sing walked with us, holding the doctor's hand. I looked over my shoulder. The dog's muzzle was in the bowl, and he was gulping down the meat. His red eyes were still on me.

Tsingtao Lily waited for us at Elizabeth's bed. Lily helped the doctor into the bed and spread a blanket over her. "Are you hot or cold, Elizabeth?"

"Sometimes hot and sometimes cold." The doctor let her head sink back into the pillow. "Right now, hot."

Lily arranged the doctor's hair on the pillow so that it evenly framed her face; then she lifted a cloth from a bowl, squeezed out much of the water, and wiped the doctor's forehead.

"You don't need to do that," Elizabeth said.

"Sure, I do." She leaned forward to kiss Elizabeth's forehead. "I once promised my father I would do one unselfish thing before I died." She brought up the cloth to Elizabeth's forehead again and smiled. "Maybe this is it."

Elizabeth tried to laugh, but it was more a rattle. Then she rolled her head to me and asked, "What are you going to name your new dog?"

捌

"You have to trust me," I said. "If you move your hand, you'll be badly wounded."

"I don't like any of this." A cigarette bounced in Red Leery's mouth as he spoke. He wasn't wearing a cap, and his red hair was bright in the sun.

The gunboat was docked at Red Cloud Ferry, and Leery sat on a bench across the table from me on the *Ingram*'s fantail. The engines had been shut down, and ashes were being hauled. The air smelled of bacon, coming from the wardroom. Two coolies were painting the three-inch gun's mount, a can of gray paint sitting on canvas next to the gun. A gooseneck can in his hand, another coolie oiled the gun's shell ejector.

The gunner's whittling project—now twenty wood links—lay on the table. A low haze over the river swirled and eddied, hiding the far shore. A sampan passed the boat, headed downstream with a poleman at the stern and two hogs in the bay. Tsingtao Lily slept in the ensign's berth. Commander Beals had agreed to take her to Chungking.

"Spread your fingers out on the table," I said. "As wide as possible."

Leery was wearing a white skivvy stained yellow at the neckline. He pressed his palm onto the wood table. "I can't get my fingers any wider."

A knife appeared in my hand, my second knife, a smaller one. Still, it was a nasty piece of equipment, with a six-inch blade, a finger guard, and an ivory handle. Six diamonds—each the size of a pea—were embedded in handle. The knife had been a gift from Eunuch Chang.

"You might want to close your eyes," I said. "Otherwise you'll flinch."

"Last time I was home I flinched when my wife threw a car battery at me," Leery said. "But generally I'm not a flincher."

I reversed the knife in my hand so that the blade was pointed down. "When Eunuch Chang showed me this, I jerked my hand aside, and my thumb was almost cut off."

"Get on with it," Leery said.

I slammed the knife down on the outside of Leery's thumb, a quarter inch from the knuckle. The blade sank half an inch into the table. With a speed that a human eye could not follow, I jerked out the knife and slammed it down again, this time between his thumb and index finger. Out the knife came again, and this time it pierced the table between his index finger and middle finger, a hair's width from the webbing. Out it came again, and the knifepoint stabbed into the table between his middle finger and ring finger. Then between his ring finger and little finger, then on the outside of his little finger, a quarter inch from the knuckle. One and a half seconds had elapsed since Leery had said, "Get on with it."

Then, without a pause, the knife retraced the pattern, piercing the table between each of Leery's fingers. The knife was a blur—moving as fast as the needle on the tailor's Singer machine at the House of Eight Orchids, up and down and back and forth between Leery's fingers and thumb, the blade punching into the table each time right next to the skin.

After ten seconds I stopped, the knife poised above Leery's hand. His face had paled, and the cigarette hung limply from his lips. I had stabbed the table thirty times in ten seconds, the blade within a molecule of Leery's skin each time.

Leery lifted his hand to stare at it, flexing the fingers. "You were damn close to cutting up my hand. Damn close."

The knife disappeared. "Knives aren't grenades," I said. "Close doesn't hurt with knives."

"Yellow Hair from Chungking," someone called from the shore.

I rose from the bench to look over the rail. Standing on the shore was Wu Longwei's bodyguard, in his long gray coat. He held a wood box rather than a Mauser machine pistol in his hands.

"May I speak with you, honorable Yellow Hair?" he called.

Watching his hands, I crossed the gangway to the dock. The box was black ebony, and he held it out as if making an offering at a shrine. The bodyguard stared at the ground. "Wu Longwei regrets his impudence and asks that you accept the six pounds of gold."

"Why the change?"

"He was unaware you were Yellow Hair from the House of Eight Orchids." The bodyguard's right hand was wrapped in a white cloth. "He regrets his hasty actions and asks that you convey his abiding respect to the eunuch Chang."

"Wu broke the deal," I said. "I'm not going to deliver his daughter to him."

"He understands. He will deal with his daughter on his own, but he asks you to accept the payment by way of apology. Do you want to weigh the gold?"

"I trust you." I tucked the box under my arm. "How's your hand?"

The bodyguard looked up. "A red-haired foreign-devil woman doctor cleaned it out and used a needle to tie the gashes." He spoke with a Szechwan accent.

"Do what she says. Don't put worm dirt on it."

"She helped Wu Longwei, too, but his face will never look the same, with all the scars and stitching," the bodyguard said. "He insists the attacker was Monwang, the six-legged demon who lives along the Yangtze, but I saw it, and it was a giant dog."

"Those old Mauser machine pistols tend to jam." I started back along the pier and said over my shoulder, "If you want to live long as a bodyguard, get something more reliable."

The gunner was waiting for me on the fantail, and we sat again at the table.

"What's in the box?" Red Leery asked.

"My fortune." I lifted the lid and pulled out ten bars of gold, magisterially placing them side by side on the table near the wood chain. Each bar weighed two-thirds of a pound.

Eunuch Chang would have been appalled, displaying valuables out in the open, but—once again—I had a strange urge to impress this American sailor. The gold reflected the sun. A foundry stamp resembling a Japanese rising sun had been pressed into each bar, and perhaps this gold had once belonged to the Japanese emperor.

A sailor walked from the starboard deck onto the fantail, a pole in his hand. He was on body patrol. His foot tucked under a scupper for balance, he lowered one end of the pole into the water near a mooring line. Aft of the *Ingram* a hundred yards, three fishermen spread a net, one on the shore and the other two in a sampan.

"Here's another body," the sailor on body patrol called from the stern. "I hate this job."

"Just shove him out into the current. In a couple months, the skeleton will wash ashore in Shanghai."

"By God, it's a white man," the sailor at the line said.

Leery rose from the table. "Anybody we know?"

"He's not so swollen up. He hasn't been in the water long. You recognize him, Red?"

Leery crossed to the rail and stared into the water between the hull and the pier. "Never seen him before. We can't just shove him out into the river, though. A white man deserves to be buried. John, help us fish him out. Grab his coat."

The *Ingram*'s aft deck was low, only a foot above the waterline. Leery pulled at the corpse but couldn't get it out of the water. He leaned farther over the rail and tried again.

Leery said, "The body arms are tied behind its back, and it has been tied to our mooring line, attached to our boat so it can't float downriver. Who the hell would do that?"

He lifted his carving knife from a pocket and slashed at the line, and we bent over the rail and lifted the body onto the deck.

I stared at the corpse. His eyes were open in sightless surprise. He was wearing a Western jacket and leather brogans. He hadn't drowned. The senninbari—the belt of a thousand red stitches that Gao Bai and I had used to strangle the Japanese secret policeman—was around his neck. The senninbari had been pulled tight.

It was my brother, William.

16

I found a rice sack to sit on in the hospital's storage room. Dusk came, and then dawn, and I was still there, staring at a box of stewed and canned tomatoes that had *Donated by the United Churches of Montana and Idaho* stamped on the side. We Chinese don't eat stewed tomatoes, which explained the dust on the box. I gazed at that box without much seeing it. Sparse light came through the storeroom's window. Countless visions of William formed in front of me, often accompanied by pangs of regret for things I had or hadn't done. I had been his advocate and protector, and he had depended on me for all those years, and he ended up floating in the Yangtze River. He could've done better than me for a brother.

The door was pushed open, and Sing slipped into the room. Her gray smock was streaked with blood, as she had been promoted from cleaning the surgery to helping the doctor with patients. Her hair was pulled back and secured with twine. When she lowered herself to sit on my lap, I shifted uncomfortably. I'd never had anyone on my lap before.

She put her arm around my neck and patted me on the back. Then she asked, "Have you been crying?"

"I never cry. I was taught not to." We were speaking Mandarin.

"Well, I've been crying for you," she said. "In my room, last night."

"You didn't even know my brother."

"But I know you." The rash on her cheeks had faded.

I shifted uncomfortably. I was unaccustomed to physical contact.

She tucked her head under my neck. "I want you to feel better."

I hesitated, then wrapped my arm around her waist. "Did Dr. Hanley send you in here?"

"She said you needed some help."

"Your nice words help." I squeezed her. "They sure do."

"Where are you going to go, Yellow Hair?"

My night with the onions and rice in the storeroom had done more than allow me to brood over William. Nothing was left of my allegiance to the House of Eight Orchids. Twenty-five years of loyalty and obedience had boiled away in a week, leaving a terrible residue of bitterness and bile.

I said, "I have something I must do, Sing."

"Are you going to leave Red Cloud Ferry? Is it about your brother?"

"William's and my Chinese father: I'm going to pay him a visit."

捌

Elizabeth Hanley patted the young lady on the shoulder. "Stay off your feet. The baby will be here in a week or ten days." She slipped her stethoscope into a jacket pocket.

The pregnant woman smiled up at Elizabeth. A week ago the doctor had told the lady to stay in bed so the baby wouldn't come early, and so a rice-straw mattress had been moved into the candle plant so the lady could run the household. Three generations of the family lived and worked in this room and the two rooms in the rear.

The pregnant woman's mother asked if we would have tea before returning to the hospital. The years had worn the mother down to a nub: hunched shoulders, a bowed head, and gnarled fingers. But she smiled brightly at the doctor as she placed cups on a table near the window, then poured tea from a pot. Four or five children hurried around the room.

I had told Elizabeth that I had to return downriver, and that it was urgent, but she had asked me to stay another day, as she was expecting a message that might be important to me, so I had been following her around until she had received it and had the chance to relay it to me. I had helped her remove an impacted wisdom tooth by pinning the man's arms while she yanked out the tooth with a pair of pliers.

She and I sat at the table, which was squeezed between large baskets of waxberries. At least a thousand white candles hung down from the ceiling.

Elizabeth sipped the tea and said, "Part of my job here is to ask for donations for the hospital. I've been hearing your gold bars click together all day."

I removed four bars from my shirt and pushed them across the table. "Is that enough?"

"With the Japanese controlling the lower river, the hospital isn't receiving money or donations. Coconut water is sterile, and I've been using it for saline because I can't get any, and our autoclave needs to be replaced, too, and—"

"You don't need to tell my why you need the gold."

"Is donating to my hospital the first charitable act of your life? How does it feel? Maybe you'll get used to it." She smiled. "But I have something for you in return. Some information. Right after you arrived in Red Cloud Ferry, I sent a message downriver, requesting that the American consul in Chungking telegraph the pastor of my church in Boise."

A sweet scent rose from my cup. We had been honored with jasmine tea, not the everyday oolong. A little girl—three years old or so—sidled up to our table and stared at the doctor's hair. The child's eyes were as round as coins, and she was wearing a white shirt and nothing else.

"Are you okay, Elizabeth?" I asked. "You don't look too healthy." I placed a hand on her forehead. "You've got a fever."

"I'll be fine."

"Isn't there medicine for malaria? You're a doctor in a hospital. You should give yourself medicine."

She shook her head, which seemed to take a concentrated effort. "I don't have any."

"What do you treat it with? Maybe I can get some for you."

"We used to have quinine, and it's sometimes effective. But we've had a lot of malaria patients, and we've used it all."

The little girl maneuvered closer.

Elizabeth bent low and switched to Mandarin. "Go ahead, little blossom. You can touch my hair."

The little girl patted the doctor's red hair, then pulled gently on several strands, then sank both hands into it. She grinned and backed away from the table, still eyeing the flame-colored hair.

"My hair is just like yours," Elizabeth said to her. "But red."

The child ran toward her mother on the mattress.

The doctor turned back to me. "The pastor then relayed the message to William Borah, a senator from Idaho. The pastor and Senator Borah have been friends for most of the century. Senator Borah is powerful. When he asks questions, he gets answers, and he asked questions at the State Department. Apparently he caused quite a stir, but he was successful."

"I don't have any idea what you are talking about," I said.

"Senator Borah asked questions about two American boys who disappeared in Chungking, China, twenty-five years ago."

My hand stilled, the tea glass almost to my mouth.

"I just received a message that was telegraphed to Chungking and then sent up the river in a packet on a postal mule. The senator found out about your mother and father."

I was as mute as a fish.

"Your father was the American consul in Chungking." Malaria made her voice weak. "Your parents had been in China three years when you and William were kidnapped. When you disappeared—which was in May 1912—your father organized a search for you."

I still couldn't generate any words.

"Because he was a senior official, he could ask the United States Marines posted in Chungking for assistance, and the navy, too, and he was friends with the Chungking police commissioner, and they all helped search for you and William. It was a huge effort."

"Wasn't huge enough, was it?" My voice was the ghost of a whisper.

"Eighteen months after the two of you disappeared, your father resigned his post, and he and your mother returned to Nebraska. Their home—your home when you were an infant—was in Lincoln."

"That was my life when I was a baby, before Chungking and the House of Eight Orchids. It doesn't mean anything to me now. I have no memories of it. I don't even know where Nebraska is."

"Your father died three years later," she said. "This was in 1917. He had gone fishing on the Platte River, and his overturned rowboat and his body were found a couple days later, near a little town on the river called South Bend."

I lowered the glass. My mouth was as dry as a kiln. The candle maker continued at his craft, dipping straw into the cauldron. He ordered his son to blow harder into the bamboo reed, which acted like a bellows to lift the flames. Steam wafted toward the hole in the ceiling. The woman who had served us tea picked waxberries from a basket and dropped them into the cauldron.

Elizabeth said, "Your mother lived in Lincoln after your father died, and she became the city's head librarian. She passed away four years ago of stomach cancer."

"I'm not much interested in all this." My voice was wavering, and I sounded false even to my own ears.

"Not interested in your family?"

I was feeling aggrieved. "The House of Eight Orchids was my family, and Eunuch Chang was as much my father as anyone." I rose from the chair.

She grabbed my hand. "Don't you want to know your last name?"

"I . . . I'm not sure." I sat back down.

"Your name is John Wade." She smiled. "And you have a middle name, so your name is John Burke Wade. You were named after your father. You are John Burke Wade Jr."

"John Burke Wade." I said the words slowly, as if tasting them. "Junior."

The candle maker rose on his toes to attach a new candle to the ceiling.

"I don't need a last name, with my family in America dead," I said. "John or Yellow Hair is enough."

She increased the grip on my hand. "You still have a family, John."

I stared at her.

"You have a sister who was born a year before your father died. She is fourteen years old, and she is being raised by your aunt and uncle in Lincoln. Her name is Anna."

I tried to say something, but the words wouldn't come.

捌

"I'm not taking one more step," I said. "This is as far as I go."

"I can't do it by myself," Elizabeth said.

With the memory of William's water-swollen body goading me, I wanted to race downstream, but Commander Beals had said that the *Ingram* had to remain in Red Cloud Ferry until the next morning, and wouldn't tell me the reason. The gunboat could travel much faster than a horse traveling on the trackers' path. And so the doctor had asked for my help while I was stranded in the village.

She gripped my arm and dragged me along. At least, she tried. She wasn't strong, and perspiration beaded on her forehead. I carried a bag of medical supplies over my shoulder. We walked along a path bordered by rotted logs covered with toadstools, and we ducked under hanging vines. Sunlight was meager in the forest. A warbler with a yellow belly flitted between the trees overhead. My shoes sank with each step, sending up the rich scent of decay, of rot.

"He was cutting down a tree," she said, "and when the tree started falling the wrong way, he jumped aside, slipped on the wet leaves, and fell hard. He has a dislocated shoulder."

"Can't you fix him by yourself?"

"This morning I tried to put it back in the joint, but I couldn't pull his arm hard enough. I'm having a bad time with the malaria right now. I'm not as strong as I should be."

"What about the spirit?" I asked.

"I've told you: a spirit has nothing to do with it."

"Maybe not in Boise, but here in China spirits have everything to do with everything."

She tapped my temple with her knuckles. "Solid bone from ear to ear."

A woodpecker hammered a tree somewhere behind us. I caught the smell of roses as I leaned closer to her. She was wearing a scent. Her blue shirt was tucked into loose cotton trousers that swished as she walked. Her hair shifted shades, depending on the light. Here, inland from her hospital, it was the color of rust. She moved gracefully, avoiding vines and mud and a patch of stinging nettles.

"We are getting close," she said. "Be polite."

"I am always polite."

"Unless you are sticking someone with a knife."

"Even then."

She pushed aside a parasol tree branch. "There he is, with his wife."

"Elizabeth, listen." I tried to slow our pace.

She tried to yank on my arm, but malaria had weakened her, and it was a paltry effort.

I said, "Eunuch Chang taught me never to show fear."

"Are you afraid?" she asked.

"I've quit breathing I'm so afraid. I need to stop right here and talk to you about this."

She led me around a stand of lacquer trees. "Too late."

The lepers were in a clearing. The man's arm was at an odd angle. His face was creased with many unnatural folds, and his right eye socket didn't appear to have skin around it. He was missing an ear. The woman—maybe his wife, though I didn't know if lepers were allowed to marry—was leaning into him, steadying him. The side of her neck was covered with red bumps. Their clothes were so faded the colors couldn't be determined.

The doctor lifted the bag from my shoulder. She brought out a pair of rubber gloves and passed them to me.

She asked, "Do you want to be the anchor or the winch?"

I shook my head. I didn't want to be either. The gloves were too small, but I crammed my hands into them.

"When I tried to relocate the arm, I ended up dragging him along the ground. So you can either hug him from behind to act as an anchor, or you can pull on his arm."

"Blessed Buddha, please preserve me."

The doctor chided me. "Leprosy is not that contagious. You have to live for years in an endemic area to catch it."

The doctor bowed to the lepers and told them the plan in her broken Mandarin.

Elizabeth and the wife positioned themselves behind the leper. The doctor hugged him around the waist. Elizabeth was a head taller than the wife. The leper held one arm in the other.

The doctor switched to English. "Grab him by the wrist." She reached over his shoulder to help position the arm. An unnatural hump was on his back.

I approached the leper's outstretched hand. It was a partial hand, missing two fingers and a thumb so that the hand resembled a talon. Horrified, I stared at it.

"Go on, John," the doctor said. Her hands were clasped together at the leper's midriff.

The wife's hair was under a brown bandana, and she wore straw sandals. She squeezed next to the doctor and also wrapped her arms around the leper.

I held my breath and gripped the leper's wrist. "What if his skin sloughs off when I pull?"

"On my signal, pull straight back. He'll cry out in pain, but you've got to do this." She ground her feet into the dirt to plant them. "Ready? Pull."

I squeezed his wrist with both my hands, and I imagined I felt worms squirming under his skin, and then I stepped back, pulling on his arm. He gasped, then yelled in pain, and his legs gave out. The two women held him upright.

"Now walk two steps to your left," Elizabeth ordered.

Keeping tension on the arm, I moved sideways, and through the leper's arm I could feel his shoulder settle back into place.

"We did it," the doctor said.

She released the leper. His wife leaned into him to help him stay upright. The hump on his shoulder had disappeared. He tentatively moved his arm. He grinned—a ghastly thing.

The lepers said a few words of gratitude, and the doctor bowed to them. She returned my gloves to the bag.

I said, "I'm going to stick my hands into a bonfire."

We started retracing our steps, through the forest toward the hospital. She held my arm again, not to pull me along but to be companionable. I'd never before walked with a woman's arm in mine.

"My fingers are tingling," I said. "It's started already."

"That's in your head," she said. "The only thing in your head."

She had been doing that, being cheerful for my benefit. I hopped over a muddy rivulet, then helped Elizabeth across.

"John, you should write your sister a letter."

"Write to an American girl?"

The doctor's voice softened. "With William gone, she's your only family."

"I have another brother: One Eye Gao Bai."

Something scurried away in the brush near our feet. I hoped it was a bamboo rat and nothing worse.

She asked, "How can a John Burke Wade Jr. be related to a One Eye Gao Bai?"

"He is my scar brother." I stopped to roll up my left pant leg. I pointed at my leg. "Take a look."

On my calf were the two Chinese symbols that together mean *brother*, in raised purple scar tissue.

I said, "Up north in Xi'an, the eastern end of the Silk Road, the Brothers of the Road for five hundred years have guaranteed safety to Silk Road travelers. They are a society of five hundred or a thousand members, nobody knows." I traced my finger along the scars. "As far west on the Silk Road as the Yellow River, a trader was safe, thanks to the Brothers."

"It sounds like a racket."

I lowered my pant leg. "If a trader who was heading for Persia paid the brothers, bandits wouldn't bother him. If the trader didn't pay, bandits would steal all his goods."

She said, "It's called extortion."

"The Brothers are fanatically devoted to each other. If one is harmed, all are harmed." I began again along the path. "And they all have 'brother' scars on their legs."

She reached for my arm again, walking near to me. Then her legs gave way, and I held her up.

"Elizabeth, you need to go to bed. You're more ill than you'll admit."

"Tell me about your friend One Eye." Her face was pink with fever.

"Gao Bai and I cut the 'brother' symbols into each other's legs, then rubbed ash into the wounds, which caused the scars to rise. We didn't know how the Brothers of the Road did it, so we created our own solemn ritual, and Gao and I promised to always defend each other."

"How old were you?" she asked.

"Eighteen. Gao and I have considered ourselves brothers ever since. Gao Bai considered William his brother, too, though William never gave himself the scar. So I do have a family."

"But not a sister. In a letter, you could tell Anna about your life in Chungking."

"Which part of my life?" I asked. "How I pick pockets? Or how I can hit someone so hard in the chest it paralyzes him? Or how—even after all the years—I still flinched every time I saw the eunuch's privates up on the shelf?"

"Anna may be waiting for a letter," the doctor said. "I'll help you write it."

"I can write my own letter."

"But if I write it, I'll make you seem normal." She tried to grin, but it must have taken too much effort, as it failed. "Making you sound normal will be tough, but it can't be too much harder than medical school."

My hand under her arm, I worked to hold Elizabeth upright as we walked.

She said, "A sister waiting in America and a dog: What could be better than that?" She gestured toward the pine-tree glade beside the road.

The giant dog was shadowing us.

17

Two Gun Sister Wong came through the inn's door, a big revolver in her hand. She pointed it at the innkeeper. "You are a traitor."

The innkeeper dropped a wood spoon. "No. I am—"

The pistol fired—the sound rolling through the dining room—and the innkeeper's right calf ripped out. He fell to the floor.

She crossed the floor and whipped the pistol butt into his head. "A traitor to China."

The innkeeper groaned, and when he tried to raise his hands to protect his head, she kicked him in the groin. He rolled to one side and lifted his legs, crying out with fear and pain.

"Time to go." Commander Beals rose from the table. "I'd leave the innkeeper a tip, but he won't be needing it." He was wearing a sailor's striped shirt under a blue jacket.

My rice and pork was only half-eaten. I followed Beals toward the door. I had heard of Two Gun Sister Wong, and I didn't want anything to do with her. She was not five feet high, and the pistol—a Webley break-top—looked like a cannon in her little hand. She kicked the innkeeper in the face.

A strip of rawhide circled her neck and was attached to the bottom of the pistol's grip, and so she didn't wear a holster. Green puttees were wrapped around her legs, and a strand of the woolen puttee held a knife against her calf. Her nose and ears were tiny, and her hair was kept tightly against her skull by a blue watch cap. As I reached the door, I was pushed aside by guerillas who rushed into the inn.

"Search the place." Two Gun Sister Wong waved the Webley at every corner of the room.

Commander Beals and I walked toward *Ingram*, the river on our right. Dusk had faded to night during our meal, and a peppering of stars was overhead. The moon was behind the mountains, and the river soughed and rippled, carrying the scent of cherry blossoms from orchards upstream.

The guerillas—about fifty of them, who were aligned with the Kuomintang—came up the river path and began setting up their bivouac. Most wore ragtag military uniforms: a KMT tunic, a German sailor's reefer jacket, padded cotton coats, Reichswehr coal-scuttle helmets, Japanese field caps, canvas gaiters, and whatever else they had picked up. Some carried Lee-Enfield rifles, others Mauser rifles, and one guerilla carried a mortar on his back. A Japanese officer's curved sword in a scabbard hung at the side of another guerilla. At the rear, six packhorses followed the column.

The guerilla unit spread out along the shoreline and in front of the shops along Red Cloud Ferry's road. Two Gun Sister Wong must have given orders that the villagers' homes weren't to be used for shelter, because none of the guerillas entered the huts. They threw blankets on the ground, and several guerillas began digging fire pits. A racket came from the inn, sounding as if tables and chairs were being upended and the stove knocked over. The villagers had vanished, which happened whenever any fighting force appeared.

I learned later from Commander Beals that Two Gun Sister Wong had been studying art at the National Southeast University in Shanghai when in February 1932 the Japanese Eleventh Infantry Division landed near Liuhe behind Chinese lines. She was known as Fragrant Sister Wong, her family name. She and six other female students were taken to the Eleventh Infantry's comfort house, where she spent four years as a sex slave. One night she used a silk stocking to strangle the sergeant who ran the comfort house, and escaped inland. She made her way upriver to Chungking and joined Yen Hsi-shan's guerillas, but when he proved to prefer planning to attacking, Fragrant Sister—known by then as Two Gun Sister—organized her own group.

Her specialty was the Red Silk Surprise, where a Japanese infantry company would come upon a lovely Chinese girl wearing a red silk robe, red silk being particularly rousing to Japanese men. Her hair would be down to her shoulders, and she would be wearing lipstick and eyeliner. At first sight of the Japanese soldiers, she would scream and run into the forest. Laughing and yelling, the soldiers would chase after her, wrestling with their belts to get their trousers down. Once she had run far enough into the trees, her guerillas would open fire. The Red Silk Surprise had never failed, until Chiang Kai-shek had awarded her a medal and lauded her in a propaganda broadcast, which alerted the Japanese army to the ambush, rendering it useless. She had refused to come to Chungking to receive the medal.

Headed toward the *Ingram* at the pier, Beals and I stepped between packhorses. A body was tied to the last horse by a rope. The ground had scraped away skin and tissue on the legs, so it was a skeleton from the hips down. A placard had been pinned to the chest that read "Traitor." Campfires flared to life. Several guerillas removed dough wads from boxes strapped to the horses and began kneading the dough.

"They shape the dough to resemble Japanese soldiers," Beals said.

Guerillas hung pots over the fire pits and brought hay and buckets of oats for their horses. The cooks passed out steamed biscuits, and the guerillas sang this little ditty, which rhymed in Mandarin, "You eat rice and I eat noodles / But let's all cook the Japs. / You can have the elbows / While I enjoy the legs. / As to the heads / Leave them for the dogs."

Two Gun Sister Wong emerged from the inn. Guerillas dragged the innkeeper from the building.

She held up a letter. "A letter from a Japanese officer. Who reads Japanese here?"

I spoke it, but I couldn't read it.

"Then I'll tell you what it says, even without being able to read it," Two Gun Sister called to her men. "It tells whatever Jap officer who conquers this town that the innkeeper was helpful to the Japanese empire. This man"—she pointed the Webley at the innkeeper's head—"is a traitor."

Without being ordered to do so, the guerilla with the Japanese sword pulled it from the scabbard. Two Gun Sister shoved her pistol into a waistband, then grabbed the innkeeper's hair and yanked him up to kneeling. The sword was raised. Yet the guerillas must have been accustomed to this procedure, because they kept singing: "You can have the elbows / While I enjoy the legs." The innkeeper's mouth opened and closed.

But then Two Gun Sister held up her hand. "This traitor isn't worth dulling your blade. Take him to the river."

The sword was returned to the scabbard, and two guerillas grabbed the innkeeper's arms and dragged him across the road onto the pebbled shore, leaving a trail of blood from the innkeeper's leg. The guerillas waded into the water, pulling the innkeeper behind them. When they were waist-deep, they pushed the innkeeper under the water and held him there. The *Ingram* was moored a few yards downriver, and sailors gathered in the bow to watch, though they might not have been able to see much in the darkness.

"Looks like they found the spy," Beals said.

Two Gun Sister Wong let her pistol hang by the rawhide, and she walked up to Commander Beals. She smiled and bowed. With her guerilla band in Red Cloud Ferry, and with the American sailors here, and with town folks knowing I was a friend of their beloved bamboo doctor, and with that giant dog following me, I was as safe here as I ever would be in China. Eunuch Chang was alive and was hunting me, I had no doubt. No one had ever betrayed the eunuch Chang of Chungking and survived. I was deathly afraid of the eunuch. The skills he had taught me over the years were only a fraction of his own arsenal.

But twenty-five years ago the eunuch had stolen me from my parents, and now he had taken my brother's life, had taken him away from me forever. I was going to repay Eunuch Chang. I owed it to William, and I owed it to myself. I was hunting the eunuch, and he was hunting me. I hoped to meet him when and where I might have a chance. I had stayed too long in the village. It was time to go.

The gunboat was a hulking black form against a darker sky. When Beals signaled the ship, Red Leery and another sailor walked across the gangway onto the pier carrying a wood box between them. They stepped slowly, and their faces were knotted. The box must have been heavy. They carried it to the end of the pier, and Leery grunted and the other sailor lowered it to the ground. Leery pulled a pry bar from his belt, inserted the claw under the box's top, and levered the box open.

Inside were twenty bolt-action Arisaka rifles and twenty bayonets packed in grease. Two other sailors carried another box from the gunboat to the shore. Leery pried open the second box's lid, revealing forty Nambu pistols. Other sailors carried out cardboard ammunition boxes. The United States Navy was supplying the guerillas with Japanese firearms, which could not be traced back to the United States, which was officially neutral in the war between Japan and China. Leery returned to the gunboat.

Beals said, "I've met Two Gun Sister twice before here at Red Cloud Ferry but have never been able to say anything to her."

"I'll help," I said.

He drew himself up and said, "I have been honored to be of service to you, madam."

When I translated this to Mandarin, Two Gun Sister's eyebrows rose, probably in surprise that a gweilo could speak her language. Then she held out her hand for Beals to shake, a Western mannerism she had learned somewhere.

She said, "I hope you will visit us many more times, and I hope that you and your children and their children live long and prosperous lives. I bless them all, and may Buddha bless them all, too."

The innkeeper's body was brought to the shore. The two guerillas dragged it toward the horses.

"I have a gift for you, madam," Beals said. "Something you weren't expecting." He motioned at the gunboat.

Leery walked from the ship carrying a rifle, I thought at first. But as he drew near, I could see that it was an automatic weapon, with a barrel sleeve with holes in it and a bipod folded against the barrel.

The commander said, "It's an MG-34, made in Germany. Let me congratulate you because you are the first owner of such a weapon along the Yangtze River."

Leery placed the weapon on the ground.

"Eight hundred rounds per minute," the commander said. "Each belt contains two hundred bullets, and I have one hundred belts for you."

Sailors brought out ammunition boxes.

Beals added, "This is the same model the Germans have been shipping to the Japanese army."

After I had translated, Two Gun Sister clasped her hands together as a bride would do when presented with a porcelain tea set, a charming gesture at odds with the big revolver hanging against her chest.

She said, "You have lightened a patriot's heart. We will do grievous damage to the invaders with your gifts."

I translated a few more sentences. The reason *Ingram* had spent two days at Red Cloud Ferry was that the guerillas had been delayed in their march to the village. Commander Beals had told me the gunboat was showing the flag on the Yangtze. During the day, yes. During the night, the boat was supplying the guerillas who were fighting the Japanese. Red Cloud Ferry was one of eight planned stops along the river to distribute weapons, Beals told Two Gun Sister. The United States wasn't as neutral in this war between China and Japan as I had thought.

The guerilla leader shook Beals's hand again and ordered several of her men to take away the weapons and ammunition. They said good-bye to each other, and Beals returned to the gunboat. I started toward the hospital. *Ingram* was leaving Red Cloud Ferry in the morning, heading farther up the river, and I was going to be on board. I wanted to say good-bye to Elizabeth.

As I walked up the dirt road, the big dog followed me, off in the trees. I stopped, and it stopped. I started again, and it started again, weaving through trees to keep up with me, but never too close.

I said, "You're too ugly to be my dog, that's for sure."

I glanced through the trees in the direction of the hospital. Red-and-yellow flames flickered beyond the trees, haphazard patterns seen through the glade. I started to run. The hospital was on fire.

捌

The west wall crawled with flames. The fire billowed and curled and sounded like the *Ingram*'s engines. The black smoke rolled into the sky carrying gold sparks. Flames rushed along the hospital's roof, threatening to engulf the building. I ran through the garden.

Sing pushed a bed into the garden, smoke following her out the door. She struggled because she was also holding the patient's saline stand. Sing was helped by a man in rags, who pulled at the bed. The bed was pushed toward the garden. The wheels sank into the gravel, and I grabbed a post and helped them move the bed to the generator shed. I glanced at the man in rags next to me. It was the leper whose shoulder Elizabeth and I had set. He must have seen the blaze from the colony. He smiled at me with his half a face. I didn't have time to shudder.

I asked Sing, "Where's Dr. Hanley?"

Her eyebrows had been burnt off, her shirtsleeve was charred, and her right hand and wrist had been burned, the flesh curled and red. She sank to the ground.

I sprinted toward the building. Just inside the hospital door I faced a wall of heat that seemed as impenetrable as a brick wall. I had to will myself forward. I stepped into the ward and called out her name. The fire was roaring and eating through the interior wall. I yelled her name again, louder. Smoke billowed into the ward and rose to the ceiling. An old man in a wheelchair with a plaster cast on a hand was trying to maneuver the chair to the door. I grabbed the chair's handle and propelled the chair out the ward door and into the garden.

I went back into the ward, and when I tried to draw a breath, the smoke seared my throat. I ran into the supply room and then into the small laboratory. Gasping against the heat, I moved into the disease ward.

"Elizabeth? Where are you?"

I could hardly hear my own words over the bellowing of the flames. A portion of the west wall caved into the ward, and orange and red sparks swirled around the room. Only one of the four beds was occupied. I pushed aside the net and lifted an old woman from the bed. She could not have weighed eighty pounds, and her bones ground together as I carried her out the side door—the heat chasing me—and lowered her to the ground near the bamboo glade. Ten other patients were out there, some lying and some sitting on the dirt. They had gotten themselves out, or Sing and the leper had helped them.

The huge dog was by the toolshed, as close to me as he had ever been. He was twisting left and right, and when I turned back toward the disease ward, he howled.

Calling her name again, I ran around the outside of the hospital as clouds of orange flame enveloped the building. The leper placed a blanket over a patient who was lying on the ground near the roses. Sing was sitting up on the gravel, but swaying, her burned hand on her lap.

I knelt down. "Where's Dr. Hanley? Have you seen her?"

She didn't say anything, and she seemed to be staring through me at the conflagration. Embers landed in the garden. Her mouth moved, but there was no sound.

I gently shook her. "Sing, where is the bamboo doctor?"

Her gaze seemed to focus. "They took her."

"Took Dr. Hanley? Who took her?"

"A lady came to the hospital in a sedan chair." Sing coughed and drew a hand across her mouth. "She and the chair bearers grabbed Dr. Hanley, and when the doctor tried to fight them, the lady slashed the doctor's arm with her fingers. She was an old lady and was wearing a beautiful green robe."

I released Sing and rose to my feet.

"Then they soaked towels in generator fuel," Sing said, "and they made torches to set the hospital on fire."

The west wall collapsed inward, sending gouts of flame skyward.

I said, more to myself, "They were nail protectors, weren't they? Not just her fingers?"

Sing looked up. "And her feet were bound in the old-fashioned way. She couldn't walk."

My mouth pulled back in a grimace. Madam Tuan had come to Red Cloud Ferry.

18

I had to look closely at the face of the cliff to see the steps, which had been carved out of the living rock. They were smaller than my foot, and placed irregularly up the stone face so that they didn't form a pattern that was easy to spot. The steps had been scored by chisels centuries ago. Handholds had also been dug out of the rock. The steps were steep and slippery, and water sprayed on me. I didn't look down.

Only two days had passed since the hospital fire. Before I had left Red Cloud Ferry on *Ingram*, I had returned Sing to her parents. She was given a joyous welcome, even by her father. She was free of the tinea, and the burn on her hand would heal.

I was behind the waterfall called Old Man's Beard. The water fell from the stone ledge high above to the boulders lining the river. The cascade was behind me, the cliff in front of me, and I was in the narrow mist-filled space between the slippery stone and the rushing water. The handholds had been artfully hidden. I found one above my head and pulled myself farther up. Moss covered much of the cliff. Several bushes had found anchor on the cliff face, and I climbed up through them, my hands feeling the granite for the next higher handhold. The gold bars in my shirt weighed me down.

Two-thirds up the cliff—maybe sixty feet above the shoreline—I reached a ledge, and I crawled onto it, my clothes sodden. The ledge wasn't much bigger than my rump. The waterfall allowed light through, and dappling flickered down the cliff face. The sheet of water—white and blue and churning—plummeted past me to the boulders below. When I tried to squeeze against the cliff face to get away from the dizzying torrent, my shoulder found air instead of granite. An opening in the cliff was just behind the ledge, a cave entrance. The eunuch had told me it would be there.

Ducking my head, I pushed myself into the cave. I crawled forward, scuffing my scalp on the stone overhead. I could feel chisel striations under my fingers. The tunnel had been scraped out of the granite. Wind came from behind, rushing past me deeper into the tunnel, so the cave must have had more than this one entrance. I left the uneven light coming through the falling water, and the tunnel became dark as I crawled forward. Stone was all around and seemed to be pressing in on me, but then after a few more yards the ceiling rose as I moved deeper into the recess. Weak yellow light was ahead, around a bend in the passage. I inched forward on my knees and hands, both shoulders grazing stone, and my head sliding along the tunnel's granite roof.

I followed the passage around the bend, and the tunnel opened to a cave lit by a dozen tar torches. As my head emerged from the tunnel into the cave, a blade came down to rest on my neck. I knew enough about blades to understand it was as sharp as my number-three knife, and it was held against my neck with precision. One swift move from the axman, and my head would drop to the cave floor. The blade was wide, an executioner's axe.

"I hope fate is guiding you," the axman said. "And not some whimsy."

I couldn't raise my head to look at him, as the blade was pressed against my neck. "I am Yellow Hair from the House of Eight Orchids."

"The one who betrayed the eunuch Chang." It wasn't a question.

For five hundred years, these monks had known everything from every corner of China. To lie to them might be fatal.

"I fled his house with my brother and a woman," I said. "Now he is hunting me."

"And you gamble with your life by coming here."

"This cave is your temple," I said. "Buddhism prohibits harming someone at a temple."

The axman said, "We aren't Buddhists, and this isn't a Buddhist temple."

"Taoism also forbids harming anyone who is inside a temple."

"We aren't Taoists, either."

The blade pressed into my neck, one feather's weight from opening the skin. I was still on my knees, my gaze on the granite under me.

"Get up."

The axe was lifted from my neck. I pushed myself to my feet.

The axman said, "Give me your knives."

A knife fell into each of my hands, and I held them out.

He smiled, revealing a gold tooth. "All of them."

"My compliments to the monks of this temple." My smallest knife appeared in my hand. "Not five people in China know I carry three." I handed the weapons to the axman.

He placed them inside his robe. "I hope for your sake you brought enough gold."

My gold bars were wrapped against my belly.

"Our headman is waiting." He carried the axe with the blade down. "If you touch any of the ancients, I will cut off your offending hand."

He led me deeper into the cave. Carrying the scent of rot, the wind swirled in many directions and fluttered the axman's gold robe. His head was shaved, and his small ears were tight against his head. Torches sputtered on the wall, and the cave's roof was lost in darkness.

Two torches framed a human body shackled to the stones with lengths of chain attached to bolts driven into the granite. Rats had been tearing flesh from the corpse, and the legs were exposed bone. The head was intact, and the mouth was a rotted gap. The eye sockets were green.

Dried blood caked the wrists and arms, as if the prisoner had tried to yank the chains from the wall.

The axman said, "He visited us last week."

If a client tried to hire the Gold Tooth monks but brought insufficient gold, the client was entombed belowground, left alive to go mad and then horribly perish. At least, that was the rumor. Kangxi, the third emperor of the Qing dynasty, had ruled China for sixty-one years, beginning in 1661. Kangxi built China into its modern shape by defeating the Three Feudatories, the Taiwan pirate Zheng Jing, and tsars attempting to expand Russia. He crushed anyone else who threatened his rule. The Gold Tooth monks—then known as Monks of the Wansing Temple—had sent a senior monk to the Kangxi Emperor to propose that Wansing monks be allowed to control southern Sichuan, where the warlords had proved to be obdurate. Outraged, the emperor ordered the monk strangled, and then he sent the Three Banner Army to the Wansing Temple on the Yangtze River. The monks were slaughtered—all who were found—and the temple was dismantled stone by stone, and the stones were carried to the empire's far corners as a reminder of the destiny of those who tried to usurp the emperor. Every other trace of the Wansing temple was destroyed, and the grounds were salted. To this day, nothing grows in the temple's garden.

Hidden in a root cellar beneath the temple, six monks had survived. Over the next decades they developed a philosophy that attachment to anything led to *dukkha*, or "suffering." Only gold endured, and only gold was reliable. The monks began a centuries-long quest to collect the metal, and they did so by performing services. Eunuch Chang had hired the Gold Tooth monks three times, in each instance when he had failed a commission. The monks' fees were always more than the eunuch would earn, but he would rather pay the monks than admit failure to a client. No one knew how many Gold Tooth monks there were, or how many temples they possessed, or whether they ever prayed.

The cave narrowed, and the axman led me around a stone corner into a room that dazzled with light. A dozen torches flickered on stands. Gold skulls lined the walls, and the torchlight reflected off them, flashing and shifting as I stepped into the room. The gold contrasted with the skulls' black eye sockets and dull white teeth. Each skull had one gold tooth. The skulls were arrayed side by side on shelves that had been carved out of the granite, walls of skulls. They stared at me with their dead eyes. Wind moaned through the cave. Hundreds of joss sticks, glowing red, were arrayed on the shelves alongside the skulls. Their smoke sped away in the wind.

An elderly monk was sitting on a bench in front of a low table, and candles on the table threw light on his round face. He waved me forward. I couldn't tell whether he was smiling or grimacing, showing his gold tooth. He wore a gold-colored robe and a black felt cap. His rimless spectacles flashed on and off in the torchlight. He looked fastidious, with a narrow nose above a prim mouth, a dainty chin, tiny ears, and if he had eyebrows I couldn't see them.

"My name is Monk Gu." His voice was just above the sound of the wind. "We do not receive many visitors. How did you find us?"

"Years ago the eunuch Chang told me about the waterfall."

"Why did you not approach one of us in Red Cloud Ferry or somewhere else along the river?" His voice warbled and whistled, as if he had been injured in the throat at some time.

"Had the eunuch already hired the Gold Tooth monks, I would not have survived approaching one of you. But here in your temple, I'm safe. This is a sanctuary."

His smile was humorless. "Our temple—and your sanctuary—ends at the cliff entrance behind the waterfall, high above the boulders. The moment you take one step back down toward the river, you no longer have sanctuary, on that slippery staircase."

"But you are holy men and wouldn't weaken sanctuary with such logic."

"You can only hope."

A tunnel entrance was behind him. Smoke from the torches escaped from the cave into the rear tunnel, streaming past a monk who was standing at the entrance. This monk was carrying a pistol, hanging at his side with the muzzle pointed at the floor. The axman remained near me.

"I have come here to donate gold to your order." I brought out three of my remaining gold bars and placed them on the table.

"And what do you want in return?" the monk asked.

"The blessings and good graces of this temple."

The monk lifted one of the bars, apparently testing its weight. "Blessings and good graces from us do not cost anything."

"The location of the gweilo who operates the hospital at Red Cloud Ferry. She is called the bamboo doctor, and she has been kidnapped by Eunuch Chang's men."

The monk leaned back. "That is much more costly."

The gold skulls were sentinels, thousands of them, shimmering with reflected light and watching me. The stabs of light were more oppressive than merry and made the skulls appear to move along the wall, advancing and retreating in golden waves, tricks of the light. Or maybe the skulls possessed an elemental power, perhaps one of judgment. I involuntarily stepped back. The axman placed a hand on my shoulder to stop me. Against the cave wall was a shelf containing small boxes, several pistols and knives, a scale, gold cord wrapped around a spool, and other items I couldn't identify.

The monk said, "You are seeking information about the operations of Eunuch Chang and his House of Eight Orchids. The eunuch is skillful. Should he learn that I have given you this information, he might try to do to the Gold Tooth Temple what the emperor failed to do three hundred years ago. So such information is costly."

"I offer three gold bars."

"These three gold bars aren't enough," the old monk said. "Not for information about Eunuch Chang's business."

The axman shifted his weapon to his other hand.

"How do I know your information is good?" I asked. "Maybe I'd be giving away my gold bars for faulty information."

Monk Gu nodded at the axman, who retrieved a knife from the shelf and passed it to me. The blade had been sharpened so many times that it was narrower than the antelope-horn handle.

"That knife belonged to Eunuch Chang. It's the one he carried from the saltworks to Chungking many years ago. We took it from the House of Eight Orchids—at night, without him knowing anything about it— as a lesson to him regarding our influence."

This was the eunuch's blade, the one he had inherited from Fu Yong at the salt spring, and the one Eunuch Chang had used to kill the Mongol Arigh. He had carried this knife along the Yellow River and across the Ch'in Ling Mountains to Chungking.

"And now I show it to you," Monk Gu said, "as evidence of our ability to know things and do things."

The axman took the eunuch's knife from me and returned it to the shelf.

"I have only three bars." I was bluffing. I had three more gold bars inside my shirt but I desperately needed the fourth as a reserve against whatever else China was going to send my way.

The monk lifted his hand toward a wall of skulls. "A monk who devotes his life to good works has his skull plated with gold and displayed here for eternity."

Intent, I suppose, on getting myself killed, I asked, "Good works?" I glanced over my shoulder, checking the path of an escape.

The axman laughed lightly, and shifted to block my way out.

"And, yes, we do good works," Monk Gu said. "Our temple is devoted to charity." He leaned forward, as if he might hear my thoughts. "And so we are always in need of the precious metal. A lot of it."

I could count on my hands the times I had been without my knives.

The elder monk stacked the bars, then unstacked them as if they were mahjong tiles. My hands were at my sides. They were formidable weapons, but not against someone who knew how to use an axe. The axman looked comfortable holding his weapon.

"We have two items of information for you," Monk Gu said. "You will benefit immensely from each of them."

The air shifted in the cavern, then shifted again, and the torch flames bent with the wind. The monks' underground home probably had many hidden entrances, not just the one behind the waterfall.

"You donated four gold bars to the hospital in Red Cloud Ferry." Monk Gu's voice piped and rattled. "We will credit you for them. And those four gold bars and these three here are the price of our information about Eunuch Chang's business."

I bowed my thanks.

Monk Gu said, "The bamboo doctor is at a farm twenty li downriver. The farm is across the river from the Lucky Son Cliff. The woman named Madam Tuan has bound and gagged her and is hiding her in the farmhouse for the night. The doctor is being guarded by a fellow with many fresh red scars on his face and arms, the one known as Ham Fist. The farmhouse has a green tile roof and camellia trees on the east and west side."

The *Ingram* had passed Lucky Son on its journey up the river.

He added, "With the gweilo woman, he is trying to lure you back to the House of Eight Orchids. He is most comfortable there and will have prepared unpleasant surprises for you."

I nodded.

The monk smiled widely. "We monks gather information as a farmer gathers sheaves, Yellow Hair. And this second item of information is critical to your well-being and happiness. It will cost your last three gold bars"—he indicated my shirt with a sweep of his hand—"and one of your knives, the one partly made of gold."

This was my second knife, my left-hand knife. How could the monks possibly have known its finger guard was made of gold? The wind shifted again, and the torch flames sputtered.

Monk Gu asked, "Do we have a deal?"

When I nodded, the axman pulled out my knives, gave the mid-sized one to Monk Gu, and returned the others to me, and I pulled the three gold bars from my shirt and handed them to Monk Gu.

Gu held up the knife to a candle. "Finely crafted and delicately balanced and immensely valuable. The Kung family never fails to produce such lovely weapons. I'm honored to touch it."

I said, "And my information that has cost me three gold bars and my knife?"

"Your dog was owned by a fisherman whose sampan overturned at Dead Raven Rapids last summer."

"That's not my dog."

"The fisherman drowned, but the dog made it to shore. The dog has been living in the wild ever since."

"That information isn't worth my gold and my knife. It isn't worth a fingernail paring cut off with my knife."

"Then how about this? The dog's name is Big Moon." He continued to grin at me, gold tooth and all.

I chewed on my lip, standing there, being examined by all those gold skulls. Monk Gu tucked the knife into his robe with a flourish. The axman stepped aside, the axe over his shoulder like a fishing pole.

I turned back toward the waterfall.

捌

I don't like mules. They are ridiculous animals, and anyone dealing with a mule looks ridiculous by the association. I'm no muleteer, and had to bribe the animal to get the slightest cooperation.

I held the carrot four feet from the animal's nose. It stared at me like I might be a moron, then flicked back its sampan-sized ears and moved toward the carrot, its hooves throwing up dust with each step. The mule smelled the carrot as if afraid I might have poisoned it—its nostrils flaring—then deigned to take the carrot between its ghastly yellow teeth. He chewed it, still eyeing me. I took five steps backward and brought out another carrot.

A plow harness had been rigged on the mule, as best as I could figure it out. I had rigged a length of rope, climbed a pine tree, and had attached the other end of the rope to the trunk near the top. A hatchet hung from my belt.

The mule moved forward for another carrot, bending the pine tree farther. The animal was the color of a chestnut, except his ears and tail were black. The hemp rope connecting the mule to the tree shivered with tension. The mule chewed the carrot with apparent nonchalance. The tree was bowed almost in half.

Near the end of the rope was a leader, a five-foot rope extension tied to the main rope. At the end of the leader was half of the trigger.

I tugged at the mule, getting him to shift my way so I could bring the rope and the leader closer to the other half of the trigger. The mule snorted and stomped a hoof but moved sideways toward me, flicking its big ears and chewing the carrot.

I didn't know where the giant dog was. Maybe he didn't like mules, either. I didn't want to use the dog's name, not even in my head, lest saying or thinking the name had ownership implications.

Pulling on the rope again, I made the mule sidle my way. The rope quavered, and the bent tree creaked. The leader was tied to the triggerbar, which had been a Y formed at the intersection of a small tree trunk and a branch. I had hacked the Y from a tree. The triggerbar was twelve inches long.

The other half of the trigger was the exposed root of a pine tree. I had cut a notch into the root. Heaving on the rope, I stretched out the leader, my feet scrabbling on the ground for purchase. The mule stared at me over his shoulder. With a lunge—my hand shaking in sympathy with the rope—I hooked the triggerbar to the notch in the root. I sprang to my feet to yank the harness buckle, freeing the mule from the rope. I handed the mule my last carrot and patted its shoulder. Freed of the harness, the mule moved off into the pine stand, probably headed back to the feed trough at his stable.

The tree was now an arced spring held down by the trigger. Although the root and the triggerbar were sturdy, they were held together by only narrow tips of wood. The slightest pull on the triggerbar would instantly free the bent pine tree. I pulled out the trip wire from a pocket and tied one end to the triggerbar. The snare was almost complete.

Elizabeth was behind a wall sixty yards away—a wall that surrounded the farmhouse with the green tile roof that Monk Gu had told me about. Bracketed by camellia trees, with their shiny leaves, the farmhouse was a quarter mile inland from the Yangtze. Tobacco and sugarcane fields bordered the river, and the farmhouse and outbuildings were near the pine forest that began at the foothills. Mountains rose behind the hills, the peaks hidden by clouds.

Behind the stone wall, I had listened for an hour to sounds from inside. I had heard Elizabeth's voice, and Madam Tuan's, and Ham Fist's, and those of the frightened farmer and his wife. Though I hadn't heard One Eye Gao Bai, he might have been in the farmhouse, too. Gao was formidable, and I couldn't risk confronting him and Ham Fist and Madam Tuan at the same time. Ham Fist had emerged through the gate to use the privy. He had been carrying a double-barrel shotgun. He had done his business, and had returned through the gate to the house.

They had kidnapped Elizabeth to lure me to the House of Eight Orchids, of course. They were heading to Chungking, and might have been waiting for a boat to take them farther downriver, knowing I would follow them. The farmer was wealthy, with an outlying pigsty, three huts for farmhands, and a stable for mules and oxen. The turpentine still—iron tubs, brass tubing, and wood barrels under a shingle roof held up by poles—was at the edge of the forest. I had borrowed one of his mules, and I had found the hemp rope, trip-wire twine, and six pitchforks in the farmer's toolshed.

Each of the pitchforks had four tines, and they were as sharp as fish-hooks. I had buried them at oblique angles so that the tines were above the ground, pointed toward the snare loop, while the handles were buried underground, anchored by boulders I had placed on the handles then covered with dirt. The snare was deadly. I began to gather old leaves and pine needles to cover the loop. The needles smelled of resin.

"The eunuch wants you alive," the voice said. "But if you move, or if I even suspect that dog is anywhere near, I'm going to pull both triggers."

My arms filled with leaves, I looked up. Forty yards away, Ham Fist was staring down the barrel of the shotgun. The muzzles were black and enormous. Both hammers were back. The stitching on his face was red and angry. He was on the path to the farmhouse, with trees on both sides of him. His eyes darted left and right, and he pointed the shotgun toward a shadow, then back at me.

"And the eunuch doesn't much care how healthy you are when you arrive in Chungking." Ham Fist's upper lip curled. "All he cares about is that your heart is still beating. That gives me a lot of leeway."

I only had two knives on me. With a shotgun pointed at me, the knives felt insignificant.

He said, "Madam Tuan knew you would follow the bamboo doctor back toward Chungking. She said you were as predictable as tomorrow's sunrise."

Ham Fist's face was distorted with wounds. An angry red welt ran across his forehead, the doctor's stitching visible even at this distance. Another wound descended from his left ear to his jawline, and another began at the jawbone under his ear and followed the curve of his chin around to the back of the jawbone on the other side. His face was also pitted with a dozen fang marks. His head resembled a ball of barbed wire. His white, knobby hand behind the shotgun's trigger had also been sewn up.

"I do not know what Eunuch Chang has planned for you," Ham Fist said, "but it is going to be long and terrible. He told me he might give you to Madam Tuan for one month, and then he will work on what's left of you."

Ham Fist was wearing black pants and a blue cotton jacket. A bandoleer was over his shoulder containing another dozen shotgun shells. He looked around for the dog again.

He said, "I've been watching you set your snare for the past ten minutes, you and the mule. And I'm not going anywhere near your loop or the trip wire or the spring tree."

I let my armful of pine needles and leaves fall to the ground.

"The great Yellow Hair reduced to using a snare." He stepped toward me, grinning with triumph. "And I'm not stepping into a snare that I can see as plain as Buddha's belly." He laughed.

Pine needles flew from the ground as a loop flew sideways, snaring Ham Fist's legs. As a pine tree snapped upright, Ham Fist collapsed to the pine needles on the ground, and the shotgun flew into the air. He flew across the forest floor toward the spring tree, and it happened too quickly for him to scream. He was dragged into the tines of one pitchfork, which was jerked up from the ground, and then into another pitchfork, and then into the third one. All of this took two seconds.

I walked across the pine needles to the tree. The righted pine tree was swaying overhead. Ham Fist was hanging upside down, ten feet above the forest floor. A pitchfork tine had pierced the back of his neck, emerging below his Adam's apple. Three other tines from the same pitchfork stuck out from his chest. The four tines of the second pitchfork were buried in his back up to the wood handle. The third pitchfork had ripped open his belly and had then been tossed aside by his violent travel across the dirt. Blood began dripping from his mouth. His eyes were open but sightless. Air clattered in his throat, and then he went silent.

"I set two snares, Ham Fist," I said. "And you only saw the decoy snare, plain as Buddha's belly."

19

By the time I was finished with Ham Fist up near the Lucky Son Cliff, Madam Tuan and the doctor were gone. The farmhouse was empty. They had left Ham Fist as a rear-guard.

I found the legendary knife maker Kung Ping's barge at Rainbow Fish Landing, eight li downriver from the Lucky Son Cliff; the *Ingram* was coaling a half mile up the river. The landing was used for tobacco shipments, but this wasn't tobacco season, so the landing was empty except for the knife maker's barge. Knife Maker Kung came through a leather flap that served as a door to the shop. He smiled, wrinkling his face from chin to hairline.

The shop was a half-cylindrical Nissen hut made of corrugated steel, one of two structures on the barge. Black smoke came from a tin stack at the roof's apex. I crossed the sandbar toward the barge, which was anchored a few yards offshore. I had left behind Ham Fist's shotgun. It was too visible. A guard on the deck raised a rifle toward me.

I called, "I am Yellow Hair from the House of Eight Orchids, a customer."

The guard waved me forward, and I stepped onto the gangplank between the sandbar and the barge. The guard was twelve or thirteen years old but held the rifle as if he knew how to use it.

He held open the leather door for me. "I heard that you are no longer from the House of Eight Orchids," the guard said. "And losing your brother: may the heavens spare me even a portion of your grief."

I ducked under a beam and stepped into the shop, standing to one side while my eyes adjusted to the low light. The forge was made of clay slurry mixed with pebbles and ashes, and the fire inside glowed red. Tin cans telescoped together served as a smokestack. I could see hammers and files hanging from a backboard against the corrugated wall, while blank blades were stacked near the forge. Against the far wall, finished knives gleamed in a glass and oak jeweler's display case. The shop smelled of oil and burning charcoal. The two men who had been working at the forge left the shop, perhaps not allowed to hear trade talk.

Knife Maker Kung motioned me to a low stool. His arms were bare, rippled and ridged with scars, and his neck and face were so scarred they resembled a cracked window. He was barefoot, and if he had a square inch of skin that wasn't scarred, I couldn't see it; the tops of his feet were covered with red and purple scars.

"Did Eunuch Chang's junk pass by Rainbow Fish Landing?" I asked.

"Earlier today, two hours after sunrise, passing downriver."

So the rapids below Red Cloud Ferry—where the junk had overturned after I cut the trackers' hawser—hadn't destroyed the junk. It had been salvaged.

"Could you see who was on board?" I asked.

"Someone with red hair, which you don't see much on the Yangtze."

"A woman?" Who else could it be?

"The junk was too far away to tell. But red hair, certainly."

"She was on deck?"

"Tied to the junk's mainmast. Wind was blowing the red hair all around. Probably a woman, but I couldn't tell."

So the eunuch and Elizabeth were four hours ahead of me.

I said, "I lost one of my knives."

"And a Gold Tooth monk found it. I've already heard."

"I don't feel right, carrying only two knives."

"Who does?"

Stock for knife handles was on shelves: deer antlers, sheep horn, walrus penis bone, mammoth tusk, and a dozen different woods.

I said, "The blade needs to be the length of my middle finger, and I want a wood handle." Wood is warmer in the hand but requires more maintenance than other handles.

"Your second knife is for throwing, as I recall," the knife maker said. "I have just the thing."

He walked to the jeweler's case, and I followed him, stepping around a bin of polishing cloths. He removed a cotton drape from the top of the case. I bent over the case, staring at its riches displayed on black felt.

I recognized a brass and iron *kilaya*, the knife of Tibetan Buddhists. But I pointed at another knife. "What is that?"

"A *kirpan*, a ceremonial knife Sikhs must wear. Every few weeks, a foreign journeyer appears at my barge—sometimes having walked for months, sometimes having come up the river from Shanghai—to obtain a blade."

The right side of the case contained the utility weapons: knives for hunting, wood carving, boning, skinning, fighting, and throwing. Kung lifted the glass to remove a slender knife with an ebony handle but no finger guard. A small brass washer—added to balance the blade—was between the wood and the brass butt. The blade had not been polished to a mirror finish to avoid reflections off the steel, but had a cloudy finish.

I asked, "May I try it?"

He lifted an arm. "The target board is over there, near the rag bin."

My arm moved, and the knife shot into the board with a smart clap.

"I don't have time to negotiate, Knife Maker Kung. How much for this throwing knife?"

"I have heard about your gold bars, and I would have charged you four gold bars," he said. "But you don't seem to be able to retain them."

"And I don't have any paper or silver money, either."

He scratched his scarred chin. "How will you pay for the knife? I worked on that knife for four days. Not my assistants, but me."

"With a service." I stepped across the shop and yanked out the knife from the wood. "Give me the knife now, and I'll perform a service for you in the future."

He smiled. "A service from Yellow Hair, adopted son of the eunuch Chang, is to be highly valued."

"I'm no longer his adopted son."

"So I've heard. But I accept your offer. Someday I will call on you."

"But I won't kill anyone for you," I said.

"Every service I would ever need from you involves killing someone. I have a list." He dropped his eyes to the knife. The wind shifted, blowing smoke down the stack and into the shop.

"China is in turmoil," Knife Maker Kung said. "No one can foresee what will happen here, and so I can't foresee what I might need in the future. But a round-eyed yellow-haired foreign devil might be useful someday. The knife is yours."

I bowed to him.

"Now I must sign it."

I gave him the weapon. No knife could truly be a Kung blade until it had been given the signature of Kung blood.

The knife maker asked, "Do you have a blood preference, Yellow Hair?"

"An arm will do fine."

He brought blade to his forearm and gashed his skin. Without the slightest suggestion of a flinch, he drew the blade three inches along his arm. Blood rose to the surface, covering the steel. Then he drew the knife up and down his arm until the blade was covered in blood.

He handed the knife to me, drops of blood falling to the floor from his arm and the knife.

I was careful not to wipe away the blood before putting the knife away in my clothing. I stepped toward the leather door.

"You are headed downriver?" the knife maker asked. More blood fell from his arm to the shop floor. "Back toward Chungking and the House of Eight Orchids?"

I nodded, and passed through the shop door and onto the gangplank. The dog was sitting by a banyan tree, looking at me.

Kung called after me, "Even with your three Kung knives, the odds will be heavily against you, Yellow Hair."

捌

The eunuch had never tended to my moral education, but I had gathered that Buddhism, Taoism, and Confucianism all taught that struggling against one's destiny is futile. One must accept one's fate. And far be it from me to question the teachings of these great religions.

"Big Moon, come here," I called, holding out a bowl of cooked fish. "Here, Big Moon."

The dog stared at me, his mammoth head low, his eyes as red as the coals in the knife maker's forge. He was fifty yards away, half-hidden by a flower pepper tree. His chest was as wide as mine, and the front legs were ham hocks. A string of saliva resembling an icicle hung from his jaw.

"Are you going to come here and eat this or not?" I lifted a piece of fish, held it up for him to see, then put it in my mouth and chewed in an exaggerated way. "It's good fresh fish." I smacked my lips and fanned the fish scent in his direction, emboldened because nobody I knew could possibly be witnessing this.

Big Moon rose from his flanks and emerged from behind the tree. He wasn't much smaller than that moronic mule, but the dog's ribs stuck out. I tipped the bowl so the dog could better see the contents.

He walked toward me ten yards and stopped.

I was at the Four Rocks Bend fish market, near Knife Maker Kung's barge. Stalls sold black carp, silver carp, grass carp, bighead carp, common carp, and crucian carp.

"Come, Big Moon." I wagged the cooked fish at him.

He padded closer on feet the size of dinner plates, his devil eyes watching my face, not the bowl. Even though I had three knives conveniently stored about my body, fear of this dog made hair on the back of my neck as straight as reeds.

Several hundred customers haggled with the vendors. Fishermen sat on logs at the shoreline, mending their fishing gear.

"Are you hungry?" My mouth was dry. "This fish is good. Have some."

The giant animal moved closer. I placed the bowl on the ground. The dog moved forward. His hot breath pushed against me. He consumed the fish in one loud, flew-flying quaff, as quickly as drawing a breath. He raised his head.

"So what now?" I was speaking English, as this monster didn't seem too Chinese—at least, not his round eyes. And they weren't red, it turned out, but brown. The red had been in my head, of course.

The dog was motionless, ten feet away. I moved a dozen steps back along the sand toward the fish market. The dog followed, and when I stopped, he stopped, still ten feet away. I climbed over a gray beach log, moving in the direction of the fish market. Big Moon leaped over the log, and stopped again, ten feet away.

I said, "I'm comfortable with that distance, if you are."

A Mongol freak show had stopped at the fish market, its junk moored out in the river. The banner hanging from the mainmast featured a three-legged man. The Kublai Khan Oddities Bazaar had been traveling the Yangtze since the time of Kublai Khan, it was said. When I was ten years old, the Kublai Khan Oddities Bazaar had been set up on a sandbar called the Number Four Washing Bar, downriver from the Chungking Wang Lung Men steps. I had paid two yuan to glimpse a

Yangtze mermaid. The fellow had pulled aside a booth's curtain, revealing a ghastly skeleton, which Eunuch Chang later that day had told me were bones of a river dolphin attached to a human pelvis and leg bones. He had sent the Rough Boys to wreck the freak show's tent and booths as a lesson regarding who they should avoid duping in the future.

Touts tried to wave me over to several booths where green and yellow flags were waving in the breeze. The main tent resembled a Mongolian yurt and was round and covered in felt. I walked around the tent toward the rope ring. Big Moon followed. A tout at a booth opened a curtain and called out about the frog boy inside. I averted my eyes. Another tout in front of a booth claimed that behind his curtain—which he would pull aside for three yuan—a man would remove paper and tobacco from a bag, and then roll and light a cigarette using only his tongue. At another booth, a fellow would lift aside the flap of his stomach to expose his intestines, for three yuan. I hurried along.

The gunship *Ingram* was coming from the coaling station down the river, as Commander Beals had said it would about then. Its bow slit the water as it came through Red Ox Gorge. Beals had said to signal him by waving a shirt, and he would pick me up. The gunboat had shown the stars and stripes as far as was navigable up the river, and had made its deliveries to the guerilla bands, and was headed back to Chungking.

Behind the tent was a hemp rope laid out in a circle on the sand. A wrestler lifted a young man off the ground, hoisted him over his head like a sack of rice, turned two circles to the hoots of the onlookers, then tossed the fellow out of the ring onto the sand. The young man scrambled to his feet, his face flushed to the color of a strawberry. The spectators' catcalls and laughter chasing him, he hurried away.

The freak show touts looked Han, but the wrestler must have been a Mongol. He was half a foot shorter than me and twice as wide. He grinned at the crowd, revealing broken black teeth.

I was going to test Big Moon's strength and allegiance.

I pushed passed several onlookers and stepped into the ring. "How much?"

The wrestler widened his smile. "If you last longer in the ring than I can hold my breath, I will pay you fifty yuan. If not, you pay me fifty yuan."

"I'll wager this knife." I held up my new Kung knife.

The wrestler's smile faded. "What is a foreign devil doing at the Four Rocks Bend fish market?"

"I'm going to throw you out of the rope ring, is what I'm doing."

The crowd was growing. A fisherman laughed and called out something in a language I didn't know.

I asked, "Do we have a wager?"

"Bataar accepts any challenge, even from skinny gweilos." He picked up sand to dry his hands and yanked on his robe to straighten it. "I'm going to break you in two before I heave you out of the ring."

The onlookers cheered. He stomped his feet in the sand and turned to the four compass points, bowing and touching his forehead.

The wrestler said, "You'll be sorry you ever came up the Yangtze."

I instinctively touched my right knife, but left it alone. The Mongol inhaled hugely and trapped the air in his lungs. Then he crouched and came at me.

Then began a bellow's roar—a low dreadful rumble that Bataar must not have heard. And when he grabbed my wrist, Big Moon appeared as if by sleight of hand, his fangs sinking into the wrestler's forearm. The dog began that crazy twisting and digging. The Mongol's bones crunched. Bataar howled with surprise and pain.

I called in English, "That's enough, Big Moon. Let go." I grabbed the giant dog around his neck—the first time I had ever touched him—and pulled him backwards. "Let go, Big Moon. That's a good dog. Let go now."

I scrambled backward, the dog's teeth still snagged deeply in Bataar's arm. I pulled the dog back and the dog pulled the Mongol. Bataar tripped forward onto the sand. I staggered under the dog's weight.

"Good dog, Big Moon. You can let him go now."

He released Bataar's arm, but the dog still hissed and blew and growled, spit flying from his mouth, his eyes drilling the wrestler. The crowd had retreated a dozen yards.

"You can take it easy, Big Moon. I'm okay." I released Big Moon's neck.

Blood seeped through the sleeve of Bataar's robe. He rose to his knees, then his feet. Sand stuck to his robe, maybe for the first time. He brushed it off with his good arm, not looking at me. Dewlaps pulled back to expose fangs almost the size of railroad spikes, Big Moon moved sideways to keep himself between the wrestler and me. The fur along his spine was sticking straight up.

I walked away from the rope circle and the crowd and the Mongol. Big Moon followed, ten feet behind me.

I said over my shoulder, "You are one fine dog, Big Moon."

The dog and I walked by the yurt toward the river. Now I had three knives and one hell dog. The odds were evening out.

20

"How do I look?" Tsingtao Lily tried to brush a strand of hair from her face, but her hand fell back to the pillow.

I moved her hair back with my fingers. "Not the best I've seen you."

I could feel the heat of her forehead. Her cheeks were sunken and pale. Her lips were cracked, and her eyes were lusterless. A Gold Tooth monk had told me where she was and hadn't charged me anything for the information. From the Mongol freak show, I had traveled downriver on a sampan for half a day and had arrived on board the gunboat a few moments before.

"How long have you been in here?" I was sitting on a stool next to her cot. I leaned toward her to hear her low voice.

"I don't know," she said. "I sleep a lot."

"Are the sailors taking good care of you?"

She groaned and tried to turn sideways but collapsed back to the pillow. "My leg."

I'd survived cholera when I was twenty-two, and I knew the symptoms. I remembered the ferocious cramping. I pulled back her blanket and straightened her leg, then kneaded her calf and pulled down her toes, freeing the muscles. These were the legs that had scandalized China in the western *Showdown at Eldorado*, a film made in Hong Kong with a Chinese cast, where Lily had performed a cancan.

She whispered, "That's better."

I replaced the blanket over her legs. A vomit bucket was near the cot, and a glass and pitcher were on a folding table. I wiped her forehead with a damp cloth.

We were in the *Ingram*'s wardroom, where four cholera-stricken sailors also lay on cots. Two coolies with buckets and rags wiped the walls, and the wardroom smelled of bleach. Every surface on *Ingram* was being disinfected.

She asked, "When will we arrive in Chungking?"

"Tomorrow. Lily, do you think maybe you should go home to Tsingtao for a while? To be with your family?"

She shook her head, a slight movement. Her English was passable, but we were speaking Mandarin.

"You are going to be weak for a long time," I said, "and maybe your mother and father could best look after you. I'll take you there myself."

"You said you would return me to Chungking."

"You are going to need a lot of care, and who will look after you in Chungking?" I held the water glass to her lips.

She sipped the water, then smiled, a feeble effort. "You are sweet."

"That's what everybody says." Not one person in my entire life.

"But you still don't know much about my life. There are a lot of people in Chungking who will look after me. I'll be fine, and don't worry about me."

From the hatch, Commander Beals said, "John, we're coming up on the junk you described."

I squeezed Lily's hand, and followed Beals along the gangway to the *Ingram*'s forward deck. Beals said, "The current here is three knots, and we're making eight knots over the ground. We'll be on them in a moment." He called up to the bridge. "Get Sergeant Johnson up here." The sergeant was a marine.

Red Leery, at his three-inch gun on the bridge, called down, "Your dog is going to need to be quarantined if you take him to the States, John."

Big Moon sat at the forepeak, his tongue out. I had placed a bowl of water near him.

"How long is the quarantine?" I asked.

"Judging from the look of your dog, it'll be about fifteen years."

The *Ingram* was moving at the speed of the wind. I had to lean against the rail to see much because coal smoke from the stacks lingered on the deck, circling Leery's gun and curling against the gunwale. The sun was a gray disk through the smoke. The junk was ahead of us, and it was Eunuch Chang's boat, no mistake. Silver dragons were inlaid on the rail. No damage from the rollover at the rapids was visible.

"What do you want me to do?" Beals asked.

"Get closer. I can't see her yet."

Big Moon moved to the rail, putting himself between Beals and me. He looked at the commander.

Beals asked, "Can't you get rid of this damned dog?"

"I've tried. Nothing works."

The *Ingram* closed on the junk. The junkmaster was at the rudder, but the boat was drifting with the current. Sergeant Johnson came onto the deck, carrying a rifle with a telescope. He was wearing olive fatigues and a cloth campaign hat. He had a seamed face and predatory eyes. He spit snoose over the rail. "Give me a target. You be the spotter, Commander. Tell me if my shot is too high or too low, and I'll adjust the scope."

Two other sailors were on the foredeck, having just arrived from the *Ingram*'s magazine. One held a shell, and the other stood near a wood cart of shells. Red Leery cranked the three-inch gun's elevator control, lowering the barrel. "I'd like a target, too."

The gunboat drew abreast of the junk. The wind shifted, clearing the air of smoke. Elizabeth came into view. Her hands were tied behind her back to the mizzenmast. She was slumped to the deck, her head on her chest. Her red hair was all about, and hid her face. She was wearing the same green dress as the last time I had seen her. One foot was out in front of her, and the other was hidden under the dress. She didn't look up. The junkmaster was a few feet behind her, the rudder handle tucked under an arm.

Madam Tuan was on a stool next to the mizzenmast, staring up at me. Her razor nail protectors were at the doctor's throat. Her yellow robe with an embroidered red phoenix hung from her loosely as if from a pole. She made a sawing motion with the nail protectors. The doctor and the mast hid most of Madam Tuan, but I could see her vulpine smile.

The marine brought up his rifle. "I'll put a bullet through that old hag's head, you want me to."

"She is hidden too well behind the mast," I said.

"No, she ain't." Sergeant Johnson worked the rifle's bolt.

Elizabeth's head rose. Her gaze found me. She may have tried to say something, but her eyes closed and her head lowered.

From the gun, Leery called, "You want me to sink that junk, Skipper?"

Beals signaled the bridge, and *Ingram* slid closer to the junk, the rails almost touching. The commander had told me that Idaho Senator Borah had spoken with the chief of naval operations, Admiral William Leahy, who had ordered the Yangtze Patrol to do anything it could to assist Dr. Elizabeth Hanley, a citizen of the great state of Idaho.

The commander said, "I'll do what you think is best, John. We can cripple the junk, or Sergeant Johnson will shoot the old lady, or the marines and sailors will board it."

"They are luring me back to Chungking," I said. "They won't harm the doctor, because they know I'll follow her. That's what they want."

"So what do you want me to do?" Beals asked.

"There's no sense risking Dr. Hanley out here."

"We can't be too much help to you back in Chungking." Beals gestured with an arm.

Between the commander and me, Big Moon snarled.

With a jerk, Beals dropped his arm. "Out here, we control the river. In Chungking, we don't control much of anything. You'll be pretty much on your own."

"I can't risk it now, with that old lady standing near Dr. Hanley."

"That lady in the yellow?" the Marine asked. "She's just a shrunken old crone."

"Sergeant, you know a lot about many subjects." My voice was grim. "But you don't know anything about Madam Tuan."

He lowered the rifle. Aft along the *Ingram*'s deck, three other marines were waiting for an order to board, bayonets on their rifles.

"Can I tell you something I learned at the Naval Academy?" Beals asked. "When you get back to Chungking, hit these people hard. Don't sit around and wait for them to make a move."

"Hitting them hard is precisely my plan."

Eunuch Chang must have despised me more than he cared for his junk or Madam Tuan or himself. His head appeared in the poopdeck's hatch, then his arms. He was carrying a US-government-issue Colt .45, and he emptied the magazine in my direction. Anger must have been marring his aim, as he missed me entirely. A sailor next to me yelped, and when he grabbed his shoulder, blood seeped through his fingers, a flesh wound.

Big Moon howled. He was down on the deck. His legs were under him at odd angles, and blood poured from his neck.

捌

A gray apron from the galley covered Commander Beals's shirt and pants. "What's your dog's name?" He lifted a square of cloth from the tray at his feet.

"Big Moon," I said. "Have you ever operated on a dog before?"

"One time I pulled a bullet out of a sailor's thigh."

Big Moon lay on the wardroom's table. His eyes were open, and he breathed in short gulps. He whimpered, and I imagined he tried not to. Blood had leaked from the wound at his neck and had covered the table under him and dripped to the deck.

After Eunuch Chang had emptied the pistol at the *Ingram*, he had stepped behind Elizabeth and had held a knife to her throat. Commander Beals had ordered his gunboat to pull away from the junk.

"Is he going to make it?" I asked.

"He doesn't look good, John. He's bleeding to death." Sweat dappled the commander's forehead.

I put my hand on the dog's head. Red Leery had found the spent bullet that had torn through the top of Big Moon's neck, so Beals didn't have to probe for a bullet inside the dog. Red stood between the commander and me at the side of the table, holding the dog's rear legs.

Beals brought up a bottle from the tray and poured fluid onto his cloth. "I'm going to open the wound and clean it out. Grab his head."

I gripped the dog's skin behind his ears. The dog's breathing became more shallow. With his fingers, Beals pushed open the wound. The dog bleated and jerked his head, but I held on.

Beals wiped the alcohol-soaked rag inside the gash. Big Moon convulsed, but I applied some of my weight to the dog, keeping him down on the table.

The skipper held up the bloody rag. "If there were dirt or rust or anything in there, I don't see it on the cloth. Maybe it's clean." He brought up a black bottle. "This is Mercurochrome. It's going to sting like hell, so hold on."

I gathered Big Moon's head in my arms, pressing his ears and his muzzle and eyes into my chest. He was silent and still, and I wondered if he had just died. Then his dewlaps flapped as he exhaled.

I touched my forehead to his head. "Hold on there, Big Moon."

The Mercurochrome splashed into the wound, and Big Moon shivered.

My head was low against Big Moon's, so I didn't see Beals bring up the needle. My eye was an inch from his, and he stared at me.

Beals said, "I'm going to start pushing this needle through."

"He don't look too good," Leery said.

"That's one stitch," Beals said. "Here we go with another. Just a couple more minutes."

Leery said, "This dog don't look like he's got a couple more minutes."

I re-gripped the dog's massive head and whispered into his ear, "Don't leave me alone, Big Moon."

捌

The butler at the American consulate had told me that Rupert Burkland had an appointment with Chiang Kai-shek at Chiang's compound in Huang Shang, and so I crossed the river in a ferry, intending to intercept him at the compound's gate. His meeting must have already ended, because he was coming down Bamboo Slanted Street in a sedan chair held aloft by two coolies. The consul was wearing a gray suit and held the sides of the chair with both hands as he bounced along. I hailed him, and he ordered the coolies to stop.

He looked down from the chair. "I saw the *Ingram* pull in an hour ago, across the river. You were on it? Commander Beals hadn't told me an army officer would be aboard." The last time Burkland had seen me, which was in his office, I had been wearing a major's uniform.

Air-raid sirens began to wind up. Coolies used a pole to raise the red lanterns on the roof of the Nationalist Bank of South China, and others lowered the consul's chair to the granite stones and fled. Burkland rose from the chair, straightening his tie. A cigarette seller and a boy pulling a Manchurian pony ran past, then a policeman in a green papier-mâché helmet. Many sirens sounded, and their rising and falling wails came from all directions.

"I don't know this neighborhood," Burkland said. "Where is a dugout?"

I led him along Pintail Street, a steep cobblestone path that led to a cliff above the river. Rickshaws and wheelbarrows had been abandoned at the sound of the sirens. We were in a flow of people running toward the dugout. The Japanese bombers came on rare days when the Chungking haze had lifted. The sky overhead was milky blue. The street was so steep that I walked sideways, a hand almost on the grimy stones. The Yangtze was below us, the *Ingram* at its dock across the river. At a stall that sold white radishes and fuzzy melons, Burkland and I turned onto Harmonious Sisters Street.

The cave entrance was ten feet wide, and low. Burkland and I ducked as we stepped into the dugout. Water leaked down the granite walls. Dozens of dugouts had been dynamited out of the stone for use as air-raid shelters in Chungking. The consul and I moved toward the back, pushed along by the crowd.

A single overhead bulb hung from the stone ceiling, and the back of the cave was dark. I stepped farther back, bumping into an old lady wearing a purple scarf over her head. Burkland and I were shoulder to shoulder, and he backed into a butcher wearing a bloody apron. A baby cried, and two men continued a loud argument that might have begun before the sirens started. A mushroom vendor tried to bring his cart into the cave but was pushed back. He left the cart outside and returned.

The sirens must have interrupted a wedding, as a young man in a blue Tibetan felt gown and black silk vest was wedged against his bride, who wore red silk. More people entered the cave, and we stepped back. Women lifted children onto their shoulders so they wouldn't be crushed. The cave smelled of tobacco, perfume, rotten teeth, and old sweat, and dank water dripped from the ceiling.

Burkland said, "You are out of uniform, Major. What's the occasion?"

"I'm doing what Eunuch Chang taught me to do; strike first and strike hard."

The consul smiled. "I've heard stories about a Eunuch Chang. But I'm not following you."

"I'm not in the marines. My name isn't Ronald Case."

He looked at me. "I've seen your identification."

"All those documents were forgeries."

He said, "Do I need to have you arrested?"

"My name is John Burke Wade Jr." It was the first time I had said my name since Elizabeth had revealed it to me. I struggled with it, and it sounded foreign, but I no longer had a home in China, and I liked the sound of my new name.

Burkland scratched his chin. "One of our earliest American consuls here in Chungking was named John Burke Wade. His photo is in my office."

"He was my father."

"That can't be. His two sons disappeared when the oldest was about five, and . . ." Burkland stopped speaking. "You are John Wade's son?"

"Eunuch Chang raised me. I am called Yellow Hair."

"I have heard rumors, and I have made inquiries." Burkland smiled again. "The Office of Naval Intelligence has told me there is no Yellow Hair in Chungking and—in a bit of uncharacteristic humor—said there is no Father Christmas, either, and they asked me to kindly not bother them again with such inquiries."

The sirens were muted this far into the cave, but the cave was filled with the sounds of coughing and wheezing and spitting. A hundred people had lit cigarettes, and the stone ceiling became hidden in smoke.

Burkland continued, "But the Kuomintang Intelligence Liaison Office has assured me that Yellow Hair indeed exists, that he is a vicious knife fighter, and that the French sent him to China to sow confusion and defeatism. But I had concluded that Yellow Hair is a myth."

Outside the cave, a whistle blew. No Japanese bombers had appeared. A false alarm. The crowd surged toward the cave entrance.

Burkland yelped. He jerked up his hand. "What the hell happened?" He held his hand up in front of him, but it was backlit by the cave entrance. "What bit me?"

I had carved the letter *Y* on the back of his hand with my number-two knife. Just some scratches that wouldn't even require a bandage.

"Damn, that hurts." He pressed his hand to his mouth. "What happened to my hand?" He looked over his shoulder, maybe looking for an animal.

We walked from the cave. I squinted against the light.

I held up the knife. A small smear of blood was on the tip. "Consul, listen closely."

"Do you always go around carving up people, for God's sake?"

"I am Yellow Hair, and I engraved my calling card on the back of your hand, but more than that, proof that what I am telling you is in earnest." I slipped the knife away. "My friend One Eye Gao Bai and I visited you in fake uniforms and presented forged documents as part of Eunuch Chang's plan to steal the gold shipment coming up the river to Chungking on the Dollar Line steamship *Monongahela*. I want to warn you about it."

Perhaps feeling undignified sucking on his hand, he put it in his pants pocket.

"Posing as marine corp and Kuomintang officers, we were going to receive the gold from the ship. The *Monongahela* arrives in Chungking tomorrow, but the gold will never. And even if you are dockside for the delivery, it still will never reach you. Unless . . ."

Burkland asked, "If you aren't part of the plan, how will it be stolen?"

"The eunuch told me the gold on the *Monongahela* will be his largest prize ever. With me or without me, he won't give up trying to take it from you." My tone was full and bitter. "I'm returning to the House of Eight Orchids, and I don't know if I will survive the visit. I'm telling you about the eunuch's plan so that, even if I am killed, you might foil the eunuch's plan and deplete his money purse.

"I know Eunuch Chang better than I know myself. He will come up with another plan. I suggest you station lots of marines and sailors around the shipment from the moment it leaves the steamship until it gets to Chiang Kai-shek. Not his valets or his bodyguards or a KMT company, but Chiang personally."

We walked back up Pintail Street, stepping around a knot of children eating the pieces of a watermelon that must have fallen off a cart. When we reached Burkland's sedan chair, his coolies swiftly returned to help him in.

Burkland said, "You and the eunuch have had a falling out, I take it."

"These past few weeks I've discovered that Eunuch Chang's way may not be my way, after all."

I left him on Bamboo Slanted Street. I had just hit Eunuch Chang hard, ruining his largest prize ever. I headed toward the House of Eight Orchids.

捌

I folded over a thick wool blanket twice, then tossed it up onto the wall so that it covered the glass shards. I had waited until daylight had faded, and now the stars were descending. The moon was not yet out.

I rose to my toes and leaped to grab the top of the wall. My feet scrambled against the wall, and I pulled myself up. I could feel the glass fragments under the blanket. I rolled over and dropped into the sand on the other side. I was inside Eunuch Chang's compound, behind the Englishman's room. When the eunuch was not in residence, the Rough Boys were allowed to roam the compound. Commander Beals had said the eunuch's junk could not possibly arrive in Chungking before morning, so I assumed Eunuch Chang wasn't here.

I stayed well clear of the irresistible snare near the whipping post. Moving on the gravel between the wall and the kitchen, I rolled my feet as I walked, as the Shaolin Temple monk had taught me, but the rocks still crunched loudly under my feet. I peered around the corner of the kitchen. Most of the compound was hidden by darkness. Light came through windows of the library and the training room. I moved forward, along a walkway toward the library, passing between camellia trees on the fragrant, azalea-lined path.

A sound came from my right, someone clearing his throat. I stepped off the path, cocking my ear in that direction. The darkness was impenetrable, so I walked soundlessly and with a hand out in a planting bed, crossed a gravel path, and moved along another planting bed, this one filled with purple cabbages.

A light illuminated the Mongol Munokio on a bridge over a lily pond, his cutlass at his side. Also on his belt was a holster. He held up an oil lamp, spit into the water, and walked across the bridge, away from me. He called out something, and another Rough Boy appeared when the lamplight reached the end of the bridge. He carried a rifle over his shoulder.

I moved toward the library, away from the pond, passing a stand of plum trees I had played in as a child. I kept to the soft flower beds, as silent as a stone. I turned the corner at the library.

"John?"

My number-one knife was out before my name was completed.

"It's me, Huiqing." She was the girl who had lit the Englishman's opium every evening. I whispered, "What are you doing out here?"

"Visiting the latrine." She stepped into my arms, looking so familiar with her hair secured behind her head with a straw. "Eunuch Chang told us you were dead. I'm so glad to see you. I missed you." I had always thought her name was apt; *huiqing* means "affectionate."

I gently pushed her away. "You can do me a favor."

"Anything."

"Go toward the pond, and walk as loudly as you can, and hum a tune."

"So the Rough Boys won't hear you?"

"Distract them for five minutes," I whispered. "That's all I need."

"Are you coming back to the House of Eight Orchids someday?"

"Eunuch Chang will never forgive me." I gripped her hand, then started toward the training room. "Good-bye, Huiqing."

Wisteria grew over an arbor that led to the building. Behind me, Huiqing began singing "The Sun Will Forever Shine on the Kuomintang." Then she spoke a few words to herself and kicked gravel. The Mongol Munokio yelled at her, but she laughed at him and continued with her song, louder this time.

I pushed open the door to the training room and walked across the padded mats. Eunuch Chang had surrounded himself with the trappings of wealth—his scrolls, the wall hangings, his longcase clock, his silk robes—but I believe he cared little for any of it. They were props, things for him to stand near or dress himself in. Without a thought, he had destroyed it all when leprosy infected the compound, which I now realized was a panicked and crazed reaction. He didn't care for any of it. Except for one item.

I reached to the top shelf and brought down the jar that contained Eunuch Chang's pao, his privates that had been cut from him forty years ago. Liquid sloshed inside, some sort of preservative.

Clausewitz taught that the best defense was an attack. That afternoon I had cost the eunuch his largest prize ever when I revealed his scheme to the American consul, and now I was taking the only thing that mattered to him, the pao in the jar. I was attacking.

I left the training room. Out in the darkness Huiqing was yelling at Mongol Munokio for some pretended offense. I slipped behind the kitchen and ran to the wall. I removed my jacket, tied the jar inside it, then put the sleeves between my teeth. I leaped up the wall, my hands landing on the blanket.

I leapt down, the jar gripped in my jaws.

捌

Tsingtao Lily peeled potatoes in the wardroom, leaning back against the bulkhead with a wood bowl of peels on her lap and a gunnysack of potatoes at her feet. She wore a galley apron and a sailor's work dungarees and shirt. Her luxurious hair was held behind her head with a length of rawhide. I had just come from the eunuch's compound.

I lowered myself to the bench next to her. "You're good with a peeling knife."

"And I've steamed a lot of rice and plucked hundreds of chickens."

My number-two knife slipped into my hand, and I grabbed a potato. I leaned toward her so the peels would fall into her bowl, and we both sliced off lengths of potato skin.

I said, "One day you're driving a Packard Deluxe Eight, and the next day you're peeling potatoes on an American gunboat. I'm not sure such things can happen in Canada or America or France. Only here in China." This had been one of the Englishman's great themes—only in crazy China—and I was happy to sound profound in front of Lily.

"I don't own a Packard." She reached for another potato.

"I've seen a dozen photos of you driving your Packard. One day the same photo of you and that car—you had a fur stole wrapped around your neck—appeared in all seven Chungking papers."

"Gold Coast Studio rented the Packard for a week," she said. "The photographs were taken by their publicity department. I don't own any horses, either. Those same photographers were assigned to take pictures of me at the Shatin stables in Hong Kong. I can't ride a horse, and those photographs were taken in the few moments I wasn't falling off the horse or climbing back on. I wore purple bruises for a week."

The scent of roses drifted from her. Strands of her hair had fallen to her shoulders, partly hiding her face.

"But you got to meet Clark Gable," I said.

"My manager and I waited in the Raffles Hotel lobby—standing between the umbrella stand made of an elephant's foot and a cage of blue and red macaws—for three hours until Clark Gable arrived with his retinue. My manager rushed over to his manager, negotiated for fifteen seconds, then passed Clark's manager a wad of currency. Clark was then led into the Long Bar, where he was seated at a table with me, the Gold Coast Studio photographer snapping photos frantically for the five minutes the managers had agreed on. Then Clark said good-bye and left the bar. Rumors of my affair with Clark Gable appeared in a hundred newspapers, along with the photos."

The knife was motionless in my hand, a half-peeled potato in the other hand.

"And those gowns I'm always wearing in the photographs—couture from around the world, from Madeleine Vionnet and Lucien Lelong, and that Dorothy Gish wide-shouldered jacket I wore in Shanghai, and that print dress with long sleeves just like the Queen Consort Elizabeth wore when she visited Paris. Those clothes are all fabricated by the studio's costume departments. They are quickly made fakes."

"How about your three dogs—Ching and Ming and Ling?"

"Those three awful dogs belong to the wife of Two Rivers Film's president. They were props, just like all the rest of it." She let her peeled potato fall into the bowl. "My entire glamorous life was a studio production, Yellow Hair."

Red Leery came into the wardroom carrying a bowl and a folded cloth. He removed one of the malaria sailor's blankets, dipped the cloth into the bucket, and wiped the sailor's arms and shoulders and neck. The sailor moaned.

Red said, "In five minutes, Tommy, you'll be cleaner than you were back home in Oklahoma City."

"I save every yuan I earn," Lily said. "And I'm going to be famous for as long as studios will cast me. I'm not going to end up a forgotten and suffering wife of a metal-fabricating-plant owner, which was my father's plan for me. Acting—and all the pretending arranged by the studios that goes along with it—will free me from spending my life serving rice and tea to ingrates, as my two older sisters do."

I peeled a potato. "You were a skilled actress in my room at the House of Eight Orchids. I almost had a heart attack when you undid the button at your neck."

"Some of me is real, John." She looked at me. "How do you know that was acting, down there with you in your room?"

"It was, wasn't it? I mean, you were acting, and you weren't really going to . . ."

"You'll never know." She laughed, a raucous belly laugh I'd never heard in any of her movies. "You'll just never know."

21

The sails were down on the eunuch's junk as the current carried the vessel toward the dock. When the junk's hull bumped the dock, two dockhands secured the lines to bollards. Eunuch Chang climbed through the hatch, then extended his hand back through the hatch to lift out Madam Tuan. Elizabeth was still tied to the mizzenmast. The eunuch grabbed her hair and lifted her head back. He freed her hands and seized her hair again to lift her to her feet. She staggered, but he held her upright. Madam Tuan's sedan chair was brought from belowdecks.

I watched from behind a boulder fifty yards upriver from the dock, the river water up to my knees. These were not the Wang Lung Men steps, with the endless circling of the water coolies, but were narrower and upstream a half mile. Some of the steps had been chipped out of granite, and others were wood. One Eye Gao Bai and the Mongol Munokio descended the cliff on the steps, Munokio's scabbard scraping each step. Six Rough Boys followed them and lined the steps. The eunuch was wearing a blue silk robe with yellow dragons embroidered on the sleeves. The wind shifted his queue. The deckhands placed a gangplank between the boat and the river, and some served as chair bearers, and when Madam Tuan was on the seat, they lifted the chair's poles to their shoulders and carried her across the gangplank to the pier.

My plan—if it could be called that—was to snatch Elizabeth before she could be taken to the House of Eight Orchids. She would be easier to grab on Chungking's streets than in the eunuch's compound. But when Gao and Munokio and the Rough Boys had appeared at the dock, my options vanished. I would have to wait.

Eunuch Chang crossed the gangplank, a hand on Elizabeth's arm. She hobbled rather than walked, clearly aching from being tied to the mast. And her malaria must have been ravaging her. Her head was down, and her hair hid her face. Munokio spoke to the eunuch, but I was too far away to hear them.

The eunuch always insisted on hearing bad news as soon as possible, and he was hearing bad news, standing there on the dock. He was being told, undoubtedly, that his pao had been stolen from the training room. Color drained from the eunuch's face.

I had lived with Eunuch Chang a quarter of a century. In all that time, I had never heard him raise his voice. He never yelled in anger. When he delivered punishment, it was with dispassion. He neither laughed nor wept. His self-control was a source of his power over others. His discipline was frightening.

On the dock, hearing the news from the Mongol Munokio, his discipline fled him. He shouted at Munokio—I could hear his voice but not make out the word—then hit him in the chest. When the Mongol doubled over, gasping for breath, Eunuch Chang flipped him off the dock and into the shallow water between the dock and the beach. The eunuch shouted at Gao, his face right in Gao's, and apparently the yelling wasn't enough, so he seized Gao's ear in the way I had learned was excruciating, and he yelled more. Then he roughly grabbed Elizabeth's arm and started up the stairs. The Rough Boys moved aside for them, then followed them up the cliff toward the town. Gao pulled Munokio from the water, rolling him onto the pier. Munokio rose to his knees but doubled over, coughing, water dripping from his shirt and pants. Even at this distance, I could see he still retained his cutlass.

I leaned back against another boulder. Eunuch Chang's pao was safely aboard the *Ingram*. Red Leery had asked me what was inside the jar, and I had told him it was better if he didn't know.

The chances of rescuing Elizabeth were slim, particularly if I wanted to stay alive. But I had badly rattled the eunuch, and so my prospects were getting better. I left the boulder and waded toward the steps.

捌

Commander Beals and I were breathing hard when we reached the top of Xi Shan, the stony summit that overlooks Chungking from the west. Two extra pistol magazines in Beals's pocket had clicked together all the way. I stepped around stunted juniper trees and pushed through a black pepper bush. Green lichen spotted the boulders, and cheatgrass grew from cracks in the stone. Xi Shan wasn't much of a mountain, and should have been called a hill, with its summit four hundred feet higher than Chungking's main street, Min Sheng.

The air was cooler at the summit. To the north was the Jialing River, which joined the Yangtze at Chungking, but the Jialing couldn't be seen from Xi Shan due to the ever-present gray haze. The *Ingram* and the *Falcon*, a British gunboat, were visible on the other side of the Yangtze, but the fields and hills beyond them were obscured by fog.

Beals sat on a boulder that faced the city. "This should do it."

He had carried the Zeiss Asiola telescope that was stored on *Ingram*'s bridge. I had brought up the wood tripod. The telescope was eighteen inches long and protected by black rubber. Stamped on the eyepiece rim was *42X*, the scope's magnification. Beals opened the tripod and mounted the scope on the tripod bolt.

"Sometimes when researching the book, I can't get close to a shrine," Beals said, "when the shrine is on a cliff or across a river. One time the

Communists were garrisoned near one, and I didn't want anything to do with them. So I use this scope and write down everything about the shrine I can see through the scope."

The haze filtered the sun, and all of Chungking below us was bled of color and was as gray as the sky. A shrike with a long gray tail landed in a pine tree downhill and chirruped loudly. The hill was so steep that when I shifted my foot, small stones rolled away.

"Extend the tripod's far leg so the scope is level on the slope." Beals passed me the tripod and scope. He was wearing a dark-blue peacoat, canvas work pants, and marine corp boots. Under the peacoat was a .45 in a holster.

"Focus by twisting that ring around the eyepiece," the commander said. "First, find the compound with your naked eye and aim the scope in that direction; then look through the eyepiece."

The House of Eight Orchids was about a mile away, in an area with more trees and wider streets than most of Chungking. Chiang Kai-shek's generals lived in the neighborhood. I found the House of Eight Orchids and brought my eye to the telescope, and the eunuch's compound seemed to leap toward me. The west wall was fuzzy, so I turned the eyepiece, and it came into focus. I'd used binoculars before, but never anything like this Zeiss scope. It made Chungking smaller and closer, and much was visible even through the haze.

I nudged the scope, and moved the view along the west wall, then over the wall to the kitchen roof, and then the training room and the orchid greenhouse. And I could see Elizabeth. She was tied to the whipping post behind the men's privy, where I had been punished for smoking the Englishman's opium pipe years ago. She hung by her arms, her head down and her legs out in front of her. I moved the viewing field, but I couldn't see the eunuch or Madam Tuan. Eight or nine Rough Boys walked the compound. Some carried rifles. I couldn't tell which one was the Mongol, and I didn't see One Eye Gao.

"Let me take a look," Beals said. "Move over so you don't move the scope off target."

I slid sideways, and Beals looked through the telescope. "They aren't treating her too kindly, looks like."

A crow flew below us.

Beals asked, "Are you going to try to get Elizabeth out of there?"

"That's what the eunuch hopes I'll do. He is down there, waiting."

"How are you going to do it?"

"I'm working on it."

"Without getting yourself killed."

"I'm working on that, too," I said.

"Why don't I send marines?" Beals asked. "They'll go into the eunuch's compound like they did at Belleau Wood and take the place straightaway."

I shook my head. "He'd disappear into the city before the marines got there and take Elizabeth with him. He's waiting for me. If I go in alone, he'll be there."

"She's not going to last long, hung from a pole like that." Beals brought his head up from the telescope. "*Ingram*'s sailors and marines would be happy to help you." He unscrewed the scope from the tripod.

"Maybe when the times comes." I rose from the boulder and dusted my trousers.

I said, "But first I'm going to take Tsingtao Lily back to the movies."

捌

Yanyu—a squat woman wearing an apron that made her resemble a Mongol yurt—applied an orange hue to Tsingtao Lily's cheek, using a horsetail brush. We were in an alley across the street from the Two Rivers Film Production Company, Tsingtao Lily's movie studio, which Gao and I had set on fire. The lot was covered with charred rubble, but the studio had moved into a vacant building fifty yards down Sinkhole Street. The studio's name had been painted above the door, but otherwise the building still looked like the Japanese Overseas Bank, made of yellow brick, with small windows, and a crenulated wall at the roofline. Buildings in the next block had been destroyed by Japanese bombs, and gray smoke still rose from the ashes.

Lily was sitting on a short stool. Yanyu hovered over her. A suitcase with fold-down legs next to Yanyu contained brushes and pencils. Yanyu diligently applied eyeliner and lip color, and then more cheek color.

Gloomy and smelling of sewage, the alley was between a mat-shed and a wicker-furniture shop, and farther down the alley were poles hung with laundry.

I opened the newspaper I had been carrying, a copy of the *Chungking Morning Post*. The enormous headline read, "Tsingtao Lily Alive." A smaller headline read, "Brave Actress Foils Yangtze Pirates' Kidnap Attempt."

I asked, "Pirates kidnapped you?"

"Pirates would get the biggest headline." Lily laughed. "Everybody loves a pirate story."

"And it says here that for the last two weeks you've been a pleasure slave to Broken-Nose Xin, the Yangtze pirate king."

She laughed again. "The studio has a fellow who sends out press releases, and he also sends bribes to the newspaper reporters and photographers."

I skimmed the story. "And you barely escaped with your life after pushing Xin the pirate king into the river, and you were last seen dazed and walking along the Yangtze's shoreline toward Chungking."

"It's wonderful, isn't it?" Lily asked. "I've been out of the action too long. Now my photo will be in every newspaper in China."

Yanyu touched the tip of a pencil to Lily's eyebrow. Across the street, a mob was gathering. A dozen newspaper photographers carried Speed Graphic and Voigtländer cameras. Reporters held notepads and pencils. A Mitchell newsreel camera was on a tripod.

"The gentleman near the door wearing the gweilo jacket and tie is the studio president," Lily said. Passersby were gathering. A fellow pushing a wheelbarrow containing white ducks tied by neck strings lowered the handles and squatted in front of the wheelbarrow. A boy tethered a black donkey to a lamppost and climbed on its back for a better view. A lice man—wearing a tank on his back, a hand pump hanging from his belt, and a signboard that read "I Fix Your Itch"—slipped off the tank and rose to his toes to survey the scene. A pickpocket named Yongrul—whose hand I had punctured with a knife when I had discovered it in my pocket three years ago—loitered near the camera crane, I suppose looking for opportunities. A dumpling vendor put down his pot, and a seamstress lowered her wood crate of needles, thread, and cloth. Children appeared from doorways and pushed toward the front of the crowd. Even refugees in tattered clothing stopped to stare. Clouds parted, and the street was washed with sunlight.

"Those policemen have been hired by the studio," Lily said.

The policemen—ten or twelve of them—wore black uniforms and green helmets with truncheons dangling from their belts. They were stationed near the studio president. Yanyu lifted a bottle of rosewater from her case and applied the scent to Lily's neck.

When Yanyu nodded, Lily rose from the stool and removed her apron to reveal a dazzling blue-sequin gown that had been artfully torn along the neckline to expose her shoulder and had been ripped in a zigzag pattern from the hem to her rear end. A red dye had been applied along one sleeve, and it looked like blood.

"Does my hair look a bit untidy?" Lily asked.

Yanyu lifted several strands of Lily's hair from the pins so that they floated down to her neck.

"I learned to limp for my role in *Autumn Flower, Life on the Run*." Lily lifted a mirror from Yanyu's case. She stared at her reflection. "How do I look?"

"Beautiful and disheveled and plucky," I said. "You will be China's heroine who escaped a terrible fate to return to her faithful fans."

"Perfect, then." She turned to me. "Will you send me your address?"

"Don't visit me," I said. "Having you around is too dangerous."

She leaned closer, taking me in with her big eyes. The effect was powerful. "I'm sorry about your brother. I didn't mean to—"

"You've broken every man's heart in China, two hundred million of them. It's your nature, like a duckling taking to the water."

She kissed my cheek. "Good-bye, Yellow Hair."

She stepped from the alley into the light. The studio president called her name and pointed. The crowd turned as one. Tsingtao Lily limped forward, and the crowd parted. She had one hand on her shoulder as if holding up the dress. Her eyes were heavenward in a plea for strength. Her bare leg flashed from the dress with each halting step. A beam of sun seemed to pick her up and follow her, and everyone else on the street faded to dun.

The cameras clicked and rolled. The policemen formed a phalanx around her. Photographers shouted, "This way, Lily." A microphone was shoved at her. She gasped for breath, swayed, but managed to hold herself upright. She began her story of her escape from Broken-Nose Xin. The crowd pushed forward.

I turned back toward the river. I had kept my promise to Lily. I had taken her home.

22

I crossed the river on the steam ferry, climbed the Wang Lung Men steps between the rows of water coolies, and made my way west through Chungking's streets. I knew I was being watched.

I walked along Turn of Good Fortune Street, passing the French Bank of China, a gray stone building with turrets and battlements that was called the Bastille. At Green Jade Street, the brokers were selling jadeite and nephrite to jewelers. The stones were displayed in trays on tables. The brokers wore cotton robes with sleeves that hung over their hands. Jewelers reached up the wholesalers' sleeves to tap out their bids on the brokers' hands, hiding the bids from others at the market. I walked around a bomb crater half-filled with putrid water. I resisted the urge to look over my shoulder, back up the street at my follower.

The town became more industrial as I moved west. The street curved toward the river. With the Japanese threatening in eastern China, two thousand factories in Shanghai and Nanking had been taken apart bolt by bolt and moved upriver to Chungking, some on junks and barges, some on the backs of men. I passed a smelter, which had clay walls on three sides and was filled with crucibles of refractory clay containing the ore. Black smoke rose from the fire under the crucibles. Next to the smelter was the bellows hut. This road had been called Purple Flower

Lane until this winter, and was now known as Smelter Lane. I had been here last night, planning my route.

The road ended at the coal yard at the shoreline. Six junks lined a dock, each darkened with coal dust on their decks and masts. The yard was a maze of ten-foot-high coal rows. On the other side of the coal yard, coolies picked up baskets of coal to take to smelters and Chungking's electrical generators.

I walked into the yard and moved between two rows of coal. I couldn't see over them. Ahead, coolies loaded baskets with coal, headed for the smelters. I turned left and passed a twenty-foot pile of crushed iron ore, also being tended by coolies. The sky was low and gray, and smelter smoke drifted between the rows. I heard the Rough Boys coming behind me.

I spun around, too late. Mongol Munokio swung the flat side of his cutlass into my temple. I staggered but caught myself. A pistol was in the Mongol's other hand, its muzzle pointed at me. His eyes were small and mean.

He said, "The eunuch wants you alive, but he said I could shoot you if I saw any of your knives." His forehead was small, and his hairline began just above his eyebrows. His neck was a stump, and his head was a plug on the stump.

My vision was blurred from the blow. Always Hungry—who I had last seen striking the post in the Rough Boys' Yard—was with him. He was about sixteen, and he had been growing a queue, which hung to his shoulder blades. He wore hempen sandals, and he carried a coil of rope. He stepped toward me. My head was filled with pain. I took a step to test my legs.

"You can't get away, Yellow Hair," the Mongol said. "There are too many of us."

Three more Rough Boys ran around the coal pile toward me.

I took off, sprinting down the aisle between mounds of coal. The Mongol wouldn't shoot me, because Eunuch Chang had no use for my dead body. The eunuch wanted to personally oversee my transition from living to dead. I ran between coal rows, the Rough Boys following me.

I turned north at the end of a row, and two more Rough Boys blocked my path. I ran back, slipping out of Mongol Munokio's grasp, and ran down a narrow path between two coal rows.

It was a dead end. I tried to scramble up the pile of coal, but it gave way under my feet, and the Mongol and Always Hungry grabbed me and threw me to the ground. The other Rough Boys—eight or nine of them now—seized me, too.

The Mongol stuck the pistol barrel into my ear. "Keep your knives inside your clothing. I'll send a bullet through your head if I see them."

They yanked me to my feet. I could have sliced up a few of them, but they weren't much older than children.

Always Hungry wrapped my wrists together with rope. He pulled out my long knife. He laughed and held it up. "Here's one of his knives. I found it, and so it's mine."

"I get his next knife," one of the Rough Boys said. "How many does Yellow Hair have, do you think?"

"Nobody is taking any of my knives," I said.

The Mongol slammed a fist into my ear, and I fell to the coal-covered ground.

"Save your talk for the eunuch," he said. "Just do as I tell you."

Once again I was pulled to my feet by many hands. I swayed, and the Rough Boys pushed me upright. My vision had a red blur at the edges, and my head seemed to be issuing pain to all the rest of me. They had tied my hands behind me.

"Get going." The Mongol grabbed my arm. "Eunuch Chang is waiting."

My tongue was thick. I stumbled forward, nausea rising from the blows.

Mongol Munokio jerked me along the coal rows. "The eunuch and Madam Tuan are arguing over who is going to get you first."

Crowding around the Mongol and me, the Rough Boys pranced and laughed at their victory.

"You are careless, Mongol," I managed to say.

Perhaps he noticed something in my tone. It brought him up. He looked down the aisle between the coal mounds. Four United States Marines were double-timing from behind a pile of coal. Rifles were at the ready, and bayonets were fixed. They wore fatigues and boots and campaign caps. They blocked the aisle and raised their rifles. They resembled a firing squad.

The Mongol's mouth opened. He turned to flee, but the gunner's mate Red Leery appeared at the top of a pile of coal behind us. A pistol was in one of Leery's hands, and a three-foot pipe in the other. Four abreast, the marines marched toward us. Three other sailors crested the pile near the gunner.

"What do we do, Munokio?" Always Hungry yelled.

The Mongol pointed his cutlass at Sergeant Johnson. He said in Mandarin, "Eunuch Chang will punish you for this."

The marine sergeant walked right up to the Rough Boys. In English, he said, "Let me explain something to you, sonny." Johnson spun his rifle so that it flipped the cutlass out of the Mongol's hand, then sent the rifle butt into Mongol Munokio's forehead.

Munokio dropped, and his cutlass landed on a coal pile.

"You hurt?" Leery asked me, sliding down the coal. His pant legs were black up to his knees.

Johnson pulled off his bayonet and used it to cut my hands free.

Leery said, "We'll put all these boys in the *Ingram*'s hold. Lock them in there."

I was still swaying, my head feeling as if it were in a vice. The marines surrounded the Rough Boys.

"How long do you want us to keep them?" Sergeant Johnson asked.

"Twelve hours." The cloud in my head was disappearing. I started to walk back along the coal. "It'll be done by then. One way or the other."

捌

"Is the chair ready?" Commander Beals asked.

"At the dock," I said. "A room has been reserved at the Straw Broom Hotel."

We carried a munitions crate along *Ingram*'s deck, approaching the gangway. Four hours had passed since my visit to the coal yard, night had come, and the river was black below us. Sergeant Johnson was on duty at the gangplank. Beals had told the marine about our mission, and the sergeant hadn't liked it, but said it was his duty to follow any lawful order, and Beals had said there was at least a 30 percent chance the order was lawful. The sergeant had replied, "That's high enough for me."

Johnson said, "Can I do something more for you, John? Other than stand here at the gangplank. I ain't working up to my full marine potential on the YangPat Patrol."

"Maybe later."

I had a blue blanket slung over my shoulder as Beals and I lugged the crate down the gangplank and onto the dock. The *Falcon* was moored behind *Ingram*. Its hatches had been covered with tar paper so that no light escaped the boat, same as *Ingram*. Beals's dark peacoat and black watch cap blended in with the dark night.

Two chair bearers waited for us. Beals and I lowered the crate.

"What's that horrible noise?" I asked.

"The *Falcon*'s boatswain plays bagpipes every night, standing in the bow. He does it to torment us."

I flipped open the latch.

"So Red Leery gets up every morning before sunrise and goes to the aft rail and blows a bugle at them. He can't play. He just blows it."

I brushed my hands together, bracing myself.

Beals stepped back. "Be careful, John."

I lifted the top of the crate. A man was inside, almost invisible in the darkness. I helped him sit up and draped the blanket over his head and shoulders. Beals backed farther away.

"Ready, Shirong?" I asked in Mandarin.

"Whatever I can do, I will do," he said from inside the crate.

I helped lift his legs over the crate's edge, then walked him toward the sedan chair, which was on the ground, the two bearers standing between the poles. I lowered him to the seat. The bearers hoisted the poles to their shoulders while Beals hurried back up the gangplank. The American consulate was hidden behind a row of camellia trees.

I gave each bearer a silver Mex, a week's income for them. "There'll be another coin for each of you when we get to the hotel."

I led them inland on Big Fish Stream Road, past the darkened consulate toward the hotel.

捌

Chungking had two airfields. The Nine Dragon Slope airfield was open year-round, and the other was a nameless sandbar in the middle of the Yangtze, available only during low water in the winter and early spring. I was on the sandbar, an unlit torch in one hand and a sulfur match in the other. Yangtze sandbars were as yellow as gold bricks, but at night the sand was gray. The black river rustled past on both sides of the sandbar, and sampans had been pushed onto the sand.

Even though the Japanese bombers had not yet attacked after sundown, Chungking maintained blackouts every night, and so the city was a black smudge to the north, vaguely silhouetted by purple clouds behind it. Most of the *Ingram*'s crew was on the sandbar, though they were lost in darkness. We were in two long lines. On the sand twenty yards from me, Commander Beals carried an unlit torch.

A low sound came from the west and quickly grew louder. Airplanes, and more than one of them, it sounded like. Commander Beals blew a whistle. When I scraped the match with my thumb, it flared to life; then I applied it to the pitch-soaked rags on the torch, which sputtered and hissed, then caught fire. Along the sandbar, other torches were lit. Two lines of torches marked the landing strip. Across the strip from me, Sergeant Johnson's face flickered in his torch's light. The engine noise grew louder.

"Japanese spies watch the airstrips, we think," Commander Beals warned. "But at least at night they can't see what we remove from the planes."

An airplane appeared, remarkably close and low. The bluejackets held their torches high, and the lights lined the sand strip. The plane, a Stinson, dropped out of the black sky and touched the sand with two wheels. A second plane followed it down, and then a third. The Stinsons were painted dark blue or black, and even the American stars on the fuselages were a dark color, maybe gray. When the third plane had come to a stop, the bluejackets stabbed their torches into the sand to extinguish them. Sailors and marines ran toward the planes.

The Stinsons' engines remained running. As I neared the first plane, the fuselage hatch slid open. A Stinson crewman started passing out boxes to the sailors. Some of the boxes—containing weapons, undoubtedly—required a sailor on each end. The Japanese had conquered the lower Yangtze. Resupply was now by air. Red Leery and I carried a rifle box to a sampan, the gunner grunting with each step.

I ran back to the Stinson. Prop wash blew my jacket against my ribs. I called to the crewman, "Do you have a box marked 'medical supplies'?"

He ducked low and disappeared aft in the fuselage. When he came back, he tossed a white box to me.

I crossed the sand to Beals and held up the box. "Quinine. Your cable did the job."

The last of the crates were removed from the Stinsons. Engine exhaust was carried in the wind. Boxes were being loaded onto sampans. The lead plane began rolling down the sand.

I took a position next to Sergeant Johnson on a sampan's forward deck. The poleman maneuvered us toward the shore, not more than a hundred yards to the south. The sampan crossed the narrow branch of the Yangtze, and when the boat scraped against the south shore I leaped off. The following night the arms would be delivered to Chiang Kai-shek.

The sampan's hull pushed onto the beach between two boulders. Other boats scraped onto the beach, though I couldn't see them in the darkness. The river whispered against the hull.

Sergeant Johnson jumped onto the sand. "Beals has ordered me to look after you."

I helped him lift the box. Rifles were inside, or maybe a machine gun or two. The medicine was under my arm.

"I'm grateful," I said.

"You don't look like you need much babysitting, though."

He held one rope handle, and I had the other. We stepped between boulders, my feet slipping on river weed. Johnson moved over a boulder. "Wheelbarrows are just up on the tracker path."

Ahead, a black shadow formed out of the night. A sharp blow sounded above the lapping of the river. Johnson grunted and fell to his knees, dropping his end of the crate. One Eye Gao Bai came at me.

My right knife dropped into my hand, but his fist chopped into my shoulder with such force and precision that my entire left side went numb down to my knees. I started to topple, and his other fist rammed into my rib cage, and so then I had no control of anything and I toppled to the sand. I was paralyzed and helpless. Sergeant Johnson had fallen onto his side, and he groaned.

Gao picked up my knife, then grabbed the back of my shirt collar and dragged me deeper into the maze of boulders. My lungs wouldn't work.

When I tried to raise a hand, he struck my biceps so that my arm instantly went dead, and then so much pain shot up and down that my head rocked back.

He held my knife at my throat. "Madam Tuan told us that the red-haired gweilo woman would lure you back home to Chungking."

I tried to take a breath, but I felt as if Gao had removed my lungs and spine. The marines and sailors yelled back and forth on the trackers' path out in the darkness, loading the wheelbarrows.

Gao said, "But the eunuch didn't believe you would be so stupid as to chase a red-haired woman devil, so he sent me to find you."

I moaned, an unseemly sound. I tried to roll onto my side, but Gao kicked my shoulder right on the point, and he knew how to do it, and a new wave of agony coursed down me.

He said, "You convinced me—on the road to the cemetery—that loyalty to the eunuch was our duty, and I believed and trusted you. Then you turned around and betrayed him."

"Gao, he made us gangsters." I worked to generate words through the pain. "I never saw it before, or I acted automatically and never let myself think about it, but despite all his duty and honor talk, we are just plain criminals."

"The eunuch wants to kill you over the course of eight days. That's why he wants you back."

I coughed. I still had two knives on me, but I couldn't feel them. When I tried to close my hand, Gao slammed his knuckles into my wrist, the way I had been taught to do, and had done so many times.

Sergeant Johnson's foot scraped against the sand, but he didn't move anything else.

"I thought you were my brother," Gao said, "and you left me."

I managed to say, "Come with me."

"Never. I am the eunuch's son, just as you said I was."

He jerked up my trouser's leg and lowered my knife. A vast new universe of pain made me bite into my tongue, drawing blood. I felt as if Gao had set my leg on fire.

He held up a three-inch square of my skin that contained my brotherhood scar. He had skinned my calf. The flap was dripping blood. Then he pulled up his pants. A bandage was around his leg. He had cut off his own brotherhood scar, too.

"I have loved you as my brother too long to give you to the eunuch,"

Gao said, "but you and I are through forever. From this moment, you are dead to me."

He tossed the square of scarred skin into the river, and then he vanished into the darkness.

捌

Perfume bottles jangled together as Red Face Zixin pushed his cart up the hill along Nutmeg Street. He was bent into his task, and his face under his black cap was even more red than usual. His black vest—containing dozens of perfume sample bottles—weighed him down. Behind him, down Nutmeg Street, a green KMT sedan with wide fenders traveled toward Chiang Kai-shek's residence. A wheel on the cart dropped into a pothole, and Red Face Zixin grunted as he lifted a corner of the cart to free the wheel. Madam Tuan had cut off one of his toes, but he didn't limp as he maneuvered his cart.

I tried not to limp as I walked from between two gray-bark poplar trees. My leg felt as if One Eye Gao Bai were still cutting away at it. "Red Face Zixin, may I offer a business deal."

He straightened himself, and wiped sweat from his forehead with the short sleeve of his skivvy. "Something for a lady? There is nothing your wife or a lady friend might want in the entire world that I do not have on this cart." He lifted a glass bottle. "This scent arrived from Paris via Shanghai on a steamer just this morning. It is essence of wisteria, and I offer it for the same price as it is found in Shanghai, with no markup for its journey up the river."

I stepped to the cart, into a cloud of cloying odors. The array of rouges and lipsticks was near the front of the cart, and the perfumes at the rear.

"I'm not interested in anything for a lady," I said.

"Then you have come to the right vendor." Red Face looked left and right in an exaggerated way. "Something for the stamina, is it? Every man can use a boost, I know." He opened a drawer and lifted out a red leather bag. "From the territory known as Alaska in the far north. Powdered testicles of a black bear. Three pinches of the powder into a glass of rice wine. No more, or you will explode, if you take my meaning."

I said, "I want to rent your cart."

"My cart?" He expanded his chest. "This is my route and my territory. I pay the Black Goose every month for this right to sell along this route."

"I only need it for thirty minutes, and I'll pay you ten Mexes." This was more money than he would make in a month of peddling perfume. "I'll return your cart in exactly half an hour, right here."

Red Face sold his perfumes along Foreign Merchants Row and was probably accustomed to dealing with Westerners.

He said, "But my best customer is just up the street."

"You'll only be a minute or two late."

His eyes narrowed, and his lips moved silently. I suppose he was figuring his profit.

"And I want to rent your clothing," I said. "I need your sample vest and your cap. I'll give you my clothing to wear for the thirty minutes."

"Impossible."

"For another five Mexes."

Again his lips moved. "My cart and my clothing? Are you up to something wicked? I have a reputation in Chungking for selling the finest—"

"Make it another ten Mexes. Twenty-five in all." I pulled a bag of coins from my pocket and lifted them to his eye level. He would work two years for this much money. Commander Beals had leant me the money.

He smiled and reached for the bag. "You foreign devils always drive such hard bargains."

23

Madam Tuan was held upright by her maids, her arms around their shoulders. They helped her from the House of Eight Orchid's gate across a few feet of gravel to Red Face Zixin's cosmetics cart. She gripped an edge of the wagon to keep herself upright, and the maids retreated to the compound's wall.

She lifted a glass stopper from a perfume bottle. "Is this new, Red Face?"

Stitched white cranes ornamented her blue robe. Her hair was held behind her head with jade combs, her face had been painted pink, and her lips were dark red. The blades on her nail protectors reflected the morning light. Across the street were the homes of senior Nationalist officers. Camellia and plum trees lined the road.

"Is this from Paris?" She sniffed the stopper. "Where did you get this lovely scent? Does Madam Chiang wear it?"

She tested the perfumes laid out in rows in front of a bin of scented scarves. I had tucked Eunuch Chang's pao under the scarves. I was wearing Red Face Zixin's vest of many pockets, and his black cap. Under my trousers, my calf was wrapped in a bandage but still felt as if flames were working on my leg. I lowered the cart's handles and turned toward her.

"You and the eunuch gave my brother, William, a choice," I said.

She looked up, and her eyes widened and mouth parted. She tried to step back on her deformed feet and had to grab the cart for support.

"William was given a choice," I said. "He could save the Japanese pilot's privates, or he could have Tsingtao Lily. You remember, of course."

She inhaled, and she rearranged her face. She took me in with her eyes, from my head to my feet, contempt deeply etched into her face. "You—a traitor to the great Eunuch Chang—dare to speak to me?"

"Now you have a choice," I said. "Your head or your throat."

She laughed, a hideous cackle. "You threaten me, Yellow Hair? With one of your pretty little knives?" She clacked her nail protectors together.

The maids stepped farther away long the wall, their glances going back and forth between Madam Tuan and me.

One of the maids whispered, "Yellow Hair, please . . ."

"So, are you going to use one of your knives on me, Yellow Hair?" She shifted her weight on her hip, which forty years ago might have been provocative.

"Your head or your throat," I said. "Which is it to be?" The scents of perfume drifted up from Red Face's vest.

"Eunuch Chang spent years teaching you about knives, and now you are going to cut a woman?" She laughed again. "I was right when I told him you would never amount to anything."

"I could never cut a woman." I smiled.

"Because you are weak," she said. "You've always been weak."

"Make your choice," I said.

She said, "I wanted to drown you when you were a child but Eunuch Chang wouldn't let me."

"Then I'll make the choice for you." I touched my throat.

Most of her throat vanished—blown out behind her—so that air was between her head and her shoulders, followed by the crack of a rifle. For an instant her head was suspended in air, flaps of skin hanging from her chin, and then she sagged to the ground, her head bouncing once.

Blood gushed onto the gravel. Her blue gown was spread out all around her. The maids ran back through the compound's gate.

Seventy yards from the cart, Sergeant Johnson stepped the rest of the way around the wall's corner, his rifle in his hand. He pulled back the bolt to eject the cartridge. Wearing a black towel over his head and black coolie trousers and shirt, Shirong—the fellow Commander Beals and I had delivered from the *Ingram* to a hotel the night before—limped after him. I pushed aside the scarves and lifted the pao from the cart.

The sergeant walked my direction, calling out, "I aimed for her Adam's apple. Too high? Too low?"

I walked toward the House of Eight Orchids' gate. "Just right."

捌

I found Eunuch Chang in the courtyard between the kitchen and the privy, where I suspected he would be waiting for me, alerted by the rifle shot. He was wearing a gold silk robe that I had seen only once before, when Chiang Kai-shek's wife had appeared at the gate. She arrived demanding to know whether the eunuch was a person or a fable, and the eunuch had donned the gold robe to greet her. The robe's borders were decorated with thousands of lapis beads. He held his hands together in front of him, each hand up the other sleeve.

"Madam Tuan said you would return, looking for the red-haired gweilo woman," the eunuch said. "I didn't believe you were so foolish, but I took her advice, took the woman from you, and now here you are."

Eunuch Chang's privates were in the jar under my arm.

He asked, "And Madam Tuan?"

I shook my head.

His eyes dropped to the ground, and he pursed his lips.

I asked, "The Englishman?"

"He was a friend of yours, so he is at the bottom of the public well on Diamond Merchant Street."

He squared his shoulders. "Here is your woman, then." He stepped aside.

Elizabeth was sitting on the ground, her legs out in front of her and her arms above her head, tied to the pole, the same pole where I had been striped for smoking the Englishman's opium many years ago. She brought up her head. Her eyes were glassy, and if she recognized me she didn't let on. Her face was as pale as candle wax, and she had lost weight so that her body seemed lost in the peasant's coarse blouse and black trousers she wore. The skin of her face that had once been so full and lively seemed stretched over her skull. She was trembling from the malaria so that her hands jerked against the ropes.

"I've come here to make a trade," I said.

He moved two steps toward me, not quite within arm's reach. "You have brought my pao." His voice was high and sweet.

Without removing my eyes from him, I lowered the jar containing his privates to the ground.

The eunuch drifted closer, his arms still up his sleeves. His temples were shaved, as always, but he had nicked the skin above his ear, a blade slip I'd never seen before. He smiled in his meager way, and his eyes were belligerent. I sensed that the House of Eight Orchids' forger and tailor and the maids were looking at us from windows and doors.

"I'll trade the pao for the bamboo doctor," I said.

"My pao is now on the ground between us." He stepped yet closer. "Why don't I just take it?"

My hands were at my side. "You are welcomed to try."

"The student challenges his master?" he said. "I will not trade. All I want in return for the woman is you, John. You stay, and she can go."

I had deprived the eunuch of his fighters: Ham Fist, Madam Tuan, the Mongol, and the other Rough Boys. And I now knew One Eye Gao Bai would not help the eunuch. So Eunuch Chang was my only worry. His feet hidden by the robe's hem, the eunuch glided closer, almost within his arm's reach.

"You deserted me after all I did for you?" he said. "I made you my son."

"You stole me from my parents and made me a gangster. I did things for you no decent person should ever do."

"Decency? Is that what this redheaded woman has taught you?" He laughed, the first time I'd ever heard him laugh. It was a brittle sound, like a kingfisher's call.

"You haven't seen all of my offer." My gaze on his right eye, I called, "Shirong. Come out."

Shirong limped out from behind the kitchen. When Shirong was twenty yards away, he removed the black scarf around his head to reveal his half-eaten face. Elizabeth and I had set this leper's shoulder back into its socket, and in gratitude he had agreed to come to Chungking with me. Eunuch Chang hissed.

Shirong was wearing his leper-colony rags. A folded scroll was under the arm the doctor and I had returned to the socket. His hands and face were corroded, his legs covered with rotted bulges. With his ravaged hands, he unfolded a scroll and held it up. It was the eunuch's most valuable scroll, the Pearl Sutra, the yellow paper with woodblock stamps, dating from the year 882. He and I had removed it from the eunuch's library a moment ago.

The eunuch began a keening, and he was undoubtedly unaware of it, a strangled lament, as unprofessional a sound as I had ever heard from him. Shirong ran his decayed hand along the edge of the yellow scroll; then perhaps thinking this insufficient, he kissed the scroll.

"I'll increase my trade offer," I said. "In exchange for the bamboo doctor, I'll give you your pao, and I'll also give you your compound."

The eunuch's eyes darted between Shirong and me. "You would desecrate your home?"

I said, "Unless you agree to a trade, Leper Shirong is going to wipe his hands over everything you own and every structure in the compound. All your knives, all your scrolls, all the plum trees, and he's even going to spit into the ponds. And he's going to pick—with his rotted hands—the eight orchids in your greenhouse. For the second time you will have to burn down the compound and cover the ground with lime."

The eunuch may have begun trembling, but I couldn't tell for sure, with most of him hidden by the robe. Elizabeth moaned.

"Release the doctor to me," I said, "and the doctor, the leper, and I will leave your home right now. You will have your pao, and the House of Eight Orchids can remain standing."

The eunuch's right eye twitched almost imperceptibly, and my knife came out and I shot it forward, catching the eunuch's blade on my knife's finger guard, the weapons sharply clanging together. My other hand slashed into his throat under his chin, and he bowled backwards, his robe flying.

I swept down and slashed the Achilles tendon of his right foot, severing it. The eunuch began a scream but bit it back. I kicked his knife away, though he surely had others in his robe. On the ground, he clutched his ruined leg.

I stared down at him, my knife in my hand. I drew a long breath.

Then I cut the rope above Elizabeth's hands, and caught her when she slumped forward. Her eyes were closed. Leper Shirong and I carried Elizabeth toward the House of Eight Orchid's front gate. We left the eunuch writhing and gasping on the ground next to his pao.

捌

I left Elizabeth and the leper at the front gate and went back into the compound. I crossed the bridge and passed the kitchen and the forger's shop, heading for William's room. I pushed open the door. Partially finished canvases leaned against the walls, some with bold colors, others more muted. His version of a Van Gogh—half-finished, showing only the deep-blue sky and bursting yellow stars, but not yet the landscape beneath them—was on his dresser, perched next to a brass incense burner. The Van Gogh had been destined for a gullible New York City art collector. His painting apron hung from a nail on the west wall.

I stood in the doorway. I wanted a token of his life, and his mother-of-pearl button—the one that matched mine and that we had both fervently hoped had belonged to our mother—was in the candy box under his bed. I lowered myself to my knees, pushed aside a three-legged stool, and reached for the tin.

My fingers found the edge of the box. It was cool to the touch. I reached farther, gripping it. Something clicked, and I tried to jerk my hand away, but it was too late.

A wire loop seized my wrist and instantly sunk into the flesh, and I was spun around and dragged across the floor, knocking over the stool and bouncing sideways into the dresser. The silver teapot and sugar tong spilled from the dresser. The wire yanked me by the wrist, and my legs swung around uncontrollably. I smashed through the bedroom bamboo wall and was dragged out into the yard.

The eunuch had moved the loop of the irresistible snare from the whipping post yard to William's bedroom, triggered by the cigar box's motion. When the boulder, which acted as the snare's power, landed in the yard at the base of the wall, I stopped moving, and lay there on the gravel on my belly, a sharp pain in my shoulder from being jerked by the wire.

My wrist still stuck in the snare's noose, I wiped dirt from my lips with my other hand and rolled over on gravel. Eunuch Chang stood above me, using the irresistible axe to hold himself upright. Blood from his foot colored his trouser leg below the robe. The sun was behind him, and I squinted. Elizabeth and the leper were on the other side of the compound near the gate, waiting for me.

He balanced himself on one leg. His voice was hoarse due to the blow to his throat. "You are familiar with the whipping post." He sent the flat of the axe into my temple.

I must have blacked out, or close to it. I distantly heard the eunuch grunt, and felt him seize both of my wrists. He rolled me, or he dragged me—I didn't know. I gasped from the pain echoing back and forth in my head. Gravel scraped by under me. When the pain eased, I found myself sitting on the gravel, my arms above my head, tied to the whip-ping post, just as Elizabeth had been a few moments before.

Eunuch Chang stood in front of me on one leg, his foot dripping blood onto the gravel. I tried to jerk my hands down, but the rope bit into the skin of my wrists. The snare's noose had been cut away from my arm. I brought one knee up and planted my foot under me, trying for leverage, but the eunuch spun the axe around and stabbed my knee with its ivory-capped handle. I hung there, just as I had those many years ago.

The eunuch stared at my face. "I tried to teach you about family and loyalty." He brought a finger to the corner of his eye. He adjusted his balance again with the axe handle; then he raised the axe. The blade glittered in the sun. "But I failed, and there is no hope for you."

He sighted down the handle at me before spinning the handle so that the blade was above his head. He swung the axe, and it split the air heading for me. It seemed a long time coming, arcing in at me, aimed at my skull. But the blade whistled above my head and sunk into the whipping post, severing the rope holding me to the post. I collapsed sideways to the gravel. The eunuch left the axe blade buried in the wood.

"I see you now, back with me at the House of Eight Orchids, and . . ." His trembling voice trailed off. He seemed to struggle, his face twisting. He inhaled, a long rattling. Then he said, "I cannot kill my favorite son." His tic eye glittered with moisture. "But you are no longer welcome here. Go. Leave me."

捌

The tri-motor Stinson's engines rumbled. The plane's wheels had sunk a few inches into the sand. The morning sun was rising over the east-ern mountains, and the Yangtze was turning blue. The airplane had not delivered weapons this time, and so a night landing had not been required. The American consul, Rupert Burkland, had ordered the plane here for me. Rays of sun touched the top of the bank building across the river. Coolies had already begun carrying water buckets up the three hundred steps.

My life since the age of two had been spent in China, and on that sand spit I carried everything I owned by that point: one bowl of chicken.

A crewman appeared at the Stinson's hatch. He called over the sound of the engines, "You coming, pal?"

"I'm bringing a dog," I said.

The crewman—wearing a short leather jacket and blue trousers—leaned out of the fuselage to look down the sandbar. A toothpick hung from his mouth. "That big dog? You're joking, right?"

Big Moon was fifty yards away. His gaze shifted between the Stinson's three roaring engines.

"We weren't told anything about a dog," the crewman said.

Big Moon was wearing a leather collar that Gunner's Mate Red Leery had made. Marine-corp gold and maroon service stripes had been stitched onto the collar. Red had stolen them from Sergeant Johnson's dress uniform. The collar was below a large bandage wrapped around his neck.

"Big Moon, I'm leaving China, and you should come with me," I called above the engines. "There's nothing for you and me here anymore."

The dog paced left and right, still staring at the airplane. Fishermen sculled sampans out into the river from both shores. The steam ferry blew its whistle, about to begin the day's first crossing. A salt junk neared a dock across the river. Trackers pulled an empty coal scow up the river, the sound of the drum carrying over the water. There was no haze, and the early sun was casting gold light on Chungking, so no one would venture too far from the air-raid caves. Smoke was still rising from the eastern edge of town, where the Yangtze and Jialing Rivers met, from bombs dropped two days ago. A run of white clouds was overhead, and a small wind rippled the river.

I stepped toward the Stinson's hatch and held up an arm, a gesture I hoped would convey to the dog that my suggestion was entirely reasonable. "Come on, Big Moon. Climb up here with me."

My name was called from the north. I ducked to peak under the tri-motor's fuselage. A water-taxi sampan was being furiously rowed toward the sandbar from the city. A fellow in the sampan was yelling and waving.

"Big Moon, get into the plane," I called. "Otherwise I'm going to have to leave you here."

The giant dog turned a circle and barked but didn't get any closer to the Stinson. "Yellow Hair," came from the sampan. "Wait."

The sampan bit into the sandbar, and the fellow jumped onto the sand. He carried a gunnysack, and he ran across the bar in a wobbly way, as if unaccustomed to land.

The pilot slid open his window. He yelled at me over the engine's roar, "Let's go. Climb aboard."

The fellow from the water taxi veered widely around the Stinson's propellers, then rushed toward me. It was Knife Maker Kung Ping. The morning sun cast the scars on his forehead and face in deep red. These were his first steps on dry land in his life.

Gasping for breath, he said, "I am here to claim my service from you. Take me with you. I want to go to the Beautiful Mountain."

"How did you know I'd be here?"

He shrugged. "News flows up and down the river. I heard it from a Gold Tooth monk."

I used my hands as a stirrup, and Knife Maker Kung planted his foot in them. The knife maker was surprisingly heavy, and I suspected he had sold his barge and his equipment and his knives and was carrying gold. The crewman grabbed Kung's arm and pulled him onto the plane.

"We're taking off," the pilot yelled at me. "Get in or don't." He slid the window shut.

The engines began to wind up. Prop wash almost pushed me back into the plane's tail. I called, "Big Moon, come. Please."

The dog stared at me but wouldn't move toward the plane. The Stinson inched forward. With a last look at Big Moon, I tossed the chicken onto the sand and grabbed the hatch rim to pull myself aboard. The plane began bumping along the sand. The crewman slammed shut the hatch. I looked out the glass portal. Big Moon followed the plane down the sand spit.

The fuselage was too small to stand, so I crawled to a seat next to Elizabeth, who lay on a litter, an olive-green blanket over her. Her crazy red hair was all over the pillow. Her eyes were open, and some color had returned to her cheeks. The quinine had already begun to work. I'd never before been on an airplane, and the crewman had to strap me to the seat, as I didn't know how. The crewman took his seat behind the pilots, facing aft. The plane bounced, picking up speed.

Then I unbuckled the strap, leaped from my seat, and pushed past the crewman up to the pilot's seat. Instruments and toggle switches surrounded him. He wore a leather cap over a headset and a brown jacket.

"I want to ask you—one American to another—to stop this plane on the sand spit for one minute. It's important."

"Or what? Are you going to stick me with one of the knives I've heard about?"

"I dropped my knives into the Yangtze this morning."

I suppose pilots by nature know how to make quick decisions. He pushed forward the throttles, and the engines' roar diminished. The bouncing Stinson slowed.

"What the hell?" the crewman called from his seat.

I yanked open the hatch and dropped to the sand. The propellers still spun. Big Moon had almost caught up to the plane, shadowing it, as he had shadowed me for days. I had no idea if he would let me approach him, but I didn't have time to do anything but run up to him. I grabbed him by the trunk, my arms almost circling him, and pulled him toward the plane. He let me yank him along until we got too near the plane, and then he dug all four feet into the spit. He was too heavy to lift.

The Stinson's crewman appeared at my elbow. "Grab one end and I'll grab the other."

We awkwardly lifted Big Moon and stumbled toward the plane, sand filling my shoes. The crewman and I shoved Big Moon through the Stinson's hatch. The crewman climbed aboard and slid the dog aft on the deck.

I levered myself into the plane, and the crewman closed the hatch. I gripped his arm in thanks. He returned to his seat. Behind me, Big Moon panted with his tongue out.

The Stinson rolled along and then with a mighty roar lifted into the air. The sandbar fell away. I looked out the window. Red Leery had said to watch for a salute, and as the plane skimmed above the river and passed *Ingram* both the forward and rear three-inch guns shot huge gouts of flame over the water. Leery had loaded the shells with baking powder. The Stinson rose toward the sun, and the Yangtze River grew smaller.

Knife Maker Kung was behind Elizabeth and me, and behind him Big Moon breathed in big huffs on Kung's neck. My forehead and calf smarted in equal measure.

Elizabeth said something, but her voice was too weak to hear above the engines. I unhooked the straps so I could lean close.

She said, "Anna is on a train called the Empire Builder right now, traveling west to Boise."

I had a sister. It would take a while to get used to the idea.

Elizabeth Hanley squeezed my hand. I leaned down to do something I'd never before done in my life. I kissed a woman. Elizabeth. On her cheek.

She grinned. "You and Big Moon are going to like Idaho."

ABOUT THE AUTHOR

Called "a master storyteller" by Clive Cussler, James Thayer has written thirteen critically acclaimed novels, many of which have been optioned for films and translated into many languages. Born in Eugene, Oregon, and raised in the state of Washington, he is a graduate of Washington State University and the University of Chicago Law School. He is also the author of *The Essential Guide to Writing a Novel*. Thayer is a member of the Washington State Bar Association and International Thriller Writers, and he teaches fiction writing at the University of Washington extension school. He lives with his family in Seattle.